Nigerian Connection

Nigerian Connection

By: Keith Hoare

Copyright © 2014 by Keith Hoare

Published by: Ragged Cover Publishing

ISBN 978-1-908090-3-55

Chapter One

Carol Sheppard was drunk on vodka. Her excuse was that it was her birthday, and she'd never be sixteen again. Her mates had bought a bottle, told her she could drink loads and no one would smell it on her breath. It had all begun as a bit of fun, but soon all three of them were decidedly drunk in the park shelter.

Across in the open grassland, a man who'd followed them was throwing a stick for a dog running freely around the park. At the same time, he was observing the three girls drinking, their talk getting louder, coupled with heaps of laughter.

A little earlier, as they'd entered the park, he'd pulled a photograph from his pocket, checking it against each girl. Satisfied that one of them resembled the girl in the photo, he'd pressed a few buttons on his mobile and raised it to his ear.

"The target didn't go to the bus, as we expected, she's in the park with her friends, drinking," he said.

"You're certain?"

"She certainly looks like the girl. We'll need to confirm once we have her. I'll call when they're about to leave; then you move the car into position."

***

Carol stared for a short time at her watch. It had too many hands, and she couldn't decide what time it really was. "I'd better go, mum's expecting me... I'll call later," she slurred, trying to stand.

With the bottle empty, the other two also stood.

One girl hugged Carol. "Have a... good... birthday - call me," she stuttered, bursting into fits of laughter when they both nearly fell over.

After a hug from the other girl, Carol left the shelter in a direction where the wind was in her face, making her feel a little less drunk. Her legs didn't seem to want to control her feet though, so she walked slowly, constantly on the edge of falling over.

The man playing with the dog threw the stick for the last time. He'd watched two of the girls stagger arm-in-arm away from the shelter, moving towards the park's south entrance. His target was going in the other direction, at times calling back to her friends and waving. Removing his mobile from his pocket, he pressed a few buttons, yet again, and waited.

"We're in luck. They've separated! Our target, as expected, is now heading towards the bus stop. I'll follow."

As Carol arrived at the park entrance, a policeman walked up to her. He wasn't wearing a tall helmet, but a flat cap.

"Been drinking, Miss?"

She leaned on the park boundary wall, looking at him with glassy eyes. "It's my birthday, are you going to arrest me?" she replied, at the same time trying to appear sexy and vulnerable.

The policeman looked at this attractive, long-legged schoolgirl attempting to soften him up and grinned. "Not if it's your birthday, but I think we should get you home safely. I'll drop you at the door; it won't be necessary to get you in trouble."

Carol felt dizzy and looked back at him with half-closed eyes. "I'd like a lift if you don't mind, I'm not sure I could find the bus stop, or if they'd let me on."

He just laughed. "You might be right there. Come on; let's get you home shall we, what's your address?"

Soon Carol was sitting in the rear of the car. The man in the park had slipped in alongside the driver. The policeman she'd been talking to earlier was driving.

"Aren't you going to put your sireny thing on? I've never been in a police car before," she slurred.

"I don't think so, love; you wouldn't want to disturb the neighbours, would you?"

"I suppose not," she replied, before closing her eyes.

The man in the passenger seat turned around to look at Carol and, leaning over, slapped her face a couple of times. She opened her eyes for a moment; then closed them again.

"She's well out of it, Bert, this is going to be easy," he said to the one driving and dressed as a policeman.

Within a few miles, they turned into an empty and unused unit on an industrial estate. They had selected this site earlier and set it up.

Bert turned. "Close the door, Mike, I'll park up and get her ready."

Mike climbed out the car and ran back to the roller-shutter door, quickly closing it. Bert began to drag Carol out of the car; this woke her and once out she began coughing, before throwing up. The two men stood and watched until the young girl finally finished.

Bert, who was still dressed as a policeman, came close to her. "Feeling better, love? Let's get these soiled clothes off you shall we?" he suggested, at the same time unfastening her coat and pushing it off her shoulders, letting it fall to the floor.

Carol, still very dizzy, and already confused as to why she was not home, suddenly began to panic when he didn't stop at the coat; he'd already unfastened her cardigan and was now doing the same with her blouse.

She pulled away and looked around, trying to find a means of escape. Bert nodded to Mike, who, quickly coming up behind her with a hankie in his hand, placed it over her nose and mouth, before pulling her head tight to his body, preventing her from struggling. Carol tried desperately to escape his grip, as the exertion and lack of air slowed her, giving up quickly when she beagan to feel faint. Bert, with the help of a sharp knife from his pocket, cut away the rest of her clothing. Finally he knelt down, removing her shoes and socks.

Mike released his hand, allowing her to breathe. She was gulping the fresh air after he'd momentarily released her, but he quickly grabbed her long hair, dragging her screaming to the wall of the unit. There he hit her hard across the face, stunning her into silence. His face was inches from hers.

"You want me to beat the shit out of you; maybe even rape you?" he demanded.

Her eyes were wide with fear. She felt a mixture of vulnerability and embarrassment, but she said nothing.

"I said, do you want to be raped?" he shouted.

Tears began to form in her eyes, before trickling down her face. "Please don't rape me, I'll do anything you want," she stuttered.

"Then from now on, do as you're told, then you'll not be harmed. Refuse, then expect to be raped, before we beat the shit out of you. Do you understand?"

"Yes," she replied meekly.

"Then face the wall and don't move."

Carol turned to the wall as requested; she was shivering in the cold of the unit, and very scared.

Bert pushed a brush into her hand. "Comb your hair, don't turn around, or move from that position, otherwise you know what to expect."

They both watched as she combed her hair. Bert took his mobile phone from his pocket. "That's good. Now drop the comb and keep your hands down at your sides," he demanded.

Carol did as she was told, and he took a photo.

"Turn round, still keep your hands at your side, your feet together. Look straight ahead."

She turned around.

Bert sighed, glancing at Mike. "Wipe her face, then push the hair behind her ears."

Mike came up to her; he'd pulled a small packet of wipes from his pocket and wiped her tear-streaked face before arranging her hair.

Again Bert took a photograph, before pressing the send button. Minutes later, with Carol still standing there, his mobile bleeped; a text had arrived. He looked down at it. 'You have the right girl, deliver her,' was all it said.

"It's a go, bundle her clothes up and bag them; then get the clothes we brought from the boot." Bert looked back at Carol. "We've a long way to go, do you want a piss?"

She timidly nodded a 'yes'.

He walked over to her, grabbing her arm, before marching her to the toilet. "In there, keep the door open, you've got one minute. After that, you dress in what we've brought."

Chapter Two

Corporal Sherry Malloy MC, a soldier in Unit T's strike force Dark Angel, with unit commander Lieutenant Colonel Karen Harris, made their way towards a steel shed on a building site in France. Both female soldiers were dressed in full combat gear, including bullet-proof jackets, and each carried M5 carbides. Karen, when on operations, also carried hand grenades attached to a diagonal ammunition strap across her chest. It was something she'd always done since returning from the Lebanon after her abduction. The shed was long and thin and set to the very edge of the site. Only moments before, the entire site had been secured by Unit T's Dark Angel soldiers, the French gendarmerie standing back, ready to take over on Karen's orders.

They walked past a number of men lying flat and face down on the ground. Their hands were tied behind their backs. Karen stopped and turned to the soldier guarding them.

"Is this everyone on the site?"

He nodded. "Yes, Colonel."

One of the prisoners turned his head to look up at Karen, realising this soldier was in charge. "You, you'll die for this," he spat out in perfect English.

Karen laughed. "So how do you expect to achieve that? After all, you'll be an old man when they let you out, and good for nothing."

"When our people find out, they will come for you," he retorted.

Karen knelt down, with her head close to his. "Then let me give you some help, so they know who to target, shall I? When you talk to your lawyer, give him a message to take to your paymaster, Pular. Tell Pular you met Karen Harris. I'm the one who has already taken out six of his brothels, and I'm not stopping until he has nothing left," she whispered into his ear.

He grinned suddenly. "You believe this is one of Pular's? You could not be further from the truth, and I'd advise you to start running. I won't need to give them your name, they will already know it." Then he began to laugh, which quickly turned into a cough, probably caused by heavy smoking.

"You should give up smoking; it'll kill you one day," Karen

9

mocked, before standing, indifferent to his threats. She received those constantly from traffickers after they'd been caught, considering it to be a macho last-ditch attempt to save face, after they realised they had been taken by a female. Her initial words had been deliberate, to see his reaction. This sort of set-up was not Pular's style, but she had to be sure in her suspicion that another trafficker was working the area. Now she was convinced that was the case - the man's reactions had been quick, without thought, convincing her that he had not said what he did to distance Pular from this operation, but more out of a cockiness on his part that his own paymasters were more violent, and would want revenge on anyone interfering in their operations. The only problem for Karen was that her unit had no intelligence on this new player.

Karen walked away and through the open door leading into the building. Inside, a passage had been made with a number of curtains hanging on a continuous steel rod down the entire length. Initially, the curtains were hiding what lay behind them, but they had been pulled back, revealing nine separate cubicles; these cubicles were created by a curtain strung between the wall, and the railing. In every cubicle was a double bed, a girl lying on each one. All the victims were apparently high on drugs, with some constantly coughing, others screaming in frustration that the next fix of the day hadn't been administered; none could escape, prevented by a chain around one ankle attached to the bed. Sherry, following Karen, already felt sick, from the pungent stink of body sweat, mixed with the unmistakable smell of vomit caused by the drugs. She noted that Karen didn't seem to be affected.

Karen stopped and looked at one of the girls with a little more interest, pulling out a picture from her breast pocket. "How is she?" Karen asked a soldier kneeling at the girl's side in French.

The soldier, one of the Unit's medical team, who had been moving down the shed checking on each girl while the site was secured, looked up at Karen. "They've been giving the girls cocaine, Colonel, just enough to keep them high and responsive. Apart from superficial injuries, this girl, like the others, will go through hell as she's weaned off, but she'll be okay," he replied in French.

"When will she be coherent enough to talk?"

The medical man shrugged. "Two, maybe three days, everyone's different. This one's obviously new, unlike the others I've looked at, so she could come out of it that much sooner."

Karen nodded and turned back to leave the shed. She had no interest in the other victims. A soldier was waiting at the entrance.

"You can release the site to the police right away. Then they can get the medical teams to the victims," Karen said to the soldier.

He saluted and ran off towards the main gate of the building site.

Once out of the shed, Sherry took the opportunity to speak. "I see you checked one girl against a photo, is she important?"

"She is, not because she's the daughter of someone with standing, but more because of how she was abducted. You see, that girl only arrived in the country from the USA ten days ago to join a research group heading for Antarctica. We know that she checked into her hotel, but never slept there. The alarm was raised two days later, when her parents were unable to contact her, following a call to them from the head of the research group asking if she'd departed for Europe. This is the seventh time it's happened in France - the other girls we've never found. This tip-off, about the building site being used as a brothel, with a request that we go in to secure the building, may be the break we've been looking for. After all, the layout, the operation, was not Pular's style, so I needed to be sure it wasn't him. Also, knowing the background of this girl, talking to her may give us a better insight as to how she was taken."

"But won't they change their tactics now?"

Karen shook her head. "It isn't usual for the abductors snatching to order to be part of the brothel operation. They usually snatch and sell on. For the supplier the loss of a site is a bonus; after all, the brothel operator will want the girls replaced while he sets up a new location. If this is not the case and the snatcher is the operator, then they will still want to replace, maybe changing their tactics in the way girls are taken. That's a chance we have to take."

"I've a lot to learn haven't I?"

"Haven't we all, Corporal. It's just a cat and mouse game we play. Sometimes we get the mouse, other times they escape down a hole. Although, on occasion, we get at the nest and destroy the lot, but

11

there's always a new one to take their place."

***

Further along the road from the site entrance, a man known only as Taras, small, thick-set and with black hair, was sitting in the back of a car watching the unfolding events. Sitting alongside him, also watching, was a man named Maksim. Tall, gaunt and with short cropped hair, this man was dangerous; he was ex-KGB and kept the many people who worked for Taras in line. His methods were more often than not violent in the extreme, making everyone who came into contact with him very afraid and fearful for their lives.

"The soldier with the ammunition belt across her chest is the Harris girl. I'm told she carries enough firepower to make her a formidable adversary in any shoot-out," Maksim muttered.

Taras nodded his head up and down slowly. "I presume that's the girl who took on an army, besides putting so many traffickers behind bars? A woman to admire and respect, do you not agree?"

Maksim shrugged with indifference. "She's been lucky, is well guarded and can be extremely dangerous if cornered. Except she's made of flesh and bone, no different to anyone else, and will die just as easily."

"What of her family, Maksim, why has none of her opponents taken them out and broken the girl's spirit that way?"

"It's a good question and I cannot answer that. We do know there is a sister along with a mother and father living in Manchester. They have a small semi in the suburbs and nothing like the large house in France the Harris girl owns."

"Interesting; perhaps it's time to add her sister to the girls we will require to replace the lost income from this raid. It will be an irony for Harris to know this action has lost her her sister. We'll put her to work in one of our houses, then let us see what Harris does."

"I will look into it, but expect a swift and deadly response from Unit T."

"I'm hoping they do react that way, after all, when their leader becomes emotionally involved, which for her sister she will, that's the time she'll make mistakes."

Maksim didn't reply. While it was easy to discount Karen, from

12

what he'd heard, emotion would not come into it. Her approach would be as a professional soldier. She controlled a strike force with real firepower and whose rules of engagement allowed them to shoot to kill without warning. Taras would need every man he could muster when she came for him. And come she would, he was very sure of that.

Chapter Three

Carol had been sitting in the back of a car for over three hours. This wasn't the one she'd originally been taken in. That had been abandoned just outside Manchester. This car was a large four-by-four, with the rear passenger windows darkened, not allowing anyone outside to see who was in it. Besides, she was handcuffed firmly to the safety belt, giving her no chance of opening a window, or trying to run away. Finally, the car had child-locks fitted, so if she had managed to release herself, the doors wouldn't open, neither would the windows.

She'd tried to sleep after making herself as comfortable as she could, but she couldn't. What had already happened to her was spinning around in her mind; she was unable to understand what she had done to make the men take her like this. At first she thought they were going to kill her, but it seemed illogical they would travel so far for this to happen now. Like every teenager, she had watched lots of TV films where people were abducted, ending up either dead, or working the streets for a pimp. She really hoped this was not going to be the case for her.

It was dark when the car came to a halt in a partially deserted car park, alongside what looked to her like a marina. Plenty of small sailing boats were lined up alongside wooden walkways, which went out into the water.

Bert opened the rear door and leaned over, releasing the handcuffs from the safety belt, before quickly attaching it to her other wrist. "We've been in touch with your family. They're prepared to pay for your release. That's good, isn't it?"

Her eyes lit up. Though very scared, the fact that she was to go home filled her with an overwhelming sense of relief, that it might soon be over. "You really mean it; dad's coming for me?" she asked hesitantly.

"Of course I mean it."

"Then when can I go home?"

He just smiled. "Very soon. But before you go, he must pay the ransom. In the meantime you can hardly sit in the car, so you're to stay on a boat. It's in this marina, and you and I are going to walk down the

14

jetty to this boat. Try to shout, make a run for it or do anything else to attract attention and your release is off. Then you will never go home. Do you understand?"

"Yes, I understand - you need to wait for the money, so I'll do anything you ask of me," she replied quietly.

"That's good, let's go."

The small sailing boat was at the very end of one of the jetties. However, even if she had wanted to escape it would have been useless. The boats, the jetty and the surrounding area were deserted. All she saw was one man walking a dog away from where she was. But Carol wasn't too concerned, after all, she would soon be going home, her nightmare was almost over.

Waiting at the boat was another man. He was tall, had black hair and was of muscular build. He was also French, his name Ancil Gorin.

He stepped aside to allow Carol to come onto the boat, then followed her up the gangplank, telling her to go down into the cabin. Once she was inside, the cabin door was locked, before he left the boat and joined Bert, who was waiting for him.

"The stupid girl believes she's going home, after her dad pays a ransom," Bert told him.

"That is good, it means she'll be less trouble," Ancil replied in perfect English, at the same time reaching into his pocket, pulling out a wad of notes. "Tell Roy we'll be in touch later in the month for our usual shipment. I'm doing him a favour taking this girl early, so I've deducted five hundred off the normal fee."

Bert counted the money and looked a little put out. "Roy's not going to be happy about this."

"That is not my problem. Roy wanted her to go this week; so it's meant a special trip with more costly arrangements, but she's a good-looking kid and still at an age brothels will take her, once we change her appearance."

"Yeah, okay. Roy will be in touch when the usual lot's ready for collection." With that, Bert walked away.

Ancil watched him leave, before returning to the boat. Going through into the cabin, he stood for a moment looking at Carol sitting on the side-bench seat. "We're going out to sea a short distance, to wait there for a call to say the money's arrived. Once that's confirmed you'll be dropped ashore. You'll have to make your own way, but there are plenty of houses around where you can knock on the door. In the meantime, you've two choices. One, you're chained up; two, while I take the boat out, you put together a couple of sandwiches from what's in the fridge and make tea."

Carol, relaxed now she was convinced she was going home, smiled. "The other man told me I'd have to wait till dad brings the money, so I won't be any trouble, or try to escape. I'll be happy to make something. I'm really hungry; I've had nothing since an apple at dinner time."

"Very well, but don't try to come out on deck, the door will be locked. Just call when you have everything ready."

After he had left her alone, Carol looked around. She'd never been on a small boat before, and it took time to sort out exactly where everything was. She put the kettle on the gas burner, at first struggling to understand how to light it. There was a rail set around the two-burner hob. Then she found a half-eaten cooked chicken in the fridge, along with other salad items. After fifteen minutes, during which time the engines of the boat had started up, and they moved out of the marina, she had the meal ready; she shouted through the door to tell Ancil.

He came in and looked at the food. "You've done well; we're out the marina now, so if you want you can sit on deck with me to eat."

While they were eating, they sat in silence. The only sound was the constant thud of the engine.

It was Carol who spoke first. "We're going a long way. How will you know when dad pays the money?"

"They'll call on the radio. It may seem a long way, but it isn't, we're just going down the coast. After the call, within half an hour you'll be ashore. Anyway, it's unlikely you will hear tonight, so go into the cabin and get some sleep. If you want the toilet, it's at the far end."

Carol thanked him and went down into the cabin. She was nervous, yes, but also happy. So after a quick wash she lay down on the long bench seat and fell asleep.

***

16

Carol was awakened by Ancil shaking her. "Come on, I've made tea. You'll be leaving in a short time," Ancil said, pushing a mug into her hands.

"What time is it?" she asked, sipping the hot tea.

"Half-past five. You've been asleep all night," he replied, at the same time taking the seat opposite.

"When you say I'm leaving, has dad paid then?"

"Yes, after tea I'll drop you ashore."

He watched her carefully as she finished off the tea. Already he could see her eyelids beginning to droop. Seconds later he stood, quickly taking her mug away as she sank back. Laying her out on the bench seat, he checked her carefully. The drug had worked fast; she was dead to the world. Going out onto the deck, he started the engine and set off again. In the distance, he could see a small fishing trawler coming towards them.

As it came to a halt he brought his own boat up to the side; then, with the help of the crew, they carried Carol out of the cabin and onto the trawler.

The skipper of the trawler stood watching. Ancil went over to him, giving him a bundle of Euros. Ancil was talking to him in French. "My car will be on the quay when you arrive back in port. In a couple of hours, the girl will be awake, but groggy and confused. This time your only task is to get her ashore for me. When I enter the port, they are bound to give my boat the once-over, coming from the UK, while you're fishing in territorial waters so they won't bother with you. Just get her ashore, and I'll look after her from there."

"I understand, she'll be ready when we dock. Is it the only collection this month?"

Ancil shook his head. "No, the collection's still on. This is a one-off as a favour. Just take care she doesn't make a run for it, or shout out."

"She'll be fine, have no worries on that score," he replied.

***

Ancil and Taras made their way down the cellar steps into the corridor. Ancil stopped to unlock the third door along, pushing it open. Carol was sitting on the bed.

17

Before she could speak, Ancil demanded she stand up.

Carol stood.

"Your parents involved the police, tried to deceive us, but it didn't work, so that's it. They get no more chances; they can't be trusted. We own you now. You have no say in your future; you do as you are told, or expect a beating."

"But dad wouldn't do that. Please try again, I want to go home," she begged, trying not to cry.

Ancil struck her hard across the face with his hand. "You speak when I say. Or I'll take my whip to you. Understand?" he demanded.

Her cheek was stinging; tears were trickling down her face; she was terrified of these men. "Yes," she replied meekly.

"Then strip, including your knickers, and be quick about it," he ordered.

She did as he asked, standing there quietly.

Taras looked her over, then shook his head and began talking in French. "What are your people playing at in England? Sending this sort of girl? She's skinny, no tits. My clients wouldn't pay for such a girl."

Ancil grabbed her left arm, pulling it up and twisting it so the palm and underarm could be seen. He too had reverted to French. "Look; she's not on the needle. We accepted her as a favour from our supplier; apparently a friend of his was having problems with her. So his friend decided that sooner than kill her, he thought she'd have a value. The girl's young, maybe even a virgin, so sell her to your clients that way. Her tits are still growing. There are many men who will pay good money for her."

Taras took Carol's hand and looked at her arms carefully. Then he opened her mouth and checked her teeth. After that, he turned her around, running his hands over her bottom, before shrugging indifferently. "Are you a virgin?" he asked her in English.

Carol didn't really know what to say, scared he'd hit her if she told him the truth.

"It's a fucking simple question, kid, have you been fucked?" Ancil cut in.

""I've never slept around, but my boyfriend loved me and I him,

18

he's taken me to bed twice," she admitted.

"That blows your virgin bonus value, Ancil," Taras mocked, again in French. ""So what's left? I've no clients that would want to wait around while she developed, the girl's only got a working life of a couple of years in the brothels at most. They have a high demand for young girls and work them hard, up to ten clients a day, but the girl is attractive, and it makes a change to have one that's not using. Call Marble; tell him by the end of the month I want her sterilised, her tits enlarged to thirty-six, so she's ready to begin work immediately she's delivered; then I'll pay ten grand for her plus Marble's cost. Also, have his hairdresser change her hairstyle and colour; she's too recognisable as she is."

Ancil frowned thoughtfully for a moment. ""She's worth fifteen of anyone's money, even like she is."

""Then offer her around at that, a private buyer may take the girl and let her develop naturally. Our clients like to see tits on a girl. I'm not desperate; we've more coming in later this month."

Taras, in fact, liked the girl; white girls always rented well; her athletic body and long legs were perfect. But he knew Ancil wanted to get shut of her, the girl was still spread across the European papers and it would be very high risk offering her around to private clients.

Ancil smiled and nodded his agreement. "Very well, ten grand, I'm happy to have her sterilised and her tits sorted, but before she's taken to Marble, you own her, so I want a deposit. I've no intention of paying Marble and still being left with her on my hands."

Taras pulled a wad of notes from his pocket and counted out two thousand. "This will cover the cost, with a little extra for your trouble. Tell him to use clean knives, if he doesn't and she dies on the table, or has complications, then I don't want her, and he owes me the two grand besides her worth."

Chapter Four

A few days after the raid on the brothel, Karen and Sherry were in Cannes, on the French Riviera. Sherry had been rather surprised when Karen called her, asking her to grab her toothbrush; they were going away for the weekend. Sherry was really pleased Karen had asked. Karen was fun to be with away from the unit. Then, with neither of them having boyfriends, really because of their work, making it difficult to strike up relationships, it meant they could both have fun playing up the lads on the beach, or in the disco.

They had just booked into a hotel and were in the bedroom.

"I like this room, Karen; it's a fantastic view over the beach. Which bed do you want?"

Karen just shrugged. "Left is fine. But I've got to meet someone. Can you unpack and I'll meet you back here to eat, around six?"

Sherry had suspected Karen's suggestion to come to Cannes for the weekend would have an ulterior motive. But she was happy with that, it made a change to get away and Cannes, though expensive, was a great place to be.

"I'm cool with that; I may even look for something to wear tonight."

"Well if you want clothes, speak to George on the porter's table. Tell him you're with me, what you're looking for, and he'll make sure you get a really good deal. He knows all the traders, believe me."

With this agreed, Karen left the hotel. Dressed in a slightly flared summer dress and high heels, she hailed a taxi. Twenty minutes later the taxi came to a halt outside a large house, set back off the road. Walking up to the front door, Karen rang the doorbell.

A lady opened the door and recognised Karen, quickly opening it wider to allow her inside. Karen walked through into a large lounge. A man was sitting down on a settee reading, his back towards her. However, as she approached he stood and turned.

"Karen, it's good to see you," he said, embracing her and kissing her on each cheek.

"It's good to see you again, Peter, how's the family?"

Sir Peter Parker, head of a special division within New Scotland

Yard, had known Karen since she was eighteen, when she escaped from the Lebanon. In fact, he had been in charge of Unit T for a short time, after the general who ran the unit had been caught with his fingers in the till. Now, with Unit T coming under an EU committee, he had no direct authority, though they still kept in touch and occasionally she would ask his advice, with Unit T and his department working together on an operation.

"The family's well, they are always asking about you. Next time you're in London we should all have dinner together."

"I'd like that. Thank you for asking me."

As she sat down, the lady who had opened the front door came through, carrying a tray with tea and biscuits.

"Would you join me for tea, or do you prefer mineral water?" Peter asked, knowing Karen drank very little tea or coffee.

"No, I'm fine with tea," she replied.

After they were left alone and the door had been shut, Peter poured, handing her a cup.

"Thank you, you still remember how I like it. So is this your house?" she asked.

He smiled broadly. "I wish, but no, it belongs to a good friend." Then he changed his tone slightly. "I was never here, Karen. You understand?"

"Of course, that goes without saying. I just hoped you'd dusted off that wallet of yours, splashed out, and we'd become neighbours. Well not exactly neighbours, I'm nearly a hundred miles from here, but if you'd decided that this was to be your new home, it would have been great. Besides, it would save me a fortune in hotel bills. I love this part of the Med."

He just laughed. "Maybe one day. In the meantime we need to talk. As you know the Russians moved in to take over the vacuum formed by your removal of the key players in the circle. Both you and I knew this was coming; after all, it was the price paid to bring down the circle. Alas, since then, people trafficking has become a whole new ballgame. These people are evil, kill without a thought and are already taking girls from EU countries. In the UK, we've lost five girls in as many weeks, the latest being a sixteen-year-old, Carol Sheppard."

"Yes, I've been watching the news reports. It's pretty obvious they're being trafficked. The patterns are similar, the people who are taking them are selective."

"I agree, but many senior officers in the force are plodders and having a hard time accepting that the abductions are the work of traffickers. They believe all the children are dead, and that they are hunting a serial killer. However, in the next few days, the British government is going to ask the EU formally, for Unit T to take over the investigation. It's very obvious that the Scotland Yard investigations have come to a halt, and they are merely treading water hoping for a break. You and I know there will be no break. These girls will already be placed and the leads are at a dead end. Because of that, they will get no further."

"You're right, they won't. The most they can expect is one or two of the girls turning up dead in the next few months. But it's a sensible course of action, for the UK to ask for our assistance. In France they've lost a number, the same as Spain, Greece and Portugal. Already we're following leads, squeezing the brothel owners by taking out their operations, besides making it very difficult for them to operate. My problem is that the perpetrators are eluding us; we can't get intelligence about those who run the operation. I suspect a number of people. Some I've met, before we hit the circle, but they're elusive there is little to track back to them."

Peter poured more tea for himself, while Karen declined, before commenting, "Tell me, Karen, what's the chance of you getting into the US without all the red tape?"

"You mean covertly, perhaps as a tourist?"

"Yes."

She merely smiled. "It's possible; I have passports in both Harris and my birth name Marshall. I also know a number of people I could visit there, why do you ask?"

"Do you remember a man named Harry Watson?"

Karen's attitude changed a little as she remembered this man. He had an operation in London; snatching children from local authority homes across the country. There were little or no complaints to the police about the missing children, apart from the general report that a child had absconded from the home, and was registered missing. As no authority had ever bothered to talk to any other about the missing children, no one noticed, until a small department in Whitehall, collating return forms from all authorities for government statistics, noticed that over sixty children were unaccounted for and had never returned, or been picked up by the police.

"I do remember him, though we had little to do with the operation to bring him down. Is he not in prison?"

"He wasn't convicted, or sent to prison, because he helped us in exposing a number of child rings that the children had been passed to."

She nodded her head up and down slowly, realising he'd answered a question she'd wanted an answer to for some time. "So that's how you broke those rings, we always wondered. But what happened to him and what has Watson got to do with the current increase in abductions, unless he's part of it?"

Peter smiled slightly. "First things first; Watson was allowed to leave the country. He chose to live in the US, so we assisted in obtaining the necessary documents to do that. I know it's not your way, but sometimes in this life you have to give a little to take a lot."

Karen almost laughed at that. "We do it all the time, many of the criminals walk, in return for information."

"I know, Karen, but the ones we release don't end up with a bullet in the back of their heads later."

She sighed. "What's a stray bullet between friends? Most, if not all deserve it, for what they did. But we are deviating, unless you want me to mete out final justice to this man?"

Peter, looking at her, took a sip of his tea. "We have no difficulty in sending someone to eliminate him, if needed, without asking for the assistance of Unit T, thank you. Watson was still operating after the circle was taken down. Most of his dealings were with the ones who had taken over. After we arrested him, and he helped us, part of the deal for him staying out of prison and a free man, was for him to tell us of any further contact. Two days ago he received such contact and called me. It seems like a new group have ambitions and want to operate in the US. They want him in on the operation there."

"Then tell the Americans, they are more than capable of sorting problems out, besides having the infrastructure to see it through."

"They do of course, but we won't be talking to them. They have no idea of Watson's past, and it stays that way. But if he's in with the people operating in Europe that you are looking for, then he might just be the person to give you a lead that will bring them down."

"I see; then you want me to go out there to see him? Find out what he knows and keep in touch."

"Exactly; this is a break for us, Karen. It's pointless sending one of my own staff; they don't have the wider picture as you do. Besides, with a wrong word Watson may back out, at this point I couldn't afford that to happen."

Karen stood and walked to the window in thought, then turned and faced Peter. "I don't like it, he sounds too good to be true and doesn't follow the usual pattern of criminals given a new life. I'm also not keen on leaving the Americans out of the loop. This could get really messy and spoil the relationship Unit T has with them."

"You're correct of course, it could be a set-up. Watson is certainly capable of playing both sides. But will you do it?"

Karen smiled broadly at that. "Of course, it's what we do. But if I end up in an American prison I want regular cigarettes and other items sent."

He frowned thoughtfully for a moment. "But you don't smoke."

"I know, I just might begin, sat in a small cell all day, and I could always barter them for something I could use."

He laughed. "Just go and see him, make your own judgement and let's begin to take out the Russian operation." He handed her a plastic wallet. "Everything that you need's in there, including his profile and known associates. We'll talk again, maybe in London when you're back." Then his tone and look changed. "This is just between you and me, even Stanley, your intelligence man is to know nothing about this conversation. My position would be tenuous if it got out, everything I'm telling you is top secret and off the record."

"It won't get out, Peter. Not from me anyway," she replied, just as serious. "I also appreciate your confidence in me."

"We go a long way back, Karen. I don't think, no I know, there is no one else in the world I'd trust with this information."

Later that same day, Karen and Sherry were walking along the Cannes seafront. Both girls were in light summer dresses and they were heading for a restaurant further down the road, which Karen had booked by telephone. They could have taken a taxi, but the night was warm, and there was plenty of time to spare.

Karen glanced at her watch. "Let's get a drink; we've three quarters of an hour before the table's available."

Stopping at a bar Karen often used when she was in Cannes, they sat down outside. A waiter took their order and left them alone.

Sherry was looking inside the bar. "It looks like a US ship's visiting. There are lots of sailors stood around inside."

Karen was thinking fast, rather than use acquaintances as she intended, maybe this could be a way into the US, if she played her cards right. "Yes it does, doesn't it?" she answered. "How about we come back later; then see if one or two of these really fit sailors would like to buy two stunning girls a drink."

Sherry grinned. "I'm up for that. But this doesn't sound like the Karen I know, suggesting we go on the pick-up."

Karen just smiled but said nothing.

***

After dinner, Karen and Sherry walked back into the bar they had left earlier, and stood behind quite a large crowd of sailors all trying to buy a drink.

"Hey guys, be courteous and let the girls through," a uniformed sailor standing at the bar shouted.

The crowd parted and they made her way through, thanking the sailors who let them pass.

The lad who'd shouted came up to them. He was six foot tall, with an athletic build and the arm emblems of a petty officer. He tried to speak a little French, believing they were both French girls.

Karen smiled and spoke back to him in French, but he shook his head, unable to understand what she said.

"Looks like he can't speak French," Sherry said in English to Karen.

"You might be right there, maybe if I spoke more slowly he'd understand," Karen replied in English. Then she looked back at him. "What is it you want to say to us?" she asked in French.

He stood for a moment, a little disconcerted, then burst into laughter. "You're winding me up, you're English."

"Of course, do we look French?" Sherry asked.

"I've no idea, but the few girls we've tried to talk to just shrug their shoulders, not understanding us. Anyway, I'm Caleb; my mate who's still trying to get us drinks, but having no luck, is Dick. To save you waiting too long, I'll get him to add your drinks. So what are you having?"

"I drink vodka and orange, Sherry likes a beer. Except I won't accept a drink unless I see it poured, so leave it to me," Karen replied, then turned to the bar and called a bartender on his way past. "Marcel, when you're free, please," she asked in French.

He glanced over and recognised Karen; a big grin came over his face. "It's good to see you again, Karen. One minute, then I'll be with you."

Minutes later they had their drinks.

Caleb grinned broadly and chuckled. "We should take you out all the time, Karen. He was putty in your hands."

Karen laughed. "Come on, let's go outside, it's too hot in here."

They went outside and found a place to stand alongside the small boundary wall surrounding the tables and chairs, which were all taken.

Sherry sipped her drink, at the same time looking at Caleb. "So how long are you in port?"

"Two more nights, then the ship sails."

"And where would that be to?"

He smiled ever so faintly. "Can't tell you that, Sherry, we never give ships' movements out, except a few of us won't be going. We're at the end of our tour of duty, so after the ship sails we'll be flying home; then I've a couple of weeks' leave, before going back to base and a new tour."

"And where's home for you, unless that's top secret as well?" Karen mocked.

"No, Karen, where I live isn't top secret, if you were in the forces you'd understand. We'd be placed up against a wall and shot if we gave certain information out."

Karen glanced at Sherry before she looked back at him. "Then it's a good thing we're not. So where do you live?"

"Groton, Connecticut. Have you heard of it?" Caleb asked.

"I have, it's a shipbuilding town and isn't there a submarine museum there?"

He grinned. "There is, that's where I got the itch to join the navy. But I'm really impressed you knew, Karen."

"Karen's full of all sorts of facts. I, on the other hand, had never heard of the place," Sherry cut in.

"That's because I was brought up in a strict convent school and we were virtually forced to learn. But enough of my past, are you lads up for a disco? Sherry and I are."

"Now that's what I like to hear. Let's all of us go and find out what Cannes has to offer then?" Caleb replied.

**

Later that night Karen was walking along the seafront, with Caleb, back to her hotel. Sherry was around a hundred yards behind with Dick. She had deliberately asked Sherry to hang back as she wanted Caleb on his own. Sherry smiled to herself; this was so unlike Karen, maybe she really fancied Caleb, but wasn't going to admit it.

Caleb grasped Karen's hand; she didn't pull back or object. "I've had a fabulous time; you and Sherry have really made the night."

Karen stopped, leaning back on the low sea wall. "I've had a good night, as well. So when you return to the US, what's your plan then?" Karen knew he had leave coming and had also, in conversation, found out he'd no steady girlfriend.

"Most of the lads have girls back home, but like I said earlier I haven't. I wanted to be a free entity to travel the world with no baggage. How about you?"

"I'm between relationships at the moment, so like you I'm a free entity. Though, in a week, I've got a holiday booked. Nothing special and the accommodation's downmarket. But I don't earn much, and it's taken all year to save up," she lied.

"Sounds great, where are you heading?"

"Orlando."

He seemed a little taken aback. "You mean you're coming to the States and never mentioned it earlier, that's wild, you'll truly love it there."

Karen sighed deeply. "Yes well, it would have been good, my friend Margo was coming, but she's bailed, so I'm not so sure now."

"What about Sherry, won't she go?"

"She would, but don't mention it to her. I've no intention of spending a week with Sherry; she can be really weird, if you know what I mean?"

He didn't, but wasn't going to admit it. Already he was planning on staying very close to Karen. She was his type of girl, and then, with his own leave coming up, maybe if they got on over the next day or so, she'd agree to him joining her in Orlando. He could say nothing more, as Sherry and Dick had caught up.

Chapter Five

The search for Carol Sheppard had been intense; however, even after two weeks of local area searches including extensive press coverage, little or no progress had been made. Police Inspector Tunbridge of Preston CID was summoned to the Assistant Chief Constable's office.

"I need an update, Inspector, on the Carol Sheppard case," the assistant chief asked.

"It's not good, Sir, the girl has completely disappeared. Of the cars picked up on the CCTV system, we found one burnt-out thirty miles away. Forensic went over it with a fine toothcomb, but the work was professional, they found few clues. This case is virtually the same as that of the girl Annabel, who went missing in Southend."

"Not just Annabel, Inspector, but three other girls we also know about. The government is concerned, the public's getting very edgy and the press are having a field day. As you're aware, widespread abductions on this scale are coordinated by a special division in Scotland Yard. However, information coming into the division points to the distinct possibility that this may be an international trafficking operation. Because of that belief the Home Office, with instructions from Downing Street, are not prepared to delay any further. They have requested the EU for Unit T to be brought into the investigation. Our chief's in full agreement; Unit T's intelligence is far superior on this sort of crime and it has a mandate across all EU borders, besides the resources to take these people on."

"I can't disagree, Sir, will they be working with us?"

"Yes, undoubtedly, for investigations at a local level that is. I've been informed that they will be sending their people to go through everything we have."

"Will their commanding officer be coming herself, Sir?" he asked, hoping she would. The inspector had read a great deal about Karen and was already looking forward to meeting her.

"You're talking about Colonel Harris, who commands Unit T?"

"Yes."

"No, at this stage she won't, I understand she's currently abroad.

A Corporal Malloy will be coming; she has been with Dark Angel for some time and has first-hand knowledge about the trafficking industry."

The inspector was disappointed. "That's a pity; I've always wanted to meet Karen."

"Perhaps she will come later, but at this point it is probably a good thing she isn't. We don't want the papers picking up that Unit T is involved, and if she came they would quickly put two and two together. Anyway, collate all the current information ready for a meeting first thing in the morning. Leave nothing out and don't take it as a slap in the face for the local police force. It really isn't. If Scotland Yard are right in their assumption that Carol has fallen victim to international traffickers, then Unit T will be her only hope of rescue."

Chapter Six

Maksim entered the drinking club off a street in Soho. As he walked up to the bar, the bartender came over immediately.

"What's it to be?" he asked.

"Vodka neat, none of the rubbish. I also want to see Roy."

The bartender pulled a bottle from under the counter, placed a small glass on the bar and filled it. "Three pounds. Who shall I say wants him?"

"Maksim, he knows I'm coming," he answered, throwing three pound coins on the bar before taking a swig of the vodka.

The bartender took the money, then went through to the rear.

A few minutes later he returned. "Through the door, up the stairs," he said, nodding towards a fire exit door at the far end of the room.

Roy Clement, a man in his early forties, was the leader of a criminal gang working mainly in London. At six foot three and an ex-boxer, he was not a man to be trifled with. When Maksim entered the small room at the top of the stairs, Roy was sitting on an old settee watching a pornography video on a fifty-inch TV.

He looked across as Maksim entered the room. "What do you reckon? Fifteen and taking it up both ends at once."

Maksim glanced at the television and shrugged. "If that's what turns you on. Personally I like a woman, not some scrawny kid."

Roy switched the television off with a remote control, then stood offering his hand. "The name's Roy, are you from Taras?"

Maksim nodded. "I am; it is time we met; you've been supplying good quality goods to us for a while now."

Roy sat down and pointed to another settee. "We do our best, and it was good of you to take the last girl at such short notice. She was a problem for one of my clients."

"You mean the sixteen-year-old?"

"Yes, how's she doing?"

"She's still being prepared. Although I'm happy you brought that up, as we now want a favour from you. Taras needs you to take someone for him. This is not a child but a woman in her early thirties.

31

She's to be delivered to a ship laid off the Welsh coast."

Roy grinned broadly. "That's no problem, it's what we do. Except recently we've taken five girls, the last less than a month back, not including the Sheppard girl. The police are getting a little jittery. Our fee is five thousand, fifty per cent upfront, and we choose when to take her, but you will get her within a month. Who is she and where does she live?"

Maksim pulled two envelopes from his inside pocket. "Your fee is in one, the other contains details of who we want."

Roy opened both and looked carefully at the details. Then he looked up at Maksim. "You're sure of this. Her sister's Karen Harris, who is well known among the criminal community. No one goes near her family if they value their lives."

Maksim grinned. "You're scared?"

"No, but I'm not a fool. Even so it would be fun to turn the tide on her for a change, but it'll cost you ten thousand. We'd need to keep our heads down for some time; her sister's not a girl you take on lightly."

"You've had experience then?"

Roy shook his head. "No, but Jacob Spine, a good mate of mine and well known among the criminal underworld for the kind of work we do, thought he could take the Harris girl on. He lost."

Maksim frowned. "What do you mean 'he lost'?"

Roy almost laughed, then suddenly changed and looked more serious. "I'm not sure what he did, but whatever he got himself mixed up in, attracted the attention of Unit T. He wound up with a bullet in his head. Professional kill if ever there was one and rumoured on good authority it was Unit T's work. Only their commander, Karen Harris, could order a kill."

"I see, the more I hear about Harris, the more she sounds an interesting adversary to take on. Very well, you'll get your extra money on delivery; injure her, and you get nothing."

***

After Maksim had left, Roy leaned back on the settee in thought. Times were good, and the money was rolling in. He pressed the small intercom button, wired between the bar and his office, telling the bartender to send Bert up.

Bert looked through the information on Sophie, Karen's sister. "I'm not so sure we should get involved Roy. It's one thing dealing with the police, but Unit T's another level altogether, especially anything to do with the Harris girl's family. Karen's bloody dangerous."

"Yes, well, we won't be involved. All we do is snatch and move whoever it is. The traffickers who want this woman will have to deal with Unit T, not us. So you and Mike get up to Manchester and check the woman out, where she goes and who she's with. Call me after you've sussed out the best time to take her, and we'll decide what to do from there."

***

Two days later, Mike and Bert were in Manchester. They had arrived early and were already watching the house where Karen's parents, along with Sophie, lived.

Bert yawned loudly. "If the information's right she'll be leaving for work in ten minutes. Should we follow, or stake out the house?"

"We stay here; after all, we know where she works, so it's pointless following. Apart from which this is a very quiet street; we'd be better taking her here rather than in the city. I'll give Roy a call after we see Sophie leave."

As Bert said, it was another ten minutes before Sophie left. Mike pressed the quick dial on his mobile telephone; Roy answered immediately.

"We're outside the house, Roy; it's a suburban street full of semis and quiet. We've been here for about two hours. Sophie has left for work, so it'd be easy to get inside the house and wait for her."

"You're certain there is no security?" Roy asked.

"Nothing around the house; there's a few general street CCTV cameras set around the local area, none are directed specifically at the entrance to the house. The gates at the bottom of the drive are open and don't look as if they have ever been shut. Unless all the security is inside, this is just like thousands of other semis."

Roy couldn't understand it; surely there would be some sort of security? Unless Karen was arrogant enough to believe that no one would have the nerve to take her family out.

"Take a drive around the block, return in roughly half an hour. If it's just the same then go inside and wait for the woman to come home. This is sounding like the easiest money we've made this year."

Chapter Seven

Stanley, Karen's head of intelligence, was sitting in his office inside Unit T's headquarters in France when one of his surveillance teams called. "You need to see this Stan," the operator said over the phone.

Stan walked through into the main surveillance area. Twelve operators were busy watching a number of screens each. He went over to the one who'd called him. "What's going on, Julie?"

"One of our covert CCTV cameras, outside the colonel's parents, has picked up a car that's been parked a short distance down the road since seven-thirty this morning. Local street camera operators also confirmed it entered the street and parked up among other vehicles at that time; more importantly, it wasn't a local car. The two people inside have not attempted to leave, they're still sitting inside. It's a London plate; I've contacted the British DVLA to obtain the car owner's address."

"Interesting; notify the local constabulary, but ask them to stand away for a moment until we get a better idea why they are there."

Stan returned to his office and picked up the phone. He dialled a mobile and waited. It was quickly answered.

"Stan, you want me?" Karen asked.

"There's a car a short distance from your family's house, Karen. It's been there for some time. It could be nothing or it could be something. The police have been informed, but are standing aside until we need them to go in."

Karen remained silent for a moment, then made a decision. "I don't like it, Stan. Who have we got close?"

"We have Corporal Malloy with two Dark Angel soldiers in Preston. They're looking into the missing schoolgirl Carol Sheppard, following the British governments request for our involvement."

"What time is it in Manchester?"

"9.35am, why do you ask?"

"Sophie will be at work by now. Have two soldiers secure the house, tell them to take the back way. Then send the corporal to pick up my sister. She's to take her to the charity offices and stay with her in the flat above, until we know just who these people are."

"Will do, Karen."

"Keep me informed Stan. I hope it's not what I suspect and just possible burglars casing the area."

***

Sherry and two other Dark Angel soldiers were in the police station when her mobile began to ring. She looked at who was calling and excused herself from the room. A few minutes later she was back.

"I'm sorry, Inspector, but we will have to continue another time. I've had an urgent call which we must respond to."

"I understand Corporal. We have the same problem at times. If I can be of any assistance, you call me?"

The three soldiers ran outside and climbed into their Range Rover. As they travelled the two male soldiers changed into combat gear, while Sherry, who was driving, told them of the call. "I'll drop you in the street outside a house behind Karen's parents. According to Stanley, there's a way through their garden and into her parents' place via a small gate. You're to secure the house and tell her parents that Sophie will be with me until the potential threat is sorted, one way or another."

After dropping the soldiers off, Sherry headed towards the centre of Manchester, where Sophie worked. She stopped outside her workplace on yellow lines, placed an official card in the car window and entered the building. The young woman looked up from her reception desk.

"Miss Sophie Marshall, can you call her for me please?" Sherry asked.

The girl frowned slightly. "Staff are not normally allowed to leave their desk unless it's lunch. Who shall I say wants her?"

"Corporal Sherry Malloy of Unit T," Sherry answered, at the same time showing her ID. "I'm here on behalf of her sister Karen."

"Oh yes, now I understand." The girl dialled an extension.

A few minutes later Sophie came through from the back. "Hi, do I know you?" Sophie asked.

Sherry showed Sophie her identification. "You need to come with me, Sophie. There's a security threat, and it's believed you're at risk."

She sighed heavily. "Do you know how many times Karen has done this to me? Five and each time it's been nothing."

Sherry grinned. "I really do understand, though one day it could be very real. But I'm under orders; you have to come, so we can protect you."

"I'll fetch my coat."

Sherry waited while Sophie returned to her desk, except before doing that, Sophie stopped off at the manager's office. "Excuse me, Mr Walsh, a soldier from Unit T is here. I need to check her authenticity before I leave with her."

Sophie's employers were well aware of who Sophie was and her association with Karen. For Sophie's safety while she was at work they had set procedures to follow. He nodded and picked up the telephone, dialling a number given to him beforehand. Then following a short conversation he handed the phone over to Sophie.

After they had confirmed Sherry was who she claimed, Sophie left with her.

They travelled a short time in silence. It was Sophie who spoke first. "So are you a Dark Angel soldier, or just from the unit?"

"I'm with Dark Angel; I've been with them two years now."

"I don't know how you do it. I'd be terrified even with what little Karen has told me."

"It's not too bad, I'm not covert like your sister, more a foot soldier."

"So is it as bad as what's portrayed in the papers out there then?"

Sherry sighed. "Now and then it's pretty bad, the criminals involved in trafficking are often very violent and have no respect for the sanctity of life. The only consolation is when they come up against us, unlike the police, they face violence head-on. Most cower back and give up. A few try to shoot their way out. It doesn't work; we take them out very quickly."

"So what made you join?"

"I was abducted, like Karen. They also killed my mother. I had no one else, then your sister let me stay with her for a short time in France, while I pulled myself together. I joined the army two postings in Afghanistan."

"Then you, as Karen did, escaped the trafficker by fighting your way out?"

Sherry laughed. "I wish, but I was a wimp, with no chance of escape. My abductors kept me locked up all day, then I was used by up to six men every night. All I did was manage to get a text message out, don't ask me how, but because of that Karen came for me. I have her to thank for my life and my sanity."

They arrived at the charity offices and Sherry turned down into the underground car park. She withdrew her gun from her pocket, took off the safety catch and climbed out, telling Sophie to stay inside the vehicle until she was sure it was safe. There was a good reason for this; it was very difficult to get inside the vehicle as the windows were unbreakable and bullet-proof. Sophie had also been told by Karen in the past, of an alarm button which once pressed, would not only set off a siren outside the vehicle, but send a call to local police for help. Five minutes later, Sherry, happy the area was safe, took the lift with Sophie to the flat above the offices.

Sophie walked around the two-bedroom flat, before flopping down on the settee. "So how long are we here for then?"

Sherry shrugged. "I don't know; they don't give me that information, or even what the threat may be; I just follow orders. Control will call when it is safe." Sherry in reality did know the threat, but wasn't able to tell Sophie without alarming her over her parents' safety.

Sophie almost laughed. "You're not a good liar, Sherry, but I won't push it any further, so long as you can assure me mum and dad are safe?"

Sherry gave a faint smile. "They're protected by two Dark Angel soldiers and the police are on hand, so they're as safe as they can be. That's all I can tell you, I honestly don't know anything else."

Chapter Eight

The car containing Mike and Bert left the street. They drove to a drive-through fast food restaurant and ate their purchases in the car, before returning to where Karen's parents lived. Climbing out of the car, they walked purposely up the driveway to the front door.

Bert took out a gun from his pocket, before pressing the doorbell. Mike had done the same, but stood back to the side, so he couldn't be seen through the glass window of the door.

Karen's father opened the door. "Yes, can I help you?"

"Are you Mr Marshall, father of Sophie?" Bert asked.

"I am, do you want her, because if you do she's at work?"

Bert grinned. "We'll wait for her inside," he answered, raising his gun so Mr Marshall could see it.

He first looked at the gun and then the man. "I don't seem to have an option, you'd better come in," he said calmly, at the same time turning back into the house.

Bert followed with Mike behind. Suddenly the father darted into the lounge, slamming the heavy wooden door shut behind him, leaving Bert and Mike standing in the hall.

A Dark Angel soldier stepped out from the kitchen entrance at the rear of the hall. He was dressed in black, with a bulletproof flak jacket and helmet with the visor down. Raised and trained directly at the two men was his M5 carbide.

"You are prisoners of Unit T's strike force Dark Angel. Drop the guns and lie face down on the floor. Refuse and I will shoot to kill, have no doubts."

Mike, behind Bert, turned to run out of the front door, but stopped dead. Another soldier was just outside; he too had his gun raised.

Minutes later both men were on the floor; one of the soldiers kicked their guns well away and leaned down, handcuffing each of them. Within five minutes the police arrived, and the men were taken away. The car they came in was loaded onto a car transporter, to be taken to the station for forensic examination.

Sophie's mother came out the kitchen with a tray full of mugs and a box of biscuits. Soon the soldiers and a police detective were sitting in the lounge along with Karen's parents.

The telephone rang, and her father lifted the receiver.

"Dad, it's Karen; are you and mum okay?"

"We are love; your people were very efficient, and the men were taken without a struggle. Mother and I are very worried. We believe they intended to take Sophie. This is something we don't want to happen. I think it's best that she moves to France with you until this can be resolved. The two that came were amateurs; they couldn't have planned this snatch themselves. So there's someone still out there who could try again."

"I agree, dad. I'll arrange for the Dark Angel soldiers, currently with you, to take her directly to the villa. Can mum pack her clothes?"

***

Sherry answered her mobile after the second ring, when Karen's name had come up on the screen.

"Sherry, can you pass the phone across to Sophie please?"

They talked for a while; before Sophie passed the mobile back to Sherry.

"Sophie is coming to France, Sherry. You're to stay with her until our soldiers come for her. Then you go back to Preston and complete your work there," Karen ordered. "Also call me before you leave Preston. I may want you to go to see Greater Manchester Police about the two who were apprehended today."

"Can I stay in this flat?" Sherry asked.

"Yes, no problem. Just take care and carry a gun at all times. Report in to control at least twice a day. I'm not sure what's going on, but we may well have touched a nerve of a trafficker group we don't know of. They might even have the belief I'd fall to pieces if Sophie was taken. Now they have failed to take her, they might just escalate their actions, making all Unit T forces vulnerable."

"I understand. I won't take risks."

The phone went dead, and Sherry replaced it in her pocket.

Sophie sighed heavily. "Looks like I've wrecked another job opportunity, which will really knock my savings, except this time the threat was real, so Karen's prior warning was good."

"I'm sorry; it must be very difficult to live under the shadow of such a high-profile sister."

"We've lived with it for a number of years, Sherry. Although more so these days, mum dreads the knock on the door with someone saying, Karen has been killed. She's convinced Karen's on a collision course with the sort of people she deals with."

Sherry looked down. "I believe every mum whose son or daughter is on the front line dreads that knock on the door. None of us are immune, you just don't think about it, but you're right, it must be very hard for those left behind. For my part, no one would miss me, or even know I ever existed. Perhaps that's a good thing, who knows."

Chapter Nine

Karen was back from America and having a meeting with Stanley at Unit T's headquarters in France.

"Right, Stan, what's the progress of current operations?"

"The two men we apprehended at your parents' house, Karen, have turned out to be very interesting. Both are petty criminals not known to carry guns. That alone will put them away, but that's not the part that interests us."

Karen frowned thoughtfully. "It isn't... then what is?"

"Their role in the attempted abduction is a police matter; it's the car that interests us. You see, the car was stolen. The plates attached to this vehicle were taken from a car of the same make and model that was parked in a long-term airport car park, so as not to flag it as a stolen vehicle. If I go back to the missing schoolgirl Carol Sheppard, the car found burnt-out, after her abduction, was also stolen and also had plates attached from a car left in a long-term parking lot. When Carol was taken, CCTV picked up that vehicle leaving Balmoral Street. DNA tests on what was left of the burnt-out car are indicating that at least one of the men was involved in the attempted snatch of Sophie, as he had also been in that vehicle."

Stan stopped for a moment to take a sip of his coffee.

"It figures; I suppose," Karen said, after some thought. "But I can't believe petty criminals would be so deep into this type of crime; unless they were working for someone. Then what would be their outlet? After all, the missing girls were spread across all the papers and news bulletins, so very few groups could handle such high-profile abductions, or even get them out of the country."

"I agree, but the next piece of the jigsaw surrounds a certain Roy Clement. We believe it was he who sent them to take Sophie, though the men have admitted nothing."

"What makes you believe that, and how did you get onto him?" she asked with interest.

"The final number called on the mobile phone, just before they left the street to go to a fast food outlet; that call was to Clement. We did a trace, and it led to a phone in his name. I also had my researchers do some checking, asking around within the criminal community about him. It would seem he likes to call himself a procurer. In fact, he's very boastful of his work. There's a drinking club in London he uses as a front. It would seem he does business in the rooms upstairs. These are rooms we need to bug urgently. We already have the authority to intercept his mobile and the landline of the club."

"Then send our team in. If he's accepted a contract to take Sophie, just who else has been taken by this man and where are they being delivered? Also bug his home; we should keep tabs on him until we are sure it was not just a one-off with Sophie."

"I agree, Karen, I'll have it implemented immediately. Are you going to take the Unit to lockdown?"

Karen thought for a moment. If she mobilised, it would break all outside communication. This was important if the Unit was on the move and had a target. She shook her head slowly. "No, I want to keep an open line to the police for the moment, but if we find a definite target then I will."

"I'll move onto the trafficker Pular then. With his loss of both girls and outlets, the pressure on his operation is very high. Since we started to pull them out, he's been trying to rebuild by making requests to his contacts in the Ukraine to find him more girls."

"But does it help us?" Karen asked.

Stan grinned. "Up to this moment we know that Pular is in the trafficking business, but he has always stood away from the brothel outlets. We have found out, however, that he likes to check up on the girls personally before buying. If we could get one in, there's a chance we can link him directly."

"A covert operation may just work," Karen said aloud. "Do you think we could set up such an operation?"

"I believe we can, we know a few low grade traffickers we've used before to take us to the big operators. Let me look into it, and I'll report back."

"Very well," Karen replied quietly. "So moving on, what of our new trafficker, has the girl we rescued from the building site been able to talk to you?"

"She has. According to her, when she arrived at the hotel, there

43

was a note in her pigeonhole saying she'd be collected within the hour, to meet the rest of the crew bound for Antarctica. She'd barely had time to unpack and change before the car arrived, and she was taken to a large house. Once inside the nightmare began. She was given a coffee, while she waited in a lounge; she began to feel dizzy, then the next thing she knew she was lying in a windowless room, naked and chained to a bed. I'll leave the rest of the report for you to read. Currently we're going through her journey to the house, using landmarks, things she remembers and the outside description of the drive up to the house. It'll take time, but I think we'll have a target."

Karen smiled. "You have been busy; I must go away more often."

Stan closed his file. "Well you're up to date now. If you don't need me any more, I want to pursue a few of our leads."

"No, you're fine; just keep me abreast of developments."

***

Later, it being a warm night, Karen and Sophie were sitting outside for dinner. The main dishes had just been taken away; now they were relaxing for a short time before their dessert.

"You've been very canny up to now over your visit to the US, Karen. When are you going to tell me about him?" Sophie asked.

Karen smiled faintly. "There's not much to tell. We met as arranged and spent time together."

"Oh, come on. How did you meet, how old is he, what does he do and what's his name?"

"His name's Caleb. He's twenty-nine, six foot three, brown hair and very fit. We met in Cannes on my weekend off. He's in the US Navy and was there on shore leave from the ship he's on. Now are you happy?"

"No, what did you do, where did you go?"

"We just walked, talked a lot. We even went to a theme park, wore silly hats and went on rides more suitable for children. I had a fantastic time, Sophie," Karen replied, her eyes sparkling.

"It sounds like you did. So with all this talk, did you mention the tiny point that you were a Lieutenant Colonel, besides being a multi-millionaire?"

Karen shifted uneasily. "Not in so many words," she said, then frowned. "Why should I, I'm not the type to go around flaunting my money, or my position. I've never done it before. God, only a few know the civilian title the Queen invested on me after I found her grandchild."

Sophie was one of the very few who knew that a royal child had been abducted. Karen had told her, though she shouldn't have, but they often told each other what was going on in their lives. Even their parents never knew.

"So what did you say your job was then?"

"Just that I worked in administration, I didn't elaborate."

"But surely he'd realise who you really are, by your name?"

"No, for security I used our surname Marshall."

The desserts arrived, and they said nothing until they finished them.

"It won't work, Karen, it's far better being straight from the beginning. I know from bitter experience once, being on the receiving end of someone who was dishonest," Sophie suddenly said, bringing Karen out of her thoughts.

"Yes well, I'm not marrying him, we're just going out, so what's it matter?" she retorted, trying to act indifferently.

"You're not telling me you travelled halfway across the world for a date, I don't believe it."

"Why not, I can afford it."

"So was it worth spending thousands on a first class airfare and a five star hotel?" Sophie asked.

Karen looked indignant. "I didn't go scheduled. I took a low-cost flight and stayed in a motel."

"Why, Karen?"

She shrugged. "I didn't want to show off, or make him think I was different. I wanted to be normal, go out with my boyfriend. Do normal things and just have fun. I'm lonely, Sophie, stuck here with nothing in my life."

"You told the US authorities though?"

"Immigration knew. I am allowed to enter the US you know, without having to go cap in hand to the authorities for permission.

Sophie sighed. "Well I hope it all works out for you, I really do."

45

Karen fiddled with the handle of her coffee cup. "I've some photos if you'd like to see them?" she asked softly.

"Why wouldn't I, I'm your sister and love to know what's going on in your life. So pull them out and let me drool over this hunk you've met."

Removing a package from her handbag, Karen handed the photos from inside to her sister. She couldn't help smiling to herself as she looked at the pictures. After all Caleb had served his purpose. Their time together would soon only be a memory; she had no intention of pursuing the relationship any further.

Chapter Ten

Caleb entered the officer's lounge aboard the ship he was serving on. It had been a good vacation, made all the better by being with Karen. He was sitting with a drink, looking at the pictures he'd downloaded off his camera onto his tablet computer.

A junior lieutenant entered the room. He walked up to Caleb. "I've been asked to find you. The captain has requested you join him in the wardroom immediately."

Caleb sighed, closed his tablet down, then left the room. Minutes later he was knocking on the wardroom door. He entered to find two people inside; the captain was sitting at the central meeting table, while a civilian was at the side table filling his cup with coffee from a flask. The civilian turned to look at him as he entered, collected his cup and sat down at the table.

"Lieutenant, thank you for attending so promptly; pour yourself a coffee then take a seat. May I also introduce Mr Stinger."

They shook hands; Caleb poured himself a coffee and joined them. He noticed the captain didn't elaborate on who this man was, but he decided not to pursue this, just see what they wanted him for.

"You enjoyed your leave then, where did you get to?" the captain asked.

"I did Captain. I flew to Orlando with a girl I'd met. We went to the theme parks and did the usual touristy bits."

"It sounds an ideal vacation. Mr Stinger would like to ask you some questions about it."

"I'm happy to answer any questions, Captain."

"Perhaps you can tell us a little about the girl you were with?" Mr Stinger asked.

"In what way?"

"Who she was; where she came from; and how you met her would be a good start, Lieutenant."

"This is necessary?" Caleb asked, slightly confused.

"Very much so, Lieutenant, when you propose to spend time with a serving soldier of a foreign power, and do not notify your commander."

"Her name was Karen Marshall. I'm also very aware of the rules, Sir. However, Karen was not in the forces."

"You know that for certain, Lieutenant? Perhaps you can tell me what she actually does for a living?"

Caleb was beginning to feel uneasy. What was this man getting at? "I don't understand. I presumed Karen worked in an office, she didn't elaborate as to what she actually did. But her attitude, the way she reacted, in fact, nothing about her would point to her being military."

"That, Lieutenant, is a very naive assumption," Mr Stinger said, before putting a photo on the table, pushing it towards Caleb. It was a photograph of Karen in a military uniform. "Is this the girl?"

"It looks very like Karen, though it's difficult to tell with her wearing that uniform."

"Perhaps then this photo of her on the beach in Cannes will jog your memory?"

Caleb looked at both photos. Of course, he recognised Karen in her bikini; after all he'd spent a day on the beach with her. "They could be pictures of the same girl," he finally answered but continued, "However, if she is military she chose not to tell me. I can assure you we never discussed what I did, my postings or anything about the ship and she never asked. I acted properly, at all times."

"I'm not suggesting you didn't, Lieutenant. However, Karen uses the name Marshall at times; after all it is her birth name; though, on official documents and in the military, she uses her mother's maiden name of Harris."

Suddenly Caleb realised just who she was. "This girl I've been with," he began very slowly, "she's not *the* Karen Harris. The one who received our Congressional Medal of Honour?" he asked, hardly daring to obtain a positive response.

"The very same, and she's no longer a lowly lieutenant, which she was when she last came to America. Karen Harris is a Lieutenant Colonel. She commands a UN Special Forces unit and is not the kind of girl who would fly halfway across the world to go out with a lad she met casually in Cannes, unless she had a very good reason for coming here."

His mouth dropped, and he remained staring at her picture. "You must have it wrong. The picture you're showing me has a likeness, but the girl I've been with was not even lieutenant material. She was shy, very naive and feminine. I even struggled to get her on some of the more hairy rides."

Mr Stinger just smiled. "Many of her adversaries believed just that. They treated her like a naive schoolgirl, and that was what contributed to their downfall. Most are now dead, by her hand. So whatever impression you got from her was what she wanted you to see. Karen isn't shy; she isn't naive or vulnerable. She's extremely dangerous, besides being very competent in whatever she does."

The room fell silent as they allowed Caleb to absorb what he'd been told.

"Tell us, how did you actually meet her?"

"I was with some lads from the ship, when we met two girls in a bar. The next day we arranged to meet up on the beach. The older one was Karen, who I took out that night and the next night, before my ship sailed."

Mr Stinger and the captain looked at each other. It was obvious, by the way Karen met Caleb, that she had selected him.

"The other girl; was she very attractive and around twenty, with blonde, short hair?" Mr Stinger asked.

"Yes, her name was Sherry."

Mr Stinger smiled. "Then you're talking about Corporal Sherry Malloy?"

Caleb gasped. "I really don't understand. Even Sherry never said she was military."

"Well she is and has already had two postings to Afghanistan, holds the Military Cross and is currently attached to Unit T, which Karen commands."

The room fell silent as Caleb thought back to his time with Karen. He'd felt sick in his stomach when they had to part in Cannes. All the time he'd kept pinching himself, unable to believe his luck in meeting her, particularly after she'd told him she was single with no boyfriend in tow. Now it would seem he'd been selected, falling for her lies completely.

Mr Stinger broke the strained silence. "Now you know who Karen is, I must ask if she gave any reason, beyond being with you, for being in the country?"

"None, I presumed she'd arranged her holiday and now wanted to spend it with me."

"Where did she stay?"

"We stayed in a motel."

"You shared a bed with her?"

"No, she wasn't prepared to go that far."

"And you didn't think it strange?"

"She was English, Mr Stinger, I don't know much about the English and their attitude towards sex on an initial, casual meeting. I wanted a long-term relationship with her, so I was prepared to respect her wishes."

"So why didn't you stay in a far better hotel, rather than a downmarket motel? After all, were you not out to impress this girl?"

"Karen had spent money on her airfare. It was she who booked the motel, not me. I would have preferred a better one, but I didn't say anything, as I didn't know her financial circumstances."

Mr Stinger sighed. "Then I'll tell you, Lieutenant, shall I?"

Caleb nodded his agreement, dreading what he was going to hear.

"Sherry is worth over a million dollars; then Karen's worth at least fifteen million we know about. Karen never stays in downmarket hotels, motels or whatever. Even then she will not rely on the hotel security but will almost certainly have at least two of her soldiers with her. So, if she'd decided to stay in a two star motel and alone, it was for a very good reason."

Caleb looked down, now very embarrassed at the way he'd been duped. Then to be told Karen was a millionaire was the final straw. "I'm confused, Mr Stinger. Why would two girls, both in their twenties, very wealthy, extremely attractive and the kind you'd expect to see in Cannes, choose to be soldiers?"

"I can't tell you for certain, but I would surmise it was because of their backgrounds. Both girls were abducted and treated badly. For them, this is a way maybe to get vengeance on their abductors. But I don't know for sure."

"Then I've been a fool, and you're right, I should have reported the meeting, especially when we met again in the US. Except I was flattered; Karen, like I said, is very attractive and particularly sexy, but with a manner of vulnerability and an easy-going nature that overwhelms you. I just didn't think she was anything other than a civilian."

Mr Stinger ignored his excuses and carried on with a question he wanted answered. "While you were on holiday, were there any times she wasn't with you?"

"One day I didn't see her. She said she wanted a little time on her own to get presents for her family. We met for dinner that night. Then one night we'd gone to our own rooms at eleven. I'd had such a good day I tried to call her on the internal phone at around twelve, just to say goodnight and how much I'd enjoyed her company. I suppose in some way I was hoping she'd ask me to join her. But she never answered; so I assumed she was asleep and thought nothing more of it, after all, she joined me for breakfast."

The captain looked at Mr Stinger, then back at Caleb. "I want a full report of your time with her. You miss nothing out, Lieutenant, even specific times when you were with her and not. You don't talk about her to your fellow officers, or even mention her name. Do you understand?"

"I do, Captain, and will give you a full report."

"Very well; do you have any photos?"

"Yes, on my tablet computer."

"Then pass the files across to me and remove everything from your camera and computer. From now on Karen was never with you; neither do you mail her and pass any emails she sends you directly to me."

When Caleb left the room, the captain looked across at Mr Stinger. "What's your opinion?"

"After hearing what the lad had to say, it's obvious she came to this country for a reason, using him as cover. Why she had to come, who she met, will be critical in our investigation to determine what she's up to. Thank you, Captain, for your assistance, perhaps you can forward the Lieutenant's report as soon as it's completed?"

***

Mr Stinger entered the CIA building two hours after his meeting on the ship. After going through security he walked down the corridor and into a room with the name of Chas Roper on the door.

Chas looked up. "Well Lenard, had she come for another reason rather than just a holiday?"

"I guess so. Karen, with one of the other female Dark Angel soldiers, set him up. I'll send you a full report later. Then she certainly left him for a day, and at times she was not in her room overnight. The girl went covert in our bloody country."

"But for who and why, that's what we need to find out. Did they hire a car?"

"No, it was all taxis."

"Then that's where we begin. Check all the local taxi companies and find out on the day she was without her boyfriend if any taxi carried a girl of her age and alone. Also have them check for records of night-time pick-ups from that motel. Send someone to the motel, talk to the desk clerk and anyone else, just in case she didn't take a taxi, but was picked up by someone."

Lenard shook his head. "It'll be a long shot. This girl's a very experienced covert operator; she won't make the simple mistake of being caught out by a logged taxi ride, or even being picked up on cameras climbing into a car outside the reception, you can be sure of that."

"Possibly, if she had considered that taxi ride to be a risk, but she had good cover; so there's a chance she may not have been as careful. In the meantime, I'll call my contacts in London. Maybe they can shed light on what she's up to."

Chapter Eleven

Mr and Mrs Sheppard made their way through a door set between two shops. There was a short hall with stairs at the far end. At the top of the stairs, they came out onto an open landing with a number of doors. One door had a sign with the bold letters L.B.N.F. attached, below which was a small notice asking people to ring the bell and wait.

The two of them looked at each other, she nodded, and he pressed the bell push.

Moments later a lady opened the door. "Yes, can I help you?" she asked with a smile.

"We have an appointment. I'm Mr Sheppard, and this is my wife."

"Yes, of course, we're expecting you; would you come this way please?"

They followed her through the open office, where three young women were working on computers. At the far end, they went through another doorway, up a flight of stairs, coming out into a large room with a long table running down the middle. Arranged around the table were twenty chairs.

"We would normally take you into one of our interview rooms, but today the head of the charity is here, and she has asked to see you. May I offer you some refreshments? Perhaps coffee, tea or a cold drink?" the lady asked.

"Tea would be very nice thank you," Mr Sheppard replied, "but isn't Karen Harris the head of the charity?"

"Yes, she is."

"Then it's really good of her to take time out to see us."

The lady looked back from the side table as she waited for the water to boil. "Miss Harris takes a great deal of interest in the charity; if she's in the area she will always see clients. Of course, she's abroad most of the time, but when she's in England, she will divide her time between our two offices."

The lady took a small tray over, with a pot of tea, milk and two cups. "If you take a seat, Miss Harris will be here very soon. Would you prefer I stay until she arrives?"

"No, we're fine thank you. This is a pleasant room, and we'd like to have a few minutes alone."

"I understand. Just lift the phone if you need me." She left the room.

Mrs Sheppard poured the tea for them both. She looked up at her husband. "I hope we're doing the right thing coming here, Tony. I feel very nervous coming to an outside agency for help."

He sipped the tea saying nothing for a short time, then he looked at her watching him. "What can we do, Meg? The police are baffled, and it's been over a month since Carol disappeared. It's very obvious they are merely playing lip service to our requests on progress. The young woman who runs this charity has extensive contacts, if anyone can find out what has happened to our daughter, she can."

Karen entered the room. She was dressed in a smart black trouser suit. Both Tony and Meg stood as she came up to them, offering her hand. "Good afternoon, I'm Karen Harris. But I'd like you to call me Karen."

"It's good of you to see us, Karen. I'm Tony, and this is my wife Meg."

"Well let's all sit down, then perhaps you can tell me what you want of us," Karen said, at the same time collecting an unopened small bottle of sparkling water, and a glass tumbler from the side table. She sat down at the top seat, poured a little water into her glass, then opened a notepad she'd brought into the room with her. "Before you begin, I know all about your daughter and her disappearance, so explanations and the police progress are unnecessary. I need to understand what prompted you to come to my charity and what you think we can do for you that the police can't?"

It was Tony who spoke for them both. "It's difficult; you see we haven't told the police everything."

Karen sighed. "I must warn you; your daughter's disappearance is a criminal investigation; it can be very serious if you withhold information that might well hamper their case, particularly if it results in the wasting of police time."

"We understand, but we didn't want the press to get hold of it and rake our daughter's name through the mud."

"Perhaps you'd better explain?" Karen said softly.

Tony had taken a sip of tea; he replaced the cup onto the saucer and then looked at Karen. "Two days ago, Meg was cleaning Carol's bedroom when she found a diary left between the mattress and the base of the bed. We wouldn't normally have opened it, after all, a young girl's thoughts that she places in her diary, should remain private. Meg also keeps a diary and looks on it as a means of venting thoughts and feelings? However, under the circumstances, we decided we should look at the most recent entries, to see if it could assist in understanding what may have happened to Carol."

Karen gave a slight smile. "I can understand your reluctance at first to look at the diary. I had one, and it is often good to re-look at a problem and perhaps get it into perspective. I also would have been embarrassed if mum had read it. But what was so important that you think it may have a bearing on her disappearance?"

"Perhaps I should explain?" Meg cut in. "Carol had written about her friend Sandy working in a local clothes store. She said Sandy had received a lot of really great clothes for free after modelling them for the owner in front of his buyers. But Sandy was leaving the area, to live with her estranged father down south and the owner, Amid, had asked Sandy if she knew of another girl who would like to model such clothes. The girl needed to be taller than the average girls of her age, slim and available to work on Saturdays until six. Sandy recommended Carol. After reading Carol's diary it would seem our daughter has been doing this for the last two months. All that time, we believed, she was just a Saturday counter assistant in the shop. Apparently there is a long platform in the large storeroom at the rear of the shop."

"Do you have her diary with you?" Karen asked.

Meg opened her bag and took out a small book. The front was covered with stickers and had writing saying 'Private - Keep Out' in bold letters. She handed it to Karen. "The last couple of months are the important ones," Meg said, as Karen took the diary.

Karen opened it and began to read.

"It is so cool. Amid's paying me twenty quid to model clothes in the back of the shop. All I do is walk up and down a platform while the buyers sit in chairs either side. I've a small curtained off area to change in. I was really embarrassed at first. Amid would be in there with me, while I changed. He'd check me and sometimes rearrange the clothes before sending me out. He said all models are used to having dressers do this for them, but his show wasn't designer clothes, just off the peg and didn't warrant him stood watching and messing with me all the time. Now after changing a few times, I'm not really bothered about him being there any more." The entry went on about a lad who'd asked her out, so Karen skipped those parts.

The following three weeks of entries had just been about the different clothes she'd worn; however, the fourth week was more sinister.

"Amid offered me an extra ten pounds today, to model a range of underclothes. That's thirty quid in a day; I'm enjoying it so much, I think I'll be a model when I leave school. Not sure if mum would be cool over me doing underwear, so it's best not to mention what I'm really doing on Saturdays."

By the sixth week, it was clear Carol was disturbed.

"I'm not going again; he can keep his thirty quid. Today I was expected to model just pants. When I objected Amid laughed and slapped my bottom, really hard, pushing me out onto the platform. I felt so embarrassed, but five times he had me change the knickers and go back out. After the first time, I told him I was getting dressed and going home, but he began threatening me. Said I'd receive a good beating if I let his buyers down. I was really scared and did what he told me.'

Wednesday of that week:

"Went into the shop to see Amid and tell him I wasn't coming any more. He took me into his office and laid out photos of me parading up and down just in knickers; some were so brief and see through, I may as well have been naked. He told me if I wasn't there Saturday he'd put them through our letterbox and on Facebook. I don't know what to do now. I daren't tell my friends; they believe I model a few clothes on occasion and are dead jealous. In the library at school there's a childline help number, maybe I should call and ask their advice.'

The following Saturday:

"I'm scared. I went to the shop today and during the interval he had me handing refreshments out, wearing just knickers. I was touched so many times; I just wanted to run out of there screaming. After they had all gone, Amid came into the changing room. He put his arm around me and slipped an extra twenty quid in my hand. Then with me still in my underwear, he pulled me close, rubbing my bottom, telling me he had great opportunities for me to earn some real money. I knew what he wanted me to do. I'd rather die than let those men touch me. I told him so. But he grabbed my arm, sat down on the chair in the room I change in; pushed my face down over his knees, before pulling my knickers down to my ankles, and laying into my bottom and the top of my legs. I was screaming for him to stop, but he wouldn't. When he finally did, he pushed me to the floor and started kicking me. Telling me I was a slut; the photos would go on the internet and all my friends would see me naked. I was crying, but he didn't let off. Finally, I gave in, promised I'd do anything he wanted if he'd stop hitting me, and not show the photos to mum and dad.'

The following Tuesday:

"It's my birthday; the girls have a bottle of vodka; we're going to drink it in the park. I've decided to tell mum and told Amid last night. He said I should think about it; he'd meet me in the coffee bar on the high street on Thursday, and we'd talk. I promised him I'd say nothing until we'd met. I think he's going to let me go after I threatened to tell mum.'

Karen placed the book on the table. The way the girl had been groomed, with gifts and money, was typical of what she'd heard from other girls in similar situations. The pattern was always the same. Initially giving the girl clothes she'd be comfortable in wearing. Having her change in front of him, each time handing her clothes that little bit more revealing, allowing the girl to become used to showing herself off. Very soon, with just a small cash bonus, she'd be down to knickers, before the next step in her abuse, when faced with the threat of her friends, her family finding out just what she'd been doing. Then she was caught.

"We don't know what to do, Karen. We had no idea our little girl was going through such hell," Meg said quietly.

"Do you have the address where Carol was working?"

Tony handed her a printed paper with all the details of the shop, even the telephone number. He said nothing.

"Thank you for bringing Carol's diary. I can understand why you were reluctant to show it to the police. If you don't mind, I'll keep it and make a few enquiries. On the face of it, the two actions could be unrelated, but with a delaying tactic by this Amid, and then Carol disappearing, I cannot rule out a connection."

Tony sighed. "We thought the same thing, Karen. All we can ask is that you do your best to find our little girl. We're not bothered what she did in that shop. We've been young and understand how attractive it initially was for her, but of course with age comes experience, it's all too easy to knock Carol for her stupidity, but would we have acted any different?"

Karen nodded her head in understanding. "I don't think we would have." Then she changed her tone. "Now this is really important. You should say nothing to anyone about this. Keep away from that shop, no matter how much you want to confront this man over what he's done to your daughter. Don't expect me to go in tomorrow, or even the next day. Your daughter will not be there, so it will be a watch and wait situation. That's if he is involved. Either way he will pay for the crime of messing about with a fifteen-year-old, have no doubt."

"We understand, Karen," Tony replied. "We're just thankful there are people like you to come to. We couldn't bear it if our daughter became part of a media circus. We just want her back home."

***

After the Sheppards left, Karen leaned back in her chair. Then she dialled a number on her mobile phone. The number only rang once before Stanley answered.

"I'm sending the details across to you on a shop. I want everything you can find out about it, and the man Amid, who owns, or may rent the premises."

"Will do, Karen; are you staying in Manchester tonight?"

"Yes, but what I do from there will depend on what you can find out for me."

58

Chapter Twelve

It was Saturday, four days after Karen had met the Sheppards, when she walked into the shop Amid ran. Her intelligence unit had been watching it, and had gathered a great deal of information as to what was going on there. Already the man had replaced Carol. Karen had deliberately delayed seeing this man, until the replacement girl was working there.

The time was just before six at night. A girl behind the counter was counting the takings; the shop was empty and the clients in the back had also gone.

"I'm sorry, we're closing, are you after something in particular?" she asked, looking up from the sheet of paper she was using to write down the takings.

"No, I've come to see Amid."

"He's in the back; do you want me to call him?"

"No, that's fine, I'll go through."

The girl shrugged and carried on, no longer interested in Karen, now she knew she didn't want anything.

***

Amid was in the small curtained-off area at the back of the raised platform that he liked to call his catwalk. Cassie, a girl of fifteen, was objecting to the clothes he had brought in for next week.

"You are off your trolley if you expect me to wear this lot," she said, holding up a bra and knickers set, with open crotch knickers and a bra so skimpy it wasn't worth putting on.

He moved closer to Cassie and suddenly gripped her face with his hand, pressing her hard against the back wall. "Listen kid, you get twenty quid for wearing what I say. So if you don't want this pretty face of yours cut up, and photos of you plastered across the Internet naked, you wear what I decide you wear. Have I made myself clear?"

Cassie squirmed out of his grasp and began to laugh. "No one threatens me. I'm going, and you can keep your job. But come anywhere near our house, put photos up on the net of me, an' my brothers will kick the crap out of you."

She made to leave, grabbing her coat, but Amid had other ideas. He grabbed her hair, wrenched her around and hit her hard in the stomach. Cassie doubled up in pain, but he wasn't finished, he pushed her to the floor, kicking her ribs. He knelt down, pulled her up, his face inches from hers. "Threaten me would you, think your brothers will help you out. Just remember, I can call on twenty men, your brothers will end up with both their legs broken, crippled for the rest of their lives. You will be so cut up that even a sewer rat wouldn't want you. Make your choice kid, or should I call some of my customers back to give you a good time, then ask you again?"

Never had Cassie been so frightened; even though her brothers were nineteen and twenty, well able to look after themselves, she believed Amid. Her brothers wouldn't have a chance, and it would be her fault.

"I'll wear them," she replied meekly.

"You bloody will, so put the bra set on now so I can see how it looks, then I want you back next week; otherwise we'll come looking for you. Do you understand?"

She nodded weakly.

Amid pushed her away, before standing and turning to leave, satisfied this girl was scared enough to do as he wanted.

Coming out of the curtained-off area, he stopped dead. Karen was standing just outside.

"Interesting conversation, Amid, but not very nice for the girl. I wouldn't think about making that threat against me."

He looked carefully at Karen. "So who are you and what do you want? As for my conversation with Cassie, it was just an employer-employee misunderstanding, wasn't it, Cassie?"

Cassie had come from behind the curtain and was standing listening to them. She just shrugged indifferently. "Yes, as Amid said, it was just a misunderstanding. Can I go now, Amid?"

"Pay her up, we need to talk," Karen told Amid.

"Excuse me, this is my shop, my employee and I'm not looking to take on. So unless you want to buy, get lost."

Cassie grasped the opportunity to leave. She went for her coat in the changing room and came back pulling it on, then put her hand out.

"I can't hang around while you discuss whatever, I've got to go, or I'll miss my bus. Can I have my wages, Amid?"

Cassie left after he'd put a twenty pound note in her hand.

Karen sat down on one of the many chairs around the room. "Let me introduce myself. I'm Lieutenant Colonel Harris of Unit T. You may, or may not have heard of the Unit, but we specialise in people trafficking. You, my friend, are in deep shit. Already I've witnessed threats against an underage girl. That alone will give you time. Then if I go into your past more deeply I'm bound to find more skeletons, maybe even sexual abuse of young girls, or even worse, that you're an accessory to the abduction of Carol Sheppard. As you can see, Amid, the charges are just growing and growing. You'll be lucky to come out in twenty years."

Amid had lit a cigarette and was looking at her very carefully. He of course knew who she was, recognising her from the papers, but initially had decided to play dumb. But why was she alone, why hadn't the police come, was this girl looking for a deal? "I do know you and your unit. But I presume by your being here alone, what you are saying might not happen. Which I would assume comes at a price?"

"You seem very sharp," Karen replied. "Nevertheless, I'm not alone; the entire shop's surrounded by my soldiers. It's very rare these days I go anywhere unaccompanied. It comes with the job, you see. But I'm digressing. You are correct; I do want something and that is information. You're also correct there is a possibility that no charges will be forthcoming, although you will not be allowed to continue. This operation is closed. Try to open up anywhere else, or even approach a young girl again, and you had better watch your back. You will become a legitimate target of Unit T. We will take you out, have no doubt about that. It's what we do."

If her statement had unnerved him, it didn't show. "So what is this information that is so important, you're prepared to walk away from me?"

"Carol Sheppard, it was you who arranged her abduction wasn't it? And before you come up with excuses, I've read her diary. It's very detailed and tells us what you had her do. Then the week she went missing was also the same week you'd agreed to meet her in a coffee

61

shop. I presume that was a delaying tactic?"

"She was going to blow the whistle, she had to be taken. Not that you could prove a link to me," he replied with a smirk on his face.

Karen hated the arrogance of these people and the way they would brush aside abuse as if it was the norm.

"You know, Amid, you have no idea just how precarious your life has become. This isn't a court of law; this is street law. If you want to become a statistic, so be it. I will find Carol anyway, with or without you. So forget the bullshit about proof, you are already convicted and are currently a target."

Amid wasn't sure if Karen was telling the truth, or not. But he dealt with men who for a fag would sort someone out for you. His world was violent, had little regard for life, or anything else for that matter. Karen also lived very much in that world, so it would be natural for her to carry out her threats; after all, she was well known in the underworld for the violence she often brought with her. But more importantly, she was more than capable of carrying out a threat herself, without any assistance.

"So if I give you the information you've asked for, what guarantee do I have you won't turn me in?"

"None, except my word. Which if you ask around I don't renege on, only, you can change the goalposts. Like, for example, by opening up again, or carrying on with whatever you were up to, believing I'd do nothing. Both ways would bring me back, and more importantly the agreement we have would go out the window. Mind you, if the police are already on to you that would be your problem, except any information wouldn't come from me."

"I need to think, maybe check you are who you say you are."

Karen removed her gun and began fiddling with it. "I believe you're missing the point, Amid. There is no thinking, no checking me out. You see, when I walk out of here that's it. I don't return. Then I might hand all the paperwork over to the police, or if I think you may be able to worm out of the charges, I'll issue the order to eliminate. Either way no one will ever know I was involved."

Amid was scared, but also annoyed. "What gives you the right to threaten people the way you do?" he shouted.

62

Their eyes met; hers were cold and indifferent. "I could ask you and many of the traffickers the same question. They, as you, believe it's all right to threaten children who can't fight back. Think it right to destroy a young life both physically and mentally. I'm telling you now, you can't. I've seen too many traffickers walk free from custody, because the victims were too scared to stand-up in court. The traffickers believe they are invincible. They are not, and those who live by the gun must be prepared for the consequences. So you have minutes left before I walk out of here. You will not see the week out, once I issue the order. Then children, like Cassie, can relax knowing their abuser cannot hurt them any longer."

Still annoyed, Amid tried another tack. "In this country the government observes and extends human rights to everyone, including their convicted criminals. Any more talk about killing me, then I'll call every paper in the land, they will force the government to have you removed, maybe even put you on trial."

Karen sighed deeply. "You know, your sort make me sick. It's me, me, me, all the time. Believe when the going gets tough you can shout for your rights." Then her attitude changed. "Let me tell you this? I was taken when I was seventeen. Naive, I believed I had a God, who would protect me. He never did; I had to fight my way to freedom. But the most important lesson I learned was how little I was thought about. I wasn't even shit under the trafficker's foot. As far as he was concerned I was owned, to be bartered and sold. Where were my human rights? Where were Carol's human rights, or even the girl you've just threatened with disfigurement, if she doesn't do what you ask? So if human rights are so important, you help me. Refuse, then as God's my witness, I'll kill you and yes, I'd happily go to prison for it, knowing there was one less child kidnapper and abuser on the street."

Amid was in a quandary. The people he knew about would kill him if they found out he'd given Unit T information. But, on the other hand, if he didn't, then he'd no doubt this girl would have him killed. There had to be a deal where he could get away with his money.

"If I give you the information you want, I need time to settle my affairs and return to my own country. Otherwise, I am dead anyway."

"How much time?"

"Two weeks."

"One week, Amid, that is all I'll give you. We will use the week to check on everything you tell me, we won't go in until you are out the country, but if you lie, don't expect to get on that aircraft."

"I agree."

"Then I want your passport and money, we will book the flight and hold the ticket. We don't do that for free; we want the cash off you. Warn anyone we're coming and again you will never get on the flight."

He laughed, but it was a forced laugh. "I'd be stupid to do that; I may as well go out in the street and announce I'm going public."

Chapter Thirteen

Following the agreement Taras made with Ancil, Carol had been taken the next morning to a man called Marble. They entered a large house through the backyard, immediately going through to what looked to Carol like a consulting room.

Already Carol was scared as to why she was here. But in minutes a man entered in a white coat, with a stethoscope hanging around his neck.

She remained standing while Ancil and Marble talked. Of course, she was unable to understand what they said, with her very limited knowledge of French. Then Ancil told her to undress.

Marble began to poke and squeeze her breasts, made measurements, then she was told to lie down on the couch. Again he ran his hands over her, checked her heart and pulse before he was satisfied. Still naked, she was taken out of the consulting room, down to the cellar and into an empty room. Inside there was a single bed in one corner with a mattress on top, but no blankets. Her ankle was chained to the steel crossbar of the bed. Two women came into the room, then while she was firmly held by one, the other woman injected her. Then she was left alone.

Carol lay on the bed shivering, tears in her eyes, unable to believe her parents had refused to pay, after first agreeing to. She didn't know what to do, what to say to these people to convince them to try again.

It was nearly an hour before the two women returned. By then Carol was lying on the bed curled up trying to keep warm. She felt strangely light-headed, not able to think straight. They said nothing, just turned her around on her back, laying her flat with one woman holding her legs apart while the other shaved her pubic hair. When they'd finished, the chain on her ankle was released, before they stood her up with one on each side and guided her down a corridor into a bathroom. There she sat in a plastic chair, while her long hair was cut into a pageboy style, before hair dye was applied. Carol didn't struggle, or go into hysterics; she just sat there completely oblivious to what was happening to her. Within twenty minutes, and satisfied the dye had taken, she was moved into the shower, where her hair was washed and her body was lathered with soap before being scrubbed vigorously. Carol could hardly stand, her head spinning as they dried her with two towels. Then sitting her back down on the plastic chair, they dried her hair before covering it with a plastic cap. Now finished, she was stood up, and led out of the bathroom, directly into a room with an operating table in the centre; all around were cupboards with different instruments laid out inside them. The bright lights of the room blinded her for a moment, as they brought her in, she couldn't really understand exactly where she was, or what they were doing to her. She was led to the table and helped to lie face up; she felt better lying down. The room wasn't spinning so much, but the lights above were dazzling, making her keep her eyes closed.

She could hear people talking; someone was wetting her breasts with what felt to her like a brush, at the same time her hand was lifted; then someone was tapping at her wrist, followed by the prick of a needle. She began to feel like a cold liquid was running up inside her arm, voices around her becoming more distant, then, nothing.

***

Carol woke, at first confused as to where she was. But soon she realised she was back in the room they'd taken her from, naked apart from knickers. She was alone, with both her wrists chained to the bed either side of her. Her breasts felt sore, then looking down she could see they were wrapped in bandages; her chest looked swollen. Below her belly button, there was another dressing attached to her body. It took her a few minutes of lying there, staring down at the bandages, and coming around even more, to realise just what they had done. She stared back down at the bandages, before going into hysterics, screaming and shouting obscenities. She wanted to rip the implants out of her body, but of course with her wrists secured she could only lie there. Tears began streaming down her cheeks, her distress very real. For two days, she lay in the bed. The women washed her, fed her and sat her on a bedpan she'd brought into the room with her. On the third day, Ancil came. She was back in the consulting room standing with her wrists firmly secured behind her back, wearing a loose hospital gown and knickers, the bandages gone. He pulled the gown open and looked at her breasts, rubbing his hands gently over

66

them both.

"You like your tits?" he asked her.

The hate in her voice was all too evident when she answered. "What do you think? Sticking those things in my body. I'm only just sixteen, still developing; now you've turned my body into a circus curiosity. Then what's the scar below my tummy button for?"

"Rubbish, every girl dreams of having tits like you've got. Besides, men like young girls with firm well-filled breasts, so you're destined for good times ahead. As for your other tiny operation, I've saved you the inconvenience of being on the pill, you're sterilised." He turned to Marble, talking in French. "She looks good, Marble, Taras will be pleased."

"Yes, well get her out of here. I've other clients waiting," he retorted.

Ancil released her handcuffs and helped Carol put on a loose tee-shirt, jeans and trainers, which he'd removed from a plastic bag. Then before they left and after Ancil had refastened her handcuffs, Marble handed him a small paper bag. "She needs these tablets, two at night and two in the morning for a week. If she's in pain, there are some painkillers she can take. The tablets are to keep her sedated, so she can't try to rip the stitches and pull the implants out. I've had girls try to do that, but by the end of the first week they normally accept them, it is also time then to take the stitches out. Keep her away from clients for at least three weeks, after that she'll be fine. The girl's now sterile but if you're shagging her, keep her on the pill until her second period; by then, if there were any eggs left in her tubes, they'll be gone."

***

It had been three weeks since Carol's operation; Ancil would come to see her each day, a woman would bring her food and take her to the bathroom. All that time, she'd been locked up, in a bedroom, with a television that only received French programmes. She was given only a tee shirt to wear and secured to the bed with an ankle clamp at the end of a chain. Even though, during the first week, the tablets were keeping her heavily sedated, she'd cried herself to sleep on many nights, terrified of her future and more importantly, that she may never see her family again. By the end of the third week, she was all but dried out of tears, and just sat for hours staring ahead of her, indifferent as to what was going on.

On the fourth week, Ancil as usual came to her room. He sat on the end of the bed looking at her. "Do you like your tits, now they've settled and healed?"

She wanted to tell him the truth, how she hated them, how she'd tried to get the nerve up to rip them out once he'd freed her wrists, but didn't know how. So she simply shrugged. "I've got used to them, and I've put the cream on as you told me and massaged it in. But my breasts were growing before, so why did I need implants?" she asked, trying to be as pleasant as she could, without going into a fit of screaming and shouting, which she really wanted to do.

"Your owners paid for them, they wanted you with nice tits from the start. Take your tee-shirt off and stand-up with your arms to either side of you."

She did as he asked; feeling revulsion for this man as he rubbed his hands over her breasts, checking the two tiny scars that had all but healed. He then checked the scar just below her navel. That too had healed, with little sign left they had ever been inside her. Carol could see the satisfaction on his face.

"Beautiful job, you should be proud walking around showing these off. You'll have no shortage of admirers believe me. But first let's get you dressed in a bra and knickers; then see how you look shall we? I bet you're fed up sitting around just in tee shirt."

She sighed softly. "I'd like to have underwear on again."

***

That evening Carol was brought into the lounge downstairs. She'd showered and had her hair washed, before being given skimpy underwear to put on. Ancil had completed her dressing, with suspenders, a short skirt, top and high heels. Carol felt the clothes were too old for her, not a young girl's clothes; she wanted jeans and a jumper. But at least she was dressed, and was surprised how different she looked.

He sat her at the dining table, fed her, even giving her a few drinks. Shortly two of his friends joined them, and they began playing cards. Carol moved to the settee watching. Tiring of that, Ancil put some music on.

"Come on, Carol, give us some entertainment, why don't you start to strip, show the lads here your tits."

"I'm not a stripper thank you," she replied indignantly.

His attitude immediately changed. "You are what I say you are, I own you, so get that in your thick head. Now start to strip girl, slowly and sexily for our entertainment, or I'll strip you; stretch you out on the table and let them break you in. It's your choice, entertain, or we rape you."

***

Carol was sitting on her bed leaning against the headboard reading. For the last week, she'd entertained Ancil and different men each night by stripping for them. While Ancil never let them touch her, after they'd gone he'd take her to his bed, all the time threatening her with the alternative of being gang raped by him and his friends, if she refused. She had no choice but to agree, each time it made her feel dirty and sick inside, with what he'd have her do with him.

She had just put her book down and dozed off when she heard noises from outside the door, before the sliding of the bolt. The door swung open; Ancil entered followed by a woman. She had never seen the woman before, and they both stood looking at her. Ancil was carrying a plastic bag, but leaned over the bed and unfastened her ankle clamp.

"Stand up - take your shirt off," he demanded.

Carol did as she was told. She felt embarrassed with her breasts protruding, in her view unnaturally, like they did every time she had to stand naked. Although Marble had done a good job, and the scarring was minimal and couldn't be seen, she didn't like her body any more.

The woman went behind Carol, put her hands under her arms, grasping her breasts. She worked her fingers gently, hardening Carol's nipples, checking all was well, and the girl had no pain. Then pulled away, nodding toward Ancil.

"Get dressed in the clothes in this bag," Ancil demanded, throwing the bag on the bed.

The bag contained a clean tee-shirt, knickers, jeans and trainers. As she dressed Ancil began to talk in a language Carol couldn't understand. Carol had learnt a little French just by watching the television, but this wasn't French, she had no idea what language it was. The woman finally pulled out an envelope from her handbag and handed it to Ancil.

He then turned to Carol. "This lady works for your new owner. You're going with her. Object, struggle, try to escape, and it will be met with a severe beating. Do you understand?"

She was glad to go, glad to get away from his abuse, but also scared as to what she was going to. So she just sighed indifferently. "I understand," she replied. Now free of her ankle clamp and with the door open, Carol was weighing up in her mind if she should make a break, close the door and lock the two of them inside. That thought was immediately dashed when two men came into the room, grabbing her tightly, one plunging a needle into her arm. In seconds she felt waves of dizziness coming over her before passing out.

Held between the two men, Carol was carried out and placed in the rear of a car. The woman shook hands with Ancil, before climbing into the car and driving off.

She drove as if she was possessed. Her speed dangerous, her shouts of abuse at other drivers getting in her way, resulted in many angry shouts back at her. But she ignored them, and they were soon out of the town, heading into the hills.

They journeyed for over an hour before the car stopped, and the woman climbed out, lighting a cigarette, after first checking Carol was still unconscious. Then after ten minutes, they were on their way once more.

After another hour and a half of driving the road had become very steep as it fell into a valley. Already it was dark, the lights on the car poor. As the vehicle rounded a particularly tight bend, two deer crashed through the bracken of the hedgerow directly in front. The woman screamed abuse as she dragged the protesting car to the right, in an effort to avoid the animals. She was well aware that to hit such large animals could damage the car seriously, and with a girl in the back, difficult questions could arise.

However, her reactions to avoid the deer were a bad error of judgement. While she missed the deer, she also lost control and already the front wheels were locked, sending the car out of balance. Seconds later it turned over, then again and again before coming to a halt back on its wheels. The woman, who was not wearing her seatbelt, had been thrown around hitting her head a number of times, and she was unconscious when the car stopped rolling. Carol was lucky. She'd fallen forward, down between the front and rear seats. Her body was jammed and didn't move as the car somersaulted. For a time, the engine screamed, before the fuel shut off valve operated preventing more fuel entering the engine; it died suddenly. Now there was just silence. Only the headlights of the vehicle gave any indication of the accident, with their beams pointing out into the dark of the night.

***

Carol stirred. She felt sick; her head was banging; her bones ached. She lay there a short time as the horror of what had happened to her over the last weeks came back. But even with these memories, she was confused. Where was she, why was she alone in the back of a vehicle?

Dragging herself up, and with every bone in her body protesting, she attempted to open the door. Except it wouldn't open. She tried the door opposite but that was the same, she was trapped. Undaunted, she lay down on the back-seat and began hitting the window of one of the back doors with the heel of her trainers. All she got for her efforts was a painful heel.

"God I'm stupid," she suddenly blurted out, "why don't I just wind down the window?" at the same time as grabbing the handle. Then, with a great deal of effort and a lot of wriggling, she was through the window, falling in a heap on the ground. She stood and stared at the wreck of the car.

"Help me," a voice came from behind her.

Carol spun around and stared down at the woman leaning against the banking to the side of the road. Her face was covered in dried blood; one arm looked in the wrong position for an arm, her legs were also covered in blood. Even with the blood all over her, Carol knew who it was.

"Me! Help you? I should bloody kill you."

The woman gave a faint smile. "Perhaps little girl, except it takes guts to kill; you don't have that sort of guts. Besides, you, like me, need help, five miles down this road is where I live, someone there will help."

Carol smiled. "I know the sort of help they'd give, especially to me. But thank you for the information; at least I know which way not to go. As for you, you're right, I couldn't kill, or even know how to do it. But as far as I'm concerned it's everyone for themselves. If my option is to run, or be raped every day, I'll take my chance and run."

"Ha, you think it's that easy to escape, when we're miles from the city? Walk away now, and we'll hunt you down like an animal. Then girl, you will learn a lesson in life you will never forget."

Silence came; both were looking at each other. Then Carol shrugged. "Like I said, I'll take that chance." Then she turned and walked away.

***

It was nearly daybreak when a lorry came slowly down the road, in the direction the car had been travelling in. The road was really a short cut off the main road into the town and as such, only locals would use it. The woman knew this, always using this road to avoid any possibility of being stopped by police patrols, when she had an illegal with her. However, with the accident, it had backfired, and she'd been resigned to a long night, before locals began to use the road, taking their produce to the market in the morning.

She had been sleeping, trying to push aside the pain she was in, during the wait. But the noise of the lorry crawling along in low gear had wakened her. She pulled herself up a little and smiled to herself. Soon her men would be out in the woods looking for the girl. Already she'd devised a punishment that would leave the girl with both physical and mental scars for the remainder of her life.

The lorry came to a grinding halt and soon, after a frantic telephone call, an ambulance and police were at the scene. A policeman was looking at the wreck and the marks around the car.

"You were alone, yes?" he asked in German.

"Of course I was alone, do you see anyone else?" she retorted in German.

He just nodded and didn't comment.

She looked at him carefully, trying to ascertain if he believed her, or was just nodding a reply, but he gave nothing away.

Two men from her big house on the edge of the town arrived. One came up to her and squatted down at her side. "You look pretty bad, Francis," he said in German.

"Yes, bloody deer, they should be shot," she replied, but grasped his arm when the two paramedics, preparing to move her, went over to their ambulance to bring the stretcher. "The girl's on the run, find her, she can't be allowed to talk, do you understand?" she demanded, before the paramedics came back.

He nodded and stood away as the woman was placed on a stretcher and taken to the ambulance. After the medical team left the scene, he returned to his car. The other man joined him.

"The police seem to think someone else was here. They're confused by the tracks," he said, after closing the passenger door.

"There was, Francis was bringing a girl. She's escaped and probably in the forest. I'll get a few of the men together, have them bring the dogs, she won't have got far."

The policeman watched the ambulance leave, followed shortly by the car with the two men inside. This was a small town; everyone knew each other. In particular, the police knew of Francis and her discreet men's club set just outside the town. In reality, they all knew it was a brothel, but turned a blind eye. The police had heard disturbing rumours that very young girls were being made available. They had been to the house a number of times but found no girl under the legal age, so they had stepped back. However, the chief of police wasn't satisfied and had sent a full report to his people in Berlin. They in turn had notified Unit T of the possibility that illegals were being used. The policeman raised his radio and called control, asking to be put through to the chief.

"We have a situation, Sir," he began when the chief came onto the radio.

"Explain please?"

"Ms Francis, who runs Club Apollo, was involved in a road accident. She claims she was alone, but I don't think she was. There are other tracks around the car, small, possibly that of a female or a child. I think whoever it is has made a run for it and is out in the forest. I saw Francis talking quietly to one of her men from the house. I have a feeling that she told him to find that person."

"I understand, send your precise location through to control, we'll sort things from here. You did a good job there."

"Thank you, Sir."

Chapter Fourteen

Karen, in her offce at Unit T, replaced the telephone handset back onto the cradle. Then she immediately raised it again and pressed a number of buttons.

"Stan, who have we got in Germany at this exact moment?"

"We have five Dark Angel soldiers on surveillance at Homilies house, awaiting the main force to join them. That unit is already airborne and about an hour out from joining up with the surveillance team. Why, is there a problem?"

Karen had spread a map out in front of her. "Sorry Stan, give me a few minutes. What's the airborne unit's grid reference?"

He gave it to her.

She looked carefully at the map once again. "Yes, perfect timing," she suddenly blurted out. "Stan, redirect the airborne unit, I'll send you a new grid reference. Transmit it and come to my office please."

Minutes later he joined her.

"Well, what's happened?" he asked.

Karen looked up from a document she was studying. "I've received a call from the chief of police in Berlin. He's been watching a brothel suspected of having underage girls there. We've also had reports about this place. Anyway, he believes the woman that runs the brothel was on her way back to the house with some other person. There was a road accident and he suspects whoever was with her has escaped and is on the run. The chief, the same as I, believe that the person is a girl, probably very young, as rumours have been circulating in the area that she's bringing in underage girls." Karen hesitated to think back to the time she had been abducted, and escaped, only to be chased by the people she'd escaped from. She felt for the girl and knew just what she would be going through. "He doesn't want to use the local police and alert the brothel. But by a stroke of luck we're forty miles from the accident. I'm not leaving a girl or anyone else for that matter out there on their own, Stan. We will find that person before the men from the brothel can. Already the chief's sending a helicopter with infrared surveillance cameras from Berlin to help with the search."

"It's a risk, Karen. But one that must be taken. If this is an underage girl, she's almost certain to have been abducted and should be able to identify this Francis woman as her abductor, we can close the brothel down and put Francis away for a number of years."

"I agree. In fact have my plane made ready. I'm going to Germany."

"You've a meeting in London tomorrow with Sir Peter. Have you forgotten?"

"No, tell him what happened and I'll see him early next week."

"No problem, I'll lodge a flight plan, I presume you want to leave as soon as possible?"

"Yes, certainly within the hour."

***

Karen's aircraft landed in a small private airport in Germany, close to the border with France. Already Unit T's helicopter was waiting. She quickly transferred, then even before they were in the air she'd changed into combat uniform, finishing off with a bullet-proof sleeveless jacket. A soldier handed her a belt fitted with a communication pouch and handgun holster. Karen checked the gun passed to her, before slipping that inside the holster. She then plugged the communication unit, also given her, to a connecting cable leading to her helmet, checking for reception from the headphones and microphone.

After twenty minutes of flight, the helicopter came down in a small clearing close to a farm. Captain Simon Pilchard, aged thirty-two, with a background of six years in the SAS, was waiting. He saluted her as she jumped down from the helicopter.

Karen saluted back. "Well, Captain, what's the progress?" she asked, after they were a distance from the helicopter and their speech was not drowned by the engine noise.

"We've deployed across six miles, and are closing towards the accident area. Taking into account the time of the accident, and the probable distance a person could travel away from the town, our target will certainly be contained. At present, we've slowed down, checking more carefully as we get close up."

"And the people from the brothel, have they done anything?"

"Yes, three males left around an hour ago. They returned to the accident area with two dogs. I believe they're also tracking whoever left the scene of the accident. Two from our own unit have moved up behind them. By the direction that the dogs are going in, it's confirmed our own assumption about the route the target decided to take. The target must have had some inkling that the town offered no protection, as most people would have worked towards that."

"That's good, are the men carrying weapons?"

"One has a hunting rifle. The other two are holding the dog leads. They could be armed, but it would be handguns. None will pose a serious threat to us."

They both climbed into a Land Rover, travelled for about a mile, before it came to a halt. "We walk now, Colonel, the vehicle could attract attention."

Chapter Fifteen

Carol felt sick and light-headed. Her body, badly bruised from the accident, was giving her pain. Anyone in this condition would have tried to get help from a local house, but Carol was scared, believing every house, every person, would keep her there until the woman's accomplices came for her. Then besides the punishment, her life would be that of a prostitute and worthless. This was not what she wanted, what she'd planned for her life. Carol was intending to go to university and become a lawyer, like her uncle. Her interest was in human rights and strangely enough, what had happened to her was in part what she wanted to fight.

Standing for a short time in the middle of the road, Carol tried to decide which way she should go. She'd been in the scouts for three years and had a general knowledge of survival outdoors, but that was with a survival pack and warm clothes. She had nothing besides the tee-shirt and jeans she was wearing. She was cold and already shivering. To the left of her it was very dark, but to the right the horizon was glowing slightly. This gave her the idea there was a very large town, or even a city there. On that assumption, she decided that was the direction where she could get help. But between where she was and the large town, or city, she must keep well away from houses, or farmsteads. Carol didn't hesitate any longer; she turned from the relative ease of walking down the road, setting off over the fields.

***

After two hours without stopping, Carol finally had to rest. The fields had quickly changed to shrubs and trees, the track non-existent, her progress becoming slow and laborious. Already she'd stumbled a number of times and injured herself. The forced rest was welcome; she still felt dizzy from the drugs they'd given her. Somehow they must have been suppressing pain, as the severe bruising she'd received from the car accident was now becoming a great deal worse, as the drugs weakened. Carol lay there staring vacantly up into the night. She was shaking; she seemed to be drifting, no longer able to concentrate. She tried desperately to pull herself together; she couldn't stay here.

Standing gingerly, she began to walk again, with every step getting harder. At times she couldn't even remember where she was, why she had to carry on, then seconds later, it would come flooding back to her, pushing her on.

Carol was now at the end of her endurance. The fear of capture, or punishment and what would follow, she no longer cared about. All she wanted was food and warmth. Her sense of direction had gone. Her ability to understand and avoid hazards was lost. The ground was uneven with a number of steep slopes. Seconds later she stumbled on the edge of one, lost her footing completely, fell and began rolling uncontrollably down the incline. Her screams of terror were absorbed into the overwhelming silence of the forest before she blacked out.

***

How long she had lain there unconscious, Carol had no idea. The dark skies were now lit by the morning sun. The area around her, that in the dark seemed foreboding, was made up of equally spaced and obviously well-managed trees. To the left of her she could see the edge of the bank, a good twenty feet above her, that she must have fallen from. Carol sat up with difficulty. Her tee-shirt was ripped with patches of blood on it. She'd lost one of her shoes, and the bare foot looked very swollen. She looked around and saw her trainer a short distance away. However, as she tried to stand to retrieve it, only then did she realise that her ankle could have been broken in the fall. The pain was excruciating, forcing her to scream involuntarily. Carol was gasping, feeling faint, so she lay back down, trying to pull herself together. As she lay there, tears came to her eyes. She was lost; no-one knew she was here, and there was no way she could move on. Her only chance of help lay with the woman in the car. That's if she'd bothered to send people to look for her, which she doubted. Then if she did, would they help, or just leave her? These and other thoughts were running through her mind while she lay there, already resigned to never seeing her family again; and yet, only a few hours before, she was full of hope and expectation, when she walked away from the accident and the woman. The enormity of her situation soon turned the tears to despair. Carol began sobbing uncontrollably.

In the hours that followed, Carol was drifting between

consciousness and unconsciousness. She'd thought she heard a helicopter, but wasn't sure. After that, she heard nothing.

It was late afternoon; the sun was still shining, Carol felt warm and with it she felt a little better. She'd tried to suck the dew off the grass around her, to help with the thirst, but it did little. She even tried to eat the grass, but that made her sick. The wrenching of her stomach highlighted the pain she still felt from the bruising.

***

The sun was going down, already covered in cloud; Carol was shivering from the evening chill of the air. Somewhere in her mind she thought she could hear dogs barking. The barking seemed to go on and on, at the same time getting louder; it filled her with hope that someone was looking for her. She tried to pull herself together and screamed for help. But her calls were pathetic and weak.

Very shortly, added to the dogs barking, she heard voices, then minutes later someone was at her side. They shook her vigorously, shouting at her to wake up. Carol opened her eyes. A man's face was only inches from hers. Who the man was she'd no idea, in fact, she couldn't care less provided he had water, or even food.

"Have you any water?" she whispered.

He pulled a bottle from his backpack, then after opening the top poured a little water between her lips. She drank it gratefully.

"How badly are you injured, can you walk?" he demanded.

She shook her head sadly. "I think I've broken my foot. I can't walk."

The man left her with the bottle and moved away to the other two stood watching.

"She's too far gone, besides, her foot is probably broken. The girl's no good to us."

One of the other men looked across at her. "I agree, she'll be useless for weeks. Put a bullet in her head and let's go."

"Can't we just leave her, she's unlikely to survive the night anyway?" the other man cut in.

"And if she's found and still alive, she'll tell them all about Francis. No, we get rid of her now. Anyway we're doing her a favour; a quick death is far better than her dying slowly out here, or even being ripped apart by wolves."

It was at that moment the dogs began barking, then a second later two Dark Angel soldiers appeared. Both were dressed in black combat uniforms, bulletproof vests and helmets with the visors down. Each carried an MP5 assault weapon.

"Drop your weapons and all of you lie face down in the grass. Try to run, release the dogs or make any other aggressive move, and we will shoot to kill. You are prisoners of Unit T's special forces group, Dark Angel," one of the soldiers shouted.

The men were not soldiers, but they did know what Unit T was. None of them was prepared to call the soldiers' bluff, immediately doing as they were instructed. While one soldier kept them under surveillance, the other ran down and handcuffed each man, checking all their pockets for hand weapons, before taking the dogs away, tying them to a tree stump. The other soldier called the main approaching group over the radio, telling them the area was secure, and they had found a girl, who they suspected may have come from the car accident.

***

Karen knelt down alongside Carol, holding a cup filled with a hot beverage. She had also removed her helmet, and another soldier had taken her gun, so as not to alarm the girl.

"Hi, I'm Karen, from Unit T. You're safe now and under our protection. The medics tell me, among other injuries, you may have broken your foot, so we are bringing our helicopter to evacuate you. While we wait, I need a little information; do you feel up to talking to me?"

Carol felt better after a hot drink and was now eating a biscuit.

"I'm okay thank you. What is it you want to know?"

"First your name, what country you are from and a little about how you got here. Only a brief explanation, details can wait until later."

Karen was a little taken aback that this girl was Carol Sheppard. They had cut her hair, dyed it, and she looked nothing like her official photo. Besides, they were in Germany, so the route the traffickers used to bring her so far must be very good.

"How did you know I was here?" Carol asked.

"We didn't. Well I say didn't, that's not entirely true. You see the local police suspected there was another person in the car, from the footprints, but we received no information as to who it was. We suspected a young girl, as the woman who'd been driving the car has a brothel, and we've received reports that they are using underage girls. The police in England are looking for you, although not in Europe. We had a suspicion they had brought you across the channel, but not where you were."

"When can I call mum and tell her I'm safe?"

"I'm afraid that will have to wait until we get you back to our camp. We need to confirm you are who you claim you are. Arrange ID then return you to the UK."

Further conversation was cut short when Unit T's helicopter arrived. It was unable to land, but hovered above, lowering a cradle for Carol to be placed in. Already the main group had moved off with the prisoners and dogs. While they may not be held over Carol's abduction - after all, they claimed they'd been hunting, coming across her after the dogs found her scent - just the fact that they all carried unlicensed handguns would keep them off the streets for some time, enough for Karen to take the investigation deeper into the traffickers' operation.

Chapter Sixteen

Immediately they had arrived at the camp hospital, Carol wanted to call her parents to tell them she was safe, but Karen shook her head. "I'd prefer you not to. You see, Carol, the trail that brought you here is one we want to backtrack, with your help. At present the world still believes you're missing, and we'd like to keep it that way, for around a week. By doing this, we could save a lot more children - that is, if we can find the people who are running the operation. I'd understand if you don't want to. I was in your situation, so I know what you've been going through."

"And you really believe I can help?"

"I'm not sure yet, first we should sit down and talk. I'll need every tiny detail of your abduction, where they took you, what happened and finally, how you escaped. Then I'll know if you can help."

Carol looked down. "You know, out in the forest, I was resigned to not seeing my family again. I knew by the morning I'd be dead. If what I can tell you helps just one other child, then I'm prepared to delay talking to my parents. After all, you came for me, and I'll always be grateful. As far as I'm concerned, I'm safe. Mum and dad would feel no better, or worse, with me gone for another week. I'll help if I can."

"Thank you, but I'll not keep you away from reuniting with your family a day longer than necessary. If we can go on alone without your help, we'll take you home. I promise you."

***

Carol had been in the hospital at Unit T's camp for two days. They had set her foot and dressed her superficial injuries. Although not broken, it was very badly sprained. While Carol was in the hospital, she broached the subject of her sterilisation and the implants to the doctor, asking if they could be removed before she went home and the sterilisation reversed. He'd explained to her they didn't have the facilities to undertake such an operation, but he would speak to Karen to see what could be done.

She had also spent part of the two days telling Karen everything that had happened to her, including any names she'd picked up.

"Did the doctor mention my medical problems, Karen?" she asked, at the end of the second day.

"He did, and we have arranged a specialist from a private clinic in Paris to come to the camp tomorrow. He's seen the x-rays and would like to examine you before he'll commit himself. We'll do everything we can to reverse what they have done, Carol, but a thirty-six bust has stretched the skin quite a lot, he will want to be certain what he recommends will be acceptable to you. As for the sterilisation, that is again very specialist, we will get advice, but it may need to wait until you are back in the UK."

She looked down, then back at Karen. "I hate them; I'm only sixteen, but I'd rather keep them than have a flabby chest."

"Let's see what he says, shall we. I'll sit in with you, if you want, he's the best surgeon in Paris. He'll know exactly what the ramifications will be of taking them out, and the alternatives, believe me. Anyway, for the rest of your stay here, would you like to move to my house, it's more comfortable and away from the barracks?"

She smiled. "I'd love to; I feel a little self-conscious being here, if you know what I mean?"

***

The driver, who had brought Carol from the Unit T camp to Karen's house helped Carol out from the vehicle. She'd been given crutches in the hospital and had practised all the time. Now she was quite comfortable using them and getting around reasonably well. Carol stared up at the house. She'd expected an old villa, or a very small house. This was nothing like that. It was huge, even the parking in front of the building could easily take twenty cars. As for the building, it was ultra-modern and impressive.

A lady came out from the main double door entrance and down the steps. "You must be Carol? Can I help you up the steps?"

Carol smiled. "No, I'm fine thank you; I've got quite good at getting around with the crutches. Is this really Karen's house?"

"Yes it is. Lots of people are surprised at the size of it. Anyway, perhaps you'd like to see your room? We have put you in the guest suite, as it is on the ground floor overlooking the pool, so you'd not be faced with any stairs."

The guest suite, in Karen's house, not only had its own lounge, but a bedroom with en suite complete with jacuzzi and a steam room. Never in her life had she been in a house like this. Carol sorted out her clothes before placing them in the drawers and wardrobe. Having arrived with only what she stood up in, Karen had made three hundred pounds available, allowing her to purchase her own clothes at the camp's shops, besides collecting clothes from the local town on the way to Karen's house. Karen believed this to be important, rather than push clothes onto her that she didn't like. The girl needed to feel comfortable and relaxed, after her experience, and this was a way to do exactly that. Now everything was put away, Carol was dressed in a light top with shorts; she made her way out onto the patio alongside the pool. Carol could see a girl lying on a lounger.

The girl looked up at her and smiled. "Hi, I'm Sophie, Karen's sister. How are you feeling?" she asked, at the same time standing up and walking to the side table.

"Would you like a drink? We've orange, Coke and a few different sorts of lagers and beers."

"Coke would be great, thank you. Do you live here, it's a fantastic place?"

"No, I live in Manchester with mum and dad. I'm just on a break; I love to come. But you're right; it is a fantastic place and wait till you taste the food; it's better than a five star hotel."

Carol settled down on a sun lounger; Sophie placed a glass at her side, before returning to her own.

"This house must be really, really expensive. Is Karen dead rich then?" Carol asked.

"I've no idea, she never tells me that sort of thing. I guess she must be well-off, but nothing is ever mentioned. Anyway, what do you like to do? Watch movies, listen to music channels, play board games? After all, you can't go swimming just yet, or do any other outdoor activities."

Carol shrugged. "I like anything really. It would be nice to swim, but I don't think I'll be here much longer than the rest of the week, so my foot won't have healed."

They fell silent for a short time, both lying back soaking up the sun. About half an hour later another girl arrived. It was Sherry Malloy.

Sophie opened her eyes. "Sherry, have you met Carol?" she asked.

"No, but I've heard a great deal about you, Carol. It's good to finally meet you. Would you like a top-up?" she replied, at the same time removing a carton of orange juice from the fridge and filling a glass.

"No, I'm fine, do you live here in the house as well?"

Sherry laughed. "I wish, but no, I'm in the barn. Today's my day off, and Karen allows me to use the pool when she's away."

Carol frowned. "Why do you live in the barn?"

Sherry by then had removed her tee-shirt and shorts, revealing a bikini, before settling down alongside the other girls. "I'm part of the security detail for the villa. The barn's converted to hold a number of soldiers. Then, being the only female in the detail, I get a small room to myself, which is cool, other times I'm in the camp."

Sophie stood. "I'll leave you two. I'm going to have a long soak in the tub before dinner. I'll see you later, Carol." Sophie grabbed her towel and walked away towards the house.

What Carol didn't know was that Sherry had been ordered to look after her, besides gain the confidence of the girl to assess her thinking. Already, the information Carol had given was proving extremely important, so keeping her in limbo meant the trafficker and his organisation were unaware that Karen was very close to catching them. With this in mind, Karen wanted the initial meeting to be low-key, friendly and casual. Then more importantly, Sherry was closer to Carol's age, so Karen was hoping Carol would be more at ease around her.

"I'd like a job like yours, when I leave school. It'd be great helping protect this house, besides having a sneaky swim when the owner is away. Do you eat in the house as well?"

Sherry shook her head. "I have done in the past, but once I became part of Unit T a lowly corporal doesn't sit down to dinner with a colonel." Sherry leaned closer, her voice low. "Mind you, sometimes

I go away with Karen, to the south coast or even the US. Then she's very different, a relaxed, laid-back fun girl. We have a fantastic time winding up the lads who try to pick us up."

Carol grinned. "I can imagine. I'd love to come with you, except Karen would look at me as a child I suppose. Anyway, what made you join up?"

Sherry shrugged. "I was taken the same as you, and at your age. I had a hard time after being sent to a brothel. I was there a few weeks before Karen came for me. The traffickers wanted me back, and they killed my mum, so I've got no one now, no relatives that is, I joined the army more for safety I suppose, because I was scared of being taken again. I've also been on two tours to Afghanistan. That was really tough; people don't understand that for every soldier reported killed, five are seriously injured. I was lucky, but lots of my mates weren't."

"God, I never realised you'd been taken. I'm really lucky to have got out. What abuse I got; it would be nothing to what you must have gone through. Even the thought terrifies me."

"But you've been missing over a month, how is it they never put you to work?"

Carol seemed embarrassed. "I was too skinny; or rather, my boobs were too small. The people who wanted me, were after using me in their brothels, seven days a week. So I got a boob job forced on me, besides being sterilised. I went from thirty-two to thirty-six overnight. Now I don't know what to do. I asked the specialist from Paris if the implants can be removed. They can, but I would be left with a load of droopy skin that has been stretched, and they can't guarantee my own boobs would grow enough to take it up. That would mean them cutting it out later and leaving more scars." She sighed. "I always wanted bigger breasts; I suppose every young girl does when they see their friends better developed than them, but not this way. I've the option to reduce them to thirty-four and see what happens from then. I have not said yes, or no; rather, I'm waiting now until I'm back home, so I can talk to mum. The only good bit that has come out of this is I never had to experience what you went through, although I came very close to it."

Sherry stood up. "I'm having a swim, then if you want you can

87

come and see my little room. I've got a couple of photo albums and some good music on my computer."

Carol grinned in delight. "I'd love to come, thank you for asking me."

Chapter Seventeen

Once Carol had gone to the villa, Karen travelled to London for a meeting with Sir Peter. They had a great deal to discuss. However, rather than go directly to London, using her own aircraft which she loved to fly, she flew on to Manchester. One of the two Dark Angel soldiers, assigned to look after Karen's parents until the recent attempted abduction of her sister could be resolved, met her at the airport. Forty minutes later, she was in the home of Carol's parents, Tony and Meg Sheppard.

Tony had returned from work, after Meg called, telling him that Karen was on her way and wanted to see them both. Now they were all sitting in the conservatory, and Meg was pouring tea. Both at this stage feared the worst, with Karen coming herself.

"I've asked you both to be here to give you the good news," Karen began. "Carol is safe and with my unit in France. We picked her up in Germany two days ago. She is now part of an ongoing operation which is why I have come here to see you personally and not gone through the police."

Meg froze, holding the teapot, staring at Karen, obviously in shock. Tony, stirring his tea, also stopped.

It was Meg who spoke first. "How is she? When can she come home?" she gasped.

Karen smiled. "Let me explain." She went on to tell them how Carol was found, what the traffickers had done to her, besides the injuries and her agreement to stay temporarily in France. "You can perhaps understand that with Carol's information there is a chance we can take out, not only the abductors, but perhaps rescue other children taken by the group?" she finished off.

Tony looked at Meg, and she nodded. "We both understand, Karen," Tony began. "Whatever you think best is all right with us. Naturally, it goes without saying that we want our daughter home. We want to shout from the rooftops to tell the world she's safe. But even that very short piece in her diary has made us realise just how dangerous and nasty these people you're after can be. So if Carol is happy to stay with you, and with your assurance she is safe from any more harm, we will go along with the need for secrecy. Although we would both like to be able to speak to her, if only on the telephone."

Karen smiled broadly. "Carol will be very safe. We are not using her in any operation, just not announcing that she has been found. She's also protected twenty-four hours a day, the same as I am, by very experienced soldiers. No one can get close to her, believe me. As for you wanting to talk to her, that's easy," she answered, opening her bag and removing her tablet computer. "I'll get our control to patch Carol through and you can all talk, besides see each other. I will also give you a phone number so you can call her at any time, and she can call you. I'm not looking at more than perhaps one or two weeks before you will all be together, so this is not long-term. The important point of all this is you must tell no-one, not her grandparents, her school friends, or even the police, otherwise the chance of finding other children alive will be lost."

They both agreed, then after the connection had been made, Karen left them alone, taking her tea into the garden, spending time looking at the flowers.

***

After leaving Carol's parents, Karen flew to London. Sir Peter's car was waiting outside the airport, and she was taken directly to New Scotland Yard, where Sir Peter had his office.

They embraced, and he kissed her on each cheek. "You get around, Karen. I hear you've come from Manchester. Were you visiting your parents?"

She shook her head. "No, Carol Sheppard's family. Between these four walls, we found Carol in Germany. She's currently being looked after in our base camp, but this is part of what we need to talk about."

He returned to his chair behind the desk. Karen took a seat.

"Interesting, but I presume, if you're not making it officially known, she's given you a lead?"

"She has, and it's leading us to a trafficker we didn't have any information on. He goes by the name of Taras, but we're struggling to find out more about him, except he originates from Russia, and we know he has a sidekick called Maksim. This is a man we've come

90

across before. He's ex-KGB and was mixed up with Pular for some time, then he went off the radar. With Carol's information, we're already following leads to this group. There is also another disturbing development; we're rescuing more girls who've been sterilised. It seems like a simple operation, originating from India, means they can do it with one tiny incision below the tummy button. It takes literally minutes but is extremely difficult to reverse. Then in Carol's case, she even had implants fitted; so I'll need to allocate more funding from the charity in order to find ways of helping these girls. A fifteen-year-old who's been sterilised cannot be left without the hope of raising a family when she's older."

"I agree; it is a new development. I will talk to the health minister. For the UK girls, we must have arrangements in place to assist them. As to your European operations, it sounds like you have those well under control. How did you do in the US with our Harry Watson?"

Karen leaned forward a little, her voice low. "I assume you have knowledge of major Italian mafia groups?"

"I do, which one in particular are you talking about?"

"The Ndrangheta."

Sir Peter looked at her for a moment. "That is a particularly dangerous and secretive group, Karen. Are you suggesting they have moved from their roots in drug dealing to people trafficking?"

"Yes and no, they are still heavily into drug-running. Except the drug industry, particularly the cocaine side, is under pressure. The intelligence collected by the Italian police, besides the more sophisticated ways of detecting these drugs, even in sealed containers, is hitting them hard. Now many of the people who make up the Ndrangheta are looking for more lucrative avenues, with most of them fleeing Italy, since the authorities began clamping down with moderate success, and settling in other EU countries, creating legitimate business outlets to front their illegal activities. The network is spreading, and so are the areas of criminality they are getting into.

"Harry Watson, who I went to see in America, already had contacts with a boss in the Ndrangheta. They have apparently joined up with a Mexican cartel known as Los Zetas. Los Zetas was already into drugs, people smuggling and kidnapping, with a territory that includes Mexico, US and Italy. This may be why the two have come together in an operation. Apparently it's their intention to take girls in the US and ship them into Europe. Besides a glut of trafficked illegals from Mexico into the US, which very rarely gets reported, there's also a very high number of American girls reported missing who are never found. In America, each state concentrates their search for the missing girls within their own region; there is not a great deal of cross-state searching, apart from FBI operations, which deal with the nationwide problem of hundreds of youngsters going missing every month."

"I see, so in doing this, most European police forces will assume they are winning the fight, with a reduced number of reported abductions, and cut back?"

Karen shrugged. "Yes precisely. After all, until a girl is obviously snatched, in the UK for instance, the police don't actively pursue a possible link into the sex industry. Take Carol Sheppard. The press were having a field day; the police did their usual running around, got nowhere, so effectively left her abduction on the back-burner, downgrading her to a missing person. Press- wise she's all but forgotten. Girls going missing in the US would have the authorities concentrating their search over there. Why extend their search to Europe, when they already have a very large trafficking problem in the US, so it is probable in their eyes, that the answer to a girl's abduction lies on their own soil?"

They both fell silent, while Sir Peter thought about what Karen had said.

Finally, he nodded his head slowly up and down. "It makes sense. As you say, the papers remain quiet here, the US does their usual investigations on their side of the water; while the European brothels are filled with good quality white girls. My tiny problem with all this; why has Watson come to us?"

"He's basically scared. The Ndrangheta knew he had gone to the US; apparently they have been keeping tabs on him, he suspects through the Los Zetas cartel. He told me they didn't seem to know he'd made a deal with you; they were under the impression he'd just bailed from the UK. So when they approached him to coordinate, it wasn't an offer, it was an instruction, on the threat of telling the authorities about his involvement in Europe. Watson wants out, afraid that if the US authorities get a whiff of this, he could go down for a long time. They wouldn't be as lenient as the UK have been, and you don't turn state evidence against the Ndrangheta, or the Los Zetas cartel, if you want to see retirement. But he believes if we can stem the flow to Europe, with good intelligence, taking out the brothels there, then the Ndrangheta would consider trafficking from the US a bad idea profitwise and effectively drop it, leaving him alone and still lily-white in the eyes of the US authorities."

"So he provides details of the ship the girls are on, we track it and where the girls are taken, then we raid the brothel in our ongoing fight against traffickers. It all sounds so very simple. For me, a little too simple to actually work."

"It does on the face of it sound simple. Except I think Watson only knows the first stage of the operation. The Ndrangheta may have an altogether different agenda for these girls; which he may have no knowledge of. After all, they are not fools; their survival over the years has proved that, so I can't see them completely trusting a man who is not one of them."

"I need to sleep on this, Karen, when is this operation supposed to begin?"

"He doesn't know. They told him they'd be in touch very soon; he was told to obtain premises close to a marina around sixty miles north of Boston, Massachusetts. They even gave him the address and contact number of the letting agent, with a bundle of money to make the down-payments."

"You have that address then?"

Karen passed Sir Peter a folder. "All the details are in there including the address. My only concern is, can we really trust him, or is it a smokescreen to hide something far more sinister?"

Sir Peter laughed. "Then you're the one to find this out. In our world, we trust no one, Karen. If he comes good, I'll applaud, but we need contingency if he doesn't."

Their eyes met briefly. Gone was the normal sparkle Karen always had, replaced with eyes that were cold and lifeless. "I will have a contingency plan, that goes without saying. You can also be very sure this man, or the cartels involved who use children as pawns in their game, will meet another side of me," she replied softly.

Even now, after knowing Karen for many years, Sir Peter shuddered inwardly at her words. Sat in front of him was a young woman who had faced death many times, never hesitating to turn to the gun when her life, or freedom, was threatened. Harry Watson would be very foolish to underestimate her.

"Right, on a lighter note Lady Karen Harris, it's about time you stepped out of your military uniform and were introduced to society. For this part, you will be joining me at a reception and dinner being hosted at the Russian Embassy tonight. Knowing you, you'll have no suitable evening wear in that tiny aircraft of yours, so after lunch, at which Georgina will be joining us, you and she can spend the afternoon finding something suitable for you to wear."

Karen grinned. She knew Sir Peter's daughter well; they often went out when she was in London, and Georgina had stayed at the villa a number of times. "It sounds like today's going to be a fun day, but is there an ulterior motive in me going to the embassy?"

"You mean beyond the fact that I will be accompanied by an extremely attractive and eligible young lady, to what may be a very boring, but necessary dinner?"

"Yes, even more so now that you are reverting to subterfuge, trying to convince a girl in her late twenties that she's still attractive."

He didn't answer right away, but their eyes met for an instant. When he replied his voice was serious. "You know, you shouldn't pull yourself down, Karen. I'll guarantee that when you walk into the room, every man's head will turn, and most of the women will be very envious of you. It is not just your looks; people will see a girl who has bucked the trend both militarily and privately. No other man or woman in the world holds the top bravery awards across three countries, and controls a very important European military unit, besides being recognised by the Queen for their dedication. Those are major achievements and proof that not all young people are time-wasters, druggies or lazy, but can actually be a force to be reckoned with. You may laugh, come up with silly excuses that your awards were the result of circumstance, which for most recipients of bravery awards is true. Often there is no time to think, to decide if this will give you a medal, or whatever. Most times it's a life and death situation." He paused for a moment, taking a sip of water from a glass on his desk. Then he looked at her watching him. "I vividly remember going with you to see the prime minister, after pulling down the criminal gang known as The Circle. Even he admitted, after you left, that your very presence in his office terrified him. And he knew you weren't coming for him. That, Karen, shows what an impact you have made in the world. Although, coming to your question, is there an ulterior motive in you accompanying me? There is, as you are to meet a certain Major Elfin Crustkin socially. He's your counterpart in Russia and knows a great deal about the underworld there, particularly the gangs who deal in drugs and prostitution. If any man knows Taras, this man will."

"And you think he will talk to me?"

"He will. The Russian authorities have been watching you for some time, and they are impressed. It was them who made the invitation; it was not instigated by our government. You will learn, by entering the diplomatic world, that most communication between governments is conducted in this way. Unless there are exceptional circumstances, all cooperation is done on an informal basis. It allows the official stance of a government to remain separate, leaving them effectively a sovereign state, well able to look after their own affairs and sometimes sort out their own dirty washing, without seeming to be in bed with countries they don't want to talk to officially. Although the reality is, in these days of international criminality, none can do it alone; they require the assistance of other nations when their nationals are causing problems, but are legally untouchable."

Karen sighed. "And there's me thinking you wanted to take me out."

Sir Peter laughed. "Come on, enough talk; let's join Georgina for lunch, shall we?"

Chapter Eighteen

Maksim was with Taras in Germany, in a large country house just outside Berlin. Taras was talking on the phone. As he spoke, Maksim could see he was becoming more and more irritated. Soon after replacing the handset on its cradle, he began bashing the desk with a clenched fist.

"That bloody stupid man, are all our associates just fools, or do they believe they are invincible?" he shouted.

Maksim frowned. "What are you talking about?"

Taras leaned forward, the palms of his hands spread on the desktop. "It seems Ancil has left a trail even a blind man could follow directly to me. He didn't bother to tell me that the Sheppard girl had escaped from Francis, and was then collected by none other than Unit T."

"That's bad. Do we know how she escaped, was it an inside job?"

Taras shrugged. "You know Francis, drives like someone possessed. She turned the car over, got herself injured and the girl just walked away. How Unit T got onto the escape so fast is anyone's guess, but they did; now the girl will be singing like a bird. Anyway, it won't be long before Unit T puts two and two together and will be calling on Ancil. We need to know just what happened, fast."

"I understand, I'll leave right away. What about Marble and Francis?"

Taras thought for a moment. "Let's understand what happened first shall we, then I'll decide just where we go from here. Although I've a mind to close the route back to me permanently, if you understand my meaning?"

***

It was just after eleven o'clock at night when Maksim pulled up at Ancil's house. The road was typically suburban, with large and expensive detached houses either side. Maksim took out a cigarette from a gold cigarette case and lit it slowly, glancing at the clock on the dashboard of the hire car.

Climbing out of the car, he walked up the short drive leading to the house, past two cars in the drive, the last one Ancil's. Maksim pressed the doorbell; somewhere inside he could hear chimes. Within a minute the door opened, a woman standing there. She was in her early thirties, good-looking, wearing a housecoat.

"Yes, can I help you?" she asked.

"I'm here to see Ancil. I know it's later than arranged, but the plane was delayed, then I couldn't get a car," Maksim replied.

A voice shouted from inside the house. "If that's Maksim, let him in."

The woman gave a weak smile, opening the door wider, allowing Maksim to enter. He followed her, pushing the door shut behind him.

They entered the lounge; Ancil was sitting in a chair. "You're late, Taras told me to expect you around nine," he said. Then he glanced at the woman. "Pour him a drink, then get lost," he barked.

She suddenly looked nervous, very different to the woman who had answered the door. "What can I get you?" she asked.

"Vodka, neat," came the reply.

She poured the drink, then left the room quickly.

"Taras said you'd be alone, who's the woman?" Maksim wanted to know.

Ancil shrugged. "A lady friend. She often stays the night when her husband's away. He works on the rigs, so it's three months fucking, after that she's gone for three months. But changing the subject, what is it Taras wants that he couldn't talk about over the phone?"

"We need to know about Carol Sheppard?"

"The Sheppard girl escaped. Well, not in the sense that she got out of one of our brothels, but more she walked away, after a car accident."

"I know that, have you contained the problem?"

"You mean, what does she know and could it get back to us, me in particular?"

"Yes."

"I don't know. Nothing has come out of Germany, and there's nothing in the papers here. Whoever's got the girl is keeping her on ice, or she died of exposure in the forest and hasn't been found."

Maksim sighed. "She's not dead, Unit T has her. What I want to know is how they knew where she was heading; after all, she could hardly have rung them up. It must, therefore, be someone in your organisation who tipped them off. Taras wants to know just who it was."

Ancil lit a cigarette, looked at the ground for a moment, then at Maksim. "It makes sense why Francis's people hadn't been in touch that she'd been found. It also means Unit T has been able to obtain useful information, which is why they are holding back the announcement of her escape. This is a different ball game altogether. Then as to the possibility of someone on my side tipping Unit T off, I don't think so. For a start, no one knew she was on the move, the girl went off the radar when Marble took her into his clinic weeks back."

"Then it's someone on Francis's side. Who knew she was going?"

Ancil shook his head. "Again this is confusing, no one knew. Francis hadn't come to collect her. She had brought payment for a new batch of North African girls who were already in the process of being shipped to us, and wanted to discuss when they'd be available. It was Taras who called, while she was in with me, to take the Sheppard girl back with her. Apparently he'd a possible private sale for the girl, wanting her available in Germany for the buyer to see."

Maksim was confused and also concerned. He had come to kill Ancil, to close a loophole to Taras, but this explanation was leading him to believe that he could be more useful alive, for the present. It was essential to see if Unit T directed their attention on to him, or Francis. The leak had to be found; getting rid of Ancil, or even Francis at this point, could send the informant to ground. He had to talk to Taras.

"Was Marble aware the girl was leaving?" Maksim asked.

"No, he was expecting her back in two days, for a final check-over. You can understand the girl was really down, besides scared and more than shocked to realise what he'd done to her, in fact she was hysterical. We had to sedate her for the first three weeks; otherwise she'd have ripped the transplants out of her breasts. Although by the fourth week, she'd eventually accepted them, and she was off medication by the time Francis took her."

"What of Francis, have you talked to her since the accident?"

Ancil shook his head. "There's no chance. The woman's under arrest, for using girls in her brothel under the legal age. According to Jacob, who looks after the gardens, the police came in force and literally took the house apart. They found a girl in a hidden room in the basement. She'd come from North Africa, sold by her father for a sack of rice apparently. That didn't matter; the girl was only twelve, so Francis will struggle to get out of that."

"What of the two held for the attempted abduction of Karen's sister?"

"When I called Roy to find out when she was likely to be ready for collection, it was then I found out his men had been caught. Roy said they'll keep quiet. They know their families will be looked after, with a lump sum waiting for them after any prison sentence. I've also been told by Roy that his legal lot defending them say it's going to be very difficult for the prosecution to make any possible abduction charge stick. After all, Sophie wasn't even in the house, they only asked to see her. The immediate problem for them is possession of a weapon."

"You forget," Maksim cut in. "The Sheppard girl could identify them as her abductors. What will happen if she does?"

"Yes, now you tell me she's with Unit T, that's a possibility, but it wasn't then. I will need to think about what I should do, as this opens up real problems. Unless of course, they don't put the two incidents together."

"Wishful thinking, Ancil. You can be certain Unit T will already be considering that as a possibility. Then they will link them to you?"

"Possibly, I know the two lads Roy uses quite well; they are the ones who always deliver girls to the boat. But the real problem is Roy; how would he'd cope if Unit T gets to him first, unlike the police, the Harris girl often uses threats to intimidate."

"What kind of threats?"

He smirked. "Live or die. You live if she gets what she wants; otherwise she'll order a kill."

Maksim's eyes narrowed. "And she gets away with that?"

"That girl can do what she wants, believe me. Her Dark Angel unit will make it look like a gangland killing, the Harris girl will be miles away when it happens and her unit, to all intents, will be at their base. Nothing will point to them; you can be certain of that."

Maksim lit a cigarette in thought. "Roy needs to die, it is our only choice. The tie between you and him is far too high a risk to ignore, especially if he's given the opportunity to tell all, to save his pathetic life."

"I agree, do you want me to have it done. Five grand will be sufficient."

"Yes, get it done, let us know when it's been carried out; but be quick."

Chapter Nineteen

"Sir Peter Parker and Lady Karen Harris," came the announcement when Sir Peter and Karen entered the reception room at the Russian embassy. This was the diplomatic part of government, prestigious and involving attendance at such functions, which for many was just to be seen. However, Karen was here for a very different reason.

As Sir Peter's Rolls Royce had pulled up outside the embassy, Karen felt nervous, which was rare, but tonight she did. In the past, with most of these occasions she attended, it was under her military rank. Except tonight she was to be announced as Lady Karen, and she wasn't sure how she should greet people. Today she'd had little time to think about it, spending a fantastic afternoon with Georgina, visiting a number of fashion houses to find the right dress, before they ended up in a coffee house, telling each other all their news. Now away from that and standing in an embassy with her name being shouted out, the reality sank in, and she was like a naive little girl standing next to Sir Peter.

"Sir Peter, it is a pleasure to see you again, and Lady Karen; we are honoured you have both found time in your busy schedules to attend," the ambassador said, at the same time shaking their hands.

Sir Peter replied for them both. "I always enjoy coming here, Ambassador; it's very unfortunate that the pressure of work prevents my coming more often."

"Ah yes, for me also, Sir Peter. I would, though, like to spend a few minutes with you," the ambassador answered, then he turned to Karen. "Perhaps, Lady Karen, you would prefer an escort more your age, who will introduce you to our many guests, rather than listen to our conversation?"

"Thank you, Mr Ambassador; I'd like that very much; not that I believe for one moment your conversation would be boring."

He smiled to himself at her response. "I assure you, Lady Karen, many often are bored. However, I will place you in the very capable hands of our Mr Crustkin," he replied, nodding towards a man standing a short distance away, who immediately responded by coming across.

Karen smiled inwardly. This was the man she had come to see, their introduction perfectly managed as if it was a script. She smiled warmly at him as he approached. He was very handsome, over six feet, with a rugged complexion and by the way he held himself and walked, obviously very fit and from a military background.

After introductions, they were left alone.

"Now they are gone, I like to be called Karen," she said, moving closer to him.

"Of course, you must call me Elfin, although I will still introduce you to others in the room by your title. It will be expected; many here like to think they are above their station, so being introduced to a real 'Lady' will make their night."

Karen laughed. "I suppose, not that I feel very special, I'm a little uncomfortable as a civilian, preferring to hide behind my military title."

"Well let's see how it goes, but first, may I get you a drink?"

"I would like a drink, except I won't accept an already filled glass from a waiter. I was caught once with a laced drink and nearly died. It is no reflection on your embassy, and I wouldn't even contemplate the fact that your drinks would not be perfectly safe. But the truth is, I'm nervous of accepting a drink without seeing it freshly opened and poured, no matter where I am."

He nodded slightly. "Our embassy is very aware that you will only accept a drink that way, Karen, and I assure you we are not offended. If you'd like to come with me, then you can make your own choice?"

Karen said nothing; it would seem they knew more about her than she thought. Even when it came down to something as simple as a drink, that is.

They approached a small bar, where waiters who were busily filling glasses, before taking away full trays, immediately parted to allow Karen forwards. She asked for vodka from an unopened bottle, with a small sealed tonic water; she watched them being poured.

Many of the waiters couldn't understand why this guest was having a drink made this way. One even whispered to his friend, "She's English", in their own language. The other nodded his understanding, as if being English answered her eccentricity.

Elfin was standing to one side. He knew everything there was to be known about Karen. So often portrayed as a formidable opponent, supported by her actions, it was hard to believe now he had finally met her. She seemed timid, nervous and out of her depth. Elfin, however, was no fool and wouldn't be caught by such immediate impressions. Already he noticed how she had sized up the room, maybe even looking for alternative exits, the threat-levels of people standing around and if there was any possible aggression directed towards her. This was the way he knew she would be thinking. Of all the military personnel in the room, she was perhaps the most dangerous, being so unpredictable; for this, he must constantly be on his guard in the way he spoke to her.

Karen turned to face him. "Okay, Elfin, I'm ready to be thrown into the lion's enclosure," she said, with a smile.

The next half-hour, before the dinner announcement, found Karen being introduced to so many people she lost count. Many seemed to know who she was and what she did for a living, probably derived from press reports about her. Others, particularly the women, looked at this titled and very attractive girl as some sort of threat, shying away from her as quickly as they could, often dragging their escorts with them.

When the announcement was made that dinner was to be served, Sir Peter came to find Karen and escort her into the dining room. Elfin moved away discreetly.

"So how is your foray into the diplomatic world going, Karen?"

"I couldn't do it every week, or even every month, it'd drive me mad. Much of the talk is 'do you know this person, or that person; are you going to such and such a place?' It's not for me, Peter."

"I agree, how have you got on with Elfin?"

She shrugged. "He's very courteous and polite. I don't get the impression he's very struck on me. Mind you, most people are like that after reading so much hype in the papers. Then, when they finally meet me, they must feel very let down."

Sir Peter steered her out of the small crowd making their way through into the dining room, to an area where they were alone. "Stop it, Karen. Don't put yourself down all the time. I can assure you the

103

Russians have a very high regard for you, or you wouldn't be here. After dinner, you will leave the main room and go with Elfin to a private room. I've already paved the way with the ambassador."

She nodded. "I'm sorry; I just feel like a fish out of water, that's all. I'll not let you or myself down and will keep focused."

He gave her a light hug. "I know you won't, Karen. But first, let's enjoy dinner, and please, eat something. Let's not send half the food back and upset our hosts."

She linked her arm in his. "Come on old person, let's eat, and I promise to clear every morsel from my plate."

***

After dinner, Karen and Elfin made their way through a private door into the back area of the embassy. They were now in a small, but comfortably furnished room. Coffee had been left in advance on a side table. Karen made herself comfortable, in a large leather chair.

"I trust you enjoyed dinner, Karen? Would you like to finish with coffee, I know it's not something you drink often?" Elfin asked, at the same time holding the coffee pot and glancing back towards her.

Karen looked back at him; again they seemed to know even the smallest of detail about her. But she didn't comment on it, only smiled. "I would like coffee, with a little milk, but no sugar, thank you for offering. I've never had Russian food before, and I was actually surprised how good it was."

He laughed, making her coffee as she'd asked, before taking a seat opposite her. "People have the impression we Russians, under the communist regime, were just peasants. I can assure you we were not."

"I wouldn't know, we didn't study communism in depth at school."

"The same with me for the west. In fact the reality was, you were the bad boys and we were perfect."

Karen gave a hint of a smile. "Likewise." Then she changed her tone. "I'm pretty busy at the moment, Elfin, and delayed returning to France in order to come here. While tonight has been an experience, I really don't have the time for socialising these days. You have a military background and perhaps understand more than others here that my job is a twenty-four hour occupation, with only the top brass having the time to socialise. I'm in the middle of a war, and it's getting worse, with more and more attempts to try and bring me down, even by attacking my family."

He shook his head. "Desperation don't you think?"

"You could be right there." She hesitated for a moment. Her following words were cold and without compassion. "Except to mess about with my family rather than face me directly, is a grave error in judgement. No one, no matter how powerful he, or she, believes they are, should have any illusions that I won't retaliate. I will. Anyway, enough about my problems, Sir Peter has told me all about you and the desire for Russia to speak to me off the record. He believes you have information that could be useful. I'd like to know what that is."

"You are correct, Karen. We do have information that we believe will be useful to you. However, a word of warning. You will be going up against what is the Russian mafia. They have always been among us, and the communist party put up with them, providing they didn't overstep the mark; even at times, they had a use and would do favours for the party. These days, since the demise of communism, they have taken over major industries and their leaders are billionaires." He leaned forward a little, his voice low. "To get that far is not always skill or experience, rather a question of having a ruthless and brutal nature. These types of people don't question or give you the benefit of the doubt, they kill. They will also go for family, relatives and friends to get at the one they want. No one is safe, and they have the money, the contacts to carry it out. You should remember that, particularly if you intend to seek to control their rise in the EU."

Karen shrugged indifferently. "We will control their rise, have no doubt about that."

"Perhaps. Anyway, two years ago you had a meeting with one of their leaders. You knew him as Ignatius."

Her eyes narrowed. "How do you know this?"

"It isn't important how we know, we know. In fact, there is very little we don't know about you, even your time in the Lebanon. But I digress. Ignatius has a man in Germany you should look into. His name is Taras. He was not happy when you took out one of his operations, which cost him plenty. It was him, through a man you do know called Maksim that an attempt was made to take Sophie. Maksim stupidly engaged a small-time crook called Clement to do the job. Clement is a fool, using men who believe they are hard. They are not, and it's only through luck that they have managed to take a number of girls without being caught. That was until they tried to take Sophie and came up against your unit. This is a man you should see quickly. One of the girls Clement abducted, had been placed with Taras via an intermediary in France, except she's escaped and is still I believe on the run. If the girl is picked up by the police, and not his men, then she will have information that could not only give them the route the girl was taken by, but could well lead the authorities to him. Particularly if Clement, or whoever he sold the girl to, wants to make a deal in exchange for a reduced, or no prison sentence. Ignatius will demand that Taras closes any possible links to himself. They will take out Clement and maybe even the intermediary, very quickly. Get to him first, then he may give you the information you need, in exchange for remaining out of prison. It will be academic; he won't live to enjoy any sort of freedom, as Taras will sort him out anyway."

Karen decided not to tell Elfin that they already had Carol, the girl he was talking about. This man worried her, and she didn't trust him, or the Russian government. She couldn't understand why they had this sudden urge to work with her. "You're telling me little we don't already know. Apart from the route beginning with Clement going as high as Ignatius, although I was aware Ignatius was part of the Russian mafia and trafficked."

"I'd hoped you'd progressed to that point. If you hadn't then it would have worried me."

Karen sighed heavily. "Then why am I here, Elfin?

"That is very simple. We want you to take down Ignatius. Politically we can't, but with our help you can. You see, Ignatius is very important on the drug distribution side of the mafia's operation. They were using an Italian group called the Ndrangheta for shipping the drugs into Europe. Unfortunately, the Ndrangheta are under great pressure on their usual routes. So much so that the flow has virtually dried up. But we discovered that the Ndrangheta found a different source and promised Ignatius a shipment as high as ten tons of cocaine, to be delivered two months from now. The value of that shipment is colossal. That money... if we can intercept the consignment, it would cripple Ignatius's group. Even if you don't get him directly, his backers will."

Karen said nothing, preferring to sip her coffee, at the same time not taking her eyes off him.

"Well, will you help?" Elfin asked.

She replaced her cup on the saucer then shook her head. "I can't, it's as simple as that. Unit T's primarily a trafficking operation. My terms of reference for Unit T do not allow me to become involved in drug trafficking. Although to be fair, drugs are very often part of the scene as they are used to control the victims, so after separating the human trafficking part out, we pass further investigation into the drug side of the operation to divisions better equipped than us. What you're asking, it would seem, is that I go for Ignatius primarily for a drug bust, then in doing so, I close up a human trafficking operation, which I won't do."

Elfin was a little taken aback. He hadn't expected an outright no. For everything to work, it was essential that Karen was on board. "I can understand your reluctance in being part of it. But we are talking upwards of eighty, maybe even a hundred youngsters already trafficked in this year alone. Surely you want to help them?"

Karen gave a shrug. "It would seem, Elfin, your intelligence on me and my unit is lacking. We don't, as a unit, go in to rescue unless the operation will bring down the trafficker. The victims are for us academic. We are not what everyone seems to believe. We're primarily a last resort strike force that can cut across borders, commandeer local police, or military units for assistance in sorting things out when all else fails. We do, however, investigate, not relying on government information, or police intelligence. Our own intelligence unit must convince me that to risk my soldiers' lives there is a ninety per cent chance of success; otherwise I won't issue the order. I will promise you one thing though. If my intelligence leads me to Ignatius, via this Taras, I will solve your problem and take him out; that's all I can promise."

Elfin stood. "Very well, Karen, we will leave it there. We will talk again, but I need direction."

Karen stood, then offered her hand. "I've enjoyed the experience, it was fun. I'm just sorry that I can't be of more help."

***

As Sir Peter drove them away, he glanced over to her. "Well, how did you get on?"

"I didn't. They wanted me to get involved in a drug bust, but I refused."

"Why Karen, you know it's mixed up in a very large trafficker operation?"

Karen didn't look at him; rather she just gazed out of the window. "They worry me, Peter. They seem to know all about me as far back as the Lebanon, and yet not a simple part of Unit T's actual role. I believe they really did know our role, but didn't want Unit T; they wanted me. Why, I'm not sure, maybe to bring Ignatius out, or something more sinister. Either way I was not taking the bait of saving victims already in the system, neither do I intend to help them. After all, they knew all about Carol, even who took her, transported her and the name of a trafficker I'd not heard of. Why didn't they act? Until I know that, I've no intention of getting into bed with them."

He touched her hand. "You are very astute, Karen. Most would jump at the chance of the prestige in preventing such a large consignment getting on the streets, but not you. Whatever you decide I'll stand by you. I agree; it would seem there are a great deal of unanswered questions; it's time we played the waiting game to see what transpires."

Chapter Twenty

The entrance door of the drinking club where Roy Clement had an upstairs office, swung open as Karen entered. She wore jeans, a white blouse and sleeveless padded jacket; her shoes were laced-up heels. With her hair tied back in a ponytail, she looked like any other girl of her age. The only slight difference to her jacket was that it had been put together with layers of Kevlar, making it practically bulletproof. At her ankle, hidden by the jeans, she carried a knife mounted in a sheath. This knife was mounted upside down, making it easy for her to draw quickly. Karen had a great deal to thank the SAS officer who gave her the knife, as many times, it had been the only weapon at her disposal in difficult situations, giving her the edge in a fight.

The bartender looked at her. This club was not a place a woman would come, and then, never on her own; unless she was on the game and after clients. "Get lost, we're fed up with your lot touting for business here," he said aggressively.

"Then it's a good job I'm not, isn't it," Karen answered indifferently.

"We also don't serve women who are on their own, so you'd better go anyway."

By now Karen had sat on a bar stool. "I wouldn't want to drink here if you were giving the drinks away. I'm here to see Clement; I believe he has an office in the back somewhere?"

"He knows you're coming?"

"No, except I know he's here, so don't come with any shit like saying he's not in. Just tell him it's Karen Harris - he'll see me."

The bartender went into the back.

Karen sat there indifferent to the rude and suggestive comments being made by other customers in the bar. This visit was from a final accumulation of information collected by the listening devices fitted in the club, Clement's car, his home and the tapping of his mobile telephone. It had become more apparent that Clement was snatching to order; already a man had called him on the phone, mentioning a girl's name, asking when she was to be delivered. Unfortunately, Karen's intelligence unit was unable to obtain a fix before he rang off. They even had a conversation recorded, besides photographs, of a man coming to see Clement at the club, wanting him to snatch a schoolgirl the same age as Carol Sheppard. Then with Amid's information that this was the man he'd dealt with, when he wanted Carol snatched, it was time Clement understood his current position in no uncertain terms.

She was brought out of her thoughts when the bartender returned. "Far door, marked 'fire escape', an' up the stairs," he said, nodding towards the back.

Roy was standing at the top of the stairs, looking down, as Karen made her way up. He looked at this girl, more attractive and taller than he'd thought. He also knew of her reputation, except looking at her she seemed nervous, unsure of herself, not the so-called tough and dangerous girl she was portrayed as.

They went into his office; Karen sat down while Roy went around the desk, sitting on the opposite side.

"So why do I have the pleasure of your company, you're not known for getting your hands dirty these days?" he demanded, with a touch of disdain in his voice.

Karen ignored his remark. "You have attempted to take my sister, for that I should kill you. Don't have any misconceptions, I'm quite capable."

He shrugged. "I suppose anyone with a gun in their hand is capable of squeezing the trigger; although the average person doesn't have access to such weapons, where you do. But you alone without a gun, that would be a different story, you'd run like a scared rabbit."

Karen grinned. "You mean like now, after all, I've not got a gun? I'm also not running." That was a lie; she always carried a gun, and currently it was located in a specially designed inside pocket of her jacket. This was a standard issue, Sig Sauer P226 handgun, with the modification of twenty rounds, rather than the usual fifteen.

"I'm not that naive to believe you'd come here unarmed, so how about you strip down to your birthday suit, then you can prove to me you've nothing to hide?" he asked, enjoying the idea of pulling this girl down.

"I can understand you'd like me to do that. Except I've not got

110

the time, we need to talk."

He sniggered. "I have tons of time, maybe when you're naked and have proved you're unarmed, I'll bend you over the table and give you a quick shag. After you've been well serviced, we'll have plenty of time to talk."

Karen smiled again. "Don't even think about it, you would be dead before you got within a foot of me."

"So what's this business you've got with me?"

"I want the name of the person who paid you to attempt to take my sister Sophie. I also want the name of the person you sold Carol Sheppard to."

"And if I don't tell you, that's assuming I know these girls you're talking about?"

"Oh, you know; we've done our homework and if it's passed across to the police you'll be going down for a very long time. But you ask what would happen if you refused my offer?" Karen fell silent for a moment, then smiled. "I'll kill you; it's as simple as that. You see I'm not the police; I don't follow the basic rules of evidence, lawyers and such. Your life is hanging in the balance. Give me the information, and I move on. If the police in their investigations put you on their hit list, that's your problem; they won't have got any information from me."

He stared at her a little stunned. "You have the gall to come here, tell me some cock and bull story that I had something to do with your sister's abduction, besides taking some other girl, and then threaten me. Get out, before I beat the crap out of you."

Karen stood; a hint of a smile crossed her face. "You can try if you want? It won't stop me putting a bullet in your head before the day's out. You see, it was a grave mistake involving my family; most criminals tend to keep well away, as they value their lives. Although I've given you a pretty good offer, your life in exchange for two names and numbers. If you choose not to accept it, that's your choice, I'll still find the people, and the world will be better off with one less bit of shit before the day's out."

Roy had had enough of her attitude and stood quickly, before virtually running around the desk to the office door, to prevent her leaving.

Karen didn't attempt to beat him to the door, in fact, she never moved.

He took her non-attempt to escape, as her being scared and began to taunt her with one hand raised and his first finger wagging. "Come on girl; let's see you get out without a beating; then like I told you earlier, I'll still put you over the desk for you to remember your visit. After all you've a nice figure for your age," he mocked.

Karen's face lit up as if in pleasure. "Oh, I see, you believe your six foot or so in height, besides your physical build, will overwhelm me. Is that not somewhat naive, after all, you've no idea of my capability?"

"You're all talk kid, it's time you were taught a lesson," he retorted.

It was at that moment, and before Karen could reply, or even react, that a commotion suddenly erupted in the bar downstairs. Roy was confused as to what he should do. Find out what was going on in the bar, or sort out the girl in front of him.

Deciding she was going nowhere - after all, he blocked the only exit - he turned back and looked at her watching him. "You and I haven't finished yet. Stay here; poke your head out into the bar and expect a good kicking," he said, with aggression in his voice.

Karen just shrugged indifferently. "I don't intend to leave till we've sorted our business. Although if you have ideas of running, don't even think about it. I will find you, except the offer will have been withdrawn."

He looked at her for a moment, sick of her arrogance, but decided not to rise to her threats, preferring to go down the stairs and find out what was going on. Coming out into the bar, he froze. His men were lying flat down on the floor, along with the bartender. Two men were standing, holding guns and wearing balaclavas.

One shouted at Roy. "On the floor, your hands above your head."

Roy fell to the floor. The other man ran over and checked him quickly for weapons. "He's clean," the man said.

"Good," the other replied. "You're coming with us, now move," he carried on aggressively at Roy.

Roy stood; the man who'd checked him pulled Roy's arms behind his back and fastened them together with a large plastic tie wrap, then pushed him towards the bar door. The other man followed at his heels.

"Just one minute, that man goes nowhere," Karen shouted. She had followed Roy down the stairs, and was quietly watching what was going on through the gap between the door and its frame. Now with Roy ready to leave, and with the two gunmen having their backs to her, she'd taken the opportunity to gain the upper hand. "I have a gun which is trained on you. Drop your own guns and don't attempt to turn around; otherwise I will fire."

One froze; the other tried to turn to face Karen, naively believing because it was a woman's voice, that she'd be all talk and wouldn't fire, even if she actually had a gun. He couldn't be more wrong in his assumption; Karen wasn't going to take the chance that he would bring his gun to bear on her, so she fired as he began to turn. He was lucky; Karen hadn't shot to kill, although she would have no problem in doing that. Her first shot was intended to disable, the bullet ripping through the shoulder of the hand that held the gun; although if it hadn't worked, she'd have let off a further two shots with the intention of killing him.

He screamed in pain, dropping the gun before finally spinning around to face her.

"That was very foolish, you're lucky I didn't want you dead; otherwise you would be. Now you, still holding a gun, carefully place it on the floor, then both of you, move away from the guns and lie face down on the floor. I'm from Unit T Special Forces and am more than capable of taking you both out, you should have no doubt about that."

The man still facing away and holding the gun knew of Unit T and their reputation. If this were one of their soldiers, then there was no chance of taking her from this position. He decided to do as she instructed, placing his gun on the floor without turning and moving away. The other, with one hand on his bleeding shoulder, also moved away. Both lay on the floor, face down, as instructed.

"That's very wise of you both. Clement, you should do the same, well away from the guns," Karen ordered.

Roy moved away. He was more than relieved at her intervention, suspecting these men had the intention of killing him.

Karen now decided she needed help; she had no chance of holding all these people at bay, although, she suspected that Clement would realise why they had come, so, just maybe, he would be more co-operative. She entered a series of numbers, with letters, into a text message on her mobile phone, before sending it. Receiving that code, the soldiers waiting outside would know she was in control, but needed help. Without the code, any communication by speech or text would indicate to them she was in trouble, and may even have been forced to send the message; then they must proceed with caution. Minutes later the soldiers entered the bar.

"Secure everyone in this room," Karen ordered. She dialled a number on her phone and waited until it was answered. "This is Unit T Special Forces. I'm the officer in charge; we have a code red situation. I'm sending the operation code and address as I speak. We also require a paramedic; there are injuries."

***

Karen's call was to the Metropolitan Police. A 'code red' call from Unit T, along with a unique texted conformation code, indicated a genuine call, telling the operator that arms were involved, which would then spark off a fully armed police response. Once on site they took over and secured the area to begin a search of the club premises. Within two hours, they had found guns, a small amount of class A drugs, and illegal spirits together with large amounts of contraband cigarettes, both of which no duty had been paid on. Overall Roy was in trouble, along with the barmen and others in the club. Then, with the usual tip-off to the press of this operation, from leaks within the police force, the press descended en masse. Added to this, when the press found out Unit T was involved, with Karen actually on site, there was much excitement. Anything Karen was involved in spelt instant headlines followed by big sales for the papers. Then, to find she was officially leading an operation in the UK was even rarer.

"Can you give us a statement, Karen?" a reporter shouted from among a large number pushing and jostling for position outside Roy's club.

This had happened within seconds of Karen coming out, flanked by two Dark Angel soldiers in civilian clothes. Already television cameras and photographers were surging forward, virtually preventing them getting to their vehicle. She stopped in front of the press and waited until they had settled a little, except for the flashguns constantly going off. She was aware that to ignore them was not the right thing to do, as it sparked off intense media speculation as to why Unit T was involved. The story was often filled with fantasy leading to public unease. So after agreement with the inspector in charge, Karen was to make a low-key announcement.

"I'm afraid at this stage I can't tell you much. Unit T was originally involved in an ongoing investigation surrounding trafficking. Arms were found on the premises, and I made the decision to have the Metropolitan Police secure the building for a complete search. I've now handed over that part of the operation to the police, who will give you all more details, as their investigation evolves."

"Are you suggesting this club was part of a trafficking operation?"

"No, the circumstances that we came here for were different. However, what transpired on these premises, which was nothing to do with us, required the attendance of police. As I said, they will be making their own announcement a little later on."

"Are you involved in the Carol Sheppard disappearance; and is this operation you're currently involved in directed towards finding her?" another asked.

"We have been made aware of Carol's possible abduction and we're assisting the police in any way we can. As Carol is still missing, and this is an ongoing investigation by the police, you must understand I cannot make further comments which might jeopardise their operation."

"Will you be at the premiere of the Peter Steen film tonight, Lady Harris?" a reporter from the back asked, changing the line of questioning somewhat, although every paper was interested to know if she would be there.

Karen looked at the young man, with him using her civilian title to gain her attention. "What paper are you from?"

"'Shout' magazine, we publish for young people."

"Yes, I've read it. Your editorials always seem very informed, but to answer your question. I wasn't intending to be in the UK today and was disappointed that I would miss it. But circumstances have dictated I will be here now, so I'll be attending." She hesitated, then smiled. "That is, of course, if there's still a ticket available for me. On a more personal note, I'm more than happy to be called Karen rather than by any of my official titles, unless I'm in uniform." She glanced down at her watch. "Now I must go, I cannot answer any more of your questions, thank you for your time."

A number of other questions were shouted out, except Karen had finished her press call and ignored them. She moved through the reporters to a waiting Unit T vehicle and climbed in. "Take me to the police station holding Clement, please," she asked, after finally closing the door.

***

Roy Clement was already in an interview room when Karen arrived at the police station. Karen had specifically asked that he wasn't to be interviewed until she had spoken to him. The inspector had agreed, knowing the critical nature of Karen's line of questioning.

"I've come to see Roy Clement," Karen told the desk sergeant, at the same time showing him her identification.

"Yes, Colonel, the Inspector said you were on your way. I was going to take a drink in as we didn't know how long you would be."

"No one has talked to him have they?"

The sergeant shook his head. "No, we've had a man inside with him. This is usual, but he's not allowed to strike up any sort of conversation."

"Thank you, I'll take his drink. Is there any chance of an unopened bottle of water for me? It's been a long day."

"No problems, if you give me a moment I'll fetch you one."

Karen entered the interview room, carrying coffee in a paper cup and her small bottle of water. She placed the cup in front of Roy, before settling down on the seat on the opposite side of a small table between them. There was no recording apparatus set up; the video had been switched off, and the policeman guarding him had left. Standing outside the room were the two Dark Angel soldiers who had accompanied her from the drinking club.

Roy looked at her. Since the time they'd spoken in the club, when he had been aggressive, he had changed and was now very subdued. "Thanks for the coffee; it seems your intervention probably saved my life. Those men were going to kill me," he said quietly. "You also lied when you said you weren't armed."

"Yes, well it's prudent not to tell people, especially civilians, that we're armed. The public gets very nervous over that sort of thing and rightly so. After all in this country, the police are very proud of their not having to resort to the gun, apart from in exceptional circumstances. But we should return to your problem. You're correct in believing, without my help, that you would now be at the bottom of a lake, or whatever they do with bodies these days. I'm unable to help you with your police prosecution for having weapons and drugs on the premises. Mind you, that will only count for a couple of years behind bars, long enough, with your help, to take out the people who want you dead."

He grinned. "I suppose you're right there, but what of my other operations, are the police going to have that information from you?"

Karen opened the small bottle of water and took a short drink, looking at him. "That depends. My offer to leave you alone still stands. You're a tiny part of an international trafficking operation and, it would seem, disposable. So if you tell me all you know, then unless the police are able to tie you in with the abductions, it won't come from me." Then her manner changed. "Have no doubt about the tenuous position you're in and always will be with Unit T. I don't like people such as you, or what you've done to so many children; it goes against the grain giving you the opportunity to walk free. But I'm a professional soldier and accept at times that to catch big fish you may need to let the sprats go. However, come out of prison and resume your operation abducting children, then we will take you out. Don't have any illusions over that."

The room fell silent; Roy was weighing up this girl sitting in front of him. The way she'd not rushed down the stairs from his office, but bided her time to place the two gunmen at a disadvantage to her. Her reaction when one tried to take her on. No panic, just one shot and the promise to kill him, made casually and with indifference. Although to be fair, she had little option. She wanted him alive, so at some stage

117

she had no option but to take the gunmen on.

"I may be able to help, after all there's a big difference to being out in a year or so on good behaviour, or a long sentence for abduction. But tell me, how did you get on to my lads so quickly in Manchester? They seemed to have had little or no chance, in taking your sister."

Karen smiled inwardly. The man was relaxing and becoming more confident about his position. Now she needed a little small talk, to reduce tension even further, and also to make him realise what he was up against. "They made a simple error, by assuming that because they didn't see security, it didn't exist. It's the same as traffickers and abductors. They are so convinced that the people they abduct will never escape, they become blasé. The problem is, sometimes they do escape, and those people then become extremely dangerous for the traffickers."

"In what way?" he asked with interest.

Karen looked down as if remembering. "I can only speak for myself. You see when you're alone for hours, days or weeks, everything that happens to you is amplified. To pass the time, you study your abductors, notice lots about them. Then casual remarks, an odd name, or location inadvertently mentioned, spin around in your mind. Soon you know all there is to know. You're able to remember people, their names, the place you're in. Everything in minute detail, always with the thought in the back of your mind, that if you do get a chance to escape, you escape with the knowledge of your location; and in particular your adversaries. When I went after my abductors, I knew the way they lived in the house, even its quirks. So when I went in, it wasn't blind, it was with the knowledge as to where they would be at that time, and more importantly what they were doing, even how to get into the secret room I was held in." She hesitated. "But enough about me, do you want to take up my offer?"

He finished his coffee, placing it down on the table, deliberately not answering immediately. "I like you, you're straight and I believe you will keep your word. Because of that and because you saved my life, even though I suspect I was more valuable alive than dead, I'll tell you everything you want to know. How the operation works, well, my small part of the operation that is, along with my contact names and numbers."

Chapter Twenty-One

The Range Rover drew up slowly in front of the cinema, one soldier driving and a second in the back alongside Karen. The crowds were huge, police everywhere, rows of press either side, with a red carpet laid down from the edge of the pavement into the cinema. Karen was wearing a long dress, with a short, sleeveless jacket, her long hair falling loosely over her shoulders. Sergeant Steve Martin from Dark Angel was to be her bodyguard and escort for the night. He was wearing a dark suit with a bow tie. The rear door of the car was opened to allow her out. At once there was a huge cheer, as many in the crowd recognised yet another celebrity. Cameras were flashing everywhere as she walked up to the entrance, Steve slightly behind her. She paused for a moment, turning round and smiling, before going inside.

Karen was met by the directors of the cinema, along with the producer of the film.

"Lady Harris, thank you for accepting our invitation. We have a seat already reserved, afterwards, we'd appreciate you taking a little time to meet some of the many people who helped to produce and act in the film. Then you're welcome to join us at the reception, with drinks and a buffet?" the film director said.

She smiled sweetly. "Thank you for having me at such short notice. I'd love to meet the people involved in the film and join your reception later."

***

The film was good, although, for Karen, there was far too much chasing and impossible stunts, but she enjoyed it nonetheless. Afterwards, she was introduced to the cast, the producer and director of the film.

"I presume the movie portrays the sort of life you lead, Lady Harris?" an actor from the film asked.

She smiled. "I wish, most of the time you're sitting behind a desk, then when out in the field it's more waiting about for perhaps ten minutes of action. The life you depict on screen is far more exciting, believe me. I'd have real fun if I could do all the high-speed car chases you had."

She moved on, talking to others, most wanting to know how real it all was. Eventually she was shown into the main reception room, where drinks were being handed out, and a buffet table ran down one wall; Karen turned to Steve. "Can you find an unopened bottle and make me a vodka and tonic please?"

He nodded and moved away. Karen walked up to the buffet and joined the small queue. The man in front of her was in a wheelchair. He had a tray on his lap, taking items from the table to place on his plate. Wanting a chicken leg and unable to reach one, he turned his head to ask the person behind him. His face lit up. "Karen, Karen Marshall. You are Karen Marshall aren't you?" he asked.

She gave a weak smile. "I'm sorry, the name's Harris, you're mistaken."

He grinned. "Of course, I should have remembered, that's your name now. You don't recognise me do you?"

Karen sighed; this was always happening. "Please, we're holding up the queue."

"I'm always doing that. Would you mind passing me a chicken leg, I can't quite reach without leaning over open food, which I don't want to do?"

Karen did as he asked, put a final item on her plate and quickly excused herself, moving away from him to a relatively empty area of the room. She didn't like her family name to be bandied around, and just wanted to eat up and go, but felt it would have been an affront to leave immediately, without trying the buffet. Steve came back to stand at her side.

"After this we're off, Steve, I'm not into this sort of socialising. Go and get yourself something to eat, I'm fine standing here," she said quietly, so only he could hear.

"Would you like me to bring you anything else from the table?" he asked, looking at the very little food she had on her plate.

She shook her head. "No, I don't really like buffet food; it's often left standing about for some time out of the fridge. I'd rather have a burger," she replied, with a smile.

A short time later, Karen hadn't seen the man in the wheelchair move up behind her. Steve had and quickly moved to a position to watch every movement, his hand just inside his jacket, the fingers gripping his gun. This was his role, to protect Karen.

"Why did you walk away? After all, you should know me. We even slept together, and you made a promise you never kept. It's understandable, who'd go out with someone in a wheelchair?" the man suddenly blurted out.

Karen turned to look at him. "Excuse me; I'd like to think I would know someone I'd slept with, thank you. I'm not in the habit of doing that and certainly not with a stranger," she answered indignantly.

"Yes, I can believe it, perhaps if I told you my name then you'd remember? The name's Garry, Garry Stafford. It was me and my mate Mark King that got you out of Sirec's house, when you were just eighteen."

She went cold inside. Eleven years had gone by since she had met this man. He looked so much older and was even beginning to lose his hair. Her thoughts flashed back to the road in the Lebanon, when after being chased by gunmen, she'd managed to destroy their cars, but Garry had also been injured. He'd wanted to be certain they were dead so he sent her back to kill them. Even today it made her sick inside, still vividly remembering being told by him to squeeze the trigger, on men who were already badly injured and offered no threat to either of them. Then with Garry badly injured and couldn't continue on with her, she had no option but to leave him, even agreeing if they got out they would meet again. But now, Garry seemed to think it was to be some sort of date, not as she saw it, a little flirtation with lad she believed was dying.

Karen sighed. "I'm sorry, I didn't recognise you. It's been a long time, Garry. People change; we move on."

"We do, except I live my life in a wheelchair, while you bask in the media spotlight; never once did you try to find out what happened to the people who helped you, or go to the memorial service of the ones who died getting you out. We sent you an invite, but we didn't exist in your world any more."

"Yes, well, I had reasons and my life hasn't been a bed of roses, so let's just leave it at that shall we? But it's been nice to see you again.

122

One day we should sit down and talk. Unfortunately, I've already overstayed my time here; I've a plane waiting to take me home."

Karen handed her empty plate to a waiter, then began to walk away.

"It's been nice to see you," he called after her. "Are those words all I'm worth, after ending up in a wheelchair for the rest of my life, because of you?"

Karen turned and looked back at him. "We need to talk, Garry. But not here, I'll be in touch. I really have to go. The flight plan has already been lodged."

"I'll look forward to your call then. But don't leave it for another ten years," he replied quietly.

She smiled. "I promise." Then she really did walk away.

As he watched her leave, a lady walked up to him.

"That's where you are, Garry. Why didn't you wait for me?"

He grinned, his eyes shining. "Do you know who I've just spoken to, mum?"

"No love, who?"

"Karen."

Her face darkened. This was a girl he had never forgotten. He had mood swings between hating her for putting him in a wheelchair, to praising her as he read in the papers about some new achievement. His mum's smile masked her real worries for him. "Did she recognise you?"

"No, but she hasn't changed. Those deep blue eyes, the sexy way she walks and stands, it's so Karen, mum. Anyway she said she'd get in touch."

"Yes, well don't hold your breath, Garry. I've said it a number of times. The world is at that girl's feet. Why should she waste her time looking up people from a time in her life I think she'd prefer to forget?"

He didn't reply, preferring to believe that now Karen had met him, she would keep in contact.

Chapter Twenty-Two

Unit T's strike force, Dark Angel, had mobilised three hours earlier. Now in lockdown, with all outside communications suspended, they were on the move. The place they finally surrounded was a house fifty miles east of Paris.

Karen glanced at her watch; it was three o'clock in the morning. She nodded to Lieutenant Lewis, her second in command. Within minutes, they moved to the house from a number of directions. Over their secure communications, she listened as each section secured its own objective.

Lieutenant Lewis moved up to her. "We're inside, Colonel, the building is secure."

Karen stood. "Let's go then," she replied, pulling her visor down, checking her gun and slipping the safety off. These precautions were part of the unit's standing orders, in case someone had been overlooked and still posed a threat.

They made their way to the open front door. Already two soldiers were standing guard; both saluted her as she entered.

Another soldier approached. He saluted. "Bad news, Colonel, the three occupants have already been shot, one is Ancil. They were professional killings."

Karen sighed, turning to Lieutenant Lewis. "Seems like Taras beat us to it then. He's determined to close up all avenues that may lead to him. I want the entire house searched. We need all documents, bank statements, mobile bills, in fact, anything that will give us information on how Ancil was living."

Karen followed the soldier who'd approached her through to the lounge. Ancil was lying slumped over his desk. Then she was taken through to the kitchen. Two women were face-down on the floor, both in a pool of dried blood. She looked at the wounds; each had been disabled by a general shot, followed by a more accurate shot through the back of both their heads. There was no doubt; this was a professional killing.

"I want to see Haynes and Jackson now," Karen told Lieutenant Lewis, who had returned and was at her side.

He ordered a soldier to find them, then turned back to Karen. "Should I contact the local police?"

"Not immediately, delay the call for around half an hour; by then I want everything scanned and sent back to our intelligence unit," Karen ordered, then she left the house.

Soldiers Haynes and Jackson caught Karen up at her Range Rover.

"You wanted us, Colonel?" Haynes asked, for both of them.

"Yes, I want an explanation as to why Ancil is dead. You were watching this house, and I can't see any report of gunshots, or visitors."

"We can assure you there were no visitors, apart from a post van yesterday at thirteen hundred hours. The delivery person was female; she went round to the back door with a parcel. We couldn't see if she went inside, but she was there only five minutes."

"You took photos of the woman?"

"Yes, Colonel, and we sent them on to our intelligence team."

Karen raised her radio. "Lieutenant, do we know how long they have been dead?"

"At a guess, Colonel, at least twenty-four hours."

"Thank you, Lieutenant."

Karen dismissed the two soldiers, before climbing into her vehicle, after asking her driver to wait outside. She closed the door and called Stan.

"Seems like we have an assassin in the guise of a postwoman, Stan. Did you do a search on this person, when the surveillance team sent the details through?"

"I did, Karen. The post van was in the area at that time, and the picture of the woman didn't throw up a known villain on ours, or police records. You're certain she was the assassin?"

"No, just surmising. I'll get the police forensic teams in to see what they can find. Now we've lost that route to Taras; we're left with Carol Sheppard's description of him and Clement's information as to where Ancil told him he lived. Have we got any further on that?"

"We think so; I'm checking it out and cross-referencing local authority records and such. I should be back to you later today or at the latest tomorrow. Is it your intention of setting up a surveillance operation?"

"Almost certainly. We need to learn a great deal more about him and his operation before he's confronted."

***

Karen returned to the local military camp Unit T had made their base, and turned in for what was left of the night. Following breakfast, she returned to her room. Using a satellite telephone, stored in a purpose-made case, she called Sir Peter.

"Peter, it's Karen, can you go secure?"

She waited.

"I'm secure, Karen. We've not talked for two weeks. What are you up to?"

"I moved on to take Ancil, but I think Taras was there before me. The hit was professional, Peter. The only visitor was a postwoman, but we have few details on her. I'm not certain she has anything to do with it, but I'm sending her photo over the wire. I assume, if she is, then she may possibly be wearing a wig. Stan's checking with the post office as she may be legitimate, but in the meantime, can you see if you can find out anything about her for me please?"

"I'll check our records. Although I'm not aware of any professional hitwoman, unless she's from Russia. That would make sense if Taras or Ignatius were involved. I'll talk to Elfin and see if he knows of such a woman."

Karen laughed. "You think he'll still talk to us then?"

"Of course, the meeting between you and him was an opening salvo. He'd have been very surprised if you'd jumped at his suggestion. They know you far better than you think, Karen."

"I'll never understand this diplomacy bit. So I'll have to leave it to you. On a different tack, I have another slight problem, Peter and more personal."

"If I can help, you only need to ask. What is it?"

"I attended a film premiere in London and was approached by a Garry Stafford. He and another soldier, Mark King, came for me in the Lebanon and destroyed Sirec's house. He said a few hurtful remarks, even told me I had no feelings, because I didn't even bother to go to the memorial service for the soldiers that didn't return. I could hardly

126

have told him at the time I was on an operation with Unit T, and never received such an invitation. Not that I'd have been allowed to go, after all, I'd dropped out of the public eye, as a girl who was abducted and escaped. But I'd like to see him and perhaps some of the other surviving soldiers, to clear the air if possible."

Sir Peter was one of the very few who really did know what happened to Karen in the Lebanon, although even for him there were gaps in the story that wouldn't be closed. He did, however, know Karen was at that time, out of control; with the very real possibility of being taken again, she'd turned for protection to a gun, given to her by this Garry Stafford. That single action went on to cause devastation when she began using it.

"Let me talk to one or two senior personnel who conducted the operation, Karen. I'd hoped it would have been a closed book by now, and for lots of reasons the government would like it so. Although it had to happen sometime, your coming face to face with one of the soldiers from the mission."

"Thank you, Peter. I'd like to meet them all again, if you can make it happen."

"Then I'll be in touch soon. Are you returning home?"

"Yes for a few days, then we're in London. One of our ongoing surveillance operations has turned up a group using young girls who are being handed around. It's a joint police operation to take the entire group out."

"How many are we talking about?"

"We have definite evidence of a large sex ring, using at least twelve girls of African descent, we know of one as young as eleven. Early this week we finally cracked the structure, and now we know the leaders of the group."

"This is important, Karen. Why the delay?"

"Mainly paperwork and clearance from the police departments involved. And then the crown prosecution is also looking at the evidence, ensuring we have enough to secure a solid conviction. There are four men running it, all Nigerians, two we know have very serious pending criminal convictions back in Nigeria. The government there has indicated that they will seek extradition, but they are unlikely to get it. The others have strings of convictions for GBH and are known to carry guns. If we don't plan carefully, to secure the victims, we believe they will kill them, rather than let them point the leaders out in court."

"So that is why, I presume, the British government is using Unit T?"

"Yes, these people are extremely dangerous, so the police have agreed that the operation is to be paramilitary, with their own armed units standing back as support."

Sir Peter was relieved that Karen had for once involved the authorities and not gone in alone. While he accepted that often it was necessary not to inform the local police, because of security surrounding an operation, at times it was good to do so, so as not to alienate her unit.

"It is good you're working with them, Karen. I also have a little news. We have heard from Watson in America. He tells me that the operation is on. The first ship is to leave in two weeks' time bound for Rotterdam. This is a priority action, Karen. You must make arrangements for when they come ashore."

Karen sighed. "Then it seems like I've got a busy few weeks ahead, so bang go my holiday plans once more."

"Holidays, since when did you take holidays, without getting yourself into some local conflict? I'd give up the holidays, Karen. Accumulate them and retire early."

"I'm not waiting forty years to collect," she replied, with indignation.

"Karen, get on with your work, like I'm doing. I'll speak to you soon," he replied, with a laugh.

Chapter Twenty-Three

Three men of Nigerian origin, known as Chuks, Eze and Iroatu, were in a room above a massage parlour located off the high street in Fulham, London, sitting on a variety of settee that had seen better days.

They had come to the parlour at the request of Igbo. Normally they would be looking after similar outlets for Igbo, who financed the overall operation, including the trafficking of children from tribes in Nigeria. Most children brought into the UK would be forced into prostitution or kept as slave workers in backstreet manufacturing sweatshops.

"He's fucking late as usual," Chuks commented, looking at his watch. "I need to be back to cash up."

The others were about to voice a similar comment when the door burst open, and Igbo walked in. He was a big man, six foot three, wearing sweatpants, with a short tee-shirt showing off his bulging arm muscles.

"You're late, Igbo. What's so important we had to drop everything and come here at this time?" Chuks demanded.

Igbo walked over to the fridge, took out a can of beer, then drank it all in one swig. He burped loudly, looking at them watching him. "The pigs are onto us. We're expecting a raid within the next forty-eight hours."

"How do you know this?" Eze demanded.

"Because the pig we pay protection money to told me. He said there was nothing he could do, as the operation was not with them, but some European outfit known as Unit T."

Iroatu nodded his head in agreement. "If Unit T is involved, then your pig is right. He can't do anything, or tell you what's intended."

"Who are they?" Eze asked, confused.

"It's a military unit that targets traffickers. It would seem they have caught up with us." Iroatu looked around at them all, watching and listening. "You can be sure they will already know everything about us. You also don't go up against them, if you want to live. They are not like the pigs; Unit T will come at you like the military back home. The firepower they carry means you'd stand little chance in a head-on fight."

Eze smirked. "You're suggesting we run? Even back home we never ran."

Iroatu stood. "Then you're a fool. Among the criminal fraternity, the unit's well-known to be extremely violent in their actions. Fight if you want, I'm out of here."

Igbo pulled another can of beer from the fridge. He banged the door shut. "No one's out of here, or standing up against a military unit. We have a contingency for this possibility and you all keep to the plan. We meet at the safe house in five hours from now," he demanded.

Eze was having none of this. "I'm not giving up seven girls who bring in over a grand a day. What's wrong with lying low till they've gone? After all, if we just close up shop, they'd never find us."

Iroatu laughed. "You really believe they are all sitting at home ignoring us, till they get the order to come? They will already be watching; maybe even have our phones tapped, our houses bugged. This is not a police 999 call; it's the mobilisation of a military strike force. Their planning will be meticulous, their order to move honed down to the time that gives them an advantage. I'm with you Igbo; we follow the planned contingency and get out while we can."

"Then it's decided, you've five hours to sort your ends of the operation. I won't wait, so make sure you are at the safe house on time."

As they began to leave the room, Igbo called Eze back. Seconds later they were alone.

"How is it you don't believe what is being told you then?" Igbo asked.

Eze shrugged. "It's shit and you know it. I've five hundred grand in my stash, accumulating every day, and you're asking me to give up a good income, because of some two-bit military unit. I was in the army; I know how they work. We'd go in quickly, take out what we could and be gone. They, like us, wouldn't hang around if they found nothing."

"So what would you do?"

"Move the girls, sit around for a month, then carry on. The

military unit would be long gone. Your contact will tell you if they intend to return."

Igbo ripped a piece off a magazine cover on the table, then picked up a pen. He wrote down the address. "Collect your money, then take your girls there and stay with them. No one knows of this house, so it'll be safe. I'll be in contact."

"Thanks, Igbo, I owe you."

The two embraced. Then they both left.

***

Karen walked into the intelligence block at just after six o'clock in the morning. The block was located in the main camp of Unit T. She went through to the security room, where the surveillance operation was being conducted on the Nigerians. The operation, codenamed 'High Street', was coming to a conclusion. Soon she would give the order to mobilise. Stanley, her head of intelligence, was controlling the operation; the man on the ground for Unit T in London was a Lieutenant Picker.

Stanley had already arrived, glancing up as Karen entered the room. "The meeting broke up around four hours back, Karen. Each of the men has gone their own way. Police surveillance is reporting that all but one returned to their homes. The one who hasn't is called Eze, he went directly to his sauna."

She looked confused. "What were the police waiting for? They don't need us; they should have taken them out when they were together."

"The inspector in charge was concerned about the area where they were meeting. It's volatile at the best of times, so to launch an operation there was asking for a reaction from local people. Maybe even ending up in a riot against police brutality."

She sighed. "That hardly seems likely. If it had been us, rather than them, we'd have been in within minutes and gone before anyone even knew we'd been there, after all, the majority would be asleep. I'm of the mind that there is another reason we don't know about."

Stanley nodded his agreement. "Your thinking is the same as mine. Pressure has been exerted to delay their arrest. Maybe they already know we are coming, whatever the reason, it has given them time to find a way out."

"Well it's not the first time it's happened, Stan. I'll be leaving within the hour to join up with the unit already there. We go at O five hundred hours tomorrow as planned. Let's hope they haven't scattered, and their usual Sunday meeting is still on."

Chapter Twenty-Four

Eze had returned to the building he operated from. This was a converted shop, the window frosted, so anyone passing by couldn't see inside. The shop floor had been set out as a small reception area, where a girl would usually be sitting behind a desk, to take payments. Entry could be made by pressing a bell on the locked street door, before speaking your name and appointment time into an intercom. To all intents and purposes, this premises was just one of the many types of business in London offering gents' massage and relaxation. Upstairs, however, there were seven private rooms for the 'special clients' where more 'personal services' would be available; the girls offering these services, usually between twelve and fifteen, were brought into the country and forced into prostitution. Their nightmare was not just confined to the shop; often they were taken out, in twos and threes, to entertain 'the more discerning clients' in private houses and hotels. They were always brought back to their meagre accommodation in the cellar, sharing a room with three other girls. Constant beatings and threats left the victims traumatised, most addicted to drugs, with little hope of rescue. For Eze, it had been a lucrative operation, giving him the high life, including a substantial bankroll. So to be told to abandon everything was, for him, not an option.

Eze backed his blacked-out people carrier down a narrow passage that ran between his shop and next door. This was where he always parked. Where, unseen by any passer-by, he could bundle his girls into the vehicle, to take to clients. This time, however, he handcuffed the girls together, leading them through the rear door of the shop and into the vehicle. Once inside, they were all blindfolded, and their handcuffed wrists further attached to a chain, already fitted in the vehicle. This was his normal way to transport the girls to venues, without the risk of their escaping.

With the last girl inside, he brought out a large holdall, throwing it in the back, before slamming the door shut. Then quickly getting into the front, he started the vehicle and set off. The first few streets he travelled along were mainly to make sure he wasn't being tailed. Once satisfied, he took a complex route, through a housing estate, onto a main road. Already he had looked up the address Igbo had given him, memorising the route.

***

Twenty minutes later he turned into the drive of a detached house, set among a number of similar houses. A man he'd never seen before came out of the front door.

The man was dark-skinned, well-built and wearing tee-shirt and jeans. He came up to the side of the vehicle; Eze wound down the window.

"You Eze?" he asked.

"Yeah, who are you?"

"Mike, Igbo told me you were coming. I'll open the garage door, then you can drive in. There's a door inside that leads through into the house. I presume you have all the girls?"

"I do."

He just nodded, walked over to the large up-and-over garage door, pulling it open, before standing to one side as Eze drove inside. Following him, Mike pulled the door down and locked it from inside.

Eze climbed out and stretched, before walking around to the back of the vehicle, opening the door and grabbing the large holdall. "We'll leave the girls for a moment; I want to check out the house," he told Mike.

They went through into the house.

"Your room's upstairs, I'll show you," Mike told him.

Eze followed Mike upstairs and through to the master bedroom. While Mike walked over to the window, looking outside, Eze remained at the door; he was confused. The room was completely empty, with not even a mattress on the floor.

"Where's the fucking bed?" he demanded.

Mike said nothing, pulling a gun with a silencer attached from inside his jacket. He turned to look at Eze, a grin spreading across his face, firing four times. Eze was dead by the time he hit the floor.

After making sure he was dead, Mike opened the holdall. It was stuffed to the top with bundles of cash in different currencies. Closing the bag, he ran back down the stairs and into the garage. Leaning inside the vehicle, he started the engine, leaving it ticking over. After standing there a minute or so, he went back into the house, slamming the door between the house and garage shut. Then carrying the holdall, he left the house, walking down the road a short distance, before climbing into a parked car. Seconds later the car sped away.

Chapter Twenty-Five

A Unit T Range Rover turned into a local army barracks close to Heathrow airport, coming to a halt outside the main building. Lieutenant Picker was stood waiting and saluted Karen as she climbed out. She was dressed in a black one-piece combat uniform, with a belt around her hips, to which a gun holster was attached. A gun was clipped firmly inside it.

"I'm told there's a problem, Lieutenant?" Karen asked.

"Yes, Colonel, police surveillance has lost track of Eze. When they entered his premises it was empty. No girls, nothing. It seems he took them all with him, pointing to the fact that he'd knowledge of us coming for him."

"And Igbo, what of him?"

"He's gone, as well. The same as Iroatu and Chuks. After their meeting, they all went home. The police took it on themselves to raid their private houses this morning. All the men had gone. Police surveillance never saw any of them leave. Also, none have returned to their premises. The police are getting ready to enter the massage parlours of all the suspects. They are certain the girls are still locked inside the cellars as usual."

Karen sighed, nodded her understanding, then climbed back into her vehicle, shutting the door. She called Stanley.

"We're wasting our time with the police, Stanley. There's a leak, the Nigerians have all bailed."

"It would seem that way, Karen. But all's not lost, unknown to the police we put a tracker on all the suspects' vehicles. Only one of the vehicles has moved; that was Eze's. I'll send through the location it's now parked up at. I suggest you tell no one, just take your soldiers and give the premises a look over. I've Googled the area. It's a detached house, among twenty similar properties. I'm currently trying to find out who owns it. I'll send you this information as soon as I can."

"Thanks, Stanley, at least you're on the ball. I'll contact you after we secure the house."

Karen opened her window. "Can you join me, Lieutenant?"

He walked over, climbing into the vehicle.

"I've issued an order to mobilise. We're now on lockdown," she told him, after he'd closed the door.

Soon the convoy of three Unit T Range Rovers was speeding away from the barracks. Karen had switched on her tablet computer, then through Google maps she located the house quickly and switched to street view. Lieutenant Picker was also looking at the screen.

"According to intelligence, this is where Eze's vehicle is parked up," Karen began. "It's about an hour outside London. We'll park on the main road, out of sight of the entrance, then approach on foot. I want the house taken. I don't want any girl injured in the operation. Already this is looking like a fiasco, after the police surveillance failed, which is why we're conducting this part without them. The rules of engagement for this incursion allow Dark Angel soldiers to shoot to kill. Except if we can take Eze alive, then let's do so, but not at the cost of any of the girls. Do you understand?"

"I do Colonel."

"Very well. Use Corporal Malloy to help secure, then she can stay with the girls. As we're short of soldiers, I'll take the rear. I'll call when I'm in position."

***

Following their arrival at the house they suspected Eze to be in, the soldiers had quickly dispersed to prearranged locations, and were now in position.

Already there had been three very surprised neighbours, at soldiers knocking on their doors, not only to prevent Eze making a bolt for their houses and taking a hostage, but also to close off all possible exits from the house.

Karen, with another soldier, both of them now fully kitted out, wearing bulletproof jackets, was knocking on the door of a house four down from where they believed Eze was. An elderly woman opened the door and stood back, shocked at seeing a girl standing there dressed as Karen was.

"Hi," Karen began, at the same time smiling. "Please don't be alarmed. I'm Colonel Harris of Unit T Special Forces. This is my identification," she told her, holding out her ID card. "We need you to stay inside your house, while I go around to the back. Will you do that for me?"

"Er, yes of course," the woman replied, a little bemused.

"Your neighbours on the left, are they at home?"

She shook her head. "No, they will be at work."

"Thank you. So if you'll go back inside, keep all your doors locked, this soldier will be keeping guard outside. I'll come and find you when our operation is completed."

"Were you on television a few days ago?" the woman asked.

"I was, but I can't stop and talk now. Like I said, I'll come and see you later."

Leaving the soldier to make sure the woman locked her doors, Karen went through into the garden. Quickly she made her way along the back of the gardens, joining up with another soldier already there. Both then moved into position, watching the rear door of the house Eze was in. She pulled her visor down, adjusted her communication microphone, then raised her sniper rifle, altering the sights slightly. Satisfied she had the exit covered, she called Lieutenant Picker to make an entry.

Karen listened to the commentary as her soldiers broke the doors down, spilling into the house. Already she could hear some coughing, with shouts of all-clear, as they moved through. Then the Lieutenant's voice came over the earphone. It was very sober, shaking a little. "The house is secure Colonel, but we need you to come immediately."

Karen acknowledged, except she didn't go to the house through the garden; rather, she made her way back one house, coming through to the front entrance. The Lieutenant was standing at the front door.

"What's the problem?" Karen asked.

"Eze is in a room upstairs. He's been shot at least four times. There are seven girls in the garage chained up in a people carrier, still blindfolded. The engine was running; they had little chance and all, I suspect, died of carbon monoxide poisoning." He lowered his voice. "Corporal Malloy has taken the deaths of the girls very badly. She was very shocked when she found them. I have her in the kitchen, sitting down, with a hot drink from my flask."

Karen sighed. "I can't believe this is happening. If you prefer to stay outside that's okay, while I go and see for myself."

"No, I'm fine. I'll come with you."

He took her upstairs, and she checked out Eze's body, then went down to the garage. Carefully she looked over each of the girls. With little sign of struggling or panic, Karen decided they couldn't have known what was happening to them, as none had vomited. They'd probably just passed out with the carbon monoxide, never to awaken.

Karen pulled her mobile out, keying in a code. Immediately she was connected to Stanley. She told him what they had found.

"It's bad, Karen. Except it's become even worse. The police have found fourteen other girls, all dead. You need to get out fast, before all hell breaks loose, when the press get wind of it. You can do nothing; let the police handle it from here."

"You're right. Can you call; have them send forensics and ambulances. We'll go as soon as they arrive."

After she came off the call to Stanley, Karen went through to the kitchen. Sherry was sitting quietly, her helmet on the table, her gun at her side.

Sherry looked up as Karen came in; immediately she stood and saluted.

Karen could clearly see the tears trickling down her face; the girl was in shock. She went to Sherry straightaway and put her arms around her, hugging her tightly.

"I'm sorry, Karen, I just fell apart, seeing them all lying there."

"Don't worry, Sherry, I think any one of us would have acted the same, if we'd come across them without knowing. Just get your gear together, then go and sit in my car. I'll be with you shortly."

Karen, the same as Sherry, was glad to get out. She walked down to the house the elderly lady lived in, knocking on her door.

The lady looked out of her lounge window, and seeing Karen standing there, opened the front door. "Are we all safe now?" she asked.

"You are; thank you for your understanding."

"Would you like some tea?"

Karen smiled. "Perhaps some other time, I still have a few bits and pieces to sort out."

"Yes, you always seem so busy, according to the papers. Would you do something for me?"

"Of course, what is it?"

"The WI will never believe me when I tell them I met the famous Karen Harris. Will your soldier use my camera, to take a photo of you standing by me?"

Karen could see the excitement in the lady's face at her being there. "I don't usually do that, but for you, I'll be happy to have my photo taken."

Chapter Twenty-Six

As Stanley predicted, news of the killings spread like wildfire and already hordes of reporters were crowding around the house where Eze and the girls had died. Sir Peter was sitting in his office, watching the pictures on television, waiting for Karen to arrive.

The newsreader had come on, with breaking news of the tragedy flashing across the bottom of the screen. "We have just had it confirmed, by the police, that the death toll on the girls for sale scandal has now risen to twenty-two," the newsreader began. "We are taking you direct to the houses of parliament, where the Shadow Home Secretary has arrived."

The picture switched across to the Shadow Home Secretary, standing outside parliament, with a number of reporters jostling for position. He began speaking. "It is now time the government began to take notice of just what's happening on our streets. The deaths of these young girls has shocked the nation. I also understand that there was military involvement. What I want to know is, why? Then what part, if any, have the police played in all this? We as a nation are entitled to know; in particular, who are these soldiers who turn up, often cause disruption and mayhem, before just disappearing without explanation or accountability?"

A reporter shouted out to him."We're led to understand that the military unit was Unit T's strike force, Dark Angel. What's your reaction to that?"

"If this is true, I want to know on whose authority they have come to our country? We're perfectly capable of putting our own military on the street, and under parliament's direct control. We shouldn't be relying on a renegade unit that answers to no one but the faceless Eurocrats in Brussels. I will be asking these questions in parliament later, during the emergency recall of parliament announced by the prime minister."

Sir Peter switched the television off. This man was spouting off about something he didn't understand, cashing in on what happened, just to gain votes. His sort, with no real interest in the serious nature of the people trade, got on his nerves.

At that moment, his internal telephone rang. It was his secretary. "Colonel Harris has arrived and is just signing in, Sir Peter."

"Can you go and meet her, then bring her directly through, please?" he asked.

A few minutes later, Karen entered his office. Sir Peter was already standing; they embraced.

"It's good to see you, Karen, even at this difficult time."

"Yes, it's been a real shock, particularly for Sherry. She's quite a hardened soldier after Afghanistan, and has seen a great deal of death. But to find seven girls like that was too much, the girl fell apart."

"Would you like coffee?"

"Yes please."

"Will you be keeping Sherry in Dark Angel?" he asked, walking over to the side table, to pour two cups.

"Of course. We need compassion as well, Peter, and besides, Sherry has been there herself and is well aware of the risks for the victims of trafficking. To see them would have reminded her, the same as me, that either of us could have been one of them, if we'd not been rescued."

He returned to his chair, carrying the coffee cups.

By then Karen had also sat down.

"So what's your assessment of the operation?"

"They knew we were coming Peter. Again, as a number of times before, it had to come from the police, my people had no idea where they were going, or that we were onto the Nigerians. But these traffickers must have had a contingency plan for such a possibility, so the informer has a great deal to answer for. You have to find him, or her. To see those girls, chained up with no chance of escape, will live with me a long time."

"I agree. Already the Home Secretary has been on to me. She is to announce in parliament that I'll be heading the internal investigation. She's insistent that I leave no stone unturned and not only find these people, but also how this happened. She needs something to place before parliament. With the election looming, they are all very worried such a high death toll will swing the debates away from health and education, more to the sex trade, with rather unsavoury details coming out as to the extent of trafficking and the grooming of young people in this country. Particularly when it emerges they are doing nothing, apart from helping fund a small European unit."

Karen sighed. "Well they've only themselves to blame, they've been warned enough times. Then, since opening up the Union to more eastern countries, that has brought with it the chance to bring these girls in legally. But once in, they're controlled by extremely violent people, with little chance of escape."

"You're correct, except it's not just the sex trade; drug running and organised crime are also on the increase. Our laws and punishments are far too lax, compared to what these people have been used to, with little deterrent. But we're deviating. What are your thoughts on why Eze was killed?"

"I'm not sure, Peter. Looking at the facts as we know them, this could have just been a falling out among the traffickers, or an opportunity for one of their minders to take Eze's money. After all, they were bailing; we know that, so it stands to reason that they would be taking their earnings with them. These people don't use banks. Why he was in that house is also a mystery. We do know the house had been up for sale a number of weeks. It was subject to a repossession order, which was why it was empty. The police are checking the estate agent, to find out who has recently viewed the house, but it's a long shot. Although it's inconceivable that they would hole up in such a house, with the risk of potential purchasers coming around for viewings, so they had to be there for some other reason."

Sir Peter listened, at the same time sipping his coffee. He placed the cup back on the saucer. "I think you might be right there, I'll look into it. In the meantime, leave the UK to me. You concentrate on the European mainland, to see if they emerge there, after all I can't see them being in this country now. We're already checking shipping leaving UK waters, bound for Africa and beyond. It's possible they might return to Nigeria, but I doubt it, two of them are wanted there by the authorities."

Karen looked at her watch. "Come on, I'll buy you lunch," she said.

He looked shocked. "You want to go to lunch? What's this Karen,

I'm normally dragging you, screaming with objections that I'm trying to fatten you up?"

She smiled. "Yes well, I do actually eat you know. I've also had nothing since last night, apart from drinks, so I'm hungry."

Chapter Twenty-Seven

Karen was staying overnight in her London flat. She'd just come out of the shower when the doorbell rang. Putting a dressing gown on, she walked through to the door, pulling it open. That was after first glancing at the small monitor. This had a camera connected to it, giving a view of the stairwell leading up to her flat. It was a lady who looked after the London branch of her charity.

"Good morning, Karen," she said with a smile, when Karen opened the door. "I thought I'd better bring you the papers. The telephones haven't stopped ringing this morning; everyone wants us to get in touch with you."

"Thanks, Margaret. Has the unit car arrived?"

"Yes, they're parked in the mews."

"Tell them I'll be about fifteen minutes."

She nodded, then went back down the stairs.

Karen opened the first paper and shuddered.

'WHY DID THEY NEED TO DIE?' was the headline across the entire front page, with the usual stock picture of a Dark Angel soldier, kitted out with a black visor down, holding a gun. This was a picture to intimidate, often with the claim it was Karen, but it wasn't. She read on, at the same time kicking the door shut, before wandering back towards the bedroom.

'This morning, the world is reeling after yesterday's shock announcement of the deaths of twenty-seven young girls and one man. We've since learned that these young girls were the innocent victims in an operation by Unit T's strike force, Dark Angel, to take down a trafficking gang. This operation was headed by Lieutenant Colonel Karen Harris, but it went disastrously wrong, resulting in carnage on an unprecedented scale. According to neighbours, the operation was personally led by Colonel Harris. But is this girl prepared to stand in front of the nation, apologise for the mess, and explain just what happened? Not on your life - she, as many times before, preferred to slink away, before the press arrived. And this action is from a girl who is always ready to bask in the media spotlight, when she succeeds.

'In parliament last night, the Shadow Home Secretary demanded that the government conduct an immediate inquiry, further demanding that this arrogant and supercilious officer must be brought in front of a parliamentary committee to explain her actions. He was also asking why a European strike force, known for aggressive and violent behaviour, was allowed to come into the country, above the police and our own military.

'In a government response, the Home Secretary has refused to make such a request to the Unit T's commander, stating that Unit T are highly professional and not as people believe a foreign unit. Unit T is a part-funded UK unit, located in France, with contributions from all other EU countries, and holds special operational status across all borders, because of its unique position. However, the government recognises the seriousness of what has transpired; and so is announcing an urgent internal investigation. This is to be conducted by Sir Peter Parker, who heads a special counter-intelligence unit in New Scotland Yard. On Sir Peter's part, his office has asked that the country should not pre-judge any actions until they understand the real security issues surrounding this operation. He, Sir Peter, promises that nothing will be swept under the carpet, and he intends to get at the truth.

'We at the Globe look at this investigation as an attempt to shift blame away from Unit T and in particular Karen Harris, who should at the very least give an explanation of just what went wrong. Until then, this girl will have blood on her hands, and the contempt of this great nation.'

Karen threw the paper on the bed, and began to dress. She could understand the anger, even she wasn't immune, personally vowing to herself to find these men and make them pay for their actions. Already she'd put her intelligence unit on full alert, to find out what they could. But she was realistic. This was a well-planned getaway, with the determination to close all loops back to them. She very much doubted they would be found, without the help of other criminal organisations; even then they could be in a country where they would be very lucky to be able to apprehend them.

At that moment, the telephone rang. She looked at the caller number and lifted the phone. "Hi, mum," she said quietly.

"Are you all right, love?" she asked.

"Why not, I'm used to this sort of thing; it's just a bit hurtful, that's all. There was nothing I could have done, mum; the girls were already dead."

"I know, love. Even I'm not naive enough to believe you would have allowed it, if you had a chance to prevent the killings. It's just that me and your dad are really worried about you. Do you know where to go from here?"

"We're working on it, believe me, but I don't hold out much hope. Anyway, I've requested additional security around your house. It's just a precaution, mum, nothing heavy. Don't give me a hard time; I need to know you're safe."

"I understand, but the police are already here. There's also a number of reporters standing around in the street. Just look after yourself. Dad sends his love, the same as me."

"Thanks mum. I have to go now, my car's waiting."

"Very well. Call us when you're home, and tell Sophie not to come back this weekend, like she intended. I think it's best she stays with you a little longer."

"She'll be mad, she's losing money. I offered to cover her lost wages, but she won't have it. So I'm at a loss as to what to do."

"Leave that to us, Karen. Maybe we can sort something with her employers, just keep her there that's all."

"Okay, goodbye, I love you both."

Replacing the receiver on the cradle, Karen took a last look around the flat, before making for the door, then running down the stairs to where the unit car was waiting. Her driver saluted her.

"All quiet?" she asked.

"Yes, Colonel, the reporters don't realise this flat has a side-entrance. We'll get you in the car and be away before they realise you've gone."

She gave a weak smile; she hated to run like this, but she had an appointment with Sir Peter, before she intended to leave the country and return to her unit.

***

"I need to make a statement, Peter. This is getting out of hand," Karen said, after joining him in the dining room of New Scotland Yard.

"I agree, the papers are whipping up a frenzy. What's going to be your approach?"

"I intend to tell it as it is. The public must know why we keep low-key, because of the very real risk of informers."

"So you now really believe it was an informer that made the traffickers decide to get out?"

She sighed. "How else, one minute they were running as normal, the next they killed everyone who might be able to link them to abduction and prostitution, then bailed. The meeting in Fulham must have been the catalyst. Someone told them we were on our way, and they'd only hours before we moved in."

"Very well, I'll set up an interview on the BBC tonight. We need to go through everything you're going to say in advance, and you must promise to keep to the script. I'm going to have a difficult enough job finding the leak, without a wrong word being said."

"I understand, Peter. But I'd like to make it clear, this isn't to keep my own reputation intact, I'm not really bothered about that. But the public should be told what we're up against and some of the comments in the papers this morning were not helpful in any respect."

***

Karen's Range Rover, along with two more, each carrying five soldiers, pulled up outside the BBC. The announcement, by news flashes throughout the day, that Karen was to appear on television in an extra programme, not in the schedule, called 'Face the Nation', even made headlines in the early evening papers. Already every seat in the audience had been snapped up, minutes after the first announcement, and there were huge crowds waiting outside to catch a glimpse of her when she arrived. Then even before the cars had stopped, soldiers were piling out, all dressed in dark suits and ties, not carrying obvious weapons. But they were, and intended to protect their commander no matter what, positioning themselves by the studio entrances and the rear areas. With so little room actually in the studio, the lieutenant in charge of her protection decided that with everyone being scanned, and bags searched before entering, Karen would be safe inside.

***

Sir Peter was at home, with his wife and daughter, watching the live scenes as they unfolded. He had declined an invitation from the producers of the programme to join her, saying that in view of him heading an investigation, it would not be appropriate, although he could understand the unit commander's decision to make their position clear.

"What that girl has to go through, Peter, I feel sorry for her," his wife said quietly.

"I agree and this time it really wasn't her fault."

She didn't say anything, listening to the commentary.

***

Following the opening credits of the programme, the presenter, Chris Howe, came out onto the set. For him, this was the pinnacle of his career. His programme, Face the Nation, attracted perhaps two million viewers in the ratings. This particular interview would attract twenty times that level, with the possibility of it leading to far better job opportunities.

As the clapping died down, he stood for a moment, collecting his thoughts. "In tonight's edition of 'Face the Nation', we are to meet a British officer, Lieutenant Colonel Harris. This officer has found herself at the centre of a storm, after twenty-seven young girls, with an average age of only thirteen, were brutally killed during one of her operations. So much interest has been generated over this interview that even countries as far away as the USA and Australia will be showing the programme live, with an estimated global audience in the tens of millions."

He listened to his earphone for a second.

"I've been informed that the officer has arrived and will be joining us very shortly. For those who may not know the background of this officer, I will give a brief outline of her life." He went on to give a potted version of Karen's life, from her abduction through to the present. When he finished, he listened for a moment to the director on his earphone.

"Ladies and gentlemen, I'd like you all to join me in welcoming our special guest tonight, the Commander of Unit T, Lieutenant Colonel Karen Harris DCB MV CMH CGC bar."

Then with background music playing, the audience clapping, be it more polite rather than with cheers, Karen came onto the set. She was dressed in a black trouser suit, with a white blouse, her long hair cascading over her shoulders. In her high heels, she was at least five inches taller than Chris. With her athletic figure and her deep blue eyes, she was not a girl you would ever consider to be in the army, and certainly not a girl in charge of an SAS-type military strike force. She was carrying a small purse, unknown to anyone apart from her unit; inside was a gun. Strapped around her ankle, out of sight, was a knife. Karen never moved away from her unit without some protection.

Chris embraced her, and she took the seat opposite his, crossing her legs in a relaxed pose.

"Is it all right that I call you Karen, Colonel?"

"Yes that's fine with me, after all, I'm not in uniform."

"Then may I first welcome you and thank you for agreeing to this interview. As you may understand, the world is shocked at the death toll during an operation under your command? What are your feelings over the vicious backlash from the press?"

The camera zoomed closer in on Karen, determined to pick up every feature and body movement that would give this girl away. However, Karen was no fool and knew how to control her emotions, her attitude. These skills had saved her life a number of times, leading her aggressors to believe they controlled her. Although to their cost, they were often blinded by her perceived naivety, her natural sexy look and couldn't see beyond to the real Karen.

"Ever since I was snatched from school to be sold, I've seen a great deal of death. My initiation into what my future held was being raped by two men, while others stood watching. I've stood helplessly on the deck of a ship and witnessed a girl's throat being cut, before she was pushed over the edge of the ship. I've rescued young girls who'd been beaten into submission, left naked in a stinking cellar, to be brought out and raped by upwards of six men before being taken back to the cellar, only for it to happen the next night and the next." Tears came to her eyes. "People believe as a soldier, I have no emotion, no thought for the person I may have to kill, but they would be wrong. I see that person as someone's child, a father or mother perhaps, and do my best to offer an alternative, even if it means they will be incarcerated for a very long time. Except in this world there are people who believe life has no value. That they can mete out abuse, injury and yes, even death, to further their own ends. Be it for wealth, or status. In the world of human trafficking, the rejection of demands from a trafficker can bring the victim punishments to the extreme and even death at times. I was threatened a number of times while I was in the hands of traffickers. Such threats made me more determined to fight for my freedom; though I'm still one of the very few who have succeeded in coming home."

Again she hesitated, her words soft with emotion.

"I feel very sad for these children who are already caught up in the depravities that exist within the sex trade, you can be very certain we will assist in hunting down the perpetrators and bring them to justice."

"Thank you, Karen, for making us all aware of the violent world you live in. On everyone's lips tonight is a simple question. What went wrong?"

She looked at him, at the same time carefully constructing her words. The press could see this as they hung on her every word.

"I need to be careful not to pre-empt the investigation by Sir Peter Parker. However, we have our suspicions, which I will voice, although Sir Peter's report may, or may not, back me up. I will, however, make this very clear from the outset. Unit T had nothing to do with the deaths of the girls, as you will soon understand."

Karen went on to say how it had been a joint operation between the police and her unit. Her unit's part was to support. However, she suspected the traffickers had got wind that there could be a raid coming up because of the police surveillance, deciding that it was time to get out as a result. She ignored the fact that the Nigerians could have been taken earlier by the police, so with that not happening there had to be an informer, being only a sumise on her part. That would come out in Sir Peter's report. Her final words held little comfort to the relatives of the girls. "Only Sir Peter's investigation or the apprehension of the traffickers will finally decide if we could have got to the traffickers earlier and saved the girls. I can't say if we could, I don't know."

Suddenly there was shouting and screaming coming from behind the closed doors of the studio entrance. Karen never flinched, but quickly moved her hand into her small purse, clicking open the clip, before slipping her hand inside and grasping the gun. She didn't intend to pull the gun out; it gave her confidence that she could defend herself if it became necessary.

Then the upper door burst open; two coloured men ran in, both brandishing guns.

"She lies, that girl killed those children, as if she'd pulled the trigger herself," one shouted at the top of his voice, then both of them began running down the audience stairs towards the stage, at the same time firing their guns at Karen. The range at that point was too far away for them to hit her, and mainly used to deter any attack on them.

The audience was in a panic. Most began screaming, others trying to get out of the way.

"Take your last breath, Harris, and go to your maker," one man screamed at her.

Karen, however, well aware there was nowhere to run, had no option but to fight. So with that decision made, she pulled the gun out of the bag completely, clicked the safety off and literally rolled off the couch, coming around to a position down on one knee, her body turned slightly, rather than facing the gunmen head-on, effectively reducing the hit area to herself. She'd also raised her gun, which was held steady in both hands. There was no panic, no letting off the gun prematurely as the men were doing. She knew its range, the number of shots she had, and more importantly she also knew, by the way they were acting, they hadn't even considered that she might be armed. On their part, they were still bounding down the stairs, firing wildly, but unable to take accurate aim at her until they came to a halt. Karen, already in a firing position, let four shots off in quick succession, two at each gunman.

All this happened in seconds and unlike them, Karen's shooting was deadly and accurate.

Both men screamed in pain, as her bullets ripped through their legs, sending them sprawling forward down the final steps. One let go of his gun, and it fell away safely, the other held on and attempted to raise it to try to take her out. But it was too late, Karen held the upper hand. Her next shot hit him in the shoulder of his gun arm. The pain was intense, and he screamed, dropping his gun and rolling over in agony.

Karen then fired one shot into the air. The studio suddenly fell silent, apart from the two men moaning. Karen stood, still holding her gun in both hands, analysing the situation and scanning the room, unsure if these two men were her only threat. In seconds, she made her decision.

"Members of the audience stay where you all are," she shouted. "My soldiers will soon take charge, but in the meantime don't anyone move, or make any attempt to leave, use a camera with flash, or do any other action. You risk being mistaken for an aggressor. Have no doubt, I or my soldiers won't hesitate to fire."

The reporters and others just stared at her in shock; this girl, everyone knew by reputation, was extremely dangerous when cornered. Except such a reputation was from hearsay, no one had ever seen her in action. And yet in less than a minute, she had taken down two gunmen and was holding an audience at bay, with a very real threat of shooting to kill.

Satisfied there was no obvious threat, Karen turned her attention to the gunmen. "Both of you face down on the floor, your hands above your head. I've only at this stage fired to disable. Make any sudden move, attempt to get at your weapons, and I will fire. But this time I will shoot to kill."

By now Unit T soldiers had entered through the exit doors. They immediately secured the studio as Karen said they would. Police followed them through the doors, quickly handcuffing the two men.

The lieutenant in charge of her protection came up to her. "No injuries, Colonel?" he asked.

"No, I'm fine. Where were you lot, how did they get through into the studio?"

"They'd come from this studio a few minutes before and were returning from the toilet, we didn't suspect they had gone to collect weapons. The only immediate problem was the man at the door said they couldn't go back into the studio while it was on air. It was then they kicked off and barged their way inside. We went to assist the security, but by then they were inside the studio. Even at that point we believed them to be just difficult members of the audience wanting to get inside again, we didn't realise they had guns until the firing began."

She nodded. "Okay, have my car brought around to the front. We leave for the unit tonight, as planned."

"The cars are already waiting at the front entrance," he answered, then walked away.

Karen returned to the small stage and a stunned Chris. She smiled. "Sorry Chris, I hope I've not wrecked your programme?"

He stared at her in shock. "But they have just tried to kill you, and you're laughing it off," he stuttered.

She shrugged. "Possibly, but they had little chance; I think it was more a publicity stunt. If I'd not put them down, my soldiers would have shot them dead. Although I may have taken a couple of bullets before that happened. Anyway I think the interview's over. If there is nothing else, you and the audience may now understand the type of world I live in."

He shook his head. "I don't know how you go on, Karen. I was terrified and yet you stood your ground. I think you're right; I'm beginning to understand about the world around us that the average person never sees."

Karen smiled and embraced him, kissing him on each cheek. "Don't worry, Chris, we'll look after you. I'd keep away from any subject on human trafficking on your show; it seems to attract a number of very unsavoury characters." With that, she began to make her way out of the studio, except the reporters had other ideas.

"You shouldn't leave yet, Karen. We need at least a statement?" a reporter shouted, at the same time heading towards her, with others joining in, urging her to talk to them.

In the television control room, although they had now broken live transmission, their cameras were still running, and if Karen was to give a statement, albeit off-the-cuff, they wanted it recorded; maybe even to use the footage for later news bulletins.

Karen stopped and looked at them watching her. "What do you

want me to say? Maybe you're thinking I deserve such attempts on my life; after all, you all seemed to believe I had a hand in killing those girls. Or do you want me to apologise for threatening you all with a gun?" Karen hesitated a second; no one commented. "I think you all need to look at just who you think I am. I'm no longer a naive eighteen-year-old, as you keep trying to portray me. I'm the Commanding Officer of a European SAS-type strike force. My job is not to save victims of trafficking; I have just one remit, laid down in the unit's rules of engagement. I suggest you all read it, after all, it's public knowledge. As to what has just happened, let any other amateurs contemplating taking me on, be warned. They will fail; they may even lose their lives in the attempt. I have the legal right to defend myself, given to me by the EU. Because without people like me, your children, your loved ones will always be at risk of being taken, the same as I was; except for those children, the traffickers know we will come for them."

Karen then turned and, flanked by two of her soldiers, left the studio.

Chapter Twenty-Eight

Karen had arrived back at the camp the day before. She was glad to be back; already her picture was festooned across the world's papers, holding a gun during the attempt on her life. To be fair, the papers spoke very highly of her professionalism, particularly in the way she'd gone all out to disable the gunmen, rather than kill them. This was made very clear by interviews reporters had conducted with experts to understand what would be going through her mind at that moment. Nevertheless, as a public relations exercise, to soften Karen's image to the person in the street, it had been a disaster.

Placing the entire episode in the back of her mind, with far more important operations going on, Karen walked into the barn alongside her home, now converted into accommodation for the Dark Angel soldiers assigned to secure her house. Most were out on patrol, the few around standing to attention as she entered.

"At ease, does anyone know where Corporal Malloy is?"

"She's in her room, Colonel, should I call her?" one soldier replied.

"Yes please, have the corporal join me outside, would you?"

Sherry caught up with Karen, still buttoning her uniform. She saluted. "You wanted to see me, Colonel?" she asked.

"I do, shall we take a walk; and while we're alone, Sherry, I'm Karen."

They took the path deeper into the forest, well out of earshot of anyone.

"You know, I've never been one to go around in circles with small talk, Sherry, so I'll come directly to the point. We're putting together a sting operation against one of the largest trafficking cartels operating out of the old Soviet Union, but it could need someone inside. The point is, I'm not suitable - besides being too old, I'm also well-known."

"You're asking me to go covert?"

Karen stopped at a bench and sat down. Sherry did the same.

"I am, we'd be working to infiltrate you through a low grade trafficker we've been involved with before. I'll not lie to you, Sherry, there are risks, and these people aren't nice. But we will be with you every step of the way."

"Can I ask a question, before I decide?"

"Of course, ask me anything you want."

"You've gone covert a number of times. Each time you had back-up, but even with that, you were often alone, abused and at high risk of being killed. What would you say, if you were me?"

Karen sat for a while in thought. "You're correct; there have been many times I believed I was invincible, found I wasn't and to save my life, I succumbed to rape and abuse. I'm not proud of it; after all, most times it was my own arrogance that got me in such a position. In my defence, I'd say my life was in turmoil. I've never got over being made to strip in front of everyone, before being inspected like some animal, while they agreed a price for me. My sex life, since then, has often been men who drugged or threatened me. Most people would say they'd rather have died, than accept such abuse. That's all well and good, but they don't give you the means to take your own life, or if they do, it's a death too horrific to contemplate." Karen fell silent for a moment, Sherry said nothing. "So we come to your question, Sherry. In Scotland, when you were pulled out of the brothel, I gave you your life back, told you to take it in two hands and not to let go. You chose to follow in my footsteps, even though you had the money to live comfortably. Now you're like me; we don't have a real life, such as boyfriends that last, or even go out partying every week, like others of our age. No one could care less, beyond our own family, if we live or die; so why do it? Why risk our lives? We do it because we're proud of what we do. We get a real buzz when we pull out a child who gives us a hug for coming for them. This is our road; there are no turn-offs. If it means we need to go that extra mile, to take out a particularly vicious trafficker, we do it, no matter what the cost to us."

Sherry nodded her agreement. "You're right; this is why we're here. Count me in; let's get the bastards shall we?"

Karen stood. "You know I'm already envious of you. I miss the buzz of being out there alone, pitting myself against others. How I wish I could go just once more. But I promise you this, Sherry. I'll always be very close. You won't be alone, like I was, believe me."

Then she smiled. "Get rid of the uniform, I'll find Sophie and we'll go down for a drink in the village, shall we?"

Chapter Twenty-Nine

Sherry had been picked up from Kennedy Airport in New York by Harry Watson, then taken to a warehouse some forty miles away. While they travelled, he told her what would happen.

"I'm not sure what Karen has told you, except by six tonight, I need to have you locked up in a warehouse, ready to leave for Europe with more girls. The girls are also on their way to the warehouse, the first taken five days ago, the last this morning. You were collected by me; the real girl you will replace is still at home, completely oblivious of how close she came to being taken, not that I think the men in Europe will be checking this out. Although if they do and call me, I'll act dumb, insisting you're the right girl. With you both being blonde, tall and of fair complexion, I can't see them being that bothered. Maybe they will tell me to get the right girl next time. You must not talk much; your accent is very English. I'll plant the seed that you've been educated in England and just come back. If anyone asks, say your mother is English and married an American, that's why you were sent to England, for your final years at school."

"How are we being taken to Europe and to what country?" Sherry asked.

"It's a container ship. Not very comfortable I'm afraid. You'll all travel in containers, not on deck, but in the hold. They have been positioned so that access is via the emergency door, at the bow of the ship, which is little used. The main crew will know nothing about you. You'll be in there two weeks. I understand you have arranged something with Karen, to keep in touch, which I don't want to know. Once you leave for Europe, I'm finished. All I'll do is to confirm by text, with the phone you've brought, that you are on your way, the name of the ship and the container's number."

Sherry nodded her understanding. "That's fine, you've done your part, it's now up to me. There is one thing I want to know. How carefully are we searched, before boarding the ship?"

He shrugged. "Probably very little, if at all. After all, you've already been abducted for nearly three days and been searched for weapons, mobiles, that sort of thing."

They said little more, as they had arrived at the warehouse. With a remote control fob, Harry opened the doors, then backed inside. Quickly he closed the doors. "Come on, let's get you settled in the back room. Others could arrive at any moment."

They both went across the offices along the back and into a room with a large padlock already fitted. Once inside he switched the light on and closed the door.

"Remove your clothes, including the knickers," he told her, at the same time pointing to a plastic bag in the corner of the room. "Then select something to wear from the bag. It's full of clean knickers and tops. The tops are short-cropped I'm afraid, but the men who are looking after you on the ship will want to be sure you can't hide anything. They will expect you to be already dressed that way, when the other girls arrive. I can't afford a single mistake; your life and mine would be in the balance if we get it wrong."

Sherry changed quickly, at the same time removing a small, slim, tube-like object, not seen by Harry, from the pocket of the jeans she'd been wearing.

Harry collected up her discarded clothes, heading for the door, but stopped before he left. "I'll Fed-ex your clothes, valuables and passport back to Karen."

"Thanks, Harry, I appreciate it," Sherry answered.

While he was out of the room, Sherry very carefully slipped the slim tube into the machined turned-up top of the knickers she'd replaced her own with, positioning it on her flat tummy area so it wouldn't be noticed. Minutes later he was back, carrying a set of ankle irons with a chain already attached, and a small plastic bottle of water. Telling her to sit down in a corner, he attached the irons with the chain, then padlocked the chain to an eye bolt, already set into the floor. After quickly checking they were firm, he left her alone.

***

It was nearly two hours later that more girls were brought into the room; two had their hands tied behind their backs, with a piece of duck tape over their mouths. One was already dressed in top and knickers, the other in her school clothes. Another three were carried in; all were unconscious. The men who'd brought them removed the duck tape

160

and wrist ties of the girls who were awake; then one demanded that the girl still in her school clothing undress, at the same time pulling a top and knickers set from the bag, telling her to put them on. She refused point-blank, indignant that he expected her to take her clothes off with everyone watching.

The man just shrugged, pulled an electric stun gun from his pocket and touched her shoulder; in seconds she collapsed, virtually without a sound, to the floor. Both men knelt down at her side and undressed her, before attaching an ankle iron to one of her ankles, leaving her lying there naked. Then they moved on to the three girls who came in unconscious, stripping them all quickly, but pulling knickers on them, before attaching the ankle irons.

Nearly an hour went by before the three girls were awake, pulling on the tops left at their sides. The girl who'd objected was also awake but had only been given a top. She was scrunched up, trying to hide her nudity.

Harry entered the room; he leaned back on the wall looking around at them. "You're intelligent and well-educated girls, so I expect you all to understand what I'm going to tell you. For centuries slavery, be it hard, back-breaking work in the fields, through to girls and boys forced into prostitution for their owners' monetary gain, has never ceased. You have all been selected for the latter. Soon you will be leaving for a new life, in a different country. Your life now is to serve your new owner. To give pleasure to his customers. There is no escape, only death awaits those who try." He grinned. "You have cost us a lot of money, so the ones who believe death may look an easy route out, think again. There are people in this world who are beyond sadistic. They pay a great deal of money for a girl they can work on. Your last weeks, days and hours would be like hell on earth in the hands of such people. Some if not all of you will at times contemplate attempting taking your own life - we won't let you, and soon you'll understand how we prevent such options. In the meantime, while we wait for your transport, I want silence; any girl who utters a word will be punished. Such punishments can be painful and degrading in the extreme, again I wouldn't test us. We have bought and sold many people and understand very well the art of control."

At that moment food, by way of a burger, was brought in for each girl, with a small bottle of water, the same as Sherry had been given. Harry left the room, leaving two men inside watching the girls.

He entered a small office; another man called Macario was already inside, sitting in a chair smoking.

"The ship's standing off the coast, Macario, I've just had contact," Harry began. "After they have eaten, we'll transfer them to the launch."

Macario nodded his understanding. "Everything's gone well so far. We've a good set of girls; they'll earn plenty in Europe. You had no trouble with the one you collected then?"

"No, she's a wimp. Went into hysterics after she'd been snatched, but I gave her a good hiding, now she just sits there quietly, saying nothing. You'll have little trouble with her. You know she's got an English accent? According to her she was educated in England and has only been back for a couple of weeks."

Macario shrugged indifferently. "I've no idea how they were selected, my job's to get them to Europe without incident. I presume the syndicate buying them will have all the girls' backgrounds."

Harry smiled to himself. By what he was saying, even he didn't know who they had taken, so exchanging the real girl for Sherry, may not have been as big a problem as he'd envisaged. He walked over to the cupboard, pulling out a large carton. "There are a few boxes of sedatives in here. Give them one each, after their food tonight, then they'll need two a day. Without them, you risk some of the girls possibly going into hysterics, as they realise what's happening to them. You must make sure they swallow the tablets; if you think they've not, the tablets will melt in a warm drink."

"Don't worry about it, they'll get their tablets, believe me."

Chapter Thirty

It had been a week since Sherry left for America. Karen knew the ship was on the way. She also knew the name of the ship and the numbers of the two containers that the girls were in. This information had come from Harry, after the girls had left. Except unknown to Harry, there had been another person on the aircraft that arrived from the UK, besides Sherry. He had followed them to the warehouse, which for Karen was important. Not because she wasn't certain they would leave from there, it was more the fact that she had to be sure what Harry had told her was the truth.

The small tracker Sherry carried had sufficient range for the man following her to know she was there, and when she left the building for the ship. So Karen was happy that all that could be done, had been done, to not only keep tabs on the girls, but to track the ship's progress as it made its way to Europe. With Sherry on board, the idea was that she would shut down the tracker to conserve power. All Karen hoped was that they didn't find it on Sherry during the voyage, and that she was in a fit state to reactivate the tracker when she was about to come on to land. It was going to be a long two weeks, before the ship was due to arrive in EU waters.

In the meantime, Sir Peter called Karen, telling her he had arranged for her to meet the SAS soldiers who had survived the raid and helped her escape from the Lebanon, after she was first abducted. The meeting was to be in a private room of a London hotel. Sir Peter told her that five of the SAS team who were in that raiding party would be there.

***

Garry looked at his watch for the tenth time. "She's late; I bet it was all talk on Sir Peter's side that she would come. The arrogance of that girl seems never to have left her."

A tall man, with greying hair, was standing looking out of the window onto the street below. His name was Jeffery Farrow, he had been the commander of the SAS group who went in not only to collect Karen, but take out warehouses of weapons bound for Africa. He turned and looked at Garry. "What did you expect, Garry? Karen has moved on; she's become perhaps one of the most famous soldiers in the world. This idea of yours that she'd want to see us, to relive a past she'd rather forget, was ill-conceived from the start."

"Then why did you come?"

Farrow stood silently. It was a good question, for which he'd no real answer. After his capture in the Lebanon, then interrogation by the gunrunner Sirec, he was a broken man. Pensioned out of the army after his release, in therapy for five years afterwards, he had taken another five years to return to a somewhat normal life.

"He came for the same reason as us all," a man Karen knew only as Chapman, suddenly said.

"And what is that?" Garry asked.

"Karen was, and still is, an enigma. A girl you want to hate, for the devastation she causes, and yet she's also a girl who you can't get out of your mind. I've seen her often in the papers, watched her interviews. But I've never seen the soldier in her everyone keeps saying she has become. I still see her as I remember her, all those years ago. A quietly confident young girl, aware of her sexuality, yet with a determination to win at all costs, while prepared to die if she failed." He glanced over to another man in the room. "What are your thoughts about Karen, Stefan, particularly on that day when we had to leave her?"

Stefan, the soldier that had been with Chapman and Karen, when the three of them had been cornered, with no obvious way to escape, shook his head slowly. "I'll never forget that day. Watching a girl prepare to die. I could see it in her eyes, the final realisation that everything she'd been through had been for nothing. After we left her hidden, holding that grenade to her chest, her finger on the ringpull in case they found her, I never believed she'd get home. But she did against all odds. I'd like to know how she really did it, not what was written in the papers."

Farrow cut in. "If Sirec was to be believed, he told me she shot her way out. Took on a lorry-full of soldiers, killed the lot of them, then walked away. Personally I don't believe it, the girl was naive, a child with an ego that made her believe she was invincible. Maybe she managed to shoot one soldier, even two, but not ten as he claimed. I think he said that to save face; after all, she'd made a fool of him by escaping, besides all the people he'd enlisted to try to re-capture her."

"You all have her wrong," another soldier who'd been with them, called Franco, added. "She was a deeply religious girl, who believed her god was testing her, but she'd failed him. She'd killed without compassion, never turned the other cheek, which in her religion was expected of her. She was also scared. Not of us, or the people chasing her, but God himself. Her fear, and it was a very real fear, was what she would say to him; all her beliefs, her convictions, had gone out the window because of her time in the hands of the traffickers. I think her life now is trying to make amends, trying to show her god, that deep down she is still the same girl, and although she had failed his test, she desperately wants his forgiveness."

Garry began to laugh. "That's typical of the Karen I knew. She has you all hoodwinked by the way she acts, the way she talks to you. Karen uses people for her own ends, tells them what they want to hear. She even did the same to me, making me believe she liked me, wanted to be with me, but she didn't. I was just a stepping stone out of the Lebanon. Then when I was of no further use, I was thrown to one side, after which she conveniently forgot me. Except for my part, I really believed what she said, and hung on to the dream. It got me through, helped me accept my future in a wheelchair. Now I despise that girl, what she's achieved at the expense of not just us, plenty of others, who she has also pushed aside."

Farrow took a seat and leaned back. "Have you not noticed, we all have different slants on her? It begs the question, did any of us ever know the real Karen, yet we were all there and spent time with her. But whatever we think of Karen, on a personal level, we all want to meet her again. Her impact on all our lives, for some of have been huge, others who remained in the army seem to still have an admiration of her."

At that moment, Sir Peter entered the room. They all turned to look at him.

"Gentlemen, I'm sorry for the delay. Karen's plane has only just landed; she's now on her way."

"When you say a plane, is this a private one, or scheduled? After all, by all accounts she likes to swan around as if she's royalty, even to the point of delaying her entrance, to prove how important she is," Garry asked, with some bitterness in his voice.

Sir Peter nodded his head up and down slowly. "I sense a little vindictiveness towards her on your part, Garry. Remember, it was you who asked Karen for a meeting, not her. She has always felt she should meet you all and explain; but for her own safety, with traffickers still trying to take her back, Karen was enlisted in the army. Her name and her looks needed, for operational reasons, to be changed. With security around her very tight, and direct orders from the chief of staff that all ties with the past needed to be broken, she wasn't even allowed to see you, when you were all repatriated. One of her missions required Karen to return to the Lebanon, to assist in finding a number of English girls, snatched by the same trafficker." He hesitated, then looked directly at Garry. "You've all been there, you know just how dangerous the place can be, but she travelled hundreds of miles alone, and rescued three of the girls. Could any one of you have gone back so soon, and if you had, would you have gone in alone? I know I wouldn't, but she did. The girl is amazing and to date has rescued over three hundred victims of people trading, not counting the number of traffickers she's taken down. Even now, she has a number of major operations going on, and can't just drop everything to do what she wants. However, after a chance meeting with Garry, Karen requested to meet you all once more. Although she is no longer the young girl you all knew, Karen is a Lieutenant Colonel; as such, you must all respect the rank. Particularly those of you who are still serving. I say that because I suspect one or two of you feel she let you down, didn't follow through on her promises, and may demand explanations that she as a serving officer cannot give. Finally, you asked, Garry, about how she's getting here. Karen does have her own small aircraft. She trained as a pilot, in her own time, and enjoys flying. But on this occasion, she is in the UK, not only to meet you all, but on unit business, so she is travelling on one of the unit's aircraft. For any of you who don't know, the unit is based in France and their aircraft has been delayed by bad weather."

"We are all well aware of her rank, Sir Peter, and respect it,"

Farrow said. "Will Karen be able to fill in the gaps as to how she really escaped from the Lebanon, after she left us?"

"I very much doubt you will get anything from her that you don't already know. Even after leaving you, Chapman, the journey to freedom was not without problems for her. Karen made the choice that those last days and hours before she was picked up, will remain untold. It's understandable, when it turned out later that she had help from an elderly lady. Because the lady lived in the Lebanon, Karen was determined not to recount those final events, in case the trafficker, or her owner, was able to put two and two together, and realise just who had helped her. Since that time, the lady has died from natural causes; it was only then that she admitted to me the help she had received."

Sir Peter's telephone began to ring. He excused himself to answer it. Then he looked around the room. "Karen has arrived. I'll leave you all now; we'll meet a little later for lunch in the adjoining suite."

There was an air of expectation when Karen entered the room. Dressed in a black trouser suit, white blouse, with her long hair hanging loosely, she welcomed each one of them, with an embrace and kiss on both cheeks.

"I'm really sorry you've had to wait; we had fog this morning, which delayed our departure. But I'm here now; I also believe Sir Peter has arranged lunch." She smiled. "He always does this to me, trying to fatten me up, but it doesn't work, I just spend longer working out."

"We all appreciate you agreeing to meet us, Colonel. We understand that you have a tight schedule, but I for one, have so many unanswered questions, I truly believe that this meeting is essential for most of us to move on," Commander Farrow said.

"If I can answer your questions, Commander, I will, except certain parts of my time in the Lebanon, are personal to me and will remain that way. As this is a private meeting, can we dispense with my army rank, I'd be more than happy if you all called me Karen?"

"I have a question, Karen. Why didn't you look me up? We had an agreement to meet, if we got back. You never even tried to find me?" Garry asked.

Karen moved to the window, glancing out for a moment, before she turned and looked at him. "Do you want the truth, Garry, or some potted version that may make you feel better in yourself?"

Their eyes met, all of a sudden he was scared of this girl, scared of what she was about to say. But he needed to know.

"I want the truth," he whispered quietly.

She shrugged indifferently. "I thought you were dying. At the time, the last thing I wanted was any sort of relationship. I despised men, hated them for what they had done to me. But I was leaving you alone and moving on. So I flirted, made out that we were more than we were, gave you a confidence boost, in what was a very serious situation for both of us. But as for any agreement, I'd no intention of seeing it through."

"I don't believe you. We were together for three days and we were really hitting it off. I think you heard I'd been confined to a wheelchair, so just avoided me. Maybe because you didn't want to be seen pushing me around. After all, that would have spoiled your street cred."

Karen sighed; 'has he still not grown up,' she thought, 'perhaps it's time for a reality check.' "Believe what you want, Garry, but my life was in turmoil, and I was desperately worried that I'd be taken again, so I was prepared to say, or do anything that would help me get home. The ironical part of all this is that within two years of being home, I was back with Sirec. We live in a world you could never imagine, and I'd fallen in love with him; if he'd not been killed, we would have been married, and I'd probably have had his children by now."

Farrow looked shocked. "Are you telling us, after people lost their lives trying to get you out, you were prepared to walk back into the arms of someone who had hunted you down like an animal?"

"No, I'm not telling you that. In fact, I'll always be grateful that you came for me and sad that a number of good soldiers never returned. It was Saeed who'd taken me from England, not Sirec. Saeed wanted me to go to a brothel, from where I'd never have escaped. Sirec, fortunately for me, had seen my photo and read all about me, so he did a deal with Saeed. The important part was that with Sirec purchasing me, he saved me from the brothels and a life I don't even want to contemplate. He also helped me, later, to bring out the five girls abducted after me. Often in this world, someone who was your enemy becomes an ally. In a war this is typical; do we ignore the Germans, or the Italians because they were on the other side? Of course we don't, time heals, allows people to forget. That was the same for me and Sirec. We were on different sides, but when together, we found common ground."

The meeting went on for some time, Karen answering their many unanswered questions. Eventually, they joined Sir Peter for lunch.

After lunch, Karen stood. "I'm glad we have all finally met and I hope I've answered most of your questions. Unfortunately, time is never on my side, my unit is waiting for me, but I'd like to leave you with one final thought. Your intervention in my life was not wasted. You and I were the catalyst, a wake-up call for governments to help those who have been taken. The battle has already begun, to reduce the scourge of every generation. There is a new determination, and although sometimes it doesn't always go to plan, I believe we are winning. It's not a quick fix; it will carry on long after I'm gone. You should be proud of that, the same as I am."

After Karen and Sir Peter had left, the room was silent, everyone with their own thoughts.

It was Farrow who broke the silence. "Karen is right, we should be proud. We helped bring out a girl who has never turned her back on others in similar situations. Finally, as she said, we are fighting back."

Garry huffed. "Yes well, I'd like to have just a little of what she's got. If you can believe the papers, she's a multimillionaire, has the world at her feet, with the recognition of a superstar. Whatever you might think, she has come out smelling of roses, while we languish in the background, all but forgotten."

Stefan shook his head slowly. "It's time you grew up, Garry. Got rid of the chip on your shoulder and forgot Karen. She was never for you and never could be. Her world is what we all joined the SAS to be part of, but it's very clear that we only ever touched the tip, where she went in. What has it brought her? We saw it on television only days back. She lives a life where she can't even walk down the street in safety; we can, and don't you forget it. As for me, I'm proud of what she's achieved, proud to have helped her on her way, as everyone else in this room is, apart from you."

Chapter Thirty-One

Macario leaned on the rail of the large container ship, watching the launch which had brought him and the girls speeding away. Already the ship was on the move.

It was going to take fourteen days to cross the Atlantic, in that time he'd work to do with the girls. Leaving the deck, he made his way down into the hold, through an emergency door. In front of him were two containers, positioned so that the doors at the front could be opened; one of the containers was securely locked. He entered the open one. A single light, fastened with thin rope, was attached to the top of a side strut. In the dim light, six girls were sitting on mattresses, three on each side and opposite each other. They all had a chain around their ankles.

"It's time to listen and listen good. We'll be at sea for two weeks, you'll not be sitting around doing nothing; you'll spend the time learning what is expected from you, by your owners." He hesitated. "I say owners, because you're all sold. Your new owners will want you to begin work the moment you arrive; they don't want a learning curve, so this container will be your school. As for the rules, while you're with me, toilet and washing is twice a day, so get used to it. Piss in here, between toilet times, then expect to sit in it for the duration. Believe me it'll stink. Rather than crop tops, you're getting shirts and knickers. I've removed all the buttons, so you don't get it into your head to try to swallow them, in an effort to choke yourself. You'll get food twice a day. After you finish, or rather after ten minutes I'll take what's left away."

They said nothing, just sat quietly watching him, the obvious resignation to what had happened to them very apparent.

"Life in a brothel is not how it's portrayed in movies. It's hard work, long hours, and you need to know how to handle and service at least eight jons a day. That jon has paid to fuck you. For him, if it's up your fanny, your arse, or in your mouth, he's not bothered, so long as he comes. Don't piss him about, believe he'll be bothered how you feel, he won't, refusal on your part will always result in a beating, so remember that. It's also in your own interest to protect yourself from diseases. You'll get your first of three HPV jabs while you're on this ship, the brothel will give you the other two; that will protect you from most diseases. Often clients have fleas, hair lice and even parasites that cling to a girl's pubic hair, some burrowing into the skin to lay their eggs. On your first visit to the shower room, preparation of your body begins. Get rid of the body hair, I want to see a body as smooth as a baby's bottom. Object, then I'll tie you down and do it for you, followed by a good beating."

Macario could see the look of horror on their faces, as the reality of being a prostitute began to sink in. "Have no illusions, those who choose to fight, should expect many beatings. For those who'd rather die, that of course is an option, after many weeks of servicing jons. We have clients who delight in beating girls up, after that, they are handed to some of the most perverted of our clients. These are people who like nothing better than torturing a girl to within an inch of her life, before stringing her up to be butchered alive. You'd last a week, maybe two, but you would get your wish to die. Be it slowly and extremely painfully, when they finally begin to skin you. I've seen a girl's guts hanging out; breasts gone, the beating heart exposed, yet she still lives. She died after five days; the shock to her body left her speechless, no longer able to beg for mercy, for that final cut to burst her heart."

After he left them, Emma, a sixteen-year-old snatched as she walked home, already shivering with the cold of the container, began to sob quietly.

Paige, who was seventeen, and snatched after she'd finished her shift at a fast food drive-in, looked across at Emma. "Don't let him get to you, at least we're alive, so there's always hope."

"What sort of hope, to face being raped every day of my life? I'll kill myself before they do that to me."

"And how do you expect to do that? Don't you think every girl here wouldn't want to do the same? I know I would, but if being dressed the way we are, and chained up, is to be the norm, it's going to be bloody difficult to achieve."

"There'll be opportunities, maybe it'll take a few days, even a week or so, but they will get complacent and then I'll do it," Emma replied.

"Yes, Emma, you keep believing that, then soon the days will turn into weeks, months, maybe even years. If we are going to get out of this, we all need to stick together and make a plan."

"What sort of plan?" Emma asked frowning.

"I don't know what sort, that will come later."

***

By the second day at sea, Macario had already taken four of the girls to the toilet and shower room. Although he allowed them the privacy to wash and toilet themselves, they had to remove their clothes before they went inside. Inside the combined room, there was nothing besides a few toilet sheets, a bar of soap, a sponge, with a towel to dry themselves. When they came out, he quickly checked the soap and sponge were still inside the shower room, while they dressed, then they were taken back to the container. With the medication they were on, he got little aggression from them. All through the first day, he had run DVDs of girls operating in brothels, showing on a television in the container. Their introduction to prostitution had begun.

Sherry was also subject to this regime, making mental notes as to their position and distance from the hold. Although the walk between the shower room and the hold was short, she didn't see, or pass, any other member of the crew. Sherry was also afraid that while she was in the shower room, even a casual check of her knickers, by Macario, would reveal the tracker in the lining, so she removed it, after the first girl was taken, and hid it in the mattress, replacing it back in her knickers when she returned. She'd been glad she did, as Macario had thrown both items of her clothing in the bin, while she used a battery shaver on her body, before going under the shower; he'd given her replacements when she came out. Two of the girls taken to the shower room before her, had come back to the container distressed, after being forced to shave themselves, but Sherry knew differently. What Macario had described was very real.

On the second day at sea, Sherry, after her shower and toilet, was not given her clothes, or even taken back to the container. Instead, Macario grasped her arm, taking her the other way to his cabin. There he forced her to sit down on a chair, quickly attaching her wrists to the chair arms with plastic ties, then stood back looking at her.

173

"Feeling cleaner after the shower are you? But perhaps wondering why you're in my cabin?"

"I suppose I am, so are you going to tell me?" Sherry asked.

He grinned, moving behind her, running his hands over her shoulders, then down across her breasts, squeezing and massaging them gently. "You're a good-looking girl; with a nice figure, firm tits, tight bum, what else could a man want? So do you work out a lot, or perhaps have a job that requires you to be fit? Maybe even a soldier in the armed forces?"

She said nothing; already despising this man for fondling her.

Macario carried on talking. "I'm not surprised you're not saying anything, after I've mentioned armed forces; after all, you're hardly going to run around and tell everyone you're actually attached to Unit T's incursion unit Dark Angel. In fact, you're even a corporal in the unit, aren't you Sherry Malloy?"

Sherry felt cold inside, hearing her name.

Macario moved his hands back onto her shoulders, hesitated for a moment, before walking around to face her, resting his behind on the side of a small table. "How do I know? Well you see, Sherry, I got a call yesterday, as to who is going where, when we land. When I told them the girl Watson had collected was no more fifteen than I was, they asked for a description. It didn't take them long to find out who you were, really, because Watson wasn't very good at keeping your identity secret; very sad actually. He was interviewed, quite unpleasantly I believe, by the Los Zetas cartel. I received a call this morning, after they had watched the remains of him eaten by the sharks. It would seem they were quite put out that he'd managed to place a covert operator in place of a girl."

Sherry didn't know how to answer, so she remained silent.

"Quiet girl are you? Not going to beg for your life, or offer yourself in exchange for freedom, like they do in the movies? I'm surprised, because you're already an old hand in the entertainment business. Oh yes, we've looked into your past. We found you've been here before, purchased by a brothel in Scotland, at the age of sixteen and entertained, what was it, five or six men a night?"

"So what are you going to do with me, now you know who I

174

am?"

"That will be up to you. The cartel's requested I look after you very well, so that they may interview you in their own way." He grinned. "Don't expect to come out of the interview alive, none ever has, and for a girl like you, it will be a very long interview I suspect. Also, don't expect to be rescued at the port. They have the port wrapped up very well; a few hundred dollars and you'll be spirited away before anyone knows you've even left the ship."

Sherry frowned. "When you say 'up to me', what are you suggesting?"

"Bright girl aren't you? I'm suggesting we join forces, to our mutual benefit? I like shagging, so you service my needs, you also show the other girls the ropes. Do both for me, and it buys you your freedom. I could easily claim you died at sea, or have taken your own life. So what do you say?"

She gave a forced laugh. "How do I know you'll not just pass me across anyway? After all, I'd still be locked up."

"True, very true, but I'm a man of my word, and I can get you off the ship before it berths."

"What about the other girls, are they getting the same offer?"

"I could use them; after all they are on the ship to learn. But unlike a lot of men in this world, I'm not into shagging fifteen and sixteen year olds. I like an older girl, a girl with experience in pleasing a man, not some blubbering child still believing their fanny is the Holy Grail. You Sherry, are perfect, very experienced, good figure, small tits which I've no problem with, as I'm into fanny and arse." Then his manner changed. "Think very seriously about my generous offer, Sherry. You're no longer covert, so whatever happens without my help, your life is in the balance. I'm offering a way out, doing something you've done many times. Refuse and I'll leave you to your fate, and shag my way through all the other girls."

After a few seconds of silence, in which he'd remained looking at her, he shrugged his shoulders with indifference. "I'll let you sit here and contemplate what I propose; maybe when I come back I'll try you out to cement the deal."

When he left the room, Sherry felt very down. This was her first covert operation, and she hadn't realised how vulnerable you could be. How Karen could keep going back in alone, she couldn't imagine, but whatever happened, she was determined to see the operation through as best she could, besides take this man out, at the earliest opportunity.

***

Macario made his way to the ship's recreation and dining room. He sat alone; only a handful knew the girls were on board, and it had to be kept that way. After finishing his lunch, he returned to his cabin where Sherry was still bound to the chair.

While he'd been gone, Sherry had made a decision. It wasn't a good decision, but with her cover blown, she had no option but to go along with him, allowing her breathing space to decide where to go from here.

"So, have we an agreement?" he demanded, as he entered the cabin, closing the door behind him.

"Yes, I'll do what you ask of me, provided that the other girls are left alone. You also provide condoms; I've hardly got any pills with me, and there's no way I'm going to be made pregnant."

He sneered. "You're not here to make the conditions, I do. Except in this case I agree; I've a load of morning-after pills, so pregnancy will be the least of your problems. Shag your way through the voyage and I'll get you off the ship before we dock."

"And the others?"

"That's up to you; start being difficult, not wanting to continue, and I'll use them. So let's start as we mean to go on, show me what you can do and that it is not all talk."

Sherry shrugged. "So what do you want? A blow job, or to fuck me?"

He laughed. "Forget the blow job, I still want my dick after the ship docks and not part of it missing down your throat."

Sherry laughed. "Read my mind did you?"

Macario didn't reply, as he released her wrists. "Right, let's have you stood up, then turn around, grip the chair arms and bend down, with your legs well apart. So I can experience how good a fuck you are," he demanded, at the same time grasping her hand and pulling her up from the chair, before beginning to unfasten his trousers.

176

When he'd finished, he sat her back down. "You're a good fuck, Sherry; I can tell you've done this many times before. This is good, because I told my employers that the girls will be ready to work on the first day they leave the ship. Because of that, they have received higher bids based on my promise. It will also give me a bonus, so I've been working out how to do it, but with you here I don't have to. You will teach them for me."

"How will I do that? They think I've been abducted the same as them."

"I'll tell them you were taken at sixteen; you're eighteen now and are being moved to a brothel in Europe. Reminding them there's no escape, the same as you found; so they would be foolish to ignore your training."

"It could work I suppose. So what advice do I give?"

"It's your job to get them practising to strip seductively, experience their bottom being smacked, shagging both ways and how to give a man a blow job. You show them how to lubricate themselves before the jon joins them, tricks to make the jon come quick, the works. Give them your techniques; tell them about life in a brothel, then demonstrate stripping and how to mount a jon with each girl, before they are put in pairs After training they are to perform in front of me. Do this, and you'll leave two days before the ship docks. Mess around, don't push them, then the deal's off, and you go to the port with the girls. I don't need to remind you what's waiting for you there."

"Er, I think I have a tiny problem with this idea; they're all girls, if you haven't noticed?"

He laughed and walked over to a box in the corner of the room and pulled out a sealed packet. "I've thought of that, I presume you've seen a strap-on dildo harness before?"

Sherry shook her head. "No, I've never had a lesbian relationship."

He began opening the bag. "Stand up, spread your legs a little, let me show you."

She stood and in minutes he'd strapped the harness around her hips and between her legs, the rubber penis stuck out in front, with a small extra length inside her, for her own pleasure. "In the bag are three of these with various dildo lengths up to twelve inches, a large jar of lubrication, and an anal douche to clean inside the arse, before applying the lubricant. I've also three sets of underwear, suspenders and nylons."

She looked down at the dildo sticking out in front of her. "You're expecting a young girl to have this thing pushed inside her. Even I wouldn't like to try it myself," Sherry said, confused as to how she was going to achieve what he wanted.

"I couldn't give a shit, at the end of this trip they will be performing up to eight times a day. So they either ram it up each other's fannies, or I'll bring some of the crew for them to practice their techniques with. I couldn't care less which. Anyway you've been told to teach them, get refusals then expect to be punished as well."

"Why should I be punished, if they refuse?" Sherry asked, alarmed at the prospect.

"This is no easy ride," he replied aggressively. "You shag, you work, or you get the same treatment as them. The only difference is you walk away, they get to spend their young lives in a brothel."

He said no more, but took her back to the shower room to wash before handing her clothes; then grasping her arm, he returned her to the hold where the container was. There he clipped the ankle iron on and left the container.

***

Between the playing of the DVDs, Sherry told the girls of her experiences in a brothel. At first they wouldn't believe it, but as they saw more and more of the recordings made in the rooms where the girls serviced the jons, Sherry could see the despondency taking over.

"So are you a prostitute?" Emma asked, the first day Macario had told them all why Sherry was there, and that he'd decided she would teach them the profession.

Sherry looked at her with indignation. "No! I'm not a prostitute and never will be. I like you was abducted, punished constantly for five days, before I finally broke. I've been raped, up to eight times a day since then, one day I'll escape, or die trying."

Lauren cut in. "It seems the same to me, whatever you want to call it."

"Yes, when I go out on the street to sell myself, then, Lauren, call

178

me a prostitute, until then I'll beat the shit out of you, if you call me that again," Sherry retorted.

Lauren quickly apologised, but the tension in the room was that much higher, after the way Sherry had suddenly turned.

It was on the third day that Emma, the youngest of the girls, had been brought back to her mattress and left without the ankle clamp. When Sherry was brought in, last as usual to go for a shower, she was carrying a bag, and Macario a kitchen chair, which he placed in the centre of the container. Before he left he also increased the length of Sherry's ankle chain, to allow her to move quite a distance around the container, but not enough to get to the door.

Once they were all alone, with the door shut, Sherry stood up. "This time had to come," she began. "You've seen what goes on, so now it's your turn to practice the practical skills. I never had the opportunity; I was thrown into a room with a jon. One I coped with, but that was followed by six more. By the end of the night, I was in so much pain, I could hardly walk. I'll show you over the next days, how to get through each day, how to prepare yourself, before we all pair up and experience six sessions, one after the other."

She pulled out a knickers and suspender set, walking over to Emma. "Put these on."

Emma took them off Sherry and threw them to one side. "I'm not wearing that stuff," she said indignantly.

"Put them on, Emma. If you don't Macario will punish you and me as well, so put them on."

"No!"

Sherry came closer and slapped her face hard, then the other side. Emma, her face stinging, was in tears.

"I said, put them on," Sherry shouted at her.

Still she refused.

The other girls began shouting at Sherry to leave her alone, but Sherry knew what an electric stick could do; she had to try to convince the girl to do as she was told. Grabbing her hair, she dragged her screaming to the chair in the centre of the container, intending to give her a good thrashing.

"You still refuse?" she shouted at her.

"I'm not a tramp like you," Emma shouted back.

However, Macario had come into the container; in his hand he carried a stick. "Leave her, Sherry, go and sit on your mattress," he shouted.

Sherry went back to her mattress, already very scared when she saw what he held.

"So Emma, you believe a girl who was abducted, then forced into prostitution is a tramp? It'll be interesting to know what you consider yourself to be over the next months. Sherry's doing her best to make you all realise just what sort of position you are all now in, but you chose to throw it in her face. She's been there; you lot haven't. All traffickers have tools of the trade. This is the punishment stick used by most traffickers. Made from a cattle rod, it gives a light shock to move an animal on; we all tweak them to suit our own purposes. I like the small pad, others the large pad, where often far stronger shocks are given. But this is a good taste of what to expect in the brothel, when you have your paddies."

Emma stood staring at him, in lots of ways not understanding what he was saying or intending to do. However, he walked up to her, touching her stomach with the tip of the rod, through the open part of her shirt. Immediately the shock threw her back. She fell to the floor. He followed, touching other parts of her body; her screams were soon down to a whimper. Then he walked over to Sherry; she cowered back, knowing what to expect after watching Emma. Soon she too was screaming, rolling on the floor in agony.

He stopped and looked around. "So does anyone else want to experience the stick?"

No one said a word.

"No, then you do as Sherry tells you to; otherwise you and Sherry will be punished."

After he'd gone, Sherry dragged herself up, looking around the container. "If anyone else refuses and gets me punished like that again, the stick will be the least of your problems, believe me." Then she walked over to Emma, who was still lying on the floor in tears, her body shaking.

Sherry bent down, grabbed her hair and wrenched it back. "I

should kick your fucking head in for getting me punished. Refuse anything else you're told to do and expect it. Now get up and put the fucking clothes on," she shouted at her.

Emma looked at Sherry, tears running down her face. "I'm sorry, Sherry, I'm so scared of my future, I never realised he'd punish you as well. I'll do anything you ask of me from now on."

"Then get dressed," she retorted, not allowing Emma an inch.

For the next hour, she had Emma dress and undress, her foot on the chair, as she removed the nylons, getting used to the feel of the underclothes, the way to release the catches and slip the nylons down her legs. Sherry, trying to mimic reality, would sit on the chair pretending to be the jon, having Emma sit astride her, facing away, as Sherry removed her bra, squeezing her breasts till she squealed, the same as jons would do to her many times. Then always, after she was naked, Sherry would put Emma over her knee, giving the girl's bottom a good slapping, showing her how to clench herself, to reduce the stinging pain.

After around an hour, Macario was back. He said nothing, just slipped Emma's ankle iron on, then released Lauren before leaving. This went on for three days until every girl could do the actions automatically, often, at times, playing the jon, as Sherry first did.

"When you were taken to the toilet, Sherry, we all had a talk," Mia began. "We're very grateful for what you are showing us; it won't be easy to accept the life, but we all hope that one day someone will come for us. All we can do is thank you, for at least giving us an insight into how to cope."

"You don't know how lucky you all are, having this time between being abducted and the brothel. Most girls are thrown in the deep end, some as young as ten, but never give up hope. In Europe, they have specialist units that are already making an impact. They have pulled out hundreds of victims, and they will find you, believe me."

"So what's next in Macario's plan for us?" Emma asked.

Sherry smiled. "The next bit's the hardest to accept, Emma. But for the jon, it's what you're there for. I'll be showing you how you grease yourself up, how you can cope with a lot of jons, without getting yourself sore. You see, you can't rely on the secretions of normal intercourse; you'd quickly run out and dry up. Then, apart from that, many jons like anal sex, and without preparation, pushing themselves up your bottom can be very painful."

"So dare I ask how you intend to show us that?" Ashley asked quietly.

"Believe me, I'm no lesbian, although tomorrow, that's how we are going to practice. I'm going to be well embarrassed, putting a dildo harness on and demonstrating. Then you'll all pair up, doing it as well, taking turns to be the jon, we'll be doing normal and anal sex. An alternative is to use the crew, personally at this stage we need to keep away from men, until you know what you're doing."

***

The days dragged on, each day the same, having the girls practise routines and understand how to look after themselves. Sherry was always taken last; he'd have her toilet and shower, and on most days he'd not allow her to dress, but take her directly to his cabin. There he'd spend an hour with her, taking her in different ways on the bed, often knocking her about if she didn't do as he demanded. For Sherry this was like being back in the Scottish brothel, when she was first abducted. Her only consolation was the abuse was from one man, this time, not the six or eight she'd been forced to service every day in Scotland.

***

It was late one night when Macario came into the container. Normally they wouldn't see him after the last toilet session and meal. All the girls were asleep; even Sherry was until he shook her gently. She woke as he unclasped her chain. Then without saying a word he grasped her hand and brought her out of the container, closing it silently.

"You've done good by me, Sherry, in fact, besides being a good fuck, you trained the girls well, I'll miss you," he began, followed by a grin. "It's time I kept my end of the bargain. The ship docks in two days; they have already slowed down; now we're in the channel. I can get you off the ship, if you can swim that is?"

Sherry looked shocked. "You mean you intend to throw me

182

overboard, and I have to swim to shore? That's not exactly keeping your end of the bargain; I'd drown."

"You won't fucking drown, you'll be in a fucking rubber dinghy. I'm hardly likely to expect you to swim twelve fucking miles. Anyway come with me."

Sherry followed him along a passage, down three flights of stairs, through to another passage opening out into an open area with a large steel door to one side.

"This is where they load stores. With the ship loaded like it is, you jump. The water's around fifteen feet below, not even diving board height," he began telling her, as he dragged a package out from a side room leading off the open deck. On top of it was a single life jacket and a tee-shirt. He handed her both. "Get your shirt off, it wouldn't be suitable in the water, then put the tee-shirt and life jacket on. Inside this package is a rubber dinghy, once it hits the water it will inflate. It also has a light attached that will begin flashing. You follow it. Jump as far out from the ship as you can; then swim like fuck, away from the ship; otherwise you'll be dragged under the screws."

Sherry stared at him. "Are you out your mind? I'd be lucky not to break a bone on the jump, then I'd have no chance. I'd rather stay on board."

"Well you're not staying on board. Besides, it's a fucking doddle; they do it all the time in training to abandon ship. You're fit; I've kept you off sedation, unlike the other girls, so this is your way out." He grasped her hand, squeezing it for a moment. "I like you, Sherry, if I could get you off any other way, I would. The people waiting for you are pissed off, you have cost them plenty, you will pay for that. Even if Unit T is there, they will not find you. As I've told you before, as soon as we dock, you'll be spirited away. You have no concept as to just what these people are like. They'll begin to skin you alive, the pain, I'm told, is excruciating. Then, girl, you will willingly give them every bit of information they want, just so they can finally put you out of your misery and kill you."

Sherry was frightened, her belief that Karen would be with her every step of the way was not giving her confidence, with what Macario was saying about the workers at the dock. She had to leave this way, no matter what. Her cover was blown, and she'd be no help to the unit anyway. Karen wouldn't even know she was no longer with the girls when they left the dock; except by then, it would be too late, the cartel would have her.

"Okay, I'll go. As you say, I've no option," she told him, removing her shirt and pulling the tee-shirt over her head, followed by the life jacket.

Macario released the access door, opening it wide. Sherry stared in horror; she'd no idea what the weather was like, being down in the hold. Now she could see it was virtually a storm, the rain was lashing the side of the ship, the wind deafening.

He dragged the dinghy package to the edge and looked back at her. "There's clothes in the dinghy, when I push this out, you go immediately, don't hesitate," he shouted at her, above the sound of the wind and rain. "Run from the far end, jump out as far as you can, then close up into a ball, before swimming like fuck after you hit the water. Good luck, Sherry."

He turned and began to push the dinghy out the door. Sherry had backed up to the far wall.

Then as it fell out, she made a decision. She ran as fast as she could, before jumping in the air and kicking Macario squarely in the back.

He never saw her coming, and he followed the dinghy off the ship. Sherry prevented herself falling out by grabbing the side of the door. However, she wasn't staying on the ship, so she backed up and took another run, virtually flying out of the open door. This for Sherry was the right way to go. If she had stood on the edge of the opening to jump, she'd never have gone, she'd have been far too frightened. This way there was no time to think, or even look down, before she shot out the door, smashing into the wind and rain head-on, tumbling through the air, falling all the time, before finally hitting the cold water. The impact knocked every bit of breath out of her, she immediately began to sink deeper into the water, before the life jacket self-inflated, bringing her back up to the surface. Sherry was fighting for her life, already she could feel the pull towards the ship as she broke the surface, gasping for air. Even in the dark and driving rain, she could see the huge ship running at her side, as she struck out, swimming powerfully and desperately, trying to break away from the drag of the ship.

The ship passing her seemed to go on forever; she'd given everything she could. Her arms became heavy, no longer able to make any effect in her swim. The noise around her, as the water was being churned up by the ship's screws, was even louder than the wind and rain. She was being tossed around, not able to fight it any more. Sherry closed her eyes; although she'd never been brought up as a religious girl, she was praying. There were tears in her eyes, washed away before they even had the chance to touch her cheeks. She knew she'd failed and would die alone. A strange inner calmness began to encompass her. The desperate fight for survival had gone.

Sherry never felt the ship begin to turn, the screws pulling away from her, the drag of the ship no longer drawing her in, but pushing her and the thousands of gallons of water around her away from the ship. Within seconds the ship had gone, Sherry lay on the surface of the water, her eyes closed, exhausted, only held upright by the life jacket. The rain was easing to just a light drizzle splashing her face, the wind, though still there, was no longer funnelled into a roar alongside the ship.

Opening her eyes, Sherry was confused at first as to where she was. Then it came back to her; she wasn't dead; how she'd survived she had no idea, but after a great effort Sherry pulled herself upright and looked around. She could see the ship's lights in the distance, but at first that was all she could see. Then as her eyes became more accustomed to the dark, she saw one more light, a small red light flashing a distance away from her. Macario was nowhere to be seen. She suspected, without a life jacket and fully dressed, he'd not have been able to come back up to the surface; he would have been dragged under the ship. Realising the life jacket would be a drag on her as she tried to reach the dinghy, she decided to ditch it. So after unclasping the straps, she worked it off over her head. Once free, Sherry struck out with renewed energy. The swim was long and difficult. Believing at first the dinghy was close, she found it wasn't and it took a last supreme effort, on her part, to finally grab one of the ropes looped around the edge of the dinghy. For a minute or so, Sherry hung on, then after getting her breath back, she pulled herself over its side, ending up sprawled on the bottom.

Looking around the small rubber dinghy, Macario it seemed had been true to his word. There was a bundle wrapped up in a plastic bag tied to one of the ropes. She opened it and found a towel, clean underclothes, jeans, jumper and trainers. There was also a small bottle of water. Stripping quickly, she dried herself as best she could, then dressed. Just with clothes on, she felt better. After taking a sip of the water, Sherry very carefully extracted her radio tracker from the knickers she'd discarded, and activated it, pushing it into the top lining of the knickers she was wearing now. Hoping it wasn't water damaged it should run for around thirty hours, enough time, she hoped, for the signal to be picked up and be located. While she waited, she constantly kept herself alert; looking around all the time for the telltale splash of water a swimmer would make, still afraid that Macario may be alive. Sherry hoped not, his was a fitting end for what he'd put her through and particularly the punishment, which she hadn't believed was justified.

***

It was less than an hour before Sherry saw the lights of a small boat heading towards her. It was pointless standing and waving; they wouldn't see her in the dark. Sherry was relieved, the tracker's radio signal that she'd activated must have been picked up, and they were coming for her.

The boat was in fact a fishing boat and within half an hour, Sherry was hauled aboard, followed by the dinghy.

The captain came up to her. "Welcome aboard, Sherry. You must be cold after being in the water, let's get you down below. We'll arrive in port in about three hours. The cartel has already sent a car to pick you up."

Sherry stood stunned. "You mean, you're not from the unit, this was a set-up? Macario knew you'd be waiting?"

The captain laughed. "We've known you were coming off the ship early for a few days now. Unit T still believes you're on the ship with the other girls. The cartel has plans for you in a few weeks' time. Then you'll become a very important pawn in the game to get Karen Harris. In the meantime, you're to be taken to a brothel. You've already had experience in one, so you'll know the ropes and settle down quickly I expect." He glanced at two crew stood waiting. "Take her down and tie her up. Give her a hot drink and food if she wants it."

Chapter Thirty-Two

A man everyone knew as Blas, an important person within the Ndrangheta, was hosting a dinner for his many friends, in a large country estate located in France, close to the German border. Among them was his contact into the Los Zetas cartel from Mexico, Sergio Vargus. The two men had left the dinner table; then while the other guests drank brandy, smoking cigars, they went through to Blas's study.

Taking seats in easy chairs, they too were carrying glasses of brandy. Blas opened a cigar box, offering one to Sergio. Then he lit his own.

"Our plan is going well," Blas began, between draws on his cigar. "The ship has entered the English Channel, in two days they will dock."

"So is Unit T still tracking the ship?" Sergio asked.

"Yes, they're following the ship's progress, but not visually. They are using the British spy headquarters, GCHQ, to track the ship."

"Then when the ship arrives at the port, what of the containers, are all the arrangements in place?"

"They are," Blas answered, at the same time re-lighting his cigar. "Our contact, in the dock, has confirmed Unit T's request to customs and the port authorities, to allow the two containers to go through the docks without a customs check. Unit T won't want to have the girls found on the ship, or on the docks. They want to take out the people running the brothels. So because of Unit T's involvement, I've been assured that the general customs inspection of the containers, holding the girls, won't happen."

"I see, but a Unit T girl is on board, what's happening to her?" Sergio asked, with interest.

"I informed Macario, on the first day at sea, of just who she is, and gave him the background information we have on this girl, so he could identify her properly. I arranged with him that she is to be lowered into a rubber dinghy, before the ship docks, and set adrift. That's happening tonight. A small radio beacon fitted in the dinghy will locate it, and she'll be picked up by a fishing boat. We know the captain; for a small fee he's already set sail to intercept the dinghy and collect the girl. Once ashore, we'll move her temporarily to a brothel, then it's intended to use her to lure their unit commander, Karen Harris, into a trap. After this is done, she'll be returned to the brothel and with luck, the Harris girl as well."

"So we will have lost five girls, which we expected, and gained one, maybe two. What about the real cargo, have you arranged a secure location, for the exchange with the Russian mafia?"

"All taken care of, this is going to be very profitable for both of us, believe me."

"It is, so how much do our Russian friends know about the plan?"

"They know nothing and it must be kept that way. This operation has a combined value of two hundred and fifty million. This is to be paid on delivery, with a bank transfer and five million dollars in currency, gold and diamonds, to cover paying off the men. We, as well as you I suspect, cannot afford a loss on such a scale. So it's imperative the Russians believe everything is running smoothly."

"I understand, and you're right, such a shipment, if lost, would set us back twenty years."

Chapter Thirty-Three

Karen had been asked to come to the surveillance room at Unit T, as a matter of urgency. The people who worked in this facility, numbering twenty-two across a 24/7 shift, were busily following leads, besides keeping in touch with all the unit's surveillance teams out in the field.

Karen found Stanley listening in on GCHQ, as they tracked the container vessel carrying the girls. It had just entered the channel, the time a little after two in the morning. The weather was not kind, with persistent rain and a choppy sea.

Stanley turned to Karen. "Sherry's tracker started up about an hour and a half back. I've checked with GCHQ, and it's now confirmed that the tracker is no longer on the ship. The coordinates of the ship and the tracker are around two miles apart and widening. According to GCHQ, the tracker didn't move position much for around an hour, now it's moving towards the French coast. Between us, that's GCHQ and myself, we suspect she and maybe others have left the ship, perhaps waited in a dinghy, or similar, and have now been picked up."

Karen looked at him. "I promised to look after Sherry and I will. So if they've managed somehow to break her cover, then rather than kill her immediately, they could be splitting her off from the girls and taking her somewhere else."

"It's possible, on the other hand, all the girls could be with her, and the containers may [?]have been just a red herring?" Stanley suggested. "After all, Sherry's orders were specific, she was only to activate the tracker once ashore, giving us a belt and braces approach in the tracking."

"I agree Stan. But the other scenario is what I just said, and she wanted to make sure we knew where she was being taken. Sherry could be thinking, if she didn't do it now, she may be prevented later, and we'd lose her completely."

"I have to agree, both are possible, so what now?"

Karen sat for a short time, deep in thought, then made a decision. "We have to assume that the transfer of the girls will still be by container. The only way we will know if that's the case is to bring

Sherry in. There's still two days before the ship docks and unloads, so we leave surveillance at the docks, keep GCHQ monitoring the ship, and divert resources to pull Sherry out."

"Then you're ordering mobilisation?"

Karen didn't hesitate. "Yes, as from," she looked at her watch. "O two thirty hours, Unit T is in lockdown, mobilise Dark Angel, we're going in to pull Corporal Malloy out."

Chapter Thirty-Four

With a rope wrapped around her waist, attached to a bench seat, and the cabin entrance locked, Sherry had been left alone. She'd been given a mug of tea and a large cheese sandwich. Both those items she was really appreciative of. Still shivering from her time in the water and her effort swimming, she was exhausted both physically and mentally. Sherry was also feeling despondent; she'd been well and truly duped. Already she'd decided that Macario had no intention of using any of the girls. He'd targeted her for his own sexual gratification. If she'd said no, that would probably have been the end of it. As it was, she'd let him do anything he wanted with her. As to the people he'd claimed would be waiting at the docks, she now knew that was another lie; they had every intention of taking her off early. Her only doubt with this scenario was the very high risk of being killed when she'd jumped off the ship; so were they really that bothered if she survived? Now her only hope rested with the tracker - first, if it had survived being in the water and second, if anyone had picked up the signal. She knew Karen would be confused, but had every confidence she'd keep to her word and come for her.

***

Sherry had been in the cabin for a long time, leaning back and falling asleep. She was woken by the engine suddenly slowing, then minutes later it went into reverse, for a moment shaking the cabin before falling silent.

A short time later the captain and another man, obviously not from the fishing vessel, by the way he dressed, came down the steps into the cabin.

He pulled out a small black case that looked like a mobile phone, but wasn't, as it only had two buttons.

"Release her," the man instructed in French.

The captain quickly released Sherry.

"Stand up, hands above your head, legs apart," he demanded of Sherry.

He began sweeping her body with the black case, his finger on

192

the button. Suddenly as it came close to Sherry's jeans it began to bleep, getting faster and faster, before diminishing when it was down at her knees.

The man looked at the Captain, talking again in French. "Seems like Macario has been pretty lax. He has allowed her to carry a tracking device of some sort."

He looked back at Sherry. "You! Strip," he demanded. "Everything off, including the knickers; then stand again with your arms above your head, legs apart."

Sherry quickly removed her clothes, standing with her arms above her head, while he scanned her once again, then scanned the heap of clothes on the floor.

"It's in the clothes, bundle them up and get one of your crew to take a car and set off for Paris. I want him a hundred miles from here, as fast as possible."

"What of the girl?" the captain asked, glancing at Sherry, still standing with her arms above her head.

"I'll take her. Cover her with a blanket while she's on deck, then have my car brought up to the gangplank. In the glove compartment, there's a pair of handcuffs, bring them will you?"

The captain collected Sherry's clothes then left the cabin, the man remained. He looked at Sherry. "You can put your arms down and sit," he told her.

She did as she was told.

He lit a cigarette and took a long draw, then moved closer to her, grabbing her hair and wrenching her head back; his cigarette, less than an inch from one of her eyes. "Tell me, how long has the device been active. Before you answer, think very carefully." He hesitated and looked directly at her. "One lie, little girl, and I'll burn your first eye out. Lie again, and it'll be your second eye. Do we understand each other?"

Sherry was terrified; this couldn't be happening. "Yes I understand," she replied meekly.

He pulled away. "So when did you activate the tracking device?"

"Once I was in the dinghy. Macario tricked me, told me he'd let me go, after all I'd paid the price with my body every day since leaving the US. It was all I could do to help Unit T find me."

He stared at her for a minute. It was obvious the girl was very frightened. "You're a bloody fool, believing that opening your legs would sway a man into helping you?"

"I suppose, but I was scared when he told me the cartel knew who I was."

"Where was it hidden, while you were on the ship, and how long does it transmit for?" he asked, ignoring her dilemma.

"It was in the top lining of my knickers. I think the tracker goes for thirty hours, but I'm not certain."

"You're not certain, or are you lying about its operating time?" he asked immediately.

"Please, I'm not lying, they say its thirty, but I've been in the water, so I wasn't even sure if it was actually working, or if the battery had been damaged."

At that moment, the captain came down into the cabin. He had handcuffs in his hand.

"The car's waiting," he told the man, handing him the handcuffs.

He took the handcuffs and looked at Sherry. "Stand up, put your hands out."

He handcuffed her then grasped her arm, urging her towards the door. "Up the steps, wait for me at the top," he demanded.

She went up; at the top, a sailor was holding a blanket, wrapping it around her before she emerged onto the deck. The man followed her up, grabbed her arm, then took her off the ship. It was still dark; no one was around. He opened the car boot, telling her to climb in. Once inside, he slammed the boot shut. A few minutes later she heard the engine start, then after a bumpy ride, they were out of the dock and on the main road.

**

It was nearly two hours before the car came to a halt, and the engine was switched off. The boot was opened. The man was standing there. "Out, and be quick about it," he demanded.

Sherry climbed out with difficulty. She was cold and very stiff, and still had the blanket from the boot wrapped around her. Sherry could see they were parked outside a large country house; the driveway looked very long. The place seemed deserted.

He grasped her arm and urged her inside, down a very plush hallway and through a door into the cellar. Once in the cellar, they went into the first room, which was lit by a single bulb hanging from a wire in the centre. There were eight mattresses spread around the walls. On each mattress, apart from one, girls were asleep.

Sherry was taken to the empty mattress; there were two blankets folded neatly on top. He took the blanket she'd come in with from her, telling her to sit down. Then he attached both her ankles to leg irons, which were already coupled through a single chain to a large steel ring, let into the floor at the end of the mattress. Releasing the handcuffs from Sherry's wrist, he stood up, then looked down at her.

"I'm told you volunteered to join the girls on the ship, knowing they were bound for the European brothels?"

She nodded; it was pointless lying, Macario had told her on the ship, they knew all about her. "Yes, for me it was an operation."

"Maybe, but now you're in a brothel, is this still an operation for you?"

"I suppose."

"That's good, because your operation has moved to the next phase, from today you'll be servicing clients six days a week. Did Karen Harris tell you that may be the case?"

"Yes, we were aware of the risk, but she'll find me, you can be very certain," she replied with confidence.

"You keep thinking that, and you'll do well here. While you hold onto that hope, don't even think about refusing our clients' advances. Here we have a very simple punishment for those girls who find it difficult to accept their new life. Refuse clients' advances, whatever, we take them into the main lounge and tie them down, on what we like to call our sample table. They're then offered as a taster for free. Most, if not all the clients take our offer up. I wouldn't recommend being raped by upwards of twenty men one after another. The pain will be excruciating; the damage internally often permanent. Think about what I've said. Here we don't mess around; we demand and get obedience." He began to walk away.

"I'm really cold, can't I have something to wear?" Sherry asked.

He turned and looked at her. "Why? you're going nowhere. This room's your home, your prison," he mocked. "Ask your minder in the morning, she'll give you a nightdress to wear in here. On the floor, you'll only get knickers when you're paraded in front of the clients, but don't expect to keep them on," he finished with a grin. Then he did walk away.

Chapter Thirty-Five

Karen's helicopter was already in the air. She was speeding across central France to join up with a small contingent of Dark Angel soldiers, ahead of her main force. This small group had been diverted to intercept the boat the tracker was indicating Sherry was on, and maybe the other girls.

Lieutenant Ross, in charge, called Karen on their secure telephone line. "We're not going to make it to the dock before the arrival of the boat, Colonel. I'm also not sure if we can rely completely on the tracker, so we would like a visual if possible."

"I agree, Lieutenant, I'll call Stanley and have him patch me through to the local police."

Minutes later she was talking to the local police inspector. "We need you to observe the boat for us Inspector," she began in French. "Please only observe and note vehicles coming and going. If one leaves before we take over, it must be followed. We cannot afford to lose sight of any vehicle, or where it's headed."

"I fully understand, Colonel, do you know the expected time of arrival of your unit?"

"Not for another hour. Our intelligence tells me at the current speed of the boat, we'd still be approximately twenty minutes away, when it docks. My intelligence team will inform you immediately if the boat changes direction and is no longer heading for the port."

"Then leave the initial surveillance to us; we will deploy our officers. Unless shooting starts, or anything unforeseen, beyond the transfer of one or more girls, our officers will stand back."

"Thank you Inspector."

***

Karen arrived nearly two hours later; she joined Lieutenant Ross and the French police Inspector.

"The boat was a local fishing vessel, it left the dock around five hours earlier," the inspector began, this time in English, so that Lieutenant Ross could understand. "It had been in the dock for around fifteen minutes when a car pulled up and a man we identified as

Cloude Flaubert, climbed out and went aboard. Five minutes later a crew member named Lavel ran to his own car with a bundle under his arm and sped off. We're tracking him; he's heading for Paris. After he'd left, Flaubert's car pulled up close to the gangplank. A girl was brought up from the cabin. The girl, we believe, had little on, coming out with a blanket wrapped around her. She was taken off the boat and put in the car boot. He was initially heading towards Paris as well, but turned off at Rennes and is now heading for Nantes."

"That's brilliant, Inspector, you must congratulate your team," Karen said, with genuine appreciation. "So no more girls have been taken off the boat then?"

"No, in fact, the captain and crew have now left and are at their homes. When do you want us to arrest them?"

"May I call you on that? Once this Flaubert arrives at where he's heading, we'll pull out our girl that he's taken, then you can arrest the captain and the crew."

"I understand and will await your call."

***

It was early evening the following day. Already Unit T had taken over the surveillance of Flaubert. They'd caught up with him after he'd arrived at the brothel with Sherry. Realising that an assault on the brothel was now her only option to pull Sherry out, Karen was forced to wait for her main unit to join them. She wanted to go in sooner, but didn't have enough troops. Now Karen was with Lieutenant Ross and her unit was at full strength.

"We're going in as soon as possible," Karen began. "We know Corporal Malloy's inside and I assume she is safe. If they hadn't had plans for her, they'd never have brought her all this way."

"Why aren't we waiting until they close?" Lieutenant Ross asked.[didn't understand first time through...now I see that the house they are surveying is a brothel, and 'close' refers to when it shuts for the day...it could be clearer]

"I really need to talk to her before the container ship docks. Every hour we delay, the ship gets closer. Her information could change everything."

Lieutenant Ross nodded his understanding. "We'll have all the
198

troops in position by seven tonight. We can go in any time after then. It's intended to enter in four locations simultaneously, take prisoners if we can, but if we meet opposition we will take them out. By not knowing their strength, or the layout of the premises, it will be a search and rescue mission primarily."

"Very well, no matter what happens, Corporal Malloy must be protected at all costs," Karen replied.

Chapter Thirty-Six

Sherry, with little sleep, was woken by a woman holding a tray, kicking her. "Wake up, eat your breakfast," she demanded.

For what had been left of the night, Sherry had been very cold, trying to keep warm by curling up in a ball under the blankets. After a breakfast of porridge, tea, and a slice of dry toast, she was taken to wash and toilet, before being brought back and given a nightdress to wear. Then with the blanket still wrapped around her, she sat on her mattress, leaning on the back wall reading a book, which the lady looking after the girls had given her.

At just after twelve, three girls had already been taken from the room. Two men came across to Sherry, unfastened her leg irons, telling her to remove the nightdress, before giving her knickers to put on. Then with one man grasping an arm firmly, she was marched upstairs and into a large lounge. At the far end of the room was a long, raised platform, with chairs spaced apart at the back; the three girls who'd left before her were already standing around on it.

Sherry realised they were not wasting time letting her sit about, but intended her to begin work immediately.

The man who'd collected Sherry from the boat came up to her, the two men who'd brought her from the cellar left to collect another girl.

"I hope you're well rested, because we've already got clients arriving, and you're here to work," he said, with a hint of sarcasm in his voice. "Your day begins now. You're on the floor until you've serviced eight clients. This is our private lounge, not the public one. Clients are invited to select a girl from the platform. He pays for you on a time basis. We will tell you how long he has with you, then we'll come for you when the time's up. After each client, you'll be taken to the bathroom to clean yourself up, then you're back on the platform. Delay, mess about, don't give the man a good time, expect punishment. Start to tell the client who you are, where you came from, and we'll find out. We know all our special clients personally; they will tell us, believe me, so expect punishment. I shouldn't need to go through again what our punishment is."

"Then if I'm asked my name, what do I say, tell them to mind their own business?" Sherry cut in.

"Your name's Charlie, after all you are one, for getting yourself caught so easily," he answered, with a snigger. Then he changed his manner. "On the platform, when clients are in the room, you walk up and down showing yourself off. I expect to look across at any time, to see you with your back straight, your tits pushed out and nipples hard, no slouching, otherwise expect a quick swipe of a strap across your bottom to straighten you up. It's in your interest to act that way. Because until you've completed your quota you'll be up there, even if it's twelve o'clock tonight. One last point, so that you don't have the idea that this is a short-term stay for you. I've been reliably informed that your Unit T lot is chasing your clothes around the streets of Paris. No one knows you're here; no one's coming for you. This is your life and will be for weeks and months to come. Do you understand?"

"Yes, I understand very well, but you're wrong, Unit T will find me, then you will pay for what you're putting me through," Sherry answered, desperately trying to convince herself that Karen wouldn't let her down.

He laughed. "Keep thinking that way if it makes you feel better. Now get up on the fucking platform and begin to earn your keep."

***

It was after six at night. She'd been selected only twice, even then it was after all the rest of the girls had been taken, and there was only her left. Each time had been for the minimum quarter of an hour, so the clients didn't really want her. Sherry hadn't minded not being selected, after all she didn't relish the idea of being raped eight times a day anyway, and it had soon become very obvious that the clients who came to this room, came for fourteen- to sixteen-year-olds, not for a girl her age. They had been taken many times. Now Sherry was getting tired. She'd had no food, not even a drink, apart from tap water while she'd washed herself after each client, and could see at this rate she'd be here until they closed.

A tall, thin man, with greying hair, entered the room. The man who'd sent Sherry up on the platform walked up to him.

"Audric, I trust you are well?" he asked in French, offering his hand.

"Very, Cloude. I'm here to see the new girls you told me were due this week."

"We have three new girls. Their ages are fourteen, sixteen and nineteen. But only the nineteen-year-old is available for at least the next hour. Would you like to see her?"

Audric followed him to the platform, watching Sherry walk up and down. Stopping her, he asked her to turn around for him. He moved closer to Cloude. "She's got a nice figure, well-toned. I'd prefer the fourteen-year-old, but I can't wait around till she's free, so instead of my usual hour, I'll take this one for half."

"I'm sure you won't be disappointed, Audric, she only came in last night. She's usually five hundred francs for an hour's session, but you can try her out for two hundred."

"Agreed, do you have my usual room free?"

"We do, shall we sort the payment out?"

Sherry was taken to a large bedroom, told that it was a half-hour session and left sitting on the side of the bed. Inside the room, besides the bed, was a small side table, with the usual pot of lubrication jelly, and packets of condoms for clients who preferred it that way. There was also a chair and a settee.

When the man had left the room, she walked over to the table, picked up the jar and smothered plenty of the lubrication jelly around the entrance and into her vagina, besides up her bottom and on her nipples. Forced to service six to eight clients a day in Scotland for nearly two months, before Unit T got her out, she knew all the problems; she had no illusions that her own body lubrication would cope with the amount of men she was expected to service, even if many used condoms. Added to that, most men fantasised about sex, particularly wanting to go up a girl's bottom, relishing in seeing the girl squirm. Not always able to do that to their wife or girlfriend, if they had one, most would take their perversions out on a woman they'd paid for.

Audric came into the room.

Sherry stood. "So how do you want me?" she asked in English.

He looked at her, replying to her in perfect English. "What's your

202

name?"

"I'm called Charlie."

"Called? Then that's not your real name?"

Sherry shrugged. "Does that really matter, you're only here to fuck me, then you go home; I have to live here. So would you prefer to call me by another name then?"

"No, I like Charlie; I was only trying to have a conversation. Let's sit together on the settee."

She sat down alongside him, and he put his arm around her, pulling her closer, running his fingers over her breast.

When Sherry first saw him in the lounge, she'd been trying to rack her brains, she was sure she'd met this man before, but where? After all, they were in France, so the only contact would have been through Karen.

For the next five minutes, Audric conducted small talk, playing and hardening her nipples, asking her age, what she liked doing?

Sherry answered automatically, like she'd done many times before. The reality was the men weren't interested anyway.

"What's your name, or don't you want to tell me?" Sherry asked, when he'd fallen silent.

He felt relaxed, beginning to like the girl with her easy-going nature. "You can call me Audric. That, unlike you, is my real name. I'm a regular here, and I think we could be seeing more of each other, providing you perform well."

"I'll do my best. I like most things, so you shouldn't be disappointed in me. Thank you for telling your name, it feels more personal now. Most won't tell you. I don't know why."

He pulled her over in front of him, kissing her hard, at the same time rubbing his hand over her bottom. Breaking away, he looked at her for a moment. "I love the tautness of your bottom. I think I'll start with giving you a good spanking."

"If you want to, but it makes me submissive, would you prefer me that way, or more domineering?" she replied shyly.

"Submissive all the time for me, Charlie. Let me sit on the chair, then you can bend over," he told her, pushing her to one side and moving over to sit on the chair.

Sherry followed and bent over his knees, feeling him pull the knickers clear of her bottom, before he began. His smacking was playful, hard yes, stinging her buttocks a little, but she could take it. Then he stopped and pushed her off his knees onto the floor.

"On the bed," he demanded, in a domineering way, at the same time pulling his jumper off and loosening the buttons of his trousers. "That smacking has really turned me on, I hope you like it both ways, Charlie, because I intend to make your body come alive."

Sherry stood, pulled her knickers up and looked directly at him. "I've been thinking. I knew I'd seen you before. Aren't you Inspector Pilon who works at police headquarters in Nantes?"

His mouth dropped open. "How do you know me, have we arrested you for prostitution?"

She shook her head. "I'm no prostitute and never will be. A girl abducted and forced into having sex by a man is rape, but for me that's academic, so long as you don't call me a prostitute, I'm happy to do anything you want. So how would you like me positioned?"

Audric was worried. While he knew the special girls in this brothel were not there voluntarily and often underage, he never pursued it officially. But Charlie was different. The men who paid the sort of money Cloude charged, came for young girls, the younger, the better. Girls aged eighteen upwards were two a penny in the public side of the business. This girl had to be here for a very different reason, perhaps a more sinister reason than the other girls; he wanted to know what. "Why are you here in the specials?"

"I'd nowhere else to go. I've always been in brothels since I was abducted at sixteen. Except, I prefer older men, they treat you more like a human being, rather than some dirt under their shoe. Why don't you let me show you how affectionate and obedient I can be. If you enjoy me, all I ask is that you tell them nothing of our conversation when you leave. I can't afford to be beaten up, for stepping out of line and making a client feel uncomfortable."

He was relieved, if she'd been around since she was sixteen, no matter what she claimed, she was a prostitute, but probably unregistered, or in the country illegally.

"It's all forgotten, Charlie. But time's going on, get yourself on the bed while I finish undressing."

She gave him a sexy smile. "Thank you for your understanding, I promise you won't be disappointed," she replied quietly, at the same time pushing her knickers down her legs, stepping out, before climbing onto the bed, lying on her side and propping herself up on one elbow watching him undress.

He lay down alongside her on the bed. "Right, Charlie, let's see if your words are as good as your actions shall we?" he said, at the same time turning her over onto her back, climbing on top of her and forcing her legs apart.

Sherry imagined that with a man of his age, after five minutes it would all be over, the rest of the time going on a little fondling; but not so with Audric. By the time they'd come to the end of the session, he'd had her in every position he could think of, his demands on her body relentless, finally finishing with her on her hands and knees, her head down and him standing at the side of the bed before he pulled out of her, giving her bottom a few sharp slaps with his hand, making her gasp. On Sherry's part, with the lack of food and little sleep, she was exhausted, her entire body shaking with his demands. She got up a little unsteadily, retrieved her knickers and slipped them back on, before sitting on the edge of the bed.

"I've enjoyed our little romp, Charlie. If I'd known you were so accommodating and prepared to do anything I wanted of you, I'd have booked an hour," he told her, as he dressed himself.

"So we're friends and you'll not tell them I knew what you did for a living?"

"Of course I won't, already I'm considering booking you for an hour tomorrow night. I know in that time I can really make your body come alive. I'll have to ask Cloude to make sure you get plenty of rest and a couple of pills down you, to get you sexed up."

"I'll look forward to that, Audric," Sherry lied.

Picking his jacket up he made for the door. "I'll see you soon, Charlie," he said, grasping the door handle.

It was at that moment that shouting, coupled with screams and even gunshots were heard, coming from the other side of the door. Audric pulled it open; men were running out of the other bedrooms in panic, pulling their clothes on as they left. He grabbed the arm of someone passing the door.

"What's going on?"

"It's a raid, fucking military by the looks of them. You'd better get the fuck out of here," he warned, then rushed down the hallway towards the stairs.

"I'd shut the door, Audric, and sit down if I were you. Unit T's Dark Angel strike force often shoots to kill, they also don't take too kindly to men who have just raped one of their own," Sherry said quietly.

He spun around, at the same time slamming the door shut. "You! You're one of them?"

"Of course. In fact, my real title is Corporal Sherry Malone MC. The MC refers to the Military Cross I received from an operation in Afghanistan. I'm a very competent combat soldier, so I'd think twice before trying to use me as a hostage. Now hand me your jacket? I've no intention of sitting here, virtually naked, when my colleagues come in the room?"

He handed her his jacket, then sat on the chair. "So you're going to turn me in?"

"Yes, and I'll tell you why. You're an officer of the law, and you allow children to be raped and abused; besides held against their will. I couldn't care less if you claim you've never been with a young girl, I know you have, all the girls in the so-called special room were children. I've stood up there on that bloody platform and watched fourteen-year-olds taken six and seven times. It sickens me to be in the same room as you and reminds me of the time when I couldn't fight back and finally had to succumb to threats. You will go down, just for raping me. Denying it will do you no good, I'll insist they take swabs from both my vagina and my anal passage. You will not get out of it. You also told me you were a regular; I'd imagine that other girls will come forward and add to the crimes you've committed with very few, if any, my age."

At that moment, the door burst open and a Dark Angel soldier, fully equipped and holding a gun entered. He looked at the man, then Sherry. "The Commander's downstairs, Corporal, the house is secure.

She has asked us to find you and send you to her immediately. Who is this man?"

Sherry stood and looked down at him. "His full name is Inspector Audric Pilon, he is attached to the local police station. Arrest him; he's to be charged with rape and the sexual abuse of minors." Then she left the room.

Sherry made her way downstairs, with Audric's jacket wrapped around her. Just at the bottom of the stairs she stopped dead. Karen was coming through from the front lounge.

"Karen," she called, then suddenly realised her mistake. "I mean Colonel."

Karen came up to her, and the two girls hugged for a moment. "I'm glad you're all right, Sherry. I came as quickly as I could, after finding out where they'd taken you, that is."

"I knew you'd come, I wasn't sure when, so all I could do was play along and hope you wouldn't leave it too long. I don't suppose you've got any spare clothes with you? Even with a jacket around me it's a bit embarrassing to stand here in knickers that are so skimpy, they are not even worth putting on."

Karen looked at her, her voice serious. "Well you shouldn't have let them take what clothes you had on a trip to Paris, should you? Anyway I've none of yours, so you could go back to the unit like that and have all the soldiers rib you, or if you ask me really, really, nicely, I might lend you some of mine, we're both about the same size, so most will fit."

Sherry stared at her. "You wouldn't dare send me back like this, I'd die of embarrassment. Where's your bag, so I can riffle it?"

"I could, but I suppose the underwear is a touch skimpy to travel in; besides, I've got to think of the other troops travelling with you," she ribbed, before bursting out in laughter. Then she turned and asked a soldier standing behind them to bring her suitcase from the Range Rover.

***

Sherry felt so much better dressed. She'd just finished giving her initial statement to the police, who had followed Unit T in and were taking over the investigation, when Cloude Flaubert, the man who'd brought her here from the fishing boat, was being taken away.

She walked up to him. "I'd be here weeks and months, would I? You believed Unit T would fall for your trick in sending my tracker around Paris? They aren't that stupid, believe me. I hope you rot in hell. I'll also be the first up on the witness stand to make sure you're convicted and sent down for a very long time."

He said nothing, preferring to look away.

Karen joined Sherry. "Come on, Corporal, now you're decent again, into my car, we need to talk. Work doesn't stop; you've already had a break, sitting around on a ship for a couple of weeks. Then if you remember we've still got five girls on that ship, which is due to dock in less than a day. I want chapter and verse of what happened."

Sherry followed Karen out to her Range Rover. "Bloody sitting around," she mumbled to herself. "I'll give her sitting around, I was very nearly drowned."

Chapter Thirty-Seven

Karen listened, asking questions at times to clarify what Sherry told her about her time on the ship and after she'd left. Sherry told her everything, except she decided to leave out the fact that Macario had made a fool of her, believing he'd help her escape in return for sexual favours. She knew that was naivety on her part and was not prepared to admit it, even to Karen. Now Sherry was to go with the police for a medical examination and to make a full statement, before she rejoined her unit.

Just as she was about to leave the car, Karen stopped her. "Sherry. You're very certain all the girls were in one container, and there weren't any other girls aboard that you never saw?"

"There was definitely only one container with girls in. Is that important?"

"Everything's important when you're trying to build a picture of the operation. You really have done a very good job."

"Thanks, Karen, I had some hard times, but it was exciting in lots of ways, thinking back."

After Sherry had gone, Karen sat for some time, casually watching the comings and goings of police and ambulances outside the house; her mind though, was preoccupied, trying to put everything she knew together. Then she called Stanley.

"I'm told you found Sherry, Karen. Is she all right?"

"I'm hoping so, but I wish I could have gone in earlier. I was surprised how quickly they put her to work, which is something I could have prevented, if I'd gone in as soon as she went inside."

"With the best will in the world, Karen, you know you didn't have the resources then and would have risked lives in an under-resourced operation. I think Sherry will understand, but in future you're going to have to be very careful using her like this, it's not fair on the girl. She's not a covert operative and is very vulnerable."

Karen sighed. "I know, now I need to do something with her to make up for it. Anyway that's my problem."

Chapter Thirty-Eight

Blas had just finished breakfast when the captain of the container ship telephoned.

"We have a problem, Blas. The cook came to me at breakfast to say Macario hadn't picked up the food for the girls. When I went to his cabin, he wasn't there, neither was he in the container. Anyway we fed and toileted the girls, before giving them sedatives. One told us that another girl, who they called Sherry, was not there when they woke this morning either. We've searched the ship and Macario is missing, so too is the girl from the container. Also, a crew member told me a lower service door used for loading food and other goods for ship use, was wide open. This would never be left like that. I suspect, although I can't see them surviving, that both have left the ship through that door. Why, I'm not sure."

"I think you're correct in that assumption, Captain. You see, the girl was picked up very early this morning in a rubber dinghy. Why Macario would also leave the ship, I can't imagine. However, for me the containers are the priority, no matter what, they must leave as arranged. Do you have anyone trustworthy enough to replace Macario and sedate the girls further, before the container is lifted off the ship? I don't want them to scream in panic."

"I do and will see to it."

"Thank you, Captain; I'll make sure you get a bonus. Call me if you find Macario on board. Even if the bastard's drunk and panned out[unfamiliar phrase], I want to know. We have plans for bigger shipments later this year, whoever goes on that ship must be reliable. Anyway, leaving him aside, call me as soon as the containers leave the dock."

**

Later that day, the captain of the container ship called Blas to confirm the containers had been loaded on lorries and left the dock. Once the containers arrived at their destination, two small vans were already waiting to take the girls onto the brothels. Eventually, the drivers called Blas to confirm that the girls were now safely delivered.

More importantly, paid informers at the port had told Blas that the Unit T surveillance group had also left the port; and were following the containers. Finally, men under the pay of Blas to watch the containers confirmed that the Unit T surveillance team had split, and were now following the two vans, with the girls inside, to the brothels. Of course, this is what Blas wanted to happen. He knew the containers were of no importance to Unit T now the girls had left, which is what he planned. Soon Dark Angel troops would move in on the brothels, and two of his competitors would be out of business, allowing him to fill the gap.

Chapter Thirty-Nine

Karen was travelling in one of her unit's helicopters, on her way to intercept the French gendarmerie and join up with their troop commanded by a Lieutenant Hamon Clavier. This was following confirmation that the containers had left the docks, travelled some sixty miles and been parked up in the large yard of a farmhouse. Already in the yard were two small vans. Two Unit T forward observers had watched as three girls were bundled inside one, with the other two girls in the other. The vans had now left the farmyard. Karen had made the decision to keep all her Dark Angel soldiers away from the brothels, leaving the French gendarmerie to rescue the girls.

The helicopter touched down in an open field. Karen, dressed in combat clothes and carrying her gun, jumped to the ground and ran across to three soldiers who had stood watching the helicopter land.

Lieutenant Clavier walked up to Karen. She felt a little weak at the knees; this man was still just as handsome as when they last met, and she really liked him. Hamon on his part had missed her. She'd been good company, and he'd hoped to get to know her a great deal better. However, the last time they were together, both were lieutenants. Now with Karen a Lieutenant Colonel, this changed their professional relationship. She was the senior officer, his commander, with full responsibility for the operation.

He saluted. "Colonel, we've been waiting for you," he said, in perfect English.

Although Karen was able to speak good French, it was really only conversational. When it came to military duties, she preferred English, then there was no misunderstanding in interpretation.

Karen saluted back; it all felt very strange, this formality, after them being out socially in the past. "I'm here primarily to look at your side of the operation, Lieutenant. You will keep full operational control of your troops."

"Thank you, Colonel, perhaps you'd like to come to our mobile command unit and I can update you as to the current situation?"

They walked side by side, quickly arriving at a large trailer with steps to the rear. Inside the control unit, three soldiers were manning the communications. Directly through this room and another door was a small but well equipped meeting room.

They both went inside, and he closed the door. Karen turned, and he kissed her gently on the lips. She never objected, even allowing him to hold her for a moment.

"I've missed you, Karen. We should get together more often."

Karen pulled away and walked over to a flask on a side-table. "You know what it's like, Hamon. Every time we made arrangements to meet, it was either you or I having to renege. We're destined to have a very distant relationship, if at all," she replied, at the same time pouring two coffees, adding a little milk to hers before turning and handing him one.

"I can't disagree with you there. Mind you, when I heard this was a Unit T request for assistance, I was very nearly on my knees begging the camp commander to let me lead it."

Karen laughed. "You on your knees, Hamon, I don't believe it. Besides, women are falling at your feet all the time. What's so important about little me?"

He smiled. "You know me too well. But you are very important in my mind. You're the only girl I've been out with who has left a lasting impression."

Karen took a seat; her manner had changed. "Yes, that's all very well, Hamon, but first let's see if we can get these girls out of the hands of the traffickers, shall we? Then maybe later we'll have time to catch up with a little socialising."

Hamon nodded, taking a seat as well. He understood the urgency, but her manner was very cutting in his opinion.

Karen was looking at the reports. The vans had taken the girls to locations nearly forty miles apart. After reading for a short time she looked up. "The drivers of the vans. It doesn't say if they stayed or left?"

"They only dropped them off, Karen. We still have a tail on the vans, but no report as yet of where they are heading."

"We must keep tabs on them. Apart from being party to abduction, they may lead us to parts of the operation we still have no knowledge of."

"I understand. So when do you want to go in for the girls?" he asked.

"I don't know exactly. It's dependent on another part of the operation coming together. The important thing for you is to be ready to go in minutes, when I give the order. I believe this is imperative, so the girls remain relatively safe, while we take down the main part of the operation."

"So if we are after the girls, what part are you playing? I understood you were short of manpower and yet you've fifty Dark Angel soldiers sitting on their arses."

"It's best you don't know, then if there is a leak and it all goes pear-shaped, no one can point the finger at you."

"You're expecting a great deal out of this, after all we're only talking about rescuing a few American girls. Maybe with the publicity you're hoping for more, perhaps trying to repair your unit's reputation after the London fiasco?"

She looked at him for a moment. "Don't you ever talk to me that way again; otherwise you and I are finished, both personally and professionally. But I'll also tell you this. It's not about London, or anything personal on my part, to repair a reputation I'm not even bothered about. This is my job, my life. Even if there had been just one girl, I'd be doing exactly the same thing. As it is, these are American citizens and the US will not be happy with me using them as pawns, when they find out I could have pulled them out weeks back. I walk a very tight rope, with lots that I do. People get killed; it's a fact of life for me. We could even lose some of the girls in this raid, and then the shit will hit the fan." She hesitated, taking a sip of her coffee; Hamon waited. "As for television, don't believe what you hear, or more precisely what I said, that was for public consumption. I'll use whatever means I have to take down a trafficking operation, even if it requires I lose one, or many victims. The Nigerians that dare to call themselves human beings after butchering so many children will surface one day. Maybe not in days, weeks or even years, but they will surface. That sort, in their own arrogance, always do. Then they will be very lucky to see the inside of a courtroom. I'll take them out and happily watch them in the death throes of their last minutes on earth."

The room was silent, apart from the slight hum of the air conditioning.

He put his hand out and touched hers. "I'm sorry, Karen, I shouldn't have said that, it was unprofessional of me. I really do have real respect for what you do. When we saw you on television and the attempt on your life, it shook every officer in the room. Your speed of response was expected, after all, you're a professional soldier. Every one of us in your situation would have probably taken them out. Then with you having no idea of the level of threat posed, in our opinion you wasted valuable bullets in stopping them, leaving yourself at risk, by maybe having to use valuable extra ammunition to neutralise the threat from them completely. Because of that, we all decided you'd taken that course of action to keep your reputation and not kill. Most papers in France, were openly surprised you didn't shoot to kill." Karen shrugged. "It wasn't that much of a risk. My Sig P226 had already been modified to twenty rounds rather than 15, so I could hold my own. Besides, I had soldiers all carrying similar weapons, seconds away from supporting me."

"It just goes to show, Karen. We couldn't see what weapon you had, so most believed it to be just a six-round handgun."

"Okay, it's forgotten, let's start again. Like I say, we wait. No one moves until I give the order. I also need an answer on the vans and where they are headed. Otherwise, I'll wait another day."

"I would really have liked us to go in sooner, even if we don't have an answer on the vans and their final destination. Another day, Karen, could mean the difference between the girls not having to stand the humiliation of being abused."

Karen seemed to him indifferent in her reply. "Yes well, that's the chance we all have to take, including the victims, I'm not risking soldiers' lives unnecessarily to pull out a girl before she's raped, you should get used to how I operate. At least we're coming for them. For many, no one comes, often they die in captivity following years of abuse." She looked at her watch; it was close to ten at night. "I need a few hours' sleep, I got none last night, with no time to get my head down in my car. Where do you suggest?"

He grinned. "I've got a room in the local barracks you can share

215

with me. Otherwise, there's a small guest house in the village about three miles from here. I'll call them and run you over?"

She laughed. "If I used your room, then I'd get no sleep. So take me to this hotel, guest house, whatever you call it, I really do need to sleep."

He grinned. "You're wrong, after a night of making love, the time you sleep will be your best sleep ever."

She looked at him for a moment. "Okay, join me, then you can prove what you claim to be true," she mocked.

He stood. "Come on, let's get you a bed shall we, but one day I'll take you up on your offer."

Karen also stood, opening the door. Halfway through she looked back, with a hint of a smile. "Sorry, Hamon, that wasn't an open invitation, just a one-off. You seem to have muffed the opportunity. Could you ask if they can make a sandwich for me as well?"

He smiled. "What are you like; you need a man to look after you, girl."

"I keep trying, but nobody wants me," she answered, then left the room before he could comment.

Just as she came out the meeting room, a soldier sitting at the control desk looked back at Hamon, who was following her. He spoke to him in French; Karen listened.

"The brothel where Nicole and Paige were taken, had a visitor a little earlier, Sir," he began. "None other than Pier Gustavo, a known pimp for the wealthy in Paris. He left less than ten minutes ago with Nicole, heading for Paris. We have a tail on him."

Hamon looked at Karen. "What do you want to do, Colonel?"

She knew of Pier, a man she'd tried to take down a number of times, but he'd clients at the very top of the main professions and her evidence was always thrown out. Now he had a girl in his car that could take him down. But could he worm his way out of it?

"Do we have enough personnel to keep tabs on him?"

"We do, but would it be to our advantage?" Hamon asked.

She sighed. "He's slipped out of our hands three times, Hamon. We already have him for a possible abduction, but even now he could claim he'd no idea who she was, maybe was just giving her a lift for the brothel. Then if Nicole testified against him, it may not hold water. But if we could tie him up with pimping her, then he'd have no get-out, they'd throw the book at him."

"I agree, this time we wait?"

The soldier was back listening to a report, again he turned. "Sorry to interrupt, Sir, but we have another girl taken from the brothel, this time it's Lauren. She's just been bundled into a car. We have the man's photo, but he's not been identified as yet."

Hamon looked at Karen. "It can't go on like this, Colonel; we'll have my men very thin on the ground at this rate and not even able to take out one brothel. There are still two more girls in that brothel; if they go separate ways, we couldn't mount surveillance on five different locations without more resources."

"You're right. Intercept Lauren. Put the man on ice until we can assess the full situation. Now I really need sleep, I'm struggling to keep focused."

***

Karen turned over and opened her eyes. She looked at her watch; it was just after half- seven. Climbing out of bed, she showered, then dressed, before leaving the room. Outside were two soldiers, they came to attention as she passed.

The owner of the guest house met her at the bottom of the stairs. "Good morning. I hope you slept well?" she asked in French. "We've never had such tight security here before. I've laid out a breakfast table in our dining room. As an alternative, we also do a full English breakfast if you would prefer?"

Karen shook her head. "No thank you. I'm fine with cereal, fruit juice and toast. I'm sorry about turning your home into a secure location; it's necessary while I am here. But your rooms are lovely, and I did sleep well."

"We understand, your officer explained how essential it was. It didn't impinge at all on our other guests. In fact, I'm not sure if any of them were aware your security people were here. Most were already in their rooms."

Karen nodded, before going through to the dining room. There were already a few guests sitting at tables. All of them wished her

217

good morning. Most then began speaking quietly to each other, giving Karen the odd glance, after recognising her from the papers. Karen on her part ignored it, after all, for her, it happened all the time.

As she finished her breakfast, Hamon joined her. "Good morning, Karen, you must have been tired, apparently you never stirred all night."

"I needed it, would you like tea? I don't drink coffee in the morning."

He laughed. "You English, you are so funny with your quirky ways. But I will try your tea, maybe I should begin to get used to it, if I want an English girlfriend."

She didn't rise to his comment, although she knew what he meant, but poured his tea, adding a little milk. Then she stood, picking her own cup up. "Come on, bring your tea, we'll go back to my room, we need to talk."

He followed her upstairs carrying his tea. Once inside her room Karen shut the door, and they both sat down in two easy chairs. "So what's the news on the vehicles?"

"They arrived at a garage which hires vans out, around five this morning, within twenty minutes of each other. We believe now the vans were hired, but we'll check that when the garage opens. The two men left in one car, already parked up there. They drove on to a large villa just outside Leon. We're watching the villa, and I've passed the address over to your intelligence unit. They are checking on the ownership and will get back to you. We intercepted the car with Lauren in. The man, who originates from Romania, has said little, apart from at one point claiming he was a taxi driver, but wouldn't give his destination. Gustavo, who took Nicole, has arrived at a known address of his. She's currently with him, so he can no longer claim he was just giving her a lift as a favour for the brothel. This is now an abduction, with a very hefty prison sentence."

Karen sipped her tea saying nothing, while she thought about what he'd said. "I agree, Nicole should be brought in, again put Gustavo on ice like the other man. That will release you more personnel for taking down the brothels. Can you make a plan as to how you are going to approach the incursion, and I'll look at it? At this stage I really want it all to ride, while we build a complete picture of the operation, but it's very obvious the girls are now being put to use. I won't hold off much longer."

Hamon could understand Karen's dilemma; he knew she would not budge until she was certain their intervention would not close doors that now seemed to be opening, even though every day would be a nightmare for the girls still in captivity. He decided to voice that. "I'm beginning to understand your strategy, Karen. I presume you look at it in the way that the girls inside the brothels are relatively safe and going nowhere. If we took out the brothel to get them out, for the trafficker it is just an outlet, they'd go and open somewhere else we wouldn't know about."

"Precisely; although once I have the next step of the ladder and am confident I no longer need stability in the brothels, where the girls are held, I won't extend their nightmare a day longer than necessary. I do know what they are going through, Hamon; don't forget I've been there."

He stood. "Right, thank you for the tea, I think I will try it again sometime, it was refreshing. Anyway, your car will be waiting outside when you're ready to leave." He glanced at his watch. "I'll set up a review meeting for ten, if that's okay with you, with a communication link to your intelligence unit."

"Yes, that's fine, I'll be there."

He nodded and left the bedroom.

Karen finished her tea, then after cleaning her teeth packed a bag. As she left the room, a soldier waiting outside collected the bag from her and took it to the car, while Karen made her way to the reception desk.

The lady brought a book out from behind the counter. "Would you mind signing my visitor's book? It isn't often, well never really, that a famous person like you has stayed at our guest house."

"I'm happy to do that, although I'm not really famous."

"You are, believe me. Would you be offended if my husband took a photo while you signed it?"

Karen smiled. "Of course not, maybe you should both be in the photo; one of my security guards will use the camera?"

The guest house owners watched as Karen walked down the path to a waiting car. To either side of her and a little behind, two Dark Angel soldiers, who had been outside waiting for her to come out, were now following. Both carried M5 carbides, Karen a holstered handgun.

"I'm glad I don't have to live like that," his wife commented.

Her husband sighed. "I agree it must be a strange existence. Although she was taller and slimmer than she looked on television and spoke very good French."

"Yes, she was taller than I imagined as well, besides being very attractive in an English sort of way. I wonder why she picked our place to stay? I'm glad she did. It will be a talking point in the bar for a long time to come."

As they turned back into the guest house, Eric, a local man, who worked as a gardener in the many large houses around the area, hurried up the drive.

They both stopped and turned back to see what he wanted.

Eric was short of breath. "Wasn't that Unit T?" he asked, breathing heavily.

The lady grinned. "It was, their commander Karen Harris stayed with us. She even signed our guestbook, and we had our picture taken with her. Why do you ask?"

He didn't answer directly but asked another question of his own. "Why was she here?"

"How do we know? We received a call late last night to see if we could put her up. When she arrived, the guest house was turned into a fortress. There were armed soldiers everywhere. It was a little scary, but exciting."

"And the rest of her unit, where did they stay?"

The woman frowned. "Why are you asking all these questions, Eric? She was a guest, that's all. She paid her bill and left. Although we didn't want her to pay, it was exciting enough with her just being here, but she insisted. Now if you want to know more, go and ask them. They must be based somewhere in the area."

Eric never answered, just nodding acknowledgement, turned and hurried away.

The husband rubbed his chin in thought. "Those were strange questions. Eric's never taken an interest in any of our guests before. Do you think we should tell someone? After all Karen could be in danger."

His wife frowned. "From Eric, I don't think so, but he could be asking for someone else. I've got the telephone number of the man who called originally to see if we had a room. I could call him if you think it's important?"

"I think it is. You saw what happened on television. That girl is always under threat, and if dad was still alive, being military himself and part of the French resistance, he'd insist they were made aware."

"I will call him. Karen was a pleasant, well-mannered girl; I'd hate anything to happen to her because we'd not warned her unit of someone's excessive interest in why she was here."

Chapter Forty

Nicole and Paige, two of the girls brought over from America, had arrived at a house in the suburbs of Paris. It was late afternoon, and they were taken to a small room with four steel framed beds, each with an easy chair alongside it. They were told to remove their clothes and were given nightdresses, their ankles secured, with ankle irons on chains welded to the steel bedframe. The chains were just long enough for them to sit in the easy chairs as well as lie on the beds. Under each bed was a plastic bedpan, in case they needed to toilet between morning and afternoon visits to the bathroom.

After they had been left alone, Paige looked across at Nicole. "Are you scared?" she whispered.

"Terrified, I'm trying to remember all Sherry taught me. She was some girl, I could never be like her."

"I know what you mean. You don't think they'll use us today do you?"

"God, I hope not, I'm knackered already, just travelling."

They had been in the room for around two hours, when two men entered; one elderly, the other in his early forties. Both were small, overweight, and the elderly man was gasping for breath.

"Both of you stand up and remove your nightdresses," the older one demanded.

The two girls did as they were told.

The younger man came closer to Nicole. Nicole, five foot eight, slim build, with long, blonde hair and deep green eyes, was very attractive for a sixteen-year-old, although not really suitable for a brothel, being so thin; except this man didn't want her for a brothel. Nicole felt embarrassed at the way he looked her over, ran his hands over her body, looking for signs of drug taking. She remembered Sherry's advice, to remain still and not give them an excuse to punish, as most brothel owners relished a girl objecting, pulling back or refusing to do anything they demanded of her, enjoying their superiority over the victim.

The two men began talking in French; neither girl could understand.

"I like this one," the younger man said, after a single glance at Nicole.

"Twenty-five thousand, you can take her now if you want, or we'll deliver," the older man said.

"I'll take her. Have you anything for her to wear?"

"We supply an outdoor coat; it's short but buttons up and a pair of heeled shoes. She'll be fine with that. We use them to take the girls to hotels. You wouldn't know they were naked underneath; it's essential they wear nothing that can conceal anything, such as a weapon or a means for them to self-harm, when they are moved."

"Very well, shall we settle up, while she's made ready?"

They left the room, but in minutes a lady came in carrying a plastic bag. Paige was told to put her nightdress back on and sit on her bed. Then she handed Nicole a coat and a pair of shoes from the bag.

"Put the shoes and coat on, then button up. You've been sold."

"Where am I going?" she asked, obviously shocked.

The woman shrugged. "I don't know, when you're dressed just sit on the side of the bed, you'll be leaving very soon."

"It's hardly dressing, a coat and shoes, what about knickers as well?" Nicole asked.

The woman suddenly slapped her face. "You ask for nothing; you wear what I tell you to wear," she screamed at her.

However, Nicole didn't cower back. "Hit me again and I'll kick your head in," she retorted.

The woman was stunned, but knew she could do nothing; the girl would be gone in ten minutes, and the buyer wouldn't allow the brothel to punish her as she deserved. "You're very lucky you've been sold; otherwise I'd relish having you beaten up," she replied.

Nicole grinned. "You believe I'm scared of you? Think again. I'll escape one day and my brothers will come. They're all US Marines, and they will kill you and the rest of the shit here. Remember that old woman; you can't hide behind threats forever."

The woman laughed. "Dream all you want, but that chance will never come. We know what we're doing."

At that moment, a man came in, released Nicole's ankle iron and took her out of the room.

Nicole glanced back from the door. "Look after yourself, Paige. Sherry told us never to give up hope. I know I won't," Nicole said, with tears in her eyes.

"Foolish girl, she won't last long with her attitude," the woman commented, then looked at Paige. "As for you, you're staying here. After food, you'll be going to the viewing room. We've a busy night so you'll be working till two. In the morning the doctor's here, he's Indian, but very nice. So you won't be getting breakfast."

Paige felt sick inside; she'd hoped for at least a short time to settle, but the doctor concerned her. "Why do I need to see a doctor, I'm not ill?"

The woman gave a sickly grin. "You're one of four to be sterilised tomorrow. All the girls who work here are done."

She looked at her, appalled at the prospect. "But I don't want to be sterilised, I'm only sixteen, I want a family," she gasped.

"Are you as stupid as the other one? This is your life, and we don't have you here to produce babies, so being fertile is pointless and only leads to you taking pills. We tried that in the past, and some kept them in their mouths, ending up with abortions and a lot of wasted days, when they should have been earning."

"But I won't be here forever, when I'm too old, can't I go home then?" she asked, desperate for them not to take away her dream of being a mother.

The woman could see the stress levels rising in the girl. This would be her first session, and she needed it to go off without any problems. The days that followed would be that much easier for the girl, by then accepting her fate. She smiled. "I'll ask for you, Paige. Show the owners you can work hard without any trouble tonight, and you will take your tablet regularly, then they will do that for you."

Paige was relieved. "I'll really try, thank you," she replied.

The woman nodded and left the room.

Paige lay on the bed, sobbing her heart out. Now split from the other girls, she had never felt as alone as she did now.

Chapter Forty-One

The girls Emma, Ashley and Lauren had been taken to another brothel from the one Nicole and Paige had gone to. Arriving late in the afternoon after being on the road for four hours, they were all very cold, hungry and becoming more despondent by the minute, as they realised just how far from the ship they'd travelled. All of them were convinced no one would find them now.

They could see nothing of where they actually were, when they finally came to a stop. The van had backed into the yard, the doors shutting before they were taken out, through a single door and down some steps. The passage at the bottom of the steps was long and narrow, with many doors off it. Ushered along the passage to the end door, they entered a large shower room with showers to each side and three-legged stools between each. Hooks above each stool had towels hanging from them.

A woman followed them in. "You have ten minutes. Get yourself showered, wash your hair and dry it."

After showering, the girls were separated into different rooms off the passage. Each room had a bunk bed, two single chairs and a small table, with a toilet and basin in a corner. There was a small high window with bars on it.

Emma was pushed into the room; the door slammed shut. A girl already inside was sitting in one of the chairs.

She looked at the girl, who was looking back at her. "Hi, I'm Emma," she said, as casually and friendly as she could.

The girl just nodded and picked up a very old and tatty book and began reading.

Emma tried again to get a conversation going, asking, "Do I sleep on the top or bottom?"

The girl looked up from the book, and began talking in a language Emma couldn't understand.

This time Emma pointed to the top then the bottom bunk, then at herself.

The girl smiled, pointing to the bottom.

She thanked her and lay down, closing her eyes.

She awoke about twenty minutes later when the door opened and a woman, with a man at her side, brought in two plastic trays. On each tray was a small dinner and a drink, with two biscuits alongside. The trays were placed on the table, and they left. The girls ate in silence.

***

It was nearly an hour before the door was opened again. The woman took the trays, placing them on a trolley. Then grasping Emma's arm she urged her out of the room, down the corridor into a very well-lit room of similar size, painted all white; along the back of the room were racks of clothes.

"Remove your nightdress; then stand with your arms at your side," the lady ordered.

Emma did this. The woman looked at her for a moment, then went to a rack, pulling out a bra and knickers set. "Put these on."

Emma took the underclothes from her and dressed.

The lady checked they fitted as she wanted, then pulled out a schoolgirl's uniform. "These as well."

Again Emma put them on, although the skirt was short and the blouse very thin and virtually see-through. Finally, she finished it off with short white socks and high heels.

Pulling a comb from her pocket, the woman combed Emma's hair and tied it back into a ponytail. She stood back looking at her for a moment then urged her out of the room and upstairs, along a plush corridor and into a room at the other end. This was tastefully furnished, with a small raised circular platform in the centre.

A man of African origin followed them in. "You're Emma and fifteen?" he asked.

"Yes," she replied.

"You're a very attractive young lady, and look nice in schoolgirl uniform. I believe you were given tuition on the ship?"

"Yes, I was shown what was expected of me," she said, not knowing what else to say.

"Then you will begin work tonight. We have a lot of clients who like our young girls dressed in the schoolgirl look. You will be in great demand. The sessions are thirty minutes long, with fifteen minutes between clients to dress and wash yourself, besides having a drink and perhaps a biscuit if you want one. In the bathroom, there's lubricants both for your vaginal and anal passages, you should use both. All girls service eight clients a day. Have no illusions, girls who refuse the advances of a client will be punished using the electric rod. I believe you've had a taste of this rod already?"

"Yes."

"That is good, so you know what to expect. This is a very high-class brothel, our clients expect the girls to be friendly and approachable. Have you understood everything I've said, do you have any questions?"

"I understand; you intend to have me raped eight times a day. Will I be on the pill? There's no way I want a baby fathered by a rapist. Then what happens when I'm on my period?"

He shrugged. "Talk to clients in that way, claiming they're raping you and you can expect regular punishment till you learn to keep your mouth shut. Until you're on your period, you will receive a pill each day. During your period, you will be sterilised so you will get your wish not to have a baby fathered by a client. The method is quick, leaves an undetectable scar and is irreversible. Now, that's enough questions. The minder will take you to the bathroom, prepare yourself quickly, your first client is already waiting."

Ashley was brought in. She was wearing a knickers and suspender set, with a small jacket just hiding her knickers in a standing position. Again the man explained what was expected of her, then she was taken to begin work.

After Ashley had gone, another man join the African in the room before Lauren was brought. She unlike the other two was dressed in jeans and a jumper with trainers.

"Your two friends have already begun work, they will service eight clients each tonight," the man began. "You, however, have been sold privately. This gentleman with me is your new owner. You're a very lucky girl to have been selected and will have a relatively easy life, compared to what you would experience here. Work hard to please him, and you will never return. Cause him problems, refuse his hospitality, and you will be brought back, punished and unlike

227

your friends, you will be working twelve hours a day with upwards of twenty clients. Keep that in the back of your mind, it wouldn't be pleasant believe me."

She said nothing, just looked across at the man. Then smiled to herself. He would rue the day he took her in, she was very certain of that.

Chapter Forty-Two

Paige, sitting on the side of her bed, was just finishing off food that had been brought by a man ten minutes before, when the lady who'd been with her earlier returned. She was carrying a plastic bag.

"You enjoyed the food?" she asked, in a manner that showed little interest in the reply.

"Yes, thank you," Paige answered.

"That is good, now it is time you got yourself ready for tonight," she replied, at the same time placing the bag on the bed and leaning down, unfastening her ankle clamp. She stood, looking down at Paige still sitting on the side of the bed. "I'm taking you to the bathroom. You will toilet and shower. I advise you to grease yourself well inside and around the entrance, including your back passage and also around your nipples. After each client, you'll return to the washroom, clean yourself up and grease yourself again. I advise you not to try and escape when we go to the bathroom, the doors leading upstairs are always locked and you will be punished. We have two levels of punishment. Either way you are stretched out on the floor with your hands and feet tied to floor rings. Then you are flogged. We use a leather strap with many tails for starters; if you persist in being difficult, then punishment is by the use of an electric rod. That is always used if you are aggressive to a client, or refuse his advances. He's paid for half an hour of your time; he owns you and can do as he likes. Providing he does not injure you. Even then you will complete your time with him, tied down if necessary. Do you understand?"

"What's there to understand? I get raped; you lot get paid. It's hardly the most complex of things."

"Then remove your nightdress and we'll go to the bathroom."

Paige felt embarrassed walking down a passage naked; passing two men, she was glad to get into the shower room. At least in there she was left alone. After toileting, she stood under the shower for a time; her whole body was shivering, although she wasn't sure if it was the anticipation, or the fear of what was about to happen to her. Either way she was very scared.

As she finished drying the woman came in. "Are you ready?"

"Nearly, I've just got to use the grease, but am not really sure how much?"

The woman grabbed the pot, put her two fingers in and showed her. "Use this much, now spread your legs." Quickly she rubbed around her vagina entrance and inside. "Bend down," she demanded. Again she did the same inside her rectum and around. "Do this each time, you won't feel the client entering you, believe me. Now do your own breasts and the nipples, it will stop them getting sore."

Back in the room, the lady put her hair up, then she was given a bra and knickers set, followed by suspenders, nylons and high-heeled shoes. This, along with a very short dress, was typical of what the clients of this brothel liked the girls dressed in.

The lady stood back. "You look very nice; many clients will bid for you tonight. Wait here - a minder will come for you."

She'd only just left the room before the minder came in. Well-built and around six foot two, he grasped her arm, virtually propelling her out of the room, and up the stairs, where he unlocked a door and continued along a well-carpeted hall to a room to one side. At least fifteen men were already inside the room, and they turned to look at who was being brought in.

"This is the second girl of the night," the minder began in French. "She's sixteen, English speaking only, and new to the house. She's inexperienced so you will need to break her in. For those who like that challenge, expect a tight fanny, silky smooth inside that will grip you well. Her availability tonight is six half-hour slots starting every three quarters of an hour. Bidding starts at two hundred and fifty euros per half hour with a maximum two half-hour slots together, before she must be allowed to rest. Payment is to be in advance; injuries that prevent the girl working on will be charged as a full night. Can we start the bidding?"

Bidding was brisk and within five minutes, Paige had been sold for two one-hour sessions and two half-hour slots. She of course had no idea what was being said, but stood very still, already terrified of what was actually happening to her.

The minder took her arm once more, and they left the room, going upstairs into a small bedroom, with one kitchen chair and a bed.

"Your first client will be here shortly. You've two one-hour sessions and two half-hours. This one is half an hour. This is your first night of six a week; be warned, girls who hold back, don't give the client the experience he expects, will be punished."

Paige sat on the edge of the bed, already she felt dirty with the grease smeared over her and the thought of having to open her legs to a stranger. Then, when the man entered the room, she was already feeling revulsion of what he would expect her to do.

He came up to her. "I'm told you're new at this, so it seems then I'll be the one to break you in. I'm looking forward to seeing you perform."

She looked at him. "If you mean you'll enjoy raping me, feel free, but don't expect me to help, you'll be shagging a sack of potatoes," she retorted.

He nodded his head up and down. "You're going to be difficult are you? Do you want me to call someone, perhaps have you beaten; then we will see how you perform?"

She smiled. "I bet that really turns your sort on, being able to have a girl punished because she's not prepared to help you rape her. And you call yourself a man, you're pathetic, is this why you come here, because no woman will have you?" she mocked.

"My wife has problems; she's unable to have intercourse."

"So, most wives are like that, then why aren't you with a registered prostitute, or do you prefer to have a sixteen-year-old snatched off the street to be raped every day of her life? I think you're lying to make me feel sorry for you, well I don't."

"Either way, little girl, you will get a good shagging, anyway I'm not into clothes, so get rid of them then lie on the bed?"

"If you want," she replied, beginning to undress. Soon she was naked and climbed onto the bed, lying down facing him.

The man had also taken his clothes off and followed her. He was leaning over her, fondling her breasts, trying to kiss her.

"I don't kiss, that tends to show I like you in some way, I don't, all you get is a shag," she said, turning her head away.

"Very well, if that's what you want; so let's start with something you can't object to, just so that you know who's boss shall we? Now

231

get off the bed."

She climbed off the bed and stood silently. He moved to the edge sitting up, before grabbing her arm and pulling her over his knees. Seconds later he laid into her bottom, making her scream, tears rolling down her face. She tried to follow Sherry's advice and clench her buttocks, but it still hurt her a great deal.

Finally, he stopped and told her to stand, a huge grin on his face. "This is fun, it's clear you've never done this before, let's see if you can arouse me shall we, before I ram my cock up your fanny? Down on your knees in front of me; then start playing with it. I want it to be gentle, feel the softness and warmth of your hands before you take it into your mouth; suck and lick like you'd do a lollypop. I presume you know how to lick a lollipop, or don't you know how to do that either?" he said, with a lot of aggression in his voice.

Paige didn't answer, but knelt down in front of him. Grasping his penis, she began playing about with it for a moment. She stared at this man's tiny penis, his pot belly, his sweating as she stroked him; already he was moaning, telling her to put it in her mouth. All she could feel was revulsion, so she moved closer, took his penis into her mouth, then turned her head slightly, sinking her biting teeth in, determined not to release.

He began screaming, trying to push her off, but lost his hardness with the pain and suddenly her teeth met. She pulled away, spitting the top of the penis from her mouth; blood was spurting everywhere.

She stood up looking down at him. "What else do you want me to do?" she asked with a smile.

His screams brought a minder running. By then Paige had moved to the wall and pulled her knickers on; she spat blood from her mouth, before wiping her face on the sheet.

The minder stopped dead staring at the man, blood pouring from around his crotch.

"That bitch has bitten my cock off, she's dead," he screamed at him, "get me a fucking doctor."

"Don't blame me, you told me to take it in my mouth and treat it like a lollipop, I didn't know it'd come off," she shouted back at him, at the same time pulling the dress over her head.

By now the woman who looked after Paige had also come into the room. She grasped Paige's arm and took her back to her room.

"You realise you will be punished?" she said quietly.

"For what? I did what he asked of me; I've never been with a man before, when he told me to put it in my mouth and bite, I did," she protested, but of course she didn't tell the complete truth, he'd never told her to bite. However, deep down she was glad. Whatever they did to her she wasn't bothered. It was worth it to hear the man scream, as she spat part of his penis out of her mouth.

The owner of the brothel came into her room. He looked at her for a short time. "You've injured a client; in fact he's demanding I kill you. What have you got to say?"

"I did as he asked; I thought he was some sort of pervert and liked pain." She shrugged. "Not that you'll believe me, you'd rather believe him. So kill me if it makes you, or him feel better. My life is over as I knew it, so I couldn't really care less."

He turned and left the room; the woman followed.

"Do you want her in the punishment room? She can't be allowed to get away with this, or you'll never break her," the woman urged.

He stood for a moment. "Prepare her, then I will come and administer the punishment. In the morning, she's first on the list with the doctor; that will shake the bitch. Then she's on mild doses of cocaine, until the aggression goes from her and she's under control."

The woman, accompanied by a minder, collected Paige and marched her down the passage, turning into the far room. She was stripped, before being laid face down on the cold stone floor; her legs spread wide, ankles clamped with ankle irons. Then her arms were pulled high above her head, attached to handcuffs fitted with rings in the floor. Paige was now very firmly held down, not able to move.

The lady looked at her. "I told you, but you ignored my warning. Now it's time to pay for that arrogance."

"Fuck you," Paige retorted.

"Cocky bitch aren't you, like the girl you came with. You don't know half of what we can do to girls with your attitude."

The owner came in. "You have injured a client; in fact lost us one. For this, you will be punished."

The minder handed him a short stick. On one side was a number of leather strips, on the other a stubby handle. Gripping the stick tightly, he started at her shoulders with hard, sharp swipes, moving down each time until he was below her knees.

Paige was screaming; by the time he reached her legs she'd passed out.

He stood back. "See, not a broken bit of skin, perhaps a little bruising, but that will go before she's recovered from her operation and ready to service clients again."

**

Paige was lying on her bed. For the rest of the night, she'd been in a great deal of pain from the punishment. Now it had almost gone, leaving just a throbbing when she moved. In lots of ways, she felt good, glad to see that man screaming as she bit him. Her determination to do the very same again had not been broken by the beating, in fact, it had galvanised her into wanting to do more to clients, before they finally gave up and killed her. For Paige, death was a far better option than years of this.

The woman came in. "It's time for your toilet and shower," she said, releasing the ankle iron.

Paige stood with difficulty and followed her. She sat on the toilet for a short time, before getting under the shower, relieved as the cool water cascaded over her back, taking the pain away slightly.

As she finished, the woman came in with a minder. He grasped her arm, and she was taken back to the punishment room. Paige was pulling back, believing they were going to punish her again. But he dragged her in. In the centre of the room was a long table, with a white sheet on it. Another man was also in the room, and she was quickly lifted bodily and laid flat on the table, her arms pulled down either side and handcuffed to the table legs. Her legs were splayed; her ankles firmly fixed to separate rings attached to the other end of the table. Then a strap was taken round her, just under her breasts, then around the underside of the table before being pulled tight. Another strap was placed around her just above the knees. Paige was now very firmly secured on the table, unable to move. Finally, she had a pad put under her head, enabling her to look down across her body.

The minders left and a man in a white coat, with a lady pushing a trolley, came in. Both put masks on and the lady plunged a needle into Paige's stomach.

Paige felt a numbness spreading in her stomach area. Already she was beginning to realise just what they were about to do to her. She tried to struggle, but she was far too firmly fixed.

"Please don't sterilise me, this is a mistake, the woman said they wouldn't do this, said I could have pills," she begged.

The doctor looked towards her. "I can assure you there's no mistake, in fact, the owner insisted you were to be the first of the day. We even decided on not putting you to sleep, so you could watch your womanhood being taken from you, with the help of a pillow placed under your head."

While he talked, he'd been massaging her stomach, working her internal organs up to the top of her tummy. Once satisfied, he took a knife and made a small cut just under her belly button, widening it, before fitting a ring keeping the cut open. Taking an instrument from the tray, with a small hook, he pushed it inside the opening, working around until he pulled out a tube.

"These young girls, it's so easy to find their fallopian tubes. Not like the older women in India," he said to his assistant, speaking in their own language. While he'd spoken he had kinked the tube and was wrapping the kinked part at the base with suture, tying a number of knots very tightly. Satisfied it was firmly tied together and blocked off, he cut off the looped part of the tube. He held it up for Paige to see, grinning behind his mask. "See girl," he said to her. "This is the first of your fallopian tubes. Used by your body to pass eggs down to the uterus. Soon I will remove your other. Then you will be sterilised. It is irreversible; you are no longer a complete woman; a fitting addition to a simple flogging."

Happy with his work he pushed the tied tube back into her body and began fishing about with the hook for her second tube. Again after tying and cutting this one, he pushed it back inside her. Pulling the ring out that held her open, he closed the wound with a single stitch. The lady wiped over the area with a sterile wipe and put a small dressing on top.

The doctor looked down at her. "I hope you found it interesting? All you have left is an eggless uterus, only good now to please men. So for you it's pointless; going back to the way you lived, dreaming that one day you'll have a family, it can never happen." He walked to the door laughing, calling the minders back. Paige was unstrapped and lifted onto a stretcher. Then she was taken to her own room. Her ankle was secured; she was left sobbing her heart out.

Chapter Forty-Three

Karen was sitting in the mobile command centre meeting room. She was alone and on a secure link to Sir Peter. Earlier she had sent him the location of the house the van drivers had returned to, after they had taken the girls to the brothels. Stanley, her head of intelligence, had drawn a blank as to who owned the property, so he suggested she talk to Sir Peter.

"Karen, the house belongs to a man known as Blas. We suspect, but have no evidence at this stage, he's a member of the Ndrangheta. With the drivers of the vans ending up there, our information is probably good and in line with Watson's claim, that this group was the one that approached him."

Karen sighed. "It's a start, Peter, except it doesn't link the trafficking operation to Ignatius which I'd hoped it would. Unless he or the Russian cartel owns the brothels; even then he will personally be standing away from the outlets, just manipulating in the background."

"Yes, I agree, it's all still a little hit and miss, we've nothing that could even implicate this man called Blas in trafficking. If we tried to link the drivers with him, he'd probably just claim they were employees and what they did in their own time is nothing to do with him. Although I really can't see this sort of abduction taking off, it's messy, high risk and for the Ndrangheta, a long way from drug smuggling. Anyway, Karen, what's your next move?"

If the truth were known, she didn't know what to do and really needed advice. "You have to help me here, Peter. I've got girls I know are almost certainly being abused. If the Americans find out that I could have prevented it, they'll be pretty upset. Although for my part, those girls being here has moved us on, with a definite link to this man Blas. I really need to leave him alone, let him believe we know nothing of his operation and see what he does next."

"I see your dilemma, Karen. My only point is; the Ndrangheta does not run brothels that I'm aware of; which suggests they have just trafficked these girls and sold on. Would they care if the brothels were raided now? I don't think they would. The only concern is like you say, for the moment you need to be standing away. Let them believe they've duped you, so they may continue their other operations, allowing you to put a far better picture together as to what they're really up to."

"You seem to believe, then, what's happened is just a test run for a larger operation?" Karen asked with interest.

"I wish I knew. You're into trafficking more than me, what sort of money will they have made out of this?"

"They may get ten or fifteen thousand a girl. Out of that there's setting up in the US then shipping them, besides the cost for the actual abductions. I really can't see them making money on such a small number; unless they intend to ship in twenty or more."

"Well keep me in the loop will you, and if I can help in any way, call me."

"I will, send my love to your wife and Georgina."

"I'll do that, Karen, take care."

***

Karen leaned back in the chair, deep in thought. She was totally confused as to why the girls really came, why they didn't try to spirit them away after finding out about Sherry? Then why did they have two containers, when the girls were only kept in one?

For ten minutes she mulled over the facts, moving them about in her mind, trying to form a new slant on the entire operation; then she suddenly hit the table with her hand, in realisation. The girls were nothing, she realised; just a means to get the containers out of the dock under the watchful eye of Unit T. It was what was in the second container that was more important than the girls. Sherry had given her the answer, by saying the girls were just in one; she'd just not seen it. Then Elfin, when she was at the Russian embassy, she remembered him telling her Ignatius was looking to purchase a large consignment of cocaine off the Ndrangheta. But of course the Ndrangheta couldn't supply on their routes, it had all but dried up, because of so many raids by the authorities. But the Los Zetas cartel could supply, and she knew the Ndrangheta and the Los Zetas cartel were working together from her conversation with Watson. Now she was convinced the second container must contain the cocaine. Just how much was in there she'd no idea, but it had to be in the tons.

"My god," she said aloud. "That's it; at last I've a chance to deal a blow to the cartels that would knock them back years."

Grabbing the telephone she called Stanley. "Can you go to your office, Stanley, and then call me on a secure line please?"

Two minutes later he called. "I'm secure, Karen, what is it you want?"

"I'm mobilising Dark Angel. I also want both helicopters armed with Stinger missiles."

"Why are we mobilising, Karen?"

"I think, no I know where there's a consignment of cocaine, tons of the bloody stuff. Enough to destroy hundreds if not thousands of lives. I believe the exchange is going down between the cartels."

Stanley said nothing for a moment, stunned at what she'd just told him. "You're serious, tons of cocaine you say?" he whispered.

"Ninety-nine per cent, Stanley. Everything points to it. Then when Sherry told me the girls were all in one container, it became obvious."

"So you believe the drugs are in the other container? Should we not involve other departments?"

"We can't, there isn't time. Besides not being sure just how much there is, which would warrant a container, it would bring informers out like ants. Every move we made they'd know, the cocaine would be spirited away, by each and everyone trying to make some easy money. Then to keep us away, they'd remind us that we don't do narcotics, and we'd be asked to stand down. As it is at the moment, we're dealing with a trafficker operation, and we'll just stumble on the cocaine as a side issue."

"I can understand that, but why the Stingers?"

"They're my insurance. If it looks like we've failed, and they try to get the container away, I'll blow it to smithereens."

"Very well, Karen. Are all Dark Angel sections to join the current surveillance team on the containers?"

She thought for a moment. "All but one division; I believe Blas is an important part of this operation. We need to keep surveillance on his house. If he moves then we follow. It's just possible that the exchange will be done separately to the payment. I want to be flexible

239

in case that happens, and we're fighting, so to speak, on two fronts."

"Very wise; what of the girls, do they wait?"

"No. I've a meeting with Lieutenant Clavier to look at his proposals to bring the girls out, before I return to Unit T. I don't believe there is any value to us in them staying there any longer."

"I think you're right. I'll keep in close touch with you. Will you be sending Corporal Malloy back to unit? She's come off operation and will need debriefing and a general check-up?"

"I don't want her with me, Stanley, but I think she should stay with the French operation, to pull the American girls out, then go back to Unit T with them."

"I agree. She will be valuable in that respect, and if Clavier's going in immediately, then she'll be back at unit perhaps just as quick, certainly within a couple of days."

Chapter Forty-Four

Karen sat down with Hamon in the meeting room of the trailer. She was looking at his proposal to take out the two brothels where the girls had been taken.

"This looks good, Hamon, you should join Unit T."

He smiled. "Any time, Karen, then at least we'd be with each other."

She nodded. "True, but we do work all over Europe, so you could find you're still hundreds of miles from me. Anyway, one step at a time, let's get the girls shall we."

"Will you be commanding the other team?" he asked.

"No, I'm afraid not. In fact I won't be here, I've been called back to our unit; another part of the same operation is coming to fruition, so this part is all yours."

"You're bailing, only two days after we've met again? Besides which, this is your operation, we're only support."

Karen remained silent for a moment, then looked at him. "I haven't bailed, but your operation must coincide with the other one I'm going to lead. They're all centred on one man called Blas who shipped the girls in; except we've intelligence he's going to a meeting, where possibly more of his girls are located. I want to hit them all at once. I'll be leaving Corporal Malloy with you; she knows the girls and will be able to identify them, but look after her for me. If you're stuck for soldiers, I'll supply a Unit T detachment. They are not Dark Angel soldiers, but the ones used for surveillance and security of the camp."

Of course, this was partly a lie, after all she wasn't going for more victims; Karen just wanted her units to be free to concentrate on the container.

"I understand; except if they're not Dark Angel soldiers, we will call on more of our own if necessary." He hesitated. "I'd hoped that you and I could get together afterwards. I'd like some time with you, Karen, away from all this."

She reached out and touched his hand. "I do as well, Hamon. Maybe we should go down to the coast, perhaps Cannes, for a few days?"

He smiled. "I'll hold you to that."

After more planning of their operation, Karen stood, as did Hamon. He put his arms around her and kissed her gently. "Take care, no heroics and keep me updated."

She nodded. "You need to know one more thing, Hamon. Unit T is mobilising and will move to lockdown, so following this meeting, there will be no direct contact with me. Stanley will give you the green light to go in. Under no circumstances move without his confirmation; that is essential."

"I understand, we will wait for the go. It must be serious if you're mobilising?"

She shook her head. "It's normal, it just makes sure informers can't get any information as to what we are doing, or where we are going, that's all."

***

Karen was already in a helicopter heading back to Unit T's camp. She had just finished a conversation with Stanley, who was now busily calling the units of Dark Angel soldiers back off leave. For them, this was usual if something big was going down and it was accepted as part of the job. However, if the truth were known, any soldier would be upset if they had been left out, with their day-to-day routines normally taken up with training, surveillance duties and keeping the villa secure. Although they all looked forward to the villa assignment; the food was good and off-duty, if Karen wasn't home, they could use the swimming pool.

As Karen's helicopter landed, a car was already waiting for her, taking her directly to the camp's headquarters. An officer approached and saluted. "Your visitor is waiting in the main meeting room, Colonel. He arrived about ten minutes ago."

"Thank you, can you arrange coffee for me, please. Also, I want a full briefing for all Dark Angel personnel, at twenty-two hundred hours."

Karen went through to the meeting room. The man stood looking out of the window, but turned when she came in. It was Elfin.

He came up to her, kissing her on each cheek. "It's good to meet

242

you again, Karen. This is the first time I've been to Unit T. With what I've seen, the security is pretty impressive, your people very courteous and efficient."

"Thank you, Elfin. You're really very honoured to be here. This is a closed unit and receives few visitors. Even the top brass have trouble arranging a pass to visit us."

At that moment coffee was brought, then they were left alone.

"I'm really quite intrigued, last time we parted we were quite far apart. Your call to the embassy requesting I see you urgently came as a shock. Within minutes I was taken to the airport, put on the earliest available flight to Paris, where a transport aircraft was being held pending my arrival."

She smiled. "Yes, I'm sorry about that, but our passenger aircraft wasn't available, so the only one that could get you here was our usual supply plane."

"That's no problem. In Russia, we were often sent from place to place on such transport. It took me back a few years believe me. So now I'm here, what is it that's so important that even my embassy couldn't tell me?"

Karen sipped her coffee, her eyes never wavering from his. "There was a reason for that, Elfin. You see, if what I'm going to tell you was overheard, picked up on a phone tap or whatever, not only would it place lives at risk, but the very operation. It also means that, in less than two hours, Unit T moves to mobilisation. For you, that will take immediate effect. It means communication with the outside world will cease. You will be searched, scanned and given a change of clothes. Any mobile or other forms of communication will be taken from you. You will not be allowed to be on your own at any time. If you try to use a phone, leave the camp, or make any effort to communicate you will be arrested, even risk being shot. If you cannot accept these terms then you must leave the camp immediately."

He could tell by her manner that she was deadly serious. "That is a very high level of security, Karen, is this normal for a mobilisation or just for me, because I'm Russian?"

"It's normal. Most of our work is carried out against a background of informers serving different masters, trying to find our movements.

We've taken down people from all walks of life, including billionaires down to the vagrants off the street. My soldiers understand the need for security at this level, and also realise their lives could be at risk, as so many in the past have found to their cost, when people inform on us. We cannot be complacent and must trust no one, no matter how important they are, or even who they are. The only slight difference for you, as for any outsider, is that you will not be allowed on your own for even a minute. So in answer to your question, is it because you are Russian, the answer is no, even Sir Peter would be subject to the same restrictions."

"Then I will accept your requirement in its entirety. It's clear you have not brought me all this way to talk, so one way or another you require my assistance."

"I do, and thank you for accepting my conditions. We will meet again in fifteen minutes after you have changed." Karen pressed a button just under the meeting room table. In seconds, a soldier entered and Elfin left the room with him.

***

When Elfin returned, he was dressed in black combat clothes, as worn by the Dark Angel soldiers.

Karen smiled. "They suit you, and you look pretty relaxed wearing them."

"Being in the Russian forces for ten years helps, Karen," he answered, at the same time taking a seat at her side.

"Now the reason why you are here?" she said. "I know, well I'm 99 per cent certain, where there's up to ten tons of cocaine. We're expecting the shipment is about to be moved to a place where the Russian mafia will take possession, or it is exchanged. It's the intention of Unit T's forces to intercept the drugs, along with the people making the transaction. They will be, I believe, Ignatius and a man we only know as Blas. As you know Elfin, that could mean we are talking up to three hundred million dollars of cocaine, with a street value of close to five billion dollars. The loss of such a large consignment, besides the payment, will cripple the cartels for a long time. Now perhaps you can understand just why Unit T is mobilising, and why I was so insistent that you understand what is at stake?"

His mouth had dropped slightly, and he was staring at this girl. A girl still in her twenties, but about to take on three of the largest cartels in the world. If she succeeded, her life would be in constant danger. They would hunt her down, of that he had no doubt. "You are certain of your information?" he gasped.

She shrugged indifferently. "Nothing is ever certain in the world I live in, but in this case, short of going and opening the container, yes, I'm very certain that it does contain cocaine. How much, that is something I don't know."

"You are aware of the risk to you personally, if you succeed?"

"Of course; but I've survived threats to my life for the last ten years, so what's the difference?"

"Very well, so what is it you want of me?"

"I want you to give my soldiers a briefing on the sort of tactics we can expect from the Russian mafia. I also want you to confirm that what is in the container is cocaine, and we are not being tricked in some way. I wouldn't know as it isn't my area, or expertise."

"That is no problem, Karen. I'll brief your men willingly. I'm a little confused though. You told me in the embassy that you kept away from drugs, so why this time?"

"No, I said that sometimes my part of an operation brings us in contact with drugs, but I place them with other departments who specialise and it is usually not much more than a kilo. We are also moving on with other operations, which are all part of the same operation, bringing out a number of girls, sold by Blas or his cartel. Once the drugs are secure, we will hand that part over to the authorities, but will insist they are destroyed there and then. The risk is too high to allow them to be moved and stored. When you are talking millions of dollars, even the most uncorrupted can suddenly see a lifestyle they could never attain. That possibility must not be allowed to happen."

He leaned back in his chair and looked at her. "You know for such a young person, your head is screwed on. But how could anyone be certain you're not corrupt?"

She smiled. "You don't. Although, in my defence, I'm already a multi-millionaire and haven't managed yet to make even a slight dent in my fortune. Every time I spend any of it, the interest rate puts it all back. So a few extra millions, or even the whole lot, wouldn't make much difference to my lifestyle, just a higher tax bill."

He was surprised. They knew Karen had money, but this was the first time she'd actually admitted it. And to be indifferent to so much money must mean she already had a substantial amount, but where had it come from? "I don't suppose you are going to elaborate, where this money of yours came from? We do know that your family, although comfortable, are not well- off."

"No, that's my personal business. I will tell you; the British government knows the source and has passed the money as being legal and legitimately obtained. I'm not a criminal, and have never accepted money in return for favours."

"I can believe that, Karen. And I'll tell you this, I wouldn't say that about most of the people I deal with."

She smiled inwardly, if only he really knew where her money had come from, perhaps he wouldn't have said those words. She glanced at her watch. "Okay, it's coming up to twenty-one hundred, the meeting's at twenty-two hundred, so how about a late dinner? Then if we get out of this alive, you can take me out and show me how the Russians celebrate."

"You're asking me on a date?" he asked, with a hint of a smile.

She stood and made to walk to the door before turning. "We don't call it a date, more a celebration that we've survived. You should already know the world we live in is not only exciting but dangerous. Come on, the kitchens are staying open for me, any longer, and the food will be in the dogs, then we'll be down to beans on toast."

They walked through the building and outside; the night was warm; everything seemed so calm, already the thought of maybe finally bringing down Ignatius was sending shivers down Elfin's spine. But he knew the mafia, this was not going to be easy and he had doubts that this young girl, and her small group of soldiers, would be a match for such ruthless and dangerous men.

"Penny for them," Karen suddenly said, as they turned into the officers' club.

"I was just thinking what a nice setting the camp is in, with the warmth of the night. When back in London, I left a cold and rainy day,

246

it's a place where I'd like to live."

"Yes, I like it. You will have to come to my house; I've a swimming pool, and often eat by the side of it."

By now they were inside and passing the bar, going through to the dining room.

"You know, Karen, that is the second invitation from you. I think, no I know, I will accept both, after all it isn't often I am able to take out such an attractive and I might add intelligent, young lady, which for a man like me is always a bonus."

She never replied, just smiled to herself. She would have celebrated anyway, with all the other soldiers, not as he might expect, alone with her. Then as a guest, he'd have stayed at the villa, the camp was not really suitable, with little spare accommodation. The villa had a separate guest suite, which was not part of the main house. So if he wanted to take her out, he'd still have to ask, she wasn't that forward.

This of course was very true for Karen. She was basically very shy when it came to anything to do with her personal life. The few times she'd been asked out, beyond a simple date, had ended up in disaster. Because of this, Karen was more comfortable with casual acquaintances; more intense and serious alternatives saw her finding excuses as to why she shouldn't be there; then she'd walk, retreating back to her house away from the world. If she had been truthful to herself, she was scared of any sort of relationship. Her experience with men was one of depravity and abuse towards her. Even Karen's sex life was often forced on her; yet as a person in charge of a Unit, she was professional and full of confidence in herself.

At the end of dinner, they were sitting with coffee; the room empty apart from them. Their talk had been general, nothing specific and no mention of the coming operation.

"The dinner was very good, Karen. Do you often eat here?"

She shook her head. "Very rarely, I go home, it's only a couple of miles away. Although there are over two hundred and sixty personnel, with thirty-five officers in the camp, besides specialist researchers, so the dining rooms can get very busy."

"I was going to call you this week. I'd found out a little information that I think you would be very interested in."

"I'm interested in anything if it adds to our databases, so what was it about?"

"A report came across my desk about a Nigerian named Iroatu. I believe he is one of the three Nigerians you are looking for?"

Karen's features hardened at the mention of this man's name. "He is a man I'd very much like to meet. Do you know where he is?"

"We believe he's taken over a brothel of Pular's in Istanbul. It's not confirmed, but the intelligence is good."

"That's interesting, although his business is destined to be a very short-lived one. Do you think it's possible Pular is also in touch with the other two?"

"It's possible, for this sort, it's the only type of business they know, besides, the rewards are great, and they can get girls from Nigeria."

"We will talk more on this, Elfin."

"Of course, I would also like to see them taken down, and you are the group that can do just that."

Karen sighed. "You know this job just goes on and on, there's never a break, because if you had one, someone could die in the hands of such people before you could pull them out. That is something I never like to see, the girls that died in the hands of the Nigerians even shook me with the brutality. I wouldn't say that the traffickers I've met weren't brutal, they were, but at least they could see the value of the people they took and wouldn't kill for killing's sake. Except it's happening more and more now."

He took a sip of his coffee. "Did you ever consider it might be because of you that the brutality is becoming more prevalent?"

"I have, after all in the past they were basically left alone, so the level of violence to the victims was more to get them to do as they were told. Now, they are trying to get rid of the evidence and people who could stand up in court and not only identify them but tell people like me about their operation. Does it sadden, or concern me? At times, but no matter what, everyone has the right to make their own decisions in this world that dictates their future. No person has the right to force a future onto anyone for profit."

"I'm in full agreement, but the public is very fickle, the press gave you a hard time over the death of so many victims of trafficking."

"It's because they don't understand, and then the press don't help, because they want to sell papers. Death, particularly children's, does just that, so they milk it as much as they can."

At that moment an officer approached, standing back, waiting for Karen to acknowledge him. She looked across.

"The soldiers are assembled in the briefing room, Colonel."

"Thank you. I'll be there in a few minutes."

He saluted and left. She looked at Elfin.

"This is it. It's time for you to see Dark Angel in action. Our two C5 transport aircraft will now be fully loaded and fuelled. They are a sight to see as they take off. All I can hope now is that this time next week all my soldiers will have returned to base safely."

"With you in charge, they stand a good chance, Karen," he said, at the same time standing, before going behind Karen, drawing her chair out as she stood.

She turned and looked at him. "I could get used to this type of gallantry," she said, giving him a smile.

Chapter Forty-Five

Sherry had been assigned to stay with Hamon. Primarily because the gendarmerie had no females, and she could not only recognise the girls, but they also knew her. She was quite happy with this arrangement; after all, she was the only Dark Angel soldier with them, and it made her feel a tiny bit more important being given this task.

Sitting in the same Land Rover as Hamon, her communicator began to bleep, then finished with a long tone. "Dark Angel has been mobilised, they have gone into lockdown, we're on our own now," she said quietly.

He looked at her. "Does it scare you?"

"I suppose, but at least all the waiting and constant training will have stopped. They will be on the move with a target in mind."

"You sound as though you enjoy operations. What about your colonel, do you two get on?"

"We do, in fact, we often go away together. You should see her on the beach; she is so different, like any girl in her twenties. Then talk about flirt, I think every man just has eyes for her, I don't get a look-in."

"I wouldn't believe that for a moment, Sherry. You're an attractive girl, and I suspect could hold your own and know it."

She laughed. "I suppose, but I just enjoy being with her. She needs a break sometimes, the strain of all this must really wear her down, so if she wants to let off a little steam in her own way, I'm up for it. Besides, we stay in fantastic five star hotels and have great dinners out. After the way I was brought up, it's another world. Have you met Sophie? She's nothing like Karen; still attractive, but two years older."

"No, I'd like to. Does she live with the parents?"

"Normally, but she's at the villa for the next few weeks, though I'm not sure why, maybe it's more secure for her there. When we go back I'll introduce you, unless Karen's home, then she will."

Of course, Sherry did know why she was there, but she would never tell a stranger the reason. That was up to Karen, if she wanted them to know.

"So do you have a house?" he asked.

Sherry shook her head. "I live in the barracks. I have my own room, so it's like having your own place I think."

"Do you pay a lot for it?"

"No, it's part of your wages. You're paid a little less, but because it's an overseas posting for me, I get a higher allowance which covers what I lose. One day I'm going to buy a house. It'd have to have fantastic views, swimming pool, then after being in France I'm addicted to the sun, so it'd probably be on the Mediterranean coast."

"So you're saving like mad then, for a deposit?"

"Yes, but in a few years I'll have enough."

Again, Sherry didn't admit that she already had in excess of a million pounds in the bank; compensation for her time in the hands of traffickers. Karen had negotiated this for her, from a fund that was topped up with the money seized from traffickers. This fund had steadily increased, paying out to date well over two hundred million to the victims of trafficking.

Hamon looked at his watch. "It's time we moved out ourselves and took up our positions. Then it's a waiting game for Karen's order to move."

***

It was just after nine in the morning when the order came to move on the brothels. Karen had decided that the action would no longer affect the operation surrounding the container; although neither Sherry nor Hamon was aware of that fact.

While they waited, Sherry had been positioned to photograph every car that arrived, log the time they were there and when they left. Another soldier was photographing the people as they climbed out of their cars with a long-range lens. Both were important for the operation as the men would be prosecuted later for the rape of underage girls, providing they were identified by the girl as their abuser, or their DNA was present.

Sherry's earphone came to life, giving her the order to re-position. She fastened her bulletproof vest, brought down her visor and clicked her gun off safety. It was time. Already her stomach was tightening, the adrenaline running in her body. She was going into the unknown, with no idea as to what she might face, although she was surrounded

251

by a very expert incursion unit, leaving her little to do.

Moving around the back of the house, she joined up with two more soldiers. They said nothing to each other, only moved to their allocated positions and waited. Sherry glanced at her watch; they were one minute ahead of the time when the main door would be broken open. Then she and one soldier would enter the back. The one left would cover the door, preventing any escape.

Fifteen seconds before they went in the soldier at her side nudged her. They both broke cover; he ran to the back door and placed a charge on the handle. Exactly on time it exploded, and the door was thrown open. Neither of them delayed and they entered the house. Checking the back rooms, they met other soldiers who had come in from the front. Now they were running upstairs, bursting every door open, switching on the lights, and securing the rooms and whoever was inside.

Sherry was moving to her next objective, the cellar, with one of the French soldiers. They moved down the steps, checking each room; most of the eight rooms had girls in, some were asleep, others just sitting reading. With just the girls in the rooms, they moved on looking for minders or adult workers. In the last room, Sherry immediately recognised Paige. She was lying on her bed staring up at the ceiling.

She looked back at the soldier following. "I know this girl, she's one of the Americans brought two days back. Can you go and find where the keys are for the ankle irons, then we can release all the girls and get them upstairs?"

He nodded, happy now there was no threat down here, and left quickly.

Sherry went inside the room; Paige looked towards the door, shocked at seeing an armed soldier.

Sherry swung her gun over her shoulder and began to remove her helmet.

"Who are you? Have you come...?" Paige fell silent midway into her words, looking at Sherry in shock, now she could see who it was, with the helmet removed. "Sherry; it is Sherry isn't it? We all thought you were dead when you never came back," she gasped.

"No, I wasn't dead, though being forced to jump out of the ship while it was still moving is not something I'd recommend. I'm sorry I couldn't get here sooner, Paige."

"No, I'm glad you've come, really I am," she said, then looked away, tears in her eyes. "I wish it had been yesterday. They sterilised me, Sherry, cut my tubes out and forced me to watch."

Paige wanted to cry, but since the operation she'd been on sedation, leaving her depressed, but unable to work herself up.

Sherry moved closer, taking Paige in her arms, holding her tightly. "I'm so sorry, Paige. I'll get you to the hospital and let them see what can be done."

She shook her head. "The doctor told me it was irreversible, you'd be wasting your time."

"Don't believe anything these people say, Paige, we'll get the best surgeons in the world for you, they will find a way, believe me."

She pulled her radio from its pouch, calling for medical assistance and a stretcher.

"Have you found Nicole, she was here as well, but some man took her?" Paige told Sherry, changing the subject.

"Yes, we have her as well. We've also pulled out the other girls."

"I'm glad, we'd all become good friends. I'd like to see them again. So are you a soldier, or have you just come to identify us?" she asked, confused.

"I'm a soldier in Unit T, a unit that tracks trafficker operations in Europe. I'm not allowed to tell you any more, but you'll be coming back to the unit for a short time after the initial hospital check-up, so all your questions will be answered there."

At that moment two soldiers carrying a stretcher came into the room. "We've come to take the girl to the hospital, Corporal, is she able to leave now?"

"Yes, carry on. I'll see you soon, Paige; you'll be well looked after, believe me."

Tears were running down Paige's face. "Thank you for coming, Sherry, I'll always be grateful. Like you said on the ship, never give up hope. I didn't, and am so glad you came when you did."

Chapter Forty-Six

The huge transport planes landed at the airport on the border between France and Germany. Already the vehicles had been unloaded and were on their way to joining up with the advance units, located close to where the containers were parked. Karen, along with Elfin, had transferred to one of the unit's helicopters. Both helicopters were still on the ground; waiting for more precise details as to where Blas was heading.

Her radio suddenly came alive. "It's Stanley, Karen. You have a problem. By the information coming back to me, it's now obvious the direction Blas is going in is not towards the containers. We now have confirmation that the lorry loaded with the container the girls were not in, is on the move."

Karen's heart sank, had she got it completely wrong? Was Blas nothing to do with the cocaine, or more importantly, did neither of the containers contain drugs? Then if one did, and the helicopters were in completely different locations, would one Stinger be enough to destroy the cargo?

"Okay, Stan, I'll be back soon, in the meantime keep me abreast of where Blas and more importantly, where the container is headed."

"Will do."

She glanced towards Elfin, telling him what had happened.

He nodded. "It's usual in big drug deals. There's been too many sting operations where the seller and buyer are caught red-handed with both the goods and the money. Often now, the leaders doing the deal will meet in a hotel, or even a car park, then use their own people to check and confirm the shipment. With your suggestion that this could be a very large haul, I'd be surprised if any cash is exchanged. Sometimes it's diamonds, gold or in the past negotiable bonds, but those were made illegal by the US sometime back. But even with gold, you'd be talking about a ton of gold for a ton of cocaine, hardly the sort of quantity to put in the back of a car. These days they are more likely to do a bank transfer into shell companies, already set up for such transactions. There would need to be a large number of shell companies, as the problem with any large bank transaction is it would attract attention and flag up in the banks when the transaction went through. So it's logged and can be followed, no matter how complicated they try to make the trail. If it's in US dollars, which is the main transaction currency, the US can even call it back. Most probably all the shell companies will have a small part of the total cost. As soon as the cocaine is confirmed, all these companies will make payment to similar companies set up by the other cartel. That way the relatively low sums don't attract attention."

"So why didn't you mention all this earlier?"

"I would have thought you'd know, Karen, and made appropriate arrangements. Although thinking about it, you don't usually deal in drug transactions, so you're out of your depth. After all your sort of deals are relatively small, around a hundred grand."

"Yes well, you don't have to be so bloody clever after the fact. So this is what we do. You will be in one helicopter and head to the container, as you're the only one who can confirm the haul is cocaine. I'll follow Blas."

"If that's what you want, I have no problem doing that."

"Then can you transfer to the other helicopter, it's time we were in the air."

Elfin climbed out and began to make his way across the tarmac. Karen grasped the arm of the soldier who was to be with him at all times. "I want him watched, any problems I want to know immediately. Do you understand?"

"Yes, Colonel, I understand."

A few minutes later, both helicopters were in the air. Karen's was heading to intercept her own team already on the move and to follow them at a discreet distance.

Chapter Forty-Seven

Ignatius was passing the time looking out of the car window. They had been on the road for nearly three hours and were due to arrive at the exchange location within fifteen minutes. Already Blas had called to confirm the time of the meeting.

Following Ignatius, when he left his house, were four other vehicles; each with five men inside. Now there was only his and one other vehicle, the other three had turned off some distance back and were heading for a rendezvous with the container. It was their intention, after checking the container contents, by using the chemist with them to confirm the quality, that Ignatius would pay Blas, then they would take the container on.

All this was very risky. They could be double-crossed. Blas may have people there, and when the cocaine had been paid for, they could overcome Ignatius's people, keeping both the money and the cocaine.

To combat that possibility, all the men, apart from the chemist, were ex-military and well- armed. Also, not all would go to the container. One vehicle would stop a short distance from the container, the men would disperse and secure the surrounding area.

***

Blas had also left for the meeting. He too, like Ignatius had his own armed support. With around five million being paid in cash, gold and diamonds, he wanted to be sure he could actually take it away safely. Although Blas did have an advantage, in that he'd selected the location for the handover of the container. Because of this, he'd already moved his men in and they were set up to ensure everything went as planned.

***

Ten miles away, the lorry that was carrying the container with the drugs inside, turned into a small drive that led up to large iron gates, beyond which was the courtyard of an old house. It came to a halt close to the entrance of the house. Already a number of men were milling around, all carrying automatic weapons. Minutes later Ignatius's men arrived. They climbed out of the cars along with the chemist. He carried a small leather case. A table had been brought from the house and was placed at the back of the lorry.

Ignatius's man in charge watched, as the chemist laid his test equipment out on the table. He then turned to one of Blas's men. "You should now open the container and we will select a package from each of the crates. After positive testing, I'll call Ignatius to complete the transaction."

The man nodded and shouted to two others to open the container.

Inside the container were twenty packing cases, each with a lid that screwed down. Ignatius's man went into the container, selecting at random ten cases that would be checked. Two men, with battery operated electric screwdrivers, began removing the lids. Inside the first crate, when opened, were well-wrapped packages. One package was selected, taken out from the container and placed on the table. The chemist made a small puncture in the bag, removing a tiny amount of cocaine. He dropped it into a glass tube and poured a little liquid from a small bottle he'd taken from his case. He watched and waited; moments later it changed colour, indicating it was cocaine and of high quality. The operation was repeated, as more packages were brought out for testing.

Chapter Forty-Eight

Karen's helicopter landed; she jumped down, and the helicopter set off again to join up with the second. Both, as Karen had ordered, were equipped with one Stinger missile each. She went over to her waiting Range Rover and climbed inside, shutting the door. Soon she was talking to Stanley.

"Sherry has confirmed that all the American girls have now been accounted for and are safe, Karen. They have all been taken to the hospital for check-ups. As for the unit following the lorry with the trailer on, their forward ground surveillance team is reporting that the Russians and Italians have joined up and are with the container. According to surveillance, they say it would seem that one group, which I presume must be the Russians, have set-up a testing table and are bringing sample packages out. Ignatius has arrived at a farmhouse, around a mile off the main road; Blas is already there. Surveillance doesn't think anyone lives there, as there are no signs of it. Both Blas and Ignatius's vehicles are now parked outside. What's your next move?"

"I've been thinking, Stan, if they make a deal and the Italians leave, should we destroy at that point, or allow the container to carry on to its final destination?"

"It has advantages both ways, Karen. One, we're up against far fewer gunmen, and second it could take us to a distribution house, which could make the operation far more beneficial."

"Yes, I agree. Unless the cocaine is split there, then loaded into more vehicles, we let the consignment carry on. Surveillance must tell us immediately if a split is looking to be the case."

"Very well, I'll send the new orders to surveillance and C Company. You, on the other hand, seem to have a problem. Four further vehicles are approaching your area, very fast. I'm not sure if they are Russian, or Italian, but they will pass close to your position in around five minutes."

Karen was confused. "You're sure they have something to do with this? It doesn't seem logical?"

Stanley also wasn't sure. "No, only that they are coming your way."

"Very well, we'll delay our incursion, until we know if it is a coincidence that these vehicles are on the same road, or a threat. Keep in touch, Stanley, there's a lot going on and a number of options."

"I will and good luck."

She broke off communication and left the vehicle. Besides her Range Rover, four more Unit T vehicles were parked up, off the road in a dell, well out of sight of the road. She walked over to the lieutenant in charge of the incursion. "Seems like we have four vehicles coming along this road in convoy. Forward surveillance should be able to tell us if they are part of the meeting or not. I want your unit on the move immediately after they have passed and in a position to secure the exits from the meeting place."

"Yes, Colonel. Is it still your intention to go in?"

Karen was thinking. "We don't have the manpower to take on more gunmen, besides the ones there already, so it's going to be a watch and wait. We know this is a payment meeting so we could delay until the Russians have gone, leaving just the Italians. Although, at this stage, I'm ruling nothing out until we know more."

Chapter Forty-Nine

Colin Munford, a member of an organised crime and drug syndicate in London, had been made aware of the transaction between the Russian mafia and the Ndrangheta cartel, some three weeks before, by Macario. Macario not only owed his syndicate money from his gambling habit, but wanted a cut of the cash they would find. Colin had agreed, and Macario was supposed to keep in touch, to give him the location of the transaction. However, with Macario not contacting him for the last few critical days, Colin believed he had double-crossed him; so Colin had taken it upon himself to keep a close watch on Ignatius. Today was the first day for over a week that Ignatius had left his home, accompanied by other vehicles; Colin was certain this would be the day when the exchange was to be made.

He had noted a number of vehicles splitting off, presuming, rightly, that they were intercepting the container. Now he was confident that the reduced personnel, still with Ignatius, posed little threat. Then even if Blas had men, which he was certain he would, most would be protecting the shipment, not with him.

Knowing that he heavily outmanned and outgunned the groups at the farm where the financial transaction was to take place, Colin's vehicles stopped short of the farm, his men spilling out and beginning to make their way towards Blas and Ignatius's men.

Moments later the fight began. Everywhere guns were going off as each group sought to gain the upper hand. Colin and two others ran ahead into the building, quickly overcoming what little resistance they met, bursting into the room where the money was being counted.

Ignatius and Blas turned and stared at Colin.

"Who the fuck are you?" Blas demanded.

"I'm Colin; I'm here for the cocaine and the money."

Ignatius smiled. "Then you are a foolish man, if you believe you can take from the Russian Mafia, or even the Ndrangheta. Both of us will hunt you down and kill you."

Colin shrugged. "Whatever, where's the cocaine?"

"It's not here. If that's what you're thinking," Blas replied.

"I can see that, even I'm not that stupid to believe you've tons of the stuff in your cars. So I want answers, where is it?"

Both Blas and Ignatius said nothing.

Colin without warning fired his gun. The bullet went into Blas's foot. He screamed and then fell to the floor, rolling about in agony.

"Where is it?" Colin asked once more.

"I can't tell you; they'd kill me," Blas shouted.

Colin again fired his gun. This time it shattered Blas's arm.

"I could do this all day; I promise you won't die, but the pain will be excruciating," he said, indifferent to Blas's screams.

"You may as well tell him, Blas, he seems determined to take your cocaine. As for the money, Colin, or whoever you really are. That's mine and goes nowhere," Ignatius told him.

"You think? Well that's where you're wrong old man," he said, raising his gun.

"No, that is where you are wrong. Don't turn around and don't even think about using your gun. I'm holding an M5 carbide, at this distance it will cut you in half. So drop the gun; otherwise you will be dead before you hit the floor," came a female voice from behind him.

Ignatius looked towards the door, and the person standing there holding a gun. He grinned, even with her visor down, dressed as she was, he knew her. "Well if it isn't Lieutenant Colonel Karen Harris of Unit T's Dark Angel. Seems like you arrived in the nick of time. This man had ideas about killing me."

Colin had gone cold inside at Ignatius's words. He had heard all about this girl and she wasn't one you could bluff. She would shoot to kill without batting an eyelid. He clicked the safety on his gun and dropped it to the floor.

"Kick it away and go to the far wall with your hands up and flat to the wall. You also Ignatius, after you've removed the gun from the holster inside your jacket," Karen demanded.

Karen entered the room, but she didn't lower her gun, until two Dark Angel soldiers followed and searched everyone for weapons, including Blas. She switched the safety on and handed her gun to a soldier standing at her side. Then she raised her visor and removed her helmet, allowing her long hair to fall over her shoulders. She looked at the three of them for a moment. "It would seem very fortuitous that we

261

were passing and heard gunshots. Perhaps someone would volunteer to tell me what is going on here?"

"You mean you are not here because of intelligence?" Ignatius asked.

"As I said, we were passing. Diverting to see what was going on, besides sorting out who was shooting at who and taking control. Now I've everyone in custody, I'm after explanations." She walked to the table and looked at the packs of hundred dollar bills, trays of diamonds and kilo bars of gold on the floor. There was also a computer, with lists of companies on the screen. "So who do these belong to then?"

"They are mine," Ignatius replied.

"For what reason, are they to pay a debt, or were you all going to play cards?" she mocked.

"We had a business deal, but it's off now, so I'm packing up and going home."

Karen gave a hint of a smile. "I presume you can prove ownership and also show us where the money came from?"

"I need to prove nothing; Blas will confirm it's mine."

"I'm afraid you have that a little wrong, Ignatius. You see people are dead, most if not all of you are carrying illegal weapons. This money, along with everything else, is evidence of something going on here. I intend to impound it, and it will be up to you, after going through the criminal legal process, to claim your property back. Although as I said, I will need to see a paper trail of the original source of the money, to convince me this is not money obtained by criminal means. If it is, then it will be impounded under EU legislation."

Karen turned and left the room, meeting a soldier outside. "Have the police arrived yet?" she asked.

"Just, Colonel. They are waiting at our perimeter until you give the okay to take over."

"Five minutes, then let them in. In the meantime, gather everything off the table, bag it and secure it in my Range Rover. I also want a photo of the computer screen and the computer. We cannot take the risk of possible bribery, and people walking."

The soldier returned to the room and began collecting the cash, pushing it all back into the large holdall it had been originally packed in. Evidence seals were used to secure the bags, with Karen signing over the seals.

Ignatius watched in horror. There was five million there, if it was taken in; they could never prove it was legally obtained. He needed to talk to her. "Can we talk, Karen, alone?"

"We can, providing what you are going to tell me is relevant. You are all under caution at this time, so anything you say could well be repeated in a court of law."

"It's relevant, or more to the point important for you," he replied.

She nodded, and he was escorted by two soldiers to the room next door. Karen followed. The door was shut, and the soldiers remained on guard outside.

"It's been a long time, Karen. You've done well, and cleaned up a particularly ruthless lot known as the Circle, with our help."

"That is true, Ignatius, and I'll always be grateful, if it hadn't been a means to an end for the Russian Mafia to fill the void left by the Circle."

"That's business; you of all people should understand they had to go?"

"I do, I also warned you that if we came up against each other again, there would be no favours. Mind you, by my intervention you're still alive, so you could say any debt to you is now paid in full."

He smiled; she was a clever girl in lots of ways. "You realise you can't take money off the Russian Mafia without repercussions?"

"I'm taking nothing. I'm required to list everything at a crime scene. You will all be taken away by the police and charged, or released if you are not party to the killings that have gone on and carry a licence for your guns. That has nothing to do with me. However, we can hardly hand over such a large amount of money to the local police to keep in their property office. It invites robbery. We also cannot give it to a potential prisoner to keep in his cell. So I'll have it placed in a secure bank vault and as I said, if you are the legitimate owner, you can claim it back. Then the list of companies on the computer screen will give the authorities very interesting reading."

"Perhaps under the circumstances you're right to do as you are doing. But I think it should not go to the bank; you should look after it, and we will come to collect. As for the shell companies, you should just turn the screen off as if they never existed. We will of course give you a finder's fee; we will also give you something you really want. Call it a bonus."

"And that is?"

"The Nigerians who butchered so many children, causing you quite a lot of aggravation and wrongful accusations of incompetence."

Karen really did want the Nigerians; she also knew with the cartels contacts it would be virtually impossible to hang onto the money, and she'd never be able to prove a link between that and the cocaine. Then the computer, with lists of companies displayed could be made meaningless in days, so even that had little value in pointing the Russians conducting a drugs deal.

"It's possible that I could arrange to keep hold of the money. After all, only you, Blas and the other man, who I'm not sure who he actually is, besides Unit T, know about it. Providing they say nothing, then we could have a deal. Otherwise, it won't be up to me, rather the French government."

"They will say nothing, believe me. Then we have a deal?"

"Of course, deals for me are what it's all about." Then her tone changed. "Don't for one moment believe I'm a fool, I'm not and any deal is controlled by me. In other words, you have to trust me; I won't trust you, or any of your people. That's my way; otherwise I go it alone. It may take longer, but time is on my side; for you and others who believe they can con me, time isn't." She began to lighten her manner. "Besides, I'm a typical woman; once we dig our heels in we won't budge."

He nodded his head up and down slowly. "We know you very well, Karen. How you operate and also that your word is always good. We'll give you the Nigerians; they are perhaps the worst of all the traffickers I've ever met. I presume you will already know of the American girls who were shipped here?"

Karen laughed. "I knew before they even left the States. We already have them. Mind you, I'm going to struggle to tie Blas to the abduction."

"You have a good intelligence set-up, Karen. You should be

proud of yourself. As for Blas, I will look into that for you; they have let us down, so I'm thinking that my people will not want to do business with them again. It is time they were removed from the map."

Karen grinned. "You know, if you keep having me knock out the opposition, there will only be you left. One day I'll remove you with no deal up for grabs to get you off the hook."

He gave an indifferent shrug of his shoulders. "That's the way of the world. People come up, others go down. You've been very lucky in your life. I'd advise that you seriously think about retiring. You have already rocked the trafficking industry, but they are small beer to the drug trade. There the players are far more ruthless, with big money to protect their interests. Some of the cartels don't just control a few gunmen, they control countries."

"I don't do drugs, that's a different division," Karen cut in.

Ignatius began to laugh. "You are classic. Here's a girl who's foiled one of the largest drug deals ever made, suggesting it was only by chance she was driving past, telling me she doesn't do drugs. If you were onto the girls, then it stands to reason you'd stumbled on the drug shipment. That means you already had both Blas and the container under surveillance. You've also gone alone on it, so you were worried about informers." He was silent for a moment. "I like you a great deal. We of the Russian Mafia respect you, but it's time to get out, Karen. You've done all you can, let others take the strain. You're not short of money, and you're still young enough to enjoy life. Extending your operations into drug trafficking will be your downfall, believe me."

"I'll think about it, in the meantime I can't hold off any longer. I'll keep your money and wait for your call. But remember, no Nigerians, then no money. Even then I want them either dead, but preferably in custody before I hand the money back."

"I'd expect you to do nothing less, Karen."

Chapter Fifty

Elfin was sitting in a Land Rover, observing the soldiers of Unit T moving forward to take the container. Karen initially was going to allow it to move on, to find out where it was going to end up. However, because of her intervention after Colin tried to take the money, she issued the order to secure the drugs.

Her soldiers met with quite a lot of opposition, taking nearly an hour to finally secure the container. This was primarily because the groups protecting the container had run out of ammunition. They had never considered a sustained attack from very experienced soldiers.

The lieutenant in charge walked over to the Land Rover, looking in at Elfin. "We've secured the container, Sir. Our Colonel would like you to confirm just what the substance is in the packages."

Elfin climbed out and made his way to the container. He looked at the test equipment on the table still outside it, then picked up a package, at first smelling it, then damping a finger and touching some of the powder. He brought his finger up to his tongue and tasted it. Finally using a little liquid from a bottle already open and still on the table, he mixed some of the powder in a small glass. The colour of the liquid changed as he'd expected.

"This is cocaine, no doubt about it. You should get these packages back into the container and secure it."

"Thank you, Sir," said the lieutenant, then he looked at two soldiers stood watching what Elfin was doing. "Get everything, including the table and test equipment into the container," he ordered, and then walked away, pulling his satellite communication unit from a pouch on his belt.

As the two soldiers carried all the packages back into the container, Elfin picked up a discarded mobile that had fallen to the ground. He'd noticed the mobile phone while he was testing the powder and kicked it gently further under the table and out of sight.

When a soldier came down from the container he stopped him. "I'm going to find a toilet in the house; do you want a hand before I go?"

The soldier shook his head. "No, Sir, we're fine."

Elfin went through into the house. It was empty; the gunmen were all outside sitting against a wall. Each had their ankles strapped together with a strong, nylon tie wrap, the same as their wrists which were tied behind their backs; other soldiers were guarding them. He found an upstairs room, where he could watch out to see if anyone approached the house, then pushed a few buttons on the mobile.

"It's me. The shipment is intact. There's ten SAS-trained soldiers guarding it. Potentially that could rise to twenty-five if the ones who went to secure the money join up now."

He listened.

"They're around twenty miles from here, which would mean they could be here within half an hour if they're needed. You must come in and strike fast."

Again he listened.

"Very well, I'll do that."

Elfin returned to the container. Already it had been loaded and locked up. He glanced around the area. The soldiers were still in a defensive position. They seemed to be waiting.

"What's the plan?" Elfin asked the lieutenant.

"We're waiting for the main group, including the Colonel, Sir. There's been a slight delay handing that side of the operation to the police. We expect them in about an hour."

Elfin opened a cigarette case, offering one to the lieutenant, before taking one himself.

"So do you often have delays then?" he asked, lighting his cigarette.

"Yes, there's a great deal of waiting around at times. It's part of the job, so we're used to it."

At that moment, the lieutenant's radio came to life.

"There are three lorries and four cars coming down the road towards you, Lieutenant," a soldier on point duty said.

"You're sure they're coming here?"

"Yes, Sir, they've slowed and are turning into the road leading directly to your position."

The lieutenant was just about to call his other soldiers when Elfin went for him, quickly sending him to the ground and snatching his handgun from its holster. Elfin, as a soldier himself, was well trained and very experienced. He raised the gun to the lieutenant's head. "You two drop your weapons, or the lieutenant dies," he barked.

They did as he asked.

"Now call the other soldiers and tell them to come into the compound."

One called them. Immediately a number of soldiers broke cover and came towards the container. At that moment, the cars and lorries turned in. Gunmen spilled out.

"These are all your group, Lieutenant?" Elfin asked.

"Yes."

Elfin turned to one of the gunmen. "Secure them, and take the weapons."

Five minutes later the container was on its way, with the cars and lorries following.

"What do we do, Lieutenant?" one of the soldiers asked, at the same time trying to release his bonds.

The lieutenant smiled. "Don't worry, our Colonel's very astute. She will have a contingency, believe me."

***

Karen was already on the road, heading towards the container when Stanley called. She placed an earphone in her ear. "What is it Stanley?"

"Your surveillance team has reported a number of vehicles entering the compound. They are not sure, but it looks as if our unit has been overcome. The container is now on its way with quite a convoy of vehicles following."

"Have we still our tracker on the vehicle carrying the container?"

"Yes."

"Then we take out the container, send in both helicopters. If the first strike doesn't confirm a complete destruction, order the second helicopter to go in."

"I'm calling them as we speak, Karen. Let's hope one is sufficient, the British will be a bit upset if we use both."

"I agree. Keep the channel open, Stan; we are now only fifteen minutes away from the compound."

***

Elfin was sitting smugly in the vehicle following the container. Karen's call and their subsequent conversation about the container had surprised him. Even before her call he'd known all about the cocaine consignment and had made arrangements to intercept it. As far as he was concerned, he'd a client who would pay a great deal for the cocaine, and he would have got it for nothing, save the hire of a few gunmen.

His meeting with Karen, at the embassy, was to ensure she had no interest in bringing Ignatius down, with his actions concerning drug dealing. He'd suspected that her intelligence might know about the US girls, so he didn't want her to get in the way of his operation. As it was, she'd been useful, by already securing the lorry, saving him the trouble.

Elfin's radio suddenly came to life. "You have two helicopters inbound, Elfin."

"Whose are they?"

"We don't know, both have a signature we have no record of."

"Shit, they sound like the ones belonging to Unit T. How far away are they?"

"At their current speed they will be within range of your convoy in ten minutes."

"Thanks, keep tracking them." Then Elfin changed the frequency of his radio, ordering the lorry carrying the container to turn off at the next turning before pulling in.

All the other vehicles followed. Elfin jumped out of the vehicle shouting at everyone. "We've two attack helicopters inbound, less than ten minutes away. Take up positions to protect the container." Then he called one of the men to him. "Check that lorry for a tracking device. There must be one for them to have found us."

After giving the gunmen their orders, he ran back to his vehicle. "Empty a couple of holdalls, and come with me," he told his driver, grabbing two himself off the back seat, pouring the contents out onto the ground.

Both men ran to the container, opened up the back, climbing inside and taking the lid off one of the crates. He and the man immediately began filling the holdalls with bags of cocaine from inside the crate, until they could get no more into the bags. Then jumping down from the trailer, they ran towards some trees for protection, crouching down. He looked at his watch, already he could hear the noise of the helicopter engines, they must be only minutes away.

He was right; the first one came in steeply, its guns blazing, forcing all aggressors to dive for cover. Seconds later the Stinger missile was launched, and the helicopter pulled away. Elfin crouched lower as the missile hit its target. The explosion literally blew the container apart, turning the contents into a fireball. Seconds later the second helicopter came in, except this time it veered away, deciding that another hit on the container wasn't necessary.

Elfin glanced at his driver. "Put the bags in the vehicle. We don't share this; it's our payment, understand?"

The man gave a hint of a smile. "I understand."

Chapter Fifty-One

Karen dismissed the lieutenant after his report. She returned to her Range Rover, closed the door and called Sir Peter direct. She gave him a short version of just what had happened over the last hours.

"My god, Karen, you never cease to amaze me. So was Elfin useful to you?"

"I was coming to that. Elfin was very useful, until he decided he should have the cocaine for himself. It was Elfin's men who took the cocaine off Unit T. This was a man I was supposed to trust?"

"I can't believe that, are you sure?"

"As sure as I can be. Apparently he had a gun and was giving the orders, so he wasn't taken as a hostage. The good news is he lost the shipment. My pilots confirm complete destruction of the container. The helicopters took a few hits, but nothing serious. You know, Peter, you begin to feel very alone, ending up trusting no one, only your own instincts. I'm supposed to be part of the military machine, all comrades and working to the same end, not that I can see much of that happening."

He felt for the girl; she sounded very down. "Now the operation is virtually over, Karen, why don't you take a break, not an odd weekend but a couple of weeks and switch the phone off? Maybe even take your sister or Sherry, and just chill out."

"I'll do that. Perhaps in a week or so. I've a lead on the Nigerians; those are three men who should be behind bars. I don't care what it takes, or how much resource I put in, but they will be caught, believe me."

"I'm with you on that, Karen. I know I shouldn't say it; after all, you always act in a professional manner, but don't let your emotions control the situation. We all have a real hatred for these people. They should stand trial and let the world see and hear just how bad it is out there for victims of trafficking."

"I understand and will do my best to bring them back, though, these are known killers with little respect for human life. I think they will want to fight it out, rather than going quietly."

"I agree with you there, but you do have a very experienced unit.

These men won't know what hit them until it's too late."

"I love the confidence you have in us, Peter. I'll talk to you soon."

***

Karen had returned to her unit's base, leaving her lieutenant to sort everything with the local police. She'd visited the location where the cocaine had been destroyed by the helicopter. All of Elfin's men had scattered, leaving only three badly damaged vehicles with the lorry that had transported the container. After looking at the devastation, she was convinced that it was no longer usable. By then, the police had arrived and were loading the damaged vehicles onto low-loaders, ready to take away for inspection.

Entering the main dining room, Sherry came up to her. She saluted.

"You did a good job Corporal; Hamon was very complimentary on how you conducted yourself."

"Thank you, but I did very little. His men are good, really good and had the place tied down in minutes. I was wondering, would you have time to meet the girls before they leave? They've all asked to meet you if I could arrange it for them."

"I was going to see them in the morning, there's a small amount of official explanations that they need to be aware of. But I'm happy to see them now before I go home to a long soak in the bath."

"I'm sorry, I didn't realise you were to meet them tomorrow. It's just that they told me how well known you are in the US; it's kept their spirits up to have been rescued by your unit, and they wanted to meet you."

"Come on then, let's go and meet them, shall we?"

As they left the dining room Karen stopped Sherry out of earshot of everyone. "You haven't mentioned anything about how we could have pulled them out far earlier than we did, have you?"

She shook her head. "No, I've mentioned nothing."

"Let's keep it that way, listen to my explanation and don't elaborate when I've gone. Particularly why they weren't taken when they left the container ship, or even back in the US at the warehouse. You and I know that we could have saved them from the humiliation and abuse in the brothel, but for operational reasons we had to let it run."

"I understand and will say nothing beyond keeping their spirits up."

Karen followed Sherry to another building. This was used to keep any victims that had been rescued during operations, before they were sent back to their own country. The building was laid out to give the impression that it was a house, rather than part of the barracks. Each room was carpeted, with plenty of comfortable corners with huge wraparound settees. There was also a kitchen that had all the appliances necessary. When occupied, social workers and trauma professionals would be there. Not in uniforms but casual clothes, lounging about on the three settees, talking to the victims in a relaxed and carefully controlled environment.

They found the girls all sat together in one of the lounges, holding mugs of coffee. They looked round to see who had come in. Everyone recognised Karen immediately, and they ran over, each giving her a hug. Then she joined them on the settee.

"It's great to see you all looking so well. I hope Sherry has been looking after you? I'm really sorry not to have been there when you came out, but we had a huge operation going on."

"We understand, Karen," Emma answered for them all. "When Sherry told us it was a Unit T operation, we all wanted to meet you. You're dead famous in the States, you know?"

"How did you know where we were taken?" Mia asked.

"We didn't at first. We knew you were on the ship; after all we'd managed to get Sherry aboard. The problem was we were waiting for it to dock to collect you, except the container numbers we had been given were wrong; you weren't inside, so the traffickers managed to get you out of the docks before we realised this. You can imagine it left us in a little panic trying to pick up the trail once more."

Karen had answered in this way, so as not to admit they could have pulled them out a great deal earlier than they had. Her delay, however, allowed the girls to be abused in the brothels before they finally came for them.

Emma, who had been badly abused, wasn't convinced. "But if you knew we were on the ship, why didn't you stop it?"

"You were in international waters and you have to remember there were hundreds of containers on that ship. The search could have taken days and even then we may not have found where they'd hidden you all. So while you were aboard, you were perfectly safe. Uncomfortable, yes, and like I said, we were waiting at the dock." Although Karen had known the container numbers, she'd taken this way to reply, so the girls were able to understand how difficult it could have been trying to find them on the ship.

"Well I for one am very grateful you were coming. If you'd taken weeks to come I'd still have been grateful," Lauren cut in. "When do we go home, I've spoken to mom, but I couldn't give her any details as to what was happening."

"I've arranged a flight to Paris the day after tomorrow. From there, you will be looked after by the US consulate before they put you on a flight home."

"Why can't we go today, or even tomorrow?" Emma asked.

"I know you want to go home, Emma, every girl here does," Karen began. "But you should understand the position you're all in. This is not the US, but Europe. You of course know that, but the distinction is important. You've entered the European Union illegally. How you got here is not an issue, except we can't just send you home. Your repatriation back to your own country requires acceptance by US Immigration. This was why we took your names, addresses and photographs of each of you. We've sent these details to the French government which in turn has informed your consulate." Karen stopped and looked around at all the girls listening intently to her. "I know it all sounds very long-winded, but dealings between governments are always at a diplomatic level, I can't just ring your moms and ask them to take you home. I've spoken to officials in the French Ministry of Immigration this morning. They tell me the US consulate in Paris is currently arranging travel documents; their attaché will be arriving here tomorrow to interview each one of you. The attaché will need to officially confirm you are who you say you are, before your own country will accept you back. You have to understand, anyone could say they had been abducted, just to get into the US or any other country for that matter. Of course, that is the diplomatic route, as by

274

now, your family will have been visited. Photos of you, maybe even your passport, if you have one, will have been collected. So all this will be a formality; even so it has to be done this way."

"God, Karen, I never realised it would be so complicated, I just thought we'd go home," Lauren said, a little stunned.

Karen smiled. "Well if we don't do it that way, we're stuck with you. You'd just end up lazing around my swimming pool, partying in the camp social club at night and eating all our food."

Mia laughed. "And here's us wanting to go home, Sherry never told us there was another option."

"Well it's too late now, you're all going home. But seriously, tomorrow is going to be a very full day for you all. We've left you alone today to settle, but in the morning you will need to fill a statement out as to exactly what happened to you, from the time you were abducted to the rescue. This is followed by your interview with the US attaché in the afternoon. I'm afraid our report is very detailed; you will need to think about what you are going to say." She stopped yet again, looking around at them all watching and listening to her. "Both myself and Sherry have been through what you have all experienced. Making a statement forces you to relive what you'd rather forget. But I can't emphasise the importance of this report. It not only forms a basis for any future prosecutions of the perpetrators, but gives us a picture of the route and the methods they are adopting. What you say could help others later if it happens again, and believe me, it will happen to other girls. We can only stick together, help paint a picture, so one day we can be more proactive in helping or preventing it happening to others. You may not believe that, but if you'd been taken even a year back, your chances of being rescued would have been very low. That is how far we've come, so it may not be perfect, and yes, often we are too late to prevent abuse, but we do our best."

"We all understand, Karen, and thank you for taking the time to tell us what's going on," Emma said.

Karen glanced at her watch. "I'm going to have to go now. As tomorrow night is your last night with us, rather than sit around here, I've arranged that you come to my house for dinner. There we will have a barbecue by the side of the pool, a little music and dancing. If you'd all like to come, that is?"

Everyone wanted to go, and they told her so; asking if Sherry was going as well.

Karen stood. "Of course she is; I also think Sherry should take you to the camp shop later; they have quite a nice range of clothes, so you should find something to wear, and I'll see you all tomorrow night." After Karen left they began talking among themselves.

"I really can't believe she was so nice and approachable," Mia said.

"Karen's always been the same, when she came for me she was just as laid-back," Sherry added.

"What sort of house is it, Sherry?" Lauren asked.

Sherry laughed. "You are not going to believe it. It's huge with around ten bedrooms."

"So is she dead rich then?" Mia wanted to know.

"I can't tell you, I don't know. You have to remember I'm just a corporal, Karen's a lieutenant colonel. We are worlds apart in status, believe me. But you're going to be very impressed, and the food is out of this world."

Chapter Fifty-Two

Ignatius spent less than two days in custody. No charges were brought against him from Unit T, the fact he was carrying a gun had not been mentioned in the police reports. This was a technical oversight, as he'd given his gun to Karen, who had not passed on the information to the French police. Blas was the same. Both he and Ignatius claimed they were in a business meeting, when Colin burst in shooting, demanding money they knew nothing about and didn't have.

Returning to his house in Germany, Ignatius was in the lounge with another Russian called Nickita. Nickita was in his late fifties, ex-KGB; he was a ruthless man, demanding respect at all times. Although if you met this man on the street, his five foot three inch stature, with a balding head and heavy rimmed glasses, gave no impression of the sort of person he really was.

"I don't like this girl, she's unpredictable and has a reputation that would make even the old guard look like pussycats," Nickita commented, after listening to what had transpired with Blas.

"You are correct in many respects, but if it hadn't been for the intervention of her unit, then I'd probably be dead, the money gone. There's a belief within our organisation that this was the work of the Ndrangheta cartel."

"That is true, but it still does not take away the uneasiness I have in us dealing with her. Then these Nigerians you intend to hand over? They have paid us good money to be lost."

"They haven't paid us three hundred million dollars. Karen never gave the names of the shell companies away; and then, she still has five million of that money which she will hand back. Personally I have no qualms about giving her the information she will need to take them out. In all my time in 'trafficking', I've never killed for the sake of it. These men have knocked the industry back years with their stupidity."

Nickita shrugged indifferently. "Very well, go ahead and give her the information she's waiting for. For me, trafficking is far too much effort for little return; we should have never gone into it. After all, just one kilo of cocaine can earn more for us than a girl working two years."

"I'll make the arrangements then."

"Ignatius, be warned, if this backfires and she doesn't hand over the money, your own life will be at risk. Make very sure she does keep her end of the bargain, for your sake."

"What option do I have?"

"Very little it would seem. So just get us our money and close this chapter."

Chapter Fifty-Three

Karen was in London; she had two appointments, one at the United States Embassy, the other with Sir Peter for lunch.

Her black Range Rover drew up outside the embassy on time. Waved through the usual tight security for visitors, after showing her military pass, she was shown into the ambassador's private office.

"Colonel, it's good to meet you again," the ambassador said, shaking hands with her.

"Yes, Ambassador, it's been a long time. I hope the family's keeping well?"

"Very well thank you. May I pour you coffee?" he asked, walking over to a side table.

Karen took her coffee and sat down. She was a little nervous being here, knowing full well it wasn't going to be just a handshake, and a thank you for finding the girls. Another man had joined them, and was introduced as Chas Roper, but not the part of government he was from. Karen in turn had asked that they call her Karen, rather than her official title.

"The American government has requested that I convey our sincere thanks to you in finding the girls abducted and sent across to Europe, Karen," the ambassador began, after they had all settled down. "It was a very professional and efficient operation. Chas here has requested that he attends this meeting; he has a number of questions he believes you may be able to help us with. You see, the investigation as to just how these girls were taken and why, is still ongoing back home."

"I will do my best to help, Ambassador, although for us too, the abduction of the girls is still part of a complex and ongoing investigation. I don't want to compromise that in any way."

"We understand, Karen, and accept any limitations that you feel are necessary. Perhaps if I ask Chas to tell you what we already know, you may feel it appropriate to fill in some of our gaps?"

"Then I'm happy to answer your questions, now we both understand our position," she replied.

"I appreciate you agreeing to help, Karen," Chas began. "But first can you tell us why you went to America under your family name, and didn't inform us you were going?"

"I went as a tourist and not officially. Sometimes it's nice to get away from everything and just be a normal person on vacation. I do have permission from your immigration department to come to your country, and use the passport issued under my family name. I often attract a great deal of media interest using my official name and title."

"I'm very aware of the different arrangements you are able to use, in visiting our country, Karen, but please give us a little credit. We know you went into our country on a covert mission. You also used a Naval Officer called Caleb, picked up by you and another girl Sherry Malloy in Cannes, to join you in Florida to support the fact that you were on holiday. Except you used this holiday to visit a Harry Watson on two occasions we know of. We looked into Watson's background and found it very interesting, he was part of an investigation into people trafficking. He has not been seen for some weeks now. Don't get me wrong, we understand you wouldn't waste your time going all that way unless it had a bearing on something big going down in Europe. We would like to know what it was all about and if it involved United States citizens."

Karen took time in answering, by taking the opportunity to sip her coffee. They waited in anticipation, hoping Chas had said enough for her to give a response of value.

"I liked Caleb; he was a nice man and we had a good time. But you are correct; I did visit Harry while I was there. But you won't find Harry Watson now, he's dead. Killed, I believe, by the Los Zetas cartel. We knew that an Italian criminal gang known as the Ndrangheta, wanted to abduct girls from your country to use in the European brothels. What we didn't know at that stage was that there was a tie-up with the Los Zetas cartel and more importantly, why."

"But why didn't you tell us?" Chas asked.

"It had been just rumours and what was proposed didn't seem credible."

"You mean the abduction of the girls?"

"Of course. Who in their right mind would go to the expense of abducting six girls from different parts of your country to take across the world and place in a brothel? The cost of doing such a thing would be stupid in the extreme. Unless the girls had been pre-sold to private buyers, then of course the value would be very high, and so it would make sense."

"And you're sure that wasn't to be the case?"

"No, not at the time, it only became apparent later when they were dumped in two brothels. Both pretty low-grade ones at that, which would pay very little for them."

"After the girls had been abducted and were still in America, why didn't you contact us then. We could have set up surveillance and pulled them out?"

Karen looked at them watching her. "It wasn't necessary to involve you. We had it under control, in fact, we'd also replaced one of the girls with one of our own and they were on their way to our own backyard so to speak. So they were perfectly safe. The point is the whole operation was setting alarm bells ringing. With the major question on our lips. Why?"

"Did you find the answer?" the ambassador cut in.

"Yes. Although it wasn't the answer we expected. We believed the girls were going to private buyers and wanted them to lead us to these buyers. That was the main reason I didn't pull them out. You see, my remit is not to help the victims; their collection is academic within an operation; I'm after the traffickers themselves."

"We are aware of your remit, Karen," Chas began. "Which is why we were a little upset that you didn't see fit to let us pull them out earlier. Although now, we understand that you were protecting them."

"You mentioned that you now know why, Karen, are you prepared to elaborate?" the ambassador asked.

"I am. The girls were a cover, a means of directing interest in the ship they came in on, for the importation from your country into Europe, of what we believe was to be upwards of ten tons of cocaine. I don't need to tell you the value of such a consignment on the open market."

"You're very certain of this?" Chas asked.

"Not at first, but when we found where the girls were bound, we began to take more interest in what was happening in the dock.

A comment made by our covert operator was the key to the answer. We were given to understand by Watson that the girls were to be transported in two containers, both of which were allowed to leave the European port without being searched, to enable us to track the girls. Our operator reported that only one container was used, not two. But both went to the same location. The Los Zetas cartel had killed Harry. Both they and the Ndrangheta were heavily into drugs, and finally I heard that the Russian mafia was in the market for buying a huge amount of cocaine. With all this information, it was obviously a drug deal going down. But it was so huge that even to mention we knew this could have attracted informers, which could have meant a change in the arrangements."

"What happened to the cocaine, Karen?" the ambassador wanted to know.

Karen gave an indifferent shrug. "After my unit had confirmed we had the actual container containing the cocaine, I blew it to pieces with one of my Stinger missiles. It should serve as a very costly warning to both the Italian and Mexican cartels; they can't ship their death into Europe without the risk of losing it all. As for the girls, they were used as pawns in this game; by both sides I'm afraid. That is one of the hazards of being abducted. Could we have brought them out earlier? Of course, but I'm afraid the cocaine had become a far more valuable prize than the girls as far as I was concerned. It was capable of destroying hundreds if not thousands of lives, if we'd lost that container."

"I don't really know what to say, Karen. This is unbelievable. You have done the world a service no one will ever know about and as you say, hit the cartels very hard. What is your view, Chas?"

"I have to agree, we couldn't have done more."

Karen suddenly had an idea. "I'm glad you agree with what we did, as I was going to ask if you could help me out."

"In what way?" the ambassador asked.

"The missile we used was one of two on loan from the UK. They are pretty expensive, and the military isn't very pleased with me so they won't lend me another. I don't suppose you have a spare one knocking about do you? After all, it was your cocaine we destroyed, well, owned by one of your criminal cartels?"

The two men looked at each other, then began to laugh.

"I will pass your request onto our President, Karen. I think he will be very interested in what has happened; one of the girls involved came from his hometown, and he knows the family well."

Karen's heart sank. When he found out how she had used the girl, the president would not be too pleased, although she put on a brave face. "Well, see what you can do, I'd appreciate any help he can give me."

She glanced at her watch. "I have to go now, I've another appointment in London, then I want to be in Manchester tonight to see my family."

They all stood and shook her hand.

"It's always pleasant to see you, Karen. You must join my family for dinner one night," the ambassador said.

"Thank you, I'd love to," she answered with a smile.

When she left, Chas returned to his seat, the ambassador to his.

"She was very straight with us over the whole operation. We'd not tied the girls' abductions with the drug shipment like she did," Chas said.

"So you knew about the drug shipment?"

"Yes we knew, but we wanted to know who the purchaser was," Chas said quietly.

"Then Karen messed it up for you?"

"I'm not sure. You see we had used a contact in the Russian embassy called Elfin to try to find out if it was the Russian Mafia buying the shipment. Logically they were the only operation large enough and with the funds. He was supposed to come back to us after he had used his contacts to find out. This didn't happen, in fact, according to another contact we have in the embassy, he's gone missing. They are very concerned, and we can't get in touch with him either. As for Karen, even she's not telling us everything, not that I expected her to."

"Like what, after all, she explained the girls and told us about the drugs."

"She did, except what happened to the money? Were the newspaper reports of gangland types of shoot-out close to the border of Germany connected with the drug shipment? Then where did the Ndrangheta come in to all this? I believe whatever happened is still going on, although the actual shipment has been destroyed."

"I'll need to make a report for the President's eyes only. What is your opinion on her request for a replacement missile?"

"You should try to get her help. Her budget is low, and she does a very good job even though at times she is a little unconventional. The value of that container was such that many charged with the task of destroying it, would have succumbed to very large financial offers to leave it alone. I don't think she would have done that, no matter how much they offered her."

The ambassador finished his notes. "Very well, thank you for attending, Chas. It will be interesting to see the final outcome. I suspect Karen will still have a few surprises left for us."

Chapter Fifty-Four

Returning to France the next day, Karen stopped off in Paris. She checked into a top hotel, spent the afternoon shopping and had only just finished dressing when the telephone rang.

"Your visitor has arrived madam, he will be waiting in the residents' bar as you requested," the receptionist on the hotel desk told her.

She thanked her; then after checking herself once again in the mirror, she left the room.

"Hi, Hamon," Karen said, as she approached him from behind. He was standing at the bar waiting for the bartender to serve him.

He turned, smiled and embraced her. "You look absolutely gorgeous tonight, Karen. Tight, short dresses really suit you."

"Thank you, have you ordered drinks yet?"

"I'm trying, mind you, I wouldn't order yours until you were here. I remember the last time you refused to take a drink from me, as you'd not seen it poured."

"Habit, Hamon I'm afraid. I once had my drinks laced and came very close to losing my life. I know it's not guaranteed, even watching them being made; it just gives me a little more confidence that I'm in control; that's all."

By now the bartender had taken their order, so, after collecting the drinks, they found a quiet corner to settle down in.

"I've checked, it's been nearly five months since we had dinner, Karen. This is not good, apart from which the snow has long since gone, and I wanted to take you to see our chalet in the mountains."

She gave him a smile. "Well all's not lost, Hamon, snow has a habit of coming back again. But I really would like to go, it sounds fantastic."

They sipped their drinks for a moment. Then Hamon put his down and looked at her. "Tell me, is this meeting a date, or official, with dinner thrown in, paid for by me?"

"Both, but more so a date if you want it that way; as for the dinner, you owe me one and I have bought a new dress to wear tonight. Besides that, the hotel room cost me a fortune."

"Yes well, I'm not that lucky; I don't stay at five star hotels in Paris like you seem to. The EU must pay you very well, that's all I can think. As for a date, I like that idea a great deal. So let's get rid of the official business first, then we can relax, maybe go to a late club."

"That sounds good," she replied enthusiastically. "So the official bit, well the potted version. I know where the three Nigerian traffickers are; I want you to come with me and bring them out."

He looked at her for a moment. "That is a strange request, what's wrong with Dark Angel?"

She shook her head. "You don't understand; it's only us two and two Russians, who have already spent time on surveillance for me. You see they're in Istanbul, well just outside. We would have to go in as tourists; the Russians will meet us there, with all the intelligence we need."

"Why do you want me?"

"You're the best. Very experienced in this sort of operation, and I'd trust you with my life. If we go the official route, it's unlikely that we'd get them extradited and by the time we do, they'd have moved on. We go in, capture, then take them to the coast, where there will be a ship waiting to take them back to the EU."

"You'd never get away with it. They'd scream abduction from the highest mountain. Then whose ship will be waiting to take them back to Europe?"

She looked a little sheepish. "It wouldn't be exactly a ship, more a small powered yacht I've had an idea to charter for the month, ostensibly for a holiday. Besides, they wouldn't be able to scream abduction, who'd believe them? I'd leave them in France, then call the police and tell them who and where they are."

"Can you actually sail a boat and more importantly, do you know how far that is and how long you'd take?"

She shook her head. "You said you could sail, last time we were together and no, I've not a clue how long it would take. I've looked at cruise ships, they only take a few days to cross the Med." Then she grinned. "But you'd have me for company. I can cook, and we could sit under the stars together, maybe even make love."

"Karen, how did I ever get mixed up with you; you're talking at least 1800 nautical miles to Marseille, even at ten knots that's eight days, then we'd need to stop off for fuel adding another day. As for the romance, we'd have three prisoners aboard; they'd need to be watched 24-7; with the only good thing I can see out of this, is that you want our relationship to become more intimate."

Karen sighed. "Well I didn't say my idea was perfect. I suppose I'll just have to use the police there, or maybe call the military, once I find out it is them, and what they are up to. They do have laws in Turkey that are pretty tough on child murderers and traffickers, that's if I can convince them to make an arrest."

He said nothing for a short time, deep in thought. This girl was mad, except if he said no, there was every chance that she'd still go alone. "You're really serious about doing this?"

"Deadly, Hamon; those men butchered so many young children in an effort to cover their tracks; I'd personally just go and put a bullet in each of their heads. But Sir Peter wants them to stand trial. To let the world see what we do with murderers. I suppose that's okay with me; they'll spend their lives behind bars even if it's in Turkey. Plenty of time for them to think about what may have been?"

"The Russians, can you trust them?"

Karen gave a weak smile; then shrugged. "Can you trust anyone in this world? But they are the Mafia, and I have quite a hold over them. Well, a few million of theirs. So even if they were not to be trusted, by killing or imprisoning me they would never get at the money. Anyway they're only taking us to the house and have done the initial surveillance. After that, they go; then we're on our own."

Hamon narrowed his eyes. "So where did you get their money?"

"It's best you don't know, but believe me they want it back and this is the only way they're going to get it."

"One other thing, does anyone at the Unit know just where you're going?"

"I've not told anyone, if that's what you mean?"

"Then, Karen, you tell someone you trust. If anything goes wrong, we're out on a limb, you in particular."

She nodded. "I promise I'll tell Sherry where I am, she'll say nothing."

He sighed. "Well I suppose I'd better tag along, someone has to look after you. But we only survey; I'm not letting you go in with all guns blazing, we get the info and talk to the police." Then he hesitated. "Maybe I have that the wrong way round. Someone has to look after me."

Karen leaned across and kissed him on the lips. "Thank you, Hamon. We do it your way. We go in two days. Now business is over, you owe me dinner and a night out."

"You're always getting your own way, Karen, but there is no chance of me staying all night with you tonight. After all, I presume as usual you have soldiers protecting you discreetly? I'm not going down in some log that will remain on a military report just because I stayed in your room. Our love life, if we ever have one, remains private."

She laughed. "You are funny, you French. What's all this boasting about being the famous lovers, climbing across balconies to be with their woman and yet you're afraid of a couple of my soldiers knowing you'd made love to me."

"You're right, what the hell; but can I rely on a particularly attractive and sexy girl waiting for me, and by the morning she will find my comments of a few days back, how well she'll sleep after a night of making love, really is true?"

Karen opened her bag and pulled out a door card, placing it on the table. "I thought you'd never ask, Hamon. Except there are no soldiers, the only one around here is you. But before you pick it up, please don't come if you just want me for a conquest, or a one-night stand. I've had that all my life and although I don't expect you to fall madly in love with me, or even ask me to marry you, I like to believe a man who takes me to bed, has enough respect for me to want to be with me for longer than a night."

He reached over and grasped her hand. "You had better believe it; I'm going to be around for a great deal longer than a night, Karen. You've escaped once; I'm not going to let it happen again."

Chapter Fifty-Five

Two days after meeting Karen in Paris, they were both in Istanbul. Karen had booked a room in advance, and now they were checked in.

Hamon shut the door of the hotel room and looked around. "We seem to have one double bed. After our time in Paris, I think you just wanted me to yourself, and there are no Nigerians here," he ribbed, at the same time placing their bags in a corner.

Karen laughed, coming up to him, kissing him gently on the lips. "I really wish that was the case and we were just a couple on holiday, except this is as serious as it gets. I don't mix business with pleasure; it dulls the mind. We need just a couple of days to get enough info to put the Nigerians behind bars. Then for the rest of the week, I'll be the perfect lover. Believe me. If you think Paris was good, that is nothing to what I'm really capable of," she said tongue in cheek. If he knew the truth; which was she'd only had one lover at seventeen. Since then, apart from a few casual relationships, that she'd bailed on in only days, her only experience had been at the hands of traffickers. They, for her, were more rapists than lovers.

"You're right, Karen. We should never mix our professional relationship with our personal one. Let's get this operation over, then you can show me more of the other side of Karen Harris."

"I'm looking forward to that, Hamon." Then she began pulling her top off, at the same time walking towards the bathroom. "Right, I'm having a quick shower, we should eat early. We're due to meet the Russians at nine tonight, they will have all the information on the surveillance they've been conducting over the last few days."

***

Karen, with Hamon beside her, was sitting in a small bar. Opposite was the Russian, Oleg. He was a well-built and thick-set man in his early thirties. His partner, called Serrei, a man in his twenties, tall, muscular and very good-looking, was standing at the bar chatting to the girl behind the counter.

"The brothel is legal and registered for ten working girls," Oleg began. "Also all the girls are registered with the government as prostitutes. That is the main house at the front. They have a welcome lounge, where the girls show-off on a small stage by pole dancing and mingle with clients, agree a price and then go to their rooms. That part of the brothel seems to be run by Iroatu, one of your Nigerians. Serrei has been inside the registered part of the brothel as a client but didn't select a girl. After rejecting the girls on offer, he was asked if he preferred a younger girl around the age of eleven. He was told for fifty dollars he could have a private viewing of younger girls. Then for a further three to five hundred dollars, he could have one of them."

"Did he take them up?" Karen asked.

"The viewing yes. He was met by Igbo, another of your Nigerians, and shown five girls - three black girls, one Asian and a white girl. The girls' ages were between eleven and sixteen. He was allowed, for his fifty dollars, to have one strip so he could see her body. He did have one strip, told them he'd think about it and left."

Karen was interested in this specials viewing room. "These girls, are they kept in the same area?"

"No, he was taken through a door off the hall, along a passage then through a steel door that had the words 'Fire Escape' printed on. Only it didn't go outside, but into another house. The layout was similar, with a waiting lounge and one viewing room. The only difference was that the girls didn't come into the main lounge, which just had a large television showing porn."

"Then we have at least five underage girls, maybe," Karen said, thinking aloud. "The problem I can see is separating the children from the Nigerians. We can't have a repeat of London. The Nigerians, do they own the brothel, or are they running the place for someone else, Oleg?"

"We don't know. It did belong to a man called Pular. He may have sold it."

"What about the local police?"

He shrugged. "I'm not sure if they will be interested, or how entrenched the local station is with the illegal operation. I've logged six from the department using the brothel. They may just be in the legal section; I don't know, without following them in, and observing if they stay in the main lounge, or go through the fire door."

Karen thought for a short time. "What do you know about the general legal operation of the brothel?"

"They open Wednesday to Sunday and close the other days. The hours seem to be midday to two in the morning. But if you count how many go in, and how many leave at that time, there would be around six staying overnight, particularly on Fridays and Saturdays. They must use the illegals then as most if not all the registered prostitutes have left. Oh, they close early on Sunday night, at twelve. They have security made up of around fifteen men, who take shifts through the times they are open and four women who we think do the cleaning. Serrei has seen the telltale bulges under the security men's jackets of shoulder holsters, so we must assume they know how to handle themselves. If they don't, so be it, but don't be complacent. Most of the security lives outside, only three live on the premises. We've surmised that, as they don't go home like the others. On the days the brothel's shut, only two of the cleaners turn up. Again we are not sure if they have other women in the house that permanently live there. If they do, we've seen none come out. As for the licensed prostitutes, they come and go all the time; none live there."

"Do the Nigerians?" Karen asked.

"We think so, the place is large enough. Although they are in and out all the time. One of the Nigerians goes out every night with a van, which they keep in an area to the side that has large doors. These are closed when the van is in so you can't see what they are unloading."

"How long would the van be away?"

"Around seven Monday to Friday, and it returns about one in the morning."

"We need to see just where that van goes. It could help in splitting them up. One of us has to follow."

"I agree; I'll hire a car," Hamon said.

The Russian stood, handing her a notebook. Serrei broke away from the girl at the bar and joined them. "Everything we've told you, plus times and dates is in there. We've completed what Ignatius wanted of us. You're on your own. We leave later tonight. Good luck, you've enough in there to bring them down."

"Thank you, Oleg, and you Serrei. Both of you have been

291

brilliant. Tell Ignatius I'll be in touch with him next week will you," Karen said, at the same time standing, then embracing each one of them in turn.

"We will tell him." Then they walked away.

Chapter Fifty-Six

Chuks walked through from the client lounge into a private room off the main entrance hall. Iroatu was already in the room, so too was Igbo.

"It seems like the investment of giving the Russian Serrei our twelve-year-old for free, was the right thing to do. He has just called to tell me Karen Harris has booked into a local hotel under the name Marshall. She's with a man from the French gendarmerie, called Clavier. They will be taking over surveillance," Chuks said, sitting down.

"What should we do," Iroatu asked. "I'm not prepared to keep moving across the world, having to keep setting up with Unit T following."

"We take them out, it's no problem," Chuks replied.

Igbo nodded his agreement. "We do, but only the man, I suggest we use the Harris girl."

"What for?" Iroatu wanted to know.

Igbo laughed. "With her on cocaine, her hair cut and dyed, no one would recognise her. Then I'll put her to work servicing clients for a few weeks, before offering her to the highest bidder. Many of her enemies would relish gutting her, like the pig she is."

"Then what are we waiting for?" Iroatu replied enthusiastically.

"There's a problem using cocaine," Chuks cut in. "They stink; throw up all the time, and it's like shagging a rag doll. The clients we have expect top quality girls, not some pumped-up junkie on cocaine all the time. They wouldn't pay the sort of money we'd want for her. I've a far better idea. When I was in the Nigerian army, we'd used the drug we nicknamed chewy, made from plants in the forest, on the convicts. Give me a week with her on chewy, followed by a final two days on overdose and the memories of her past life will be destroyed irreversibly. But more importantly, she'd be off any drugs. The girl will be normal, except she'd have lost all memories of who, or where she came from, being totally reliant on us, every day of her life from then," Chuks finished, with a hint of satisfaction in his voice.

"I'd be surprised if you break her that easily," Iroatu commented.

"You look after the clients, Iroatu, leave the girl to me, I'll break her, you can be sure of that."

Iroatu had another concern. "I hope you're not going to use her afterwards in this brothel. We get far too many tourists; one's bound to recognise her and inform the authorities, if not in this country then back home, especially when it becomes public knowledge that she's missing."

Chuks shook his head. "You're right, except I could replace Charlene, bring her inside and use the Harris girl to service our lucrative hotel round for a few weeks. After her hair is cut and dyed, no one will know her. With her memory destroyed, even if any client asks her questions about her past, maybe believing they're with Karen, she'd genuinely not be able to tell them. Added to this, using the hotel round, she'll become very experienced in working with difficult clients without objection. After that, we'll offer her to the more discerning clients who pay well. She's still very attractive; some don't like the young girls, preferring one older, well broken in, submissive and prepared to do anything they want."

"That's a good idea, Chuks, so you'll be keeping her at the farm then?" Igbo asked.

"Yes, it's best we don't work her from here. She'd have to be put with the young girls, and they could mention something to a client. It'll be a bit of a pain running back and forth for the next week, till we get a new batch from Africa for breaking in there, but for me it'll be well worth the trouble, watching her slowly being destroyed."

"So let's do it?" Iroatu said with enthusiasm.

"All in good time," Chuks replied. "I'll check out the hotel they're staying in. Ask around and make sure they're alone."

At that moment a young African girl knocked on their door and came in carrying a tray with drinks. She was thirteen, brought in only three days before and put to work as a taster for the clients by delivering drinks to them.

Chuks watched her as she placed the drinks and took the empties. She left the room. "We got a good batch this last time. Just the right age I think. After Friday we'll be down to only two specials, the rest already sold. So until we get the next batch, put that girl up for bids tonight, Igbo, with a starting price of four hundred dollars. It's time she understood what was expected of her."

"No problems, Chuks. Nazim is in later, he'll outbid everyone."

***

The following night, after the last clients had left, Igbo and Iroatu were alone in their lounge when Chuks came in.

"I've had a call from the night porter at Karen's hotel. He told me both have just gone to their room, and he'll let us in through the rear hotel door. They've probably been watching this place and gone back when we closed. Let's go and collect her." He grinned. "This is one snatch I'm really looking forward to, she cost us plenty in London, now she's about to pay us back."

***

Chuks was driving the van used to take girls to private parties; the other two Nigerians were with him.

"When we get there, Iroatu, you put a bullet in the man's head. Igbo, you get her out the bed. Once she's ready to go, we collect and bag everything up of hers and don't forget the bathroom. I've arranged with the owner of the hotel to claim the man came alone. He's a regular at the brothel, and I said we'd give him a few free sessions for his trouble," Chuks told them.

Parking up behind the hotel, they were let in by the night porter at the rear entrance as arranged; then quickly made their way up the emergency exit stairs to the floor where Karen and Hamon had a room. Chuks, using the porter's spare key to open the door, pushed it slightly open. Then with a bolt cutter slid between the door and the door jamb, he cut through the night chain. They all moved inside; two heads could be seen in bed, with a light duvet covering them, both were obviously asleep. Iroatu walked over to Hamon's side and shot him immediately through the head, while Igbo grabbed Karen's hair and wrenched her head back, pushing his gun into her face; Chuks closed the bedroom door, before turning on the light.

"Off the bed very slowly, any sudden movement and I'll blow your fucking head off," Igbo, still holding her hair, said quietly.

Karen could see the quickly enlarging pool of blood around

Hamon's head as she slid off the bed and stood, with the man still gripping her hair. She felt sick inside; she knew he was dead, and it was her fault. Chuks came up to her, sticking duck tape over her mouth, before binding her wrists in front of her with more tape. Pulling a bag over her head, Chuks kept a tight grip on her arm, while Igbo took her case from out of the wardrobe, then began filling it with her clothes from the drawers. They searched everywhere, including the bathroom and soon everything was packed in her suite case. Then she was guided through the bedroom door, down the corridor and into the fire escape stairwell. Minutes later she was pushed into the back of a van, and it sped away.

***

Karen was not taken to the brothel. She was driven out to the old farmhouse the Nigerians had talked about and taken down into the cellar, stripped of her tee-shirt and knickers, before being sat on a chair firmly bolted to the floor. This was located in an otherwise empty room, apart from a bucket in the corner with a short blue painted rod inside, the other end of the rod leaning on the back wall. Alongside the bucket was a cat-o'-nine-tails, a multi-tailed leather whip with a stubby handle.

Both her wrists had been handcuffed to the chair arms; her ankles secured by ankle irons, with a chain attached between them. The chain was long enough to have allowed her to walk around, if her wrists were not secured to the chair, but she'd not have been able to run. Karen was left alone, still with the bag over her head.

Karen was already very scared. The last time she was in the hands of traffickers, she had been eighteen. Then she had value, to be sold to a private buyer, or used in a brothel. This time would be different, she was all too aware at her age, most brothels wouldn't take her. Even the Nigerians had no girls over twenty, so the very least she could expect would be pain and abuse of her body, before they killed her. Her hair-brained scheme to take them down was now in pieces and Hamon dead. Only Sherry knew where she was, but she had promised to tell no-one; except Sherry was expecting a text every other day, saying Karen was okay, and today one such text had been sent.

296

***

It was over an hour before Chuks came back to the farm. He was alone; the other two had returned to the brothel. His delay had been deliberate, giving time for the fear of what might happen next to build up inside her. He pulled the bag off her head, removed the tape covering her mouth, then stood back looking at her for a moment before moving closer, grabbing her hair, forcing her head back, his face inches from hers. The aggression in his manner made her shrink back further into the chair.

"You cost us plenty in London and should already be swimming in a pool of your own stinking blood alongside your boyfriend. But we've decided that, for you, it was too simple a death. From now on, you will suffer the humiliation of what should have happened to you ten years back, every fucking day of your miserable life. Maybe you're wondering how we found you? Let me say just this. Never send a man into a brothel who's broke, particularly one who likes twelve-year-olds. They will sell anything, even you, to fulfil their lust." Chuks let go of her hair and stood back.

Karen couldn't believe how stupid she'd been, not to take simple precautions, such as placing a chair up to the door, in fact, anything that would have given them prior warning of an intruder. She'd acted as if she was invincible, now she was going to pay the price.

"Anyway, time's money and you have a choice. This time next week, with a new name I've chosen for you, which is Amber, you'll be servicing six to eight clients a night. I presume by your age you know how to shag?"

She looked back at him, hate in her eyes. "You're dead, Unit T will come for you one day, and you can forget any ideas about putting me to work, it won't happen. I'm Karen Harris and will never lower myself to be a prostitute. So you'd better get it over with and kill me."

Chuks grinned from ear to ear. "Oh, Amber, and you notice I'm already calling you by your new name, I'm glad you flatly refused to accept my offer to provide you with meaningful work. I'd have been very disappointed if you'd just agreed and accepted the job. But your belief I'd end it all for you, by placing a gun to your head, won't happen. You see, Amber, many girls in your position over the years, sitting on a similar chair, naked and vulnerable, have said exactly the same thing to me. Except even you should understand if everyone we abducted wanted to die and we obliged, we'd have no girls to use. But for me, you're special and you cannot even begin to imagine the pleasure I'm going to have in breaking you in for your new life as a prostitute. Because have no doubt, before I've finished with you, you will be telling me your new name, what you do for a living and even be prepared to show me."

He said no more, but slipped his hand into his pocket and pulled out a dog's toy rubber bone, attached to each end was a boot lace. Moving closer to Karen, Chuks forced her mouth open, pushing the wide rubber bone between her teeth, before tying the laces together at the back of her head. He checked it was firm, then walked over to the bucket, pulling out the blue painted rod. At the end of the rod was attached a very large pad dripping with water. He gave it a squeeze on the side of the bucket and came back to her.

"I presume in your job, you've come across the cattle stick, normally used to give shocks to cattle to move them on? Of course you have, you may even have had it used on you in the past. After all, it is now the mainstay of a trafficker and brothel owner's tools of the trade? We, though, have gone a little further when it comes to breaking the spirit of a new girl determined not to conform; we've increased the power twenty-fold, attached a far larger wet pad to give better contact to the body, but more importantly, it will leave little or no marks, bad for business you see, despite the pain it inflicts and even after, being excruciating I believe. Let's see if that's the case shall we, as you experience it first-hand. Bite the bone good and hard, Amber, without the rubber bone, the last girl bit right through her tongue; we can't have you losing your tongue just yet."

Karen stared at the padded rod wide-eyed; already her body was shaking, fear building up inside her.

Chuks released her wrists, dragging her off the chair to the floor. Then using his foot he kicked her over onto her face, before pressing the pad into the hollow of her back, his thumb touching a button on the end of the rod. The electric shock that ran through her body instantly contorted her violently; it very nearly snapped her spine. She clenched her jaw hard, her teeth sinking into the rubber bone, tears of distress streaming down her face, as he moved the pad about her naked body, sending her into convulsions. Then he stopped and returned to the bucket, wetting the pad once more.

Walking back with the now re-wetted pad, he bent down, rolling her over onto her back this time. Chuks then touched her stomach, laughing as once again the shock contorted her body. Six times he found a new spot, delighting in seeing her body suddenly move violently. He stopped, replacing the rod back into the bucket. Helping her back onto the chair, he removed the rubber bone from her mouth. Karen slumped forward; she was sobbing her heart out; her body still twitching uncontrollably. Chuks glanced at her with satisfaction; it was obvious the distress and pain she was in.

"So what's your name?" he demanded.

"Amber," she whispered.

"I can't hear you, what is your name?" he shouted, at the same time slapping her face.

"Amber, my name's Amber," she yelled back at him.

"And what are you?"

"I'm to be a prostitute," she shouted again.

"Not to be, you are, say it then say it again and again until I tell you to stop," he screamed at her.

"I'm a prostitute... I'm a prostitute...I'm a prostitute..." she kept shouting, terrified of him using the rod on her again.

"Silence, what do prostitutes do?" he shouted.

"They allow themselves to be taken for money," she replied, at a more normal level.

"Taken, that's a posh word, Amber. Shagged, screwed, fucked would be far better descriptions, don't you think?"

"Yes, if you want."

Chuks was relishing seeing this girl squirm. "Now that's established, let's see if this newly- found profession has been taken to heart and you're not just mouthing the words when it comes to doing what a prostitute does for a man?" He began unfastening his pants. "Get up, turn around, bend down with your hands on the chair arms, head touching the chair seat and legs apart."

She stared at him in horror; he was going to rape her. She didn't dare move.

He almost laughed. "Hoping the cavalry is coming to your rescue, are you? It's not going to happen; you're not in a movie; this is life, as raw as it gets. For you, your initiation into prostitution starts in this room. Now get in position, wet your fanny if you want, most do. Otherwise, we begin all over again with more punishment."

Scared as she was, she couldn't do it and never moved.

"Still the fighting spirit I see. Too proud to open your legs," he said, followed with a forced laugh.

He came closer to her, grabbed each of her wrists, one at a time snapping the handcuffs attached to the chair's arms on her. "Can't have you striking out, can I?" he said laughing, grabbing her hair and wrenching her head back. He then pulled the rubber bone from his pocket.

Karen saw the bone in his hand; her face was a picture of terror; he actually intended to punish her again. "Please I can't take it again, I'll do what you ask," she implored.

"Too late, you'll learn with us that you only get one chance to do as you're told. Hesitation, or panic just because later you see we're serious, has no value," he replied, forcing the bone into her mouth, before walking over to the bucket and returning with the rod. Releasing her wrists he pushed her to the floor, immediately using the rod again on her body.

Karen was now close to passing out, as again the shocks contorted her body. She wanted to scream, but the rubber bone in her mouth prevented that.

He stopped, replacing the rod in the bucket once more.

Karen was shaking uncontrollably on the floor; every bit of her body was giving her pain, tears running down her face. Her eyes were closing, her body shutting down; she could take no more as she finally passed out.

Chuks bent down and removed the rubber bone from her mouth, then after gathering up the bucket he threw part of the contents in her face. The cold of the water suddenly brought her back to reality.

"What's your name and what do you do?" Chuks kept shouting

at her, as she came round.

"Amber, I'm a prostitute," she finally replied, her voice shaking.

He stood back and smiled. "You've got spunk girl, except your reluctance to accept the inevitable is pointless, after all it's only rewarded you with more pain, but have no doubt, I will do this all night and before you leave this room, you will have shown me that you can give a man pleasure. You've five seconds to decide."

Karen had taken all she could, with no more fight left and knowing he'd no intention of killing her, there was no option but to do as he demanded. With great difficulty, the pain of strained muscles bringing her close to screaming, she stood up, then turned round and began rubbing between her legs gently, before bending down to grip the chair arms as tight as she could, otherwise with the pain she was experiencing, she'd have collapsed back onto the floor. Finally, she spread her legs, closing her eyes tightly as he entered. Chuks wasn't gentle, grasping her hips and pounding into her. She was struggling to remain standing, her legs giving way when Chuks suddenly moved his hands to her shoulders, pushing her down even further until her head was virtually touching the chair seat, before he began slapping the tops of her legs, hard and stinging, demanding she kept still and her bottom up.

Soon he was finished, and began fastening his pants, telling her to sit back on the chair.

"You've got yourself a tight fanny, Amber, men will like that. Seems to me it's been under-used for too long, that's a shame, so it's a good job we came along to put it to use," he mocked. "Now just to get everything in that thick head of yours, tell me again what your name is, and what you do for a living and more importantly, explain how you intend to satisfy your clients?"

"I've already played your silly games, besides being beaten and raped, what more do you want?" she answered quietly, tears running down her face.

He moved closer, gripping her face between his fingers and thumb, squeezing her tight, forcing her to look at him. "You call this a silly game do you, believe deep inside you're still Karen Harris, and you've just been raped?"

Karen never responded.

"I'm asking a question," he shouted at her. "Or are you that arrogant that you need more punishment to convince you this is no game? Then so be it, one chance like I told you earlier, but you already seem to have forgotten that."

The terror of what he'd said was all too apparent in her face, as she cowered back in the chair, her hands coming up trying to stop him wrenching her mouth open and pushing the rubber bone in.

He pulled back a little. "Don't want the bone then? Well clench your teeth together, Amber, because you'll wish you had," he shouted at her, going over to the bucket and picking up the cat o' nine tails off the floor alongside it. "It's time you felt our cat."

Coming back, carrying the cat, he grabbed Karen's hair, sweeping her up off the chair to the floor, pushing her face down, using his foot on the small of her back to hold her down. Then stepping away slightly, he laid into her with the cat, beginning at her shoulders, each blow moving down her body until he was hitting the soles of her feet. Without the rubber bone in her mouth and with Chuks being very experienced in knowing how to punish a girl in this way, Karen was screaming in agony, tears running down her face. As the cat kept coming down, the pain sharp and stinging, the screams reduced to a whimper, with urine spreading around under her legs.

"So is it still a game?" he shouted, stopping for a moment to hear her answer.

"No," she whispered, her body shaking.

Again the cat came down on her body. "I can't hear you, is it a fucking game?" he screamed at her.

"No!" she shouted back.

"Then if it's not a game, sit on the fucking chair," he shouted at her once more.

Karen dragged herself around, holding onto the chair for support, the pain in her legs and bottom intense, as she sat on the chair.

"Do you still believe you're Karen Harris who's just been raped? Think carefully before you answer, get it wrong, then we're back to the stick, until you not only finally accept who and what you are, but tell me."

302

Chuks was relishing breaking her spirit, soon the next stage of her induction would begin and he needed her to keep telling herself just who and what she was.

"My name's Amber, I now prostitute for a living," she began, hesitating for a moment before continuing. "I was wrong in what I said; I wasn't raped, but offered myself willingly for your pleasure."

Chuks smiled to himself; it was obvious just how much it took for her to say those last words. He also knew Karen could take no more physical or verbal abuse today. She'd close down, close her mind and would no longer listen to what he may say to her, no matter what he did. Now it was time to keep her this way. Grasping her arm, he stood her up. "Follow me," he demanded curtly.

She shuffled along behind him, the chain attached between the ankle irons was short, preventing her walking properly.

They went into another room. There was a mattress on the floor, a toilet against the wall, with a small sink to wash in. He stopped her alongside the mattress, while he attached a chain, set in the floor, around the chain of her ankle irons with a padlock, snapping it closed. Then he pushed her down onto the mattress. Going over to a cupboard at the far end of the room, he pulled out a nightdress and a blanket, before returning and throwing them both at her. "Put it on and while you do, listen hard. These four walls are your prison; it's where you live and sleep from now on. Scream or shout all you want, no one will come, or even hear you; the nearest house is five miles away. The only time you'll ever see the light of day is when you're taken to service our clients; then you return here, to wait until the next day, when you start again."

He took out a case from his pocket, opened it and removed a syringe. Karen looked at the syringe in fear; she knew from past experience what drugs could do, and it frightened her. Chuks kicked her over onto her face, at the same time dropping down, before pushing the needle into her bottom, injecting the deadly liquid.

Karen remained on her face; her head was beginning to spin.

After a few minutes watching her, he pulled her over onto her back, looking into her eyes. Already he could see the start of dilation. "Welcome to the beginning of your new life, Amber. Already you have

303

begun the journey that will sink you deeper into a world of silence and despair. Plenty of time before that finally happens, for you to think back on your miserable life, your family, your friends and how it all has gone so horribly wrong for you. This is your first of a number of doses you'll have of a drug we call chewy, given to the criminals of our tribe before being put to work in the fields. Their minds, their aggressions, destroyed, with one thought left, to serve their master."

Even before he'd finished talking, for Karen, his voice seemed a long way away, and she was unable to understand what was happening around her.

Chapter Fifty-Seven

Sherry was in Paris. She'd taken ten days' leave and intended to spend the first week just being a tourist. Already she'd booked tours from the hotel and was planning her days. It didn't worry her being alone. She could have accepted an invitation from the lads at the camp to go clubbing in a Spanish resort, but she declined and ended up in Paris.

Unpacking her bags in the hotel room, she was half-listening to the television. She'd put it on the world news from London to catch the weather. Her French, both in speech and understanding, wasn't very good so far, so she preferred English.

The final story was just being read before the weather report. "Hamon Clavier, son of Pier Clavier, the French industrialist and a large land-owner, has been found dead in an Istanbul hotel. The Istanbul police have told news reporters that Mr Clavier was shot while he slept, and all his valuables stolen. The hotel manager said he'd arrived alone, only two days before, and the hotel will from now on be stepping up their security, particularly at night."

Sherry stopped unpacking and was staring at the television showing Hamon's photo. She went to her bag and pulled out her mobile, looking at the text from Karen, and particularly the time it was sent. She was confused by the hotel manager's claim that Hamon was alone, unless there had been a robbery and Karen had gotten out, so as not to blow her cover. Her promise to Karen not to tell anyone at unit now left her in a dilemma. Karen could have everything under control even with Hamon dead, but by the same ruling she could be in serious trouble and need help.

Sherry paced the room, not knowing what to do for the best. Karen must know that Hamon was dead; she'd also know it would be headline news in France. If that were the case, why hadn't there been further contact from Karen, just to say she was okay? But there hadn't, the last text time was before Hamon died. Then with Karen not even mentioned, she had to be alive, maybe even taken when Hamon was killed. The only people Sherry could see who might have taken her was the Nigerians. If that were true, then Karen could be in deep trouble, maybe being used in their brothel. Sherry made a decision; she had to go to Istanbul and follow up the information as she knew it. There was no way she could sit about in Paris enjoying her break not knowing.

Chapter Fifty-Eight

Karen began to come around later in the morning. Her head was spinning; she felt strangely detached from her body. Tears began to form in her eyes, before trickling slowly down her face. She couldn't stop them; everything was an effort, the depression overwhelming. But she was determined to pull herself together, dragging herself up to a sitting position. However, the drug had also helped to suppress the pain of her punishment, though it was now weakening; the pain was becoming more excruciating from the strained muscles, when her body had been twisted by the electric shocks. She felt nauseous and could only crawl across the floor to the toilet, lifting her head over the pan, retching - each time the pain taking her close to passing out. Eventually, she pulled herself up onto the toilet; the chain set in the floor attached to her ankle chain, was just about long enough to allow her to sit. How long she sat there she'd no idea, as she drifted in and out of consciousness. Finally, she stood, flushed the toilet and washed herself down from the sink. There was no soap or towels, or even a toothbrush, so she cleaned her teeth as best she could with her fingers. Back on the mattress Karen sat there staring vacantly ahead. She could still clearly remember the punishment, followed by more beatings, when she refused to allow herself to be raped; somehow she couldn't get worked up, it was as if she just accepted what he was doing to her. Then as to his demand that she forget her own name and use the name Amber, or expect more punishment, she might say it out loud, but she was a strong-willed girl and just because he told her to forget her name didn't mean she would. To do so would be to admit he'd won. She'd been sitting up for some time before Chuks arrived.

"You're awake then. What's your name?"

"I'm called Amber."

"Not what you're called, what is your name and what are you?" he shouted.

"My name's Amber. I'm a prostitute," she answered.

"Then don't forget it, and if I ever ask you again, that's what I want to hear, not 'I'm called', do you understand?"

"Yes," she replied. "I can't think straight at the moment. I'm in so much pain."

Chuks ignored her distress, and opened a small box which he'd brought into the room, removing a paper plate with a mixed rice dish covered in cling film. Taking off the cling film, he passed her the plate. "Use your fingers, you get no utensils."

She never said anything, just began to eat the food.

He watched until she finished, taking the plate from her and putting it back in the box; then handed her a drink of lukewarm tea in a large paper cup, again taking it from her when she'd drunk it all.

Taking out a small case from his pocket he took out a syringe.

Karen cowered back, but he rolled her over onto her side, pushing the needle into the upper part of her leg. Karen could feel the cold of the liquid moving up inside her leg before it went away. Already she was feeling dizzy, the room spinning as once again the drug took hold.

He then turned and left the room.

***

Chuks returned later in the day. Karen was lying down; her eyes open but not really looking at, anything.

"Sit up," he demanded.

She dragged herself up, leaning against the wall.

"I've brought you a towel, soap and toothpaste, you can wash when I've gone," he told her, at the same time handing her some food. The food was very much the same, rice with bits of vegetables , followed by a drink of warm tea.

"So what's your name and what do you do?" he demanded, placing the empty plate, and the cup back in the small box.

"My name's Amber and I prostitute for a living," Karen replied. To say anything else would have been pointless.

"That is good, you're answering immediately," he said to her, at the same time releasing her ankle irons. "Now we know what you are, take off your nightdress, wet your fanny and lie down on the mattress with your legs nice and wide?"

She just looked at him. "So it's your intention to rape me every day then?" she asked softly.

"Rape! Rape!" he cried, "Have you forgotten already?"

He grabbed her arm, pulled her up, then keeping hold of the arm

308

dragged Karen, stumbling after him, along the corridor and into the punishment room, pushing her to the floor, pulling her nightdress up, exposing her body. Taking the stick from the bucket, he came back to her. Karen was still lying there, the terror very apparent in her eyes. The chewy she'd already been given had slowed her reactions, preventing her from any sort of meaningful retaliation.

He didn't hesitate; pushing the padded stick into her stomach, pressing the button, he watched her body react uncontrollably as the pad was moved to different spots.

Karen was screaming; the pain intensified as, once again, the electric shocks sent her into convulsions.

"So is it rape, to take a woman who's just told me she prostitutes for a living?" he shouted at her, "or do you want even more punishment to finally make you accept what you are?"

Karen finally could take no more. The chewy was playing havoc with her mind and her body, but even that couldn't dull her mind from the punishment he meted out on her. "I had it wrong," she whispered. "I'm a prostitute, if you want me, I'll offer myself willingly."

"Then get up, remove the nightdress and bend over the fucking chair and open your legs wide with your head well down."

Karen did as she was told, except unlike the last time he was far more aggressive to her, knocking her around, then when she fell to the floor, he started kicking her, demanding she got up and bent over again. As she did this, he pulled a tube from his pocket, squeezing the contents around her back passage and up into her rectum. Seconds later he was forcing himself inside her, ignoring her screams of pain and distress. Finally, when he'd finished he pushed her to the floor.

"Pick up your fucking nightdress, then get back to your mattress - delay, and I'm following behind with the stick, which I'll ram up your arse and shock you into moving," he shouted at her, as he fastened himself up.

Karen didn't delay; she grabbed the nightdress and stumbled back to the other room; she knew he was right behind her, as he continued pushing her forward using the stick in her back, but he didn't push the button which would have given her a shock. Once on the mattress she pulled the nightdress over her head and sat down.

Chuks knelt at her feet, fastening her ankle irons. He looked up at her while he did this. "You're a bloody good fuck girl, even up your arse was nice and tight, when you're taken under duress that is. You must learn to do this without the threats; then I know you've finally accepted your new life and are doing it willingly. So from now on when I bring food, I want you to offer yourself as a payment for your keep. Do you understand?"

"Yes, I'm not stupid."

"That's debatable, to be caught as easily as you were. So was the man your lover, did he give you a good fucking that night, before dying and going to heaven, after we put a bullet in his head?"

She looked at him, the hate obvious in her expression. "You may have won, but you're not entitled to know my thoughts, or anything about my life before you took me. You can use that stick all you want, force me to do your bidding; that's where it ends. I don't have to talk to you beyond that."

He nodded his head up and down slowly. "You think so do you? Before I went into trafficking, I was in Nigeria during the military coup of General Abacha. It was brutal; me and my partners were able to torture, maim and rape our way across Nigeria. If I want to know your thoughts, your past, you will tell me; otherwise, we'll forget the rod. I'll tie you to the fucking chair, then begin by crushing teeth with pliers. Then if you still don't want to answer, I'll start snipping fingers and toes off, until you tell me everything I want to know." He grinned. "You'll notice I'm intending to take parts of your body that will not stop you servicing our clients, but I assure you the pain will be made even worse when I use a red hot iron to seal the wounds. Chuks moved closer to her, his face inches from hers. "This is your only warning. If I ask you a question, I don't want a lippy answer, because I'll not ask again. Did Hamon fuck you, or do you still hold this idea that what happened before in your life is private, and I've no right to know? Because if that's your thinking, what other lies are coming out your mouth? I want an answer before I set about crushing a few teeth, exposing the nerves, listening to your screams of agony?"

Karen was terrified at the very thought, still remembering the last time she delayed doing something, and she was punished. "I wouldn't let him touch me, until we'd finished gathering evidence and put you behind bars," she replied, already embarrassed admitting it, besides being sad that a man prepared to risk his life for her, she'd treated that way.

He just grinned. "I thought you'd see sense. But if that's the way you treat your men, it's no wonder you are alone and unwanted. Except soon you'll have no such inhibitions, willingly offering yourself without conditions. As it is, I'm not really that interested in your miserable life. When the chewy takes hold, that is the time I will relish, as I increase chewy to four injections a day. Such an overdose will rip your head apart. Even if I begin snipping, to get you to talk about your past, you won't be able to tell me. You see, by then, everything you knew about yourself, your memories, who you were, the names of your family and friends will be irreversibly lost forever. Finally, when the injections stop, a girl the industry has despised for years will be just a shell. Perhaps for a girl like you it will be for the best, after all it will be that much easier to focus on servicing your clients, rather than worry about home and what you did for a living all the time."

He rolled her over onto her side. Then taking the small box from his pocket, he removed the syringe. "Do you want to know why I told you that, Amber?" he asked, at the same time pushing the needle into her bottom and injecting the chewy. "I want you to lie there, no longer in control of your body, offering yourself willingly, but most importantly counting the days, like a prisoner on death row, knowing in less than a week, the overdose coming will irreversibly destroy your life as you know it, and you can do nothing about it. Sleep well, Amber, I'll be back tomorrow."

After he'd gone, Karen lay where he'd pushed her. Try as she might, she couldn't get worked up about his rape of her. Except what really hurt deep inside, was his assessment of why she still had no one in her life, summed up in so few words. Now she could no longer even think of that, as the same as other times she'd had the injection, her head was beginning to spin, her muscles no longer giving her pain; there was just the constant sick feeling in her stomach. She just wanted to go to sleep.

Chapter Fifty-Nine

It was the second day of Karen's captivity. She was leaning on the back wall, sitting on the mattress, when Chuks came in the morning. The night had been very long, the silence of the room playing on her mind, the single light in the room annoying; she wanted to sleep, close her eyes for the last time and never awaken. His threat to take the memories from the past away forever was not as Chuks believed a source of fear, but a welcome end to the nightmare that had played out in her thoughts, her dreams, for too many years now. She was counting the days, the hours when he intended to do exactly that, in the hope that what he claimed would actually materialise.

"Slept well did you, Amber, thought about your future? Frightened of losing the past are we?" he mocked, as he came into the room.

She gave a faint smile. "No, I'm not frightened; in fact I welcome it, finally a chance to sleep without the constant nightmares of the past I've had to accept. Your naive attempt to make me beg to keep my memories won't work. So give me the overdose now, or in days, it makes no difference."

"That's shit, you are frightened, but I like your attempt to play the reality down. I don't believe a girl with the lifestyle you've enjoyed over the last years, would want to change it for life as a prostitute," he said, at the same time unpacking her food.

"That's where you're wrong. All my life I've only ever had sex forced on me, made to perform, as you all call it, under duress. For me, prostitution would be no different, in fact, I'd probably enjoy it; there are no emotional ties. After all, drugs were forced into me in the past, destroyed any hope of a family, my reputation attracts men who just want to get inside my pants anyway, not look after me as I always dreamed a man would. So this new life you've told me I'm to have, is no different, I'll still have nothing, or rather nothing that I dreamed about."

"I'm glad you're now believing you will enjoy being shagged regularly, Amber. It's time to get a move on! So what's your name and what do you do for a living?"

She sighed inwardly, drawing in her breath. "My name's Amber, I'm a prostitute."

"What do prostitutes do?"

"We both know what they do, isn't it enough that I'm admitting what you want me to be?"

He looked down at her for a moment. Her arrogance was not going away, even after her little speech about enjoying being a prostitute. Reaching down, he unfastened the ankle clamp. Then grabbing hold of her arm, he dragged her up.

Karen began struggling, trying to stop him dragging her back into the punishment room. She had little chance, weakened by the drugs and the lack of food; he soon had her in the room. Forcing her to face the chair, he attached her wrists to the clamps on the chair arms. Then he collected the cat, before pulling her nightdress up over her head, and positioned her, by pushing her head down to touch the chair seat, kicking her legs well apart. Then he laid into her, starting at her shoulders and moving slowly down to her feet with each blow. Her cries of distress, soon reducing to a whimper. He broke off, satisfied she'd suffered enough.

"So are you now prepared to accept I own you, to do as I want with you?"

"Yes," she whispered.

"I can't hear you?" he shouted, hitting her once more with the cat.

"Yes, I now accept you're my owner. I'll do anything you want of me," she repeated loudly.

He slowly nodded his head up and down. "That's good; you're learning obedience, like a bitch should have for her master," he said, reaching around her and releasing her wrists. "Now get the nightdress off, face the chair once again, hands on the arms, head touching the seat, with your bottom well up. I intend to get you used to having it both ways, without the screams of yesterday."

After he'd finished, he took her back to the mattress, attaching the ankle irons, before handing her the dinner. "Eat your food. Then turn over for your injection. Expect punishment followed by your training to perform as a prostitute morning and night, until I give you an overdose. If the punishments are not getting through into your thick head, I'll begin to crush teeth, followed by snipping off of your fingers and toes, leaving you with a permanent reminder of who owns you. Believe me girl, soon the very thought of my name will instil fear in you that you can't even imagine."

He left her lying down on the mattress, the pain as he'd pushed inside her was still there, but she didn't object, all she could think about was him giving her more chewy, knowing it would dull the pain and take away the disgust of his demeaning her all the time.

Chapter Sixty

Three days after the announcement of Hamon's death and with no more text messages, Sherry had taken the first flight available to Istanbul. Then hiring a small car at the airport, she drove to the same hotel Karen, and Hamon had been booked in. The hotel was having a quiet time after the murder, so she'd a choice of rooms, but asked for one on the third floor, one floor above where Karen and Hamon had been. She spent time considering talking to Lieutenant Ross, who was second in command of the unit, but decided against it. Karen shouldn't have been where she was, without at least informing them of her intentions. She was also not absolutely certain that Karen wasn't operating in a covert situation, and didn't need any help. However, Sherry had formulated a plan that would tell her for certain if Karen was okay. That was providing Karen kept to the way she operated, particularly in a covert operation. It required her finding a way into the room where Karen had stayed in the hotel.

At three in the morning, when all was quiet and dressed in black, including a baseball hat covering her blonde hair, she went from her bedroom onto the balcony, then climbing over, she lowered herself, with not much difficulty, to the balcony below. Now it was an easy task to move from one to the next, until she reached the balcony of the room Karen and Hamon had been in. The balcony door was shut and locked. With the knowledge that all the balcony doors were the same type in the hotel, and of an era before modern double-glazed units, she'd worked out how to get through by experimenting with her own door. It was a bit drastic, but she could see no other way. So placing her jacket over a small glass square, one of a number that made up the balcony door and the one closest to the catch, she pushed it with her elbow, eventually smashing it. Reaching inside and releasing the catch, she was soon in the room. Everything had been cleaned up after the killing, ready for occupancy, but had not been used. Knowing what to look for, she made her way immediately into the bathroom and knelt down at the side of the toilet, reaching in behind the cistern, trying to feel for what she suspected might be there, which would prove Karen had been forcibly taken. Then she felt it, grasping the item and pulling it out - it was Karen's gun. Some time ago Karen had told Sherry about her original abduction. How she'd been shown where to stash a gun, without it being obvious, by an SAS lad called Garry, just as a precaution. She'd told Sherry she always did that now, advising her to do the same. But Sherry couldn't bring a gun through the airport security so she would have needed to procure one, probably with difficulty, if Karen's hadn't been there. Sherry put her hand in further, finding a spare clip and a small sheet of paper. On it was the address of the brothel they were watching, where Karen had suspected the Nigerians were. Sherry wondered if Karen put the short note with the gun in case they were taken, although she wasn't sure on that point. Sherry left by the room door, after first checking no one was around, she was soon back in her bedroom. With a gun, Sherry was able to move forward, whereas before, without any weapon, she'd have been helpless. It was coming up to a quarter to four; the day had been long. So still dressed, the gun at her side, she lay down on the bed, falling asleep very quickly. As for anyone trying to get through the corridor and inside her room, without her knowledge, they would have no chance. She'd placed a chair under the lock with a glass vase on the seat. The whole lot would come crashing down if any sort of entry were attempted, waking her immediately.

***

The following day, Sherry had an early breakfast then checked out of the hotel. Now having what she wanted, she drove up the coast in her hire car looking for a new hotel to stay in, finding what she was looking for nearly twenty-five miles away from the other hotel. It was large with over three hundred rooms and she was able to book a room for a week at a good rate. The room was at the front with views across the ocean. It had a large double bed, a balcony and a mini-bar, which she quickly took a few bottles from, pushing them into her bag.

Happy with her room, she left the hotel heading to the address of the brothel written on the sheet of paper. She wanted to weigh the building up, take her bearings in daylight, for when she went in, after they closed in the early hours. It was a decision she'd made, now she was certain Karen was in trouble. Was she scared of doing it alone? Yes, except Sherry was not without experience, even though she was only twenty. Two postings in Afghanistan and then a number of Dark Angel operations had been good training. In fact army-wise, with the resulting discipline that came from it, she was streets ahead of Karen. For her, you wouldn't witness a staged movie approach with guns firing at random, hitting nothing. Sherry's incursion would be cautious, but fast, with every bullet she fired certain of its target. She would take no prisoners; in fact she couldn't, for her it would be shoot to kill.

It was coming up to half-ten in the morning when she was at last sitting in her little car, parked among a number of other cars on the street where the brothel was located. She decided, with it being more a late venue, the place would be deserted, intending, after a short time of observation, to drive around the area, particularly around the back of the house. As she sat there making notes and small sketches, a van backed out to the side of the house, after two large doors had been opened from the inside. The man who got out to close them again was a black-skinned man. Sherry looked at him and then down to a small set of photos she had, for identifying the Nigerians. This man was one of them. Now Sherry was happy, the address was correct and the identification of this man named Chuks, confirmed at least one of them was here.

Sherry watched the van leave, then took the decision to follow. She'd got all she could at the brothel for now. Then providing the van wasn't going into the busy areas of the city, would decide if she was going to take this Nigerian on outside the brothel. At least if she did, it would be one less later.

Tailing the van was easy, the roads, although not overly busy, had sufficient vehicles all going the same way, so she was able to move into the flow and be just one of the many drivers heading in that direction. Within ten minutes, the van turned off down an otherwise deserted road. Sherry came to a halt. She pulled her tablet computer out her bag, googling her position, in order to look at the satellite images and see just where this road led. It didn't, it came to a dead end after going past three houses spread along the road, with quite a distance between each.

Cautiously she turned onto the road, then drove at a normal

speed, as if she knew where she was heading, passing the odd house, at the same time looking for the white van. She saw it parked up at the last farm, so she turned the car off the road, parking it out of sight to any car passing. It was time to approach on foot.

Chapter Sixty-One

Every day for Karen, the routine was the same both morning and night. He'd first take her to the punishment room, always beginning with punishment by the rod, or cat, each time not stopping until her screams were down to whimpers and she was begging him to stop. Chuks wanted his ownership of her, supported by the punishments, to be constantly at the forefront of her mind and so powerful that even the chewy couldn't override them. To reinforce this he had her stand up in front of him, after the punishment, to tell him who owned her, who fed her, who gave her shelter and how she was to pay for this. She would reply word for word, or he'd touch her with the rod, giving her an electric shock, making her repeat from the beginning. Chuks would then take her, his abuse of her body degrading and often painful. On Karen's part, she no longer cared, what little dignity she had was all but gone, doing everything he wanted of her.

Back on the mattress, she began to eat her food.

"I think at last, you're really learning obedience, now it has become part of your life? Very soon, you will be servicing our clients. Are you looking forward to this new life, Amber?"

She shrugged indifferently. "Why not, I don't have an aversion to sex, besides, I've nothing else to look forward to, apart from sitting here looking at blank walls," she answered.

Chuks smiled to himself; the girl's spirit was broken, the drug was already destroying her ability to think rationally, the fear of him foremost in her mind so she was scared of actually admitting she hated the abuse, when all too often he could feel the tension, as her body struggled to accept him.

Finishing her food, Karen turned on her side ready for the injection. She desperately wanted the chewy; it made her forget his abuse and dulled the pain he always left her in.

He pulled out the syringe, filled it to the usual level, then stopped for a moment. He looked at her already waiting, then back at the bottle. "What the hell," he said drawing yet another dose into the syringe. Then he quickly injected her; rubbing her thigh to get the liquid dispersed, before giving her a slap on the bottom. "I've enjoyed breaking you in, Amber, but as you said, you're nearly thirty; I prefer girls far younger, more obedient and prepared to please, without the constant threat of punishment. So I've given you your wish. That was the first of four overdoses. Even before I leave, you'll begin to feel the full effects of chewy. I don't envy your night girl, the hallucinations, the pain in the head, as the drug begins to rip you apart. You may not even be awake, when I come in the morning, but I'll not let you down, I'll give you double with your next double shot to make sure the chewy carries on with its work."

Chuks had been right; already the increased dose began to take hold as he left the room. This was nothing like the last injections. Her entire body was shaking uncontrollably; the inside of her head was banging; she couldn't think, or even control her movements any more. Visions of Chuks, screaming at her, coupled with images from her past, were flashing through her thoughts; her eyes were fixed staring ahead, but could see nothing. She was retching; her last meal spewed across the mattress. For about an hour this went on, her hands holding her head, trying to stop the banging inside, the pain unbearable. She began crying, tears streaming down her cheek, her mouth dribbling. She'd not only wet herself, but also her bowels had released; the smell of it all making her throw up again, but she had nothing left in her stomach. Finally, Karen slipped into unconsciousness. She could take it no more.

Chapter Sixty-Two

Sherry had moved closer to the farm. She wasn't certain why Chuks had come here. The place looked deserted from the outside, but inside could be very different. Convinced this farm must have some sort of connection with the brothel, not that she could immediately see what, she decided to sit it out for most of the day, to see if anyone came out.

Settling herself down, then using the telephoto lens of her camera, Sherry studied each upper and lower window carefully, trying to see any movement, but there wasn't any.

It was then that Chuks came out. She zoomed in on him, clicking her shutter a few times. She watched him lock the door then throw a box in a large skip to the side of the entrance. Climbing back in the van, he set off back towards the main road.

Sherry sat for a short time, confused. He'd locked the door as if no one else was inside, but what had he thrown away? She decided that a casual approach down the road would be a good choice. She could knock on the door; tell them she'd got lost, or some other explanation.

Three minutes later she was at the door, knocking hard. No one came or shouted from inside. Walking over to the skip, she looked inside. There were a number of various types of boxes; a few had been ripped open; she suspected by animals, or birds scavenging, there were paper plates and cups scattered around. She lifted the new box that had been thrown and opened it. Inside was a paper plate, the food on it untouched. Then she shuffled the boxes apart, to look underneath them, finding bags of rotting food. But they had been there for a week or so, and already half-eaten by scavengers.

"They have someone in here, but why here away from the brothel?" she asked herself.

Coming away from the skip, Sherry was now certain this place was deserted, with not as much as a caretaker or guard, so she walked round the building looking for a way in. There was only one back door which was firmly shut, the windows to either side small square panes, none opening, so she would need to bash the window in completely to get through. Looking at the upstairs windows, only the one above a lean-to part of the building was possible. It looked like a bathroom window, definitely an opener, and it was not closed completely, as if the wood had swelled in the past, which now prevented it shutting properly.

Sherry dragged a piece of rusting farm machinery close to the side wall of the lean-to, then climbed up, gingerly making her way over the tiled roof to the window and trying to pull it open, but it wouldn't move. Climbing back down, looking around for something she could use as a jemmy, eventually she found a small pile of iron fence rods, flattened out at one end in the form of a spike, to make it difficult to climb over once fitted. Taking one back up on the roof, she jammed it in the window, pulling as hard as she could. Seconds later the window suddenly gave way, with Sherry very nearly falling off the roof as she stumbled, dropping the improvised jemmy. The noise of it crashing down over the roof tiles and hitting the machinery below startled her. Sherry stood silently, her gun ready in her hand, the safety off. No noise came from inside the house, so eventually she climbed through the window, pulling it closed behind her.

Like any trained incursion soldier, she proceeded slowly and cautiously through the house, every room considered a risk, having to be certain no one was in any of them, so by the time she was going down the cellar steps, ten minutes had elapsed already.

In front of her was an open door, she looked inside. There was a chair in the centre with fitted restraints, a tipped-over bucket in the corner with a rod to the side of it. Sherry knew what the rod was; this type of rod had been used on her for punishment on the ship.

In the next room were old boxes and bags, but she recognised one of the suitcases. It was Karen's. A door at the end of the cellar passage had a bolt slid across at the top. Sherry thought it strange, unless it led outside, but she thought it more likely they were keeping someone locked up in there. She slid the bolt carefully and silently, her gun ready, the safety off. Then with the bolt released, she lifted the latch and kicked the door open, standing back, the gun now held firmly in both hands. The room was lit by a small single bulb hanging from the ceiling; wire was strung across from it through a small hole in the wall. The only person inside was Karen, lying on a mattress. Karen seemed asleep and didn't stir when the door opened.

Sherry went over to her, looked down and immediately saw the ankle irons. Going back out of the room, before closing the door softly and sliding the bolt back, she began searching around for a key, but found nothing.

Returning outside, she checked the skip once more, counting the discarded boxes. She surmised that based on the number with food left in them that hadn't rotted, Karen had been here since Hamon had been killed, and was being fed twice a day. Then, although the rooms upstairs had double beds in them, they didn't look as if they had been used recently. The general dust around and the lack of anything else in the rooms, or even used condoms in the skip, indicated that Karen was the only prisoner. That may mean they would have her working from here, taken perhaps to the brothel, then returned after they closed. It made sense; they wouldn't want her kept chained up in a licensed brothel, which could be inspected by the authorities at any time. More importantly for Sherry was that Karen would have to be released to go to the brothel, so whoever came for her would have keys, bringing no more than one, or even two people at the most to collect her.

Looking at her watch, Sherry couldn't see them wanting her until seven or eight at night. Although, Karen could be fed earlier, but not much before six, she didn't think. After all, she'd only just had breakfast. Running back to her car and opening a farmer's gate, Sherry parked in the field close to the hedge. It was obvious the gate had been little used, with the grass around the entrance undisturbed by a tractor, or walked on for some time. Going back to the road, checking the car couldn't be seen, unless you stopped and looked into the field, Sherry was satisfied. Then collecting a sandwich, bought in the hotel bar, a can of coke and a small bottle of water, from the mini bar in her room, Sherry walked back to the farmhouse and went inside. It was time to settle down and wait.

Chapter Sixty-Three

Chuks' visit in the morning, when Sherry had followed him from the brothel, had been to feed Karen and give her the second double dose of chewy. Karen had eaten very little; even so, although the chewy was ripping her mind apart, it still didn't prevent her offering herself to him, with the fear he had instilled in her over the days. Chuks had declined; the girl stank. He also couldn't see any advantage in punishing her, the dose of chewy so high, it would serve no useful purpose. Except, he was satisfied by her offering herself in this state, she was showing how much control he had over her now. Chuks stood, ready to leave, but watched her for a moment. Karen had started shaking, foaming at the mouth. He smiled to himself; the chewy was doing its job. Then he left the room laughing. As for Karen, Chuks now dominated her thoughts. He was a man who fed and gave her shelter, expecting in return the absolute desire to please him in any way he wanted.

***

When Chuks returned in the evening, he had the intention of giving her a massive overdose, with the same the following morning. This he knew would ultimately destroy her, maybe even leave her in such a condition she wouldn't even be able to think or speak. But he no longer cared, already he was fed up of having to keep coming. He wanted her working, earning money. If she couldn't speak, think, whatever, it didn't matter. The clients wouldn't bother so long as she was able to shag.

"Come on, what's up with you, wake up," he demanded, giving her a shake.

She stirred and slowly opened her eyes.

"So has the pain gone that you had this morning? Can you eat all your dinner tonight?"

"I think I can; the pain's not as bad as it was," she answered, even so her speech was slurred and it took her a short time to reply.

"Then get your food down and be quick about it," he said, with little interest that she was even slightly better.

Karen took the food and began eating, she was very hungry.

She finished the food, and he took the plate, before handing her the drink. It was lukewarm as usual, but she drank it down.

"Do you want me to undress, I'm well enough to give you pleasure?" she asked, not waiting for him to prompt her.

"You stink, from shitting everywhere. You're getting extra chewy tonight, so before you're incapable of even walking, let's get you under a shower; maybe it'll wake you up more. After showering and you smell better, I'll accept your offer and take you into a bedroom. Then rather than standing up holding onto a chair, you can lie down on a bed, what do you think, Amber?"

"And a shower is?" Karen asked, although in her mind, she was certain she should know, but couldn't seem to visualise what it would look like, or what it did.

"To wash you," he replied, without thinking why she shouldn't know.

"Then yes, I'd like a shower," she answered quietly, ignoring his suggestion of taking her to a bedroom.

"What about my following it with the shagging, you've told me many times you like to be shagged, so wouldn't you prefer to do it on a bed?" he asked, enjoying having this once proud girl, offering herself freely to him all the time.

For some reason, she knew exactly what Chuks meant by that word. "I've got used to you shagging me as you do, I enjoy it and look forward to you coming. But lying down, on something you call a bed, sounds to be more comfortable than holding onto a chair. So yes, I'd like to try it that way."

Chuks looked at her for a moment, why didn't she know what the words shower or bed meant? Could it be she was no longer able to associate words with objects they described? Had the chewy really done its work, destroying the word association and he'd not realised it? He decided if that was the case, she may have lost other basic memories. It was time to test her.

"Tell me, Amber, how old are you?"

She tried to think positively. "I don't know."

"What about your family, give me the names of your two brothers?" He was watching her carefully, deliberately suggesting she

325

had brothers, when he knew all she had was a sister.

Karen frowned, desperately trying to think, she knew the word brothers, but couldn't remember what they actually were. "I'm not sure, if I knew what brothers were I suppose I could have."

"How did you arrive here, and who were you with?"

"Arrive where?" she asked.

"This country?"

She looked down at her clasped hands, wondering why he was asking questions she had no answer for. Then she looked up at him. "I don't understand arrive, as for who I came with…" she hesitated. "That must be you, I know no one else."

He added to the question. "Well you must know where you were brought up, what country you used to live in, before coming here?"

She was still looking at him, obviously confused. "Don't I live here? I've never lived anywhere else before. But where this place is, I'm not sure you've ever told me."

He grinned. "So who owns you and what did you learn over the last days?"

Karen looked relieved; this was a question she could answer. "I know that," she replied with a faint grin. "You own me."

"I do, but what else have you learnt and why?"

"I've learned how to offer my body to you willingly for your enjoyment."

"Why have I taught you?"

"It's my payment for a place to live and my food."

"You are correct, and what is a prostitute?"

Karen hesitated. "I'm one, aren't I?"

"You are, and being a prostitute, Amber, means that when you're with any man, you must allow him to shag you without objection."

"Is that what you want me to do for you?"

"It is."

"Then I will willingly do that."

"At last, Amber, finally, you understand that I'm your master, for using you as I think fit. Are you looking forward to being shagged regularly?"

She nodded enthusiastically. "Yes I am, when is this man

coming?"

He smiled slightly. "Very soon, Amber. I'll get you cleaned up; your hair cut and dyed; then I'll put you to work."

"I'll do my best for you," she answered quickly, already looking forward to not being alone for hours on end.

He reached down, releasing her ankle irons. Then helping her to stand up, he pushed her arms above her head and pulled off the nightdress, throwing it into a corner.

"Right, enough talk, through the door and up the stairs, wait in the kitchen, you can't get out, the door is locked, so don't bother to try. I'll follow with a towel and a clean nightdress."

Karen walked gingerly and very slowly to the door, then steadying herself, by touching the wall, she made her way along the passage and up the cellar steps.

As Karen reached the third step, Chuks, who'd already picked up the nightdress and a towel, was standing at the bottom of the steps, watching her going up, when without even a prior warning there was a single gunshot, the bullet ripping through him like a knife into butter.

He gasped just once, before collapsing to the floor.

Sherry, who had waited in the storeroom for hours until someone came, and also to be in a position for her to take them on, pushed the door fully open and came out. With her gun held firmly in two hands, she walked up to him.

He looked up at her.

"This is for the children you killed in London, I hope you rot in hell," she said with indifference, before shooting him in the head. Checking he was dead, she rifled through his pockets, finding keys, wallet, cell phone and a gun.

Karen at first was shocked, by the deafening noise of the gunshots, but ignored it and carried on up to the kitchen. There she just stood waiting for Chuks.

Sherry ran up the cellar steps to find her. "Karen, are you all right?" she asked quietly, seeing her standing there, seeming not to recognise her. Realising something was amiss, she went up to Karen, putting her arms around her, pulling her close. "God you stink," Sherry commented, wrinkling her nose. "Are you on some sort of drug, you don't seem all here?" she asked.

"I'm to have a shower, where is it?" Karen replied, not answering any of Sherry's questions.

Sherry looked into her eyes; she could see the dilation. "That's a bloody good idea; let's get you under a shower shall we? It may even wake you up," she replied, at the same time taking her hand and leaving the kitchen to go upstairs. Sherry knew where the bathroom was, after all that was the room she'd got into the house by.

Leaving Karen under the shower, Sherry returned to the cellar, collecting the towel Chuks had been carrying, including Karen's suitcase from the storeroom.

Running back upstairs, she checked Karen was all right. She wasn't; she was leaning against the back of the shower cubicle, her eyes closed. Sherry gave her a shake. "Wake up and finish your bloody shower," she shouted at her.

This brought Karen around; in fact the tone of Sherry's voice was a command, so she mumbled an apology, before she continued washing. Satisfied Karen was actually doing as she was told, Sherry left the building through the bathroom window.

Outside Sherry moved cautiously around the farmhouse, her gun at the ready. She found no one in the van, or anyone waiting around. Satisfied Chuks had been alone, she returned to the bathroom the way she'd left.

Karen had come around even more, partly because the water had run out of hot and suddenly turned cold, very cold, virtually shocking her awake. Now the cold shower had brought her back to reality, she was drying her hair wondering where Chuks had gone, not realising Chucks was dead, and Sherry was here. When Sherry returned through the window in the bathroom, Karen looked towards her confused. "Who are you, and why are you coming through that way?" she gasped.

"If you don't know me now, you never will," Sherry answered. "Anyway at least you no longer stink, but it's best we don't hang around here. I've brought your suitcase up; it's on the bed in the bedroom next door. Sort out what you want to wear; then we'll talk back at my hotel."

Karen frowned. "Will you show me, I don't really know what that is?"

"What?"

"A bedroom, you've just mentioned a bedroom. Is it somewhere which has a bed in it? Chuks told me he was going to use a bed this time, rather than have me standing holding onto a chair."

"How can you talk to me normally; then not know what a bedroom is? Are you taking the piss?" Sherry asked, already confused by Karen's stupid comments.

Karen looked down. "I do know the word, it's just that I can't imagine what it actually looks like."

"Come on, let's get you dressed at least," Sherry said, grabbing her hand, taking her through to the bedroom. "Right, this is a bedroom, inside there is a bed, that," she told her, pointing to the bed. "On the bed is your suitcase, it has clothes in it for you to put on. Now sort out what you want to wear, then let's get out of the bloody place."

Karen began to rummage through the clothes in the suitcase. "These are very nice, and you say they are mine?"

"Yes, put these knickers on, while I sort something else for you," Sherry answered, pushing her out of the way and selecting the clothes herself.

When she'd dressed, Sherry gave her a pair of trainers.

Karen stood then finally fastened her belt. "It feels good to have clothes on again; I hated what Chuks had me wear."

"Yes, remember that feeling, when next time I'm virtually naked, and you're ribbing me after losing my clothes," Sherry retorted.

Karen just looked at her, not understanding what this girl was talking about.

Taking the suitcase, Sherry urged Karen back down into the kitchen. Both girls carried guns, except rather than just burst out of the farmhouse, Sherry stopped her, just inside the closed door.

"I'm going to leave the way I came in," she began. "I've already been outside and couldn't see anyone. We can't afford to be complacent. I'll do one final check. If it's clear I'll call you Colonel, so unlock the door and come outside, otherwise if I use Karen, we have a problem, or I'm being held against my will, so it's up to you then."

She looked at Karen for a moment. "You've understood what I've just said, didn't you?"

Karen nodded slightly. "Yes I understand, it's just at times I get very dizzy, like I'm not really here. So you want me to stand here and face the door. If someone comes in, I fire this gun?" she answered, looking down at the gun in her hands.

"Bloody hell, Karen, you're one mixed-up girl. Fuck the caution; you'll end up killing me," she said with alarm, walking over and taking the gun from her. "Just stand back, I'll open the door and check once more."

Sherry unlocked the door gingerly, opening it slightly; keeping close to the wall, she went outside. She could still see no movement, so she decided Chuks must have come alone after all. "It's all clear, Karen, let's go," Sherry called back behind her.

Karen never answered back.

She sighed, returning to the room. Karen was standing looking out the doorway, but didn't seem all there.

"Karen, get a bloody grip will you?" Sherry demanded.

She looked at Sherry. "My name's Amber. So rather than keep mixing me up with someone named Karen, can you at least call me by my real name? Then I'll know you're talking to me, and not somebody else."

Sherry grasped Karen's hand. "Come on, Amber, or whoever you think you are. We'll sort this out at the hotel; I'm bloody starving."

Once outside and locking the front door, the two girls ran to the car. Soon they were on the main road; Sherry was heading in the direction of the hotel.

***

Arriving at the hotel, she parked up. They went direct to the room; Sherry, carrying Karen's suitcase, dropped it on the floor, then glanced down at her watch. "I've still got a few hours to wait; I need food, so I'm getting a pizza, do you want one?"

Karen became more attentive; food had been mentioned. "So long as it's not rice with bits of veg in it. Can I have something to drink, not warm tea though."

"Are you right in the head, or taking the piss?" Sherry asked.

"How can bloody pizza be rice?"

Karen never replied, just sat on the edge of the bed, looking down at her hands.

Sherry left the room, locking it carefully; ran down the stairs, and through the reception, ending up at a pizza takeaway further down the road. As she waited, her thoughts went back to Karen and the way she was behaving. She knew something was seriously wrong, but whatever it was, it certainly wasn't cocaine, or any of the drugs she'd seen people high on. Karen seemed to have a memory block of some sort that didn't stop her actually talking and making sense, but she didn't seem to be able to associate what some words described, and yet in other ways she knew what tea, or rice was. Tonight she intended to take out the other two Nigerians; could she take the risk and leave Karen on her own? She wasn't sure, but decided if she left later than planned, Karen may well be asleep.

***

Karen was lying back on the bed, her eyes closed, when Sherry returned.

She walked over, giving her a shake. "I've got the food, I'll be out on the balcony."

Karen joined her in minutes, tucking into the pizza and drinking the coke. "This is really good, I'll get this again. What do you call it?"

"It's pizza, Karen, I told you this only half an hour ago. So snap out of it and concentrate," Sherry replied sternly.

"Then stop calling me Karen, I'm confused enough without you trying to change my name all the time," she shouted back, slamming the empty plate onto the side table, before walking to the edge of the balcony, looking down at the pool below. She turned to face Sherry; there were tears in her eyes. "I'm trying, I really am," she said quietly. "It's just that I can't imagine what some of the words you mention look like. I keep thinking I know, in fact, I know I should, but like pizza, I'd no idea what it was, all I could think of because you mentioned food, is what Chuks gave me, rice with bits in."

"So what can you remember?" Sherry asked.

Karen was silent for a few minutes, turning around again, leaning on the balcony. Sherry got fed up of waiting for her to say something, so carried on eating.

"I'm in a room, sat on the mattress," she suddenly blurted out. "I'm alone for long periods of time, it's dark and quiet, so quiet, I can almost hear my own heart beating. Every few hours Chuks comes. I'm taken and punished." She paused. "I have to tell him he owns me, that he's my master, and I must offer myself willingly, before I get food. Chuks takes me, always finishing up my backside. He's so big; it hurts so much, but I don't struggle to prevent him, I get punished if I do, so I just take it." Tears were streaming down her face. "I'm so confused, I don't even know who I am, or where I come from."

Sherry went to her, pulling her close, Karen was sobbing uncontrollably.

"Chuks was drugging you; it must still be in your bloodstream; that's why you can't think. You should go to bed, sleep it off. Maybe when the drug loses its grip, you'll know who you are."

Karen was listening to her, realising that what she told her did seem to make sense. "I think I will lie down; I still feel dizzy, and my head is banging. Do you have any chewy, it dulls the pain I'm in?"

"No, Karen, you've got to learn to live without it from now on."

***

Sherry glanced at her watch. It was coming up to eleven at night; time to get ready. She wanted to be at the brothel on surveillance before they closed. The two of them had watched television for a time. Sherry had fetched them supper; they'd eaten in silence; Karen was lying on the bed when Sherry went through to the bathroom.

Ten minutes later she was out, dressed in black jeans and a black jumper, holding a black baseball hat to hide her blonde hair. She walked over to Karen, who was still lying on the bed.

Karen turned her head to look at her as she approached.

Sitting on the edge of the bed, Sherry looked down. "I have to go out, Amber. If I don't come back, I've left a number on the paper alongside the clock, call it, and read them the name I've written down and the code number. The code number's important; it's the unit's unique number, so they know it's you. Tell them where you are, and you need help. They will come."

Karen just looked back at her with a vacant expression, saying nothing.

Sherry, realising she must still be heavily influenced by the drug Chuks was giving her, decided all she needed was rest and she would probably fall asleep once she'd gone. So she made her way to the door, then turned. "Whatever you do, you must remember to dial the number and give them the information." She said no more and left the room.

Chapter Sixty-Four

After Sherry had gone, Karen tried to sleep, but sleep wasn't coming easy, she just lay there wide awake; then, while the effort in even moving her limbs, caused by the drug, had gone, the headache that had been with her since the two overdoses had only eased. Even so, while the physical symptoms were receding, every time she tried to bring together memories of her past life, they would be fragmented, or images which didn't seem to want to come together; so she would discard them as no longer having any importance. The injections of chewy, coupled with Chuks' constant demands that she should think of nothing else, apart from her name, and what she did for him, were now imprinted in her mind; reinforced by the punishments he'd meted out on her, when she answered in a way he didn't like. Now as she lay there, all that was left which made sense was Chuks. It was Chuks, as far as she was concerned, who totally controlled her life, from being given a place to sleep, her food, then more importantly, what was expected of her in return; Karen still didn't have the strength, or the impetus, to pull herself out of the vicious circle Chuks had created, with the help of the chewy. Just thinking about him terrified her, even when he wasn't there.

It was with these thoughts that Karen decided the girl who had brought her to the hotel must also work for Chuks. Where had she gone? Then Chuks said he would bring men to shag her, so where was he, and where were the men? Already bored of being inside, she began wondering if she'd not understood, and Chuks had expected her to find these men? If that were the case, when Chuks found her still here, he'd punish her. The only excuse she had, was that she seemed to remember Chuks said he would bring them; not for her to go out and find them herself. All these thoughts were going round in her mind, and the more she thought about it, the more she'd become convinced that she'd got herself confused, it wasn't Chuks who found clients, it was her, the same as the other girl must be doing. Karen finally decided that rather than risk being returned to the punishment room, she should do as Chuks wanted of her and go out.

Going through to the bathroom, Karen, after tying her hair back, began to put on make-up. Normally she'd use very little, just to give her a colour, except this time her eye make-up was heavy, her lips red and thick, the cheeks more like a clown. It was if she'd no real idea of how to put the make-up on, like she was a child doing it for the first time. Standing in front of the mirror, she looked herself over. She didn't even recognise who she was looking at; her face looked drawn, her fingernails were broken and ragged, her body didn't glow, just looked dull and lifeless. Her time with Chuks, the aggressive way he'd always taken her, had made an impression. Already Karen was missing the times she'd experienced with him desperately, so the very thought of doing it with another man, even if the man didn't have the aggression of Chuks, excited her. Looking through her suitcase, she decided to wear something similar to the nightdress she'd always worn. There was nothing like that, so she selected a loose fitting summer dress, with knickers and high-heeled shoes. Karen wondered if she really needed the knickers; Chuks never gave her any to wear so she couldn't see a use for them. But she decided to leave them on for the time being, the dress was short, and she'd have to sit around in the public bars, before going to a man's room. Now ready, she picked up her handbag, along with the door card, and left the room.

***

Soon Karen was settled at the bar of the hotel she was staying in, drink in hand, watching the entertainment. She'd been there about fifteen minutes, trying to decide how to choose someone to approach, when a man came to the bar holding half a glass of beer, standing at her side.

He glanced at her. "Is this seat taken?"

"No," Karen replied.

The man sat down, looking towards the small raised stage. "What do you think of the singer?" he asked, striking up a conversation.

Karen looked at the singer. What did he mean by think, was this the singer's name? She had no idea, so she shrugged indifferently. "Okay, I suppose."

He nodded. "Yes, I thought that as well."

He sat for a while listening to the singer; then finishing his drink he called the bartender over, before glancing at Karen. "Would you

335

like a refill?"

While he had been sitting there, Karen had considered getting into conversation with him. That was after looking around and seeing the majority of men were with someone. Except with him offering her a drink, getting into a conversation was no longer a problem. She guessed he'd be in his middle twenties, and he had a rugged, well-tanned complexion. A good three inches taller than her, he was wearing tee-shirt and jeans, the tee-shirt exposing a well-toned muscular body, not overweight, and he didn't revolt her in any way. Karen gave him a smile, after deciding he may be her first client. "I'm told this is a lager, may I have the same please?"

He ordered the drinks, but couldn't understand why the bartender should be telling her what the drink was called, it looked obvious to him. Discounting it, and deciding not to ask why she needed to be told, he took the usual route of introduction. "The name's Shaun," he said, extending his hand.

"I'm Amber," she answered, shaking his hand. His grip was firm, and he lingered holding her hand for that little bit longer, before releasing her.

"Are you on holiday?" he asked.

Karen had no idea what a holiday was. So she shook her head. "No, only tonight, I think." Whether being here was a holiday, she didn't know, but she hadn't wanted to ask him, she was confused enough.

"Your English is very good, but I don't recognise the accent. Are you from the UK?"

What was he talking about, English, UK? How did she know? If this place is called UK then she must be English. Karen decided not to make her answer complicated. If he wanted to believe her to be English and from the UK, that was good enough. "Yes I am. Where are you from?" she asked, pushing the question away from her.

"Originally I'm from London, but I work here now," he replied, not elaborating what work he did. "So what do you do for a living, Amber?"

Karen hesitated, the use of her name and his direct question to tell him what she did for a living, took her back to the cellar, with

Chuks inside her room, and his constant demands to keep repeating the answer to this question, every time he saw her. But this man wasn't Chuks; so she hesitated, afraid of how he would react. "I'm with a man called Chuks."

Shaun had picked up his drink just before she replied, but stopped halfway and put it back onto the bar top. He looked at her for a moment. "Is this Chuks you work for, a Nigerian?"

Karen remembered Chuks told her he was in the Nigerian army, so that must be what Shaun meant by asking. "Yes, do you know him?" Karen asked, hoping he did, then he could be one of the men Chuks had intended for her.

"I do, in fact, I work as a minder at the house, but I've never seen you there."

"I don't know of this house you talk about. All I know is Chuks owns me and I work for him."

Shaun drank up quickly; then looked directly at her, keeping his voice down, so only she could hear. "This hotel doesn't like girls like you, trying to pick up around their bars. If you are here for what I think you are, we should go for a walk on the seafront, then we can talk?"

Karen felt relieved; Chuks should have no excuse to punish her; at least she was talking to a man who knew him. Not that she could understand why the hotel didn't like her talking to a man, she'd done nothing wrong. "Yes, if you want," she answered, finishing her lager.

They left the hotel area, heading towards the seafront. Then once away from the hotel, he carried on quizzing her. "So is Chuks here? Has he a room in the hotel? If he has; he's got to be out his mind."

"I'm in a room with another girl, but she's gone out working and Chuks hasn't arrived yet. Why are you here?"

"I live a few miles down the road. I'd seen you go to the bar, noticed nobody joined you, so I decided to buy you a drink, then offer to take you to the nightclub. I nearly dropped my beer when you mentioned Chuks. The last thing I expected was to find one of his working girls trying to pick up at the bar. If the manager found out, he would call the police and get you locked up for the night. Their bars are family bars and they want to keep it that way. So why didn't you just say you were on the game, a call girl, or whatever and available?"

337

Karen frowned. "I'm not any of those, Chuks told me I'm a prostitute."

He couldn't believe the girl was so thick as to not know that a prostitute was also called a call girl, after all at her age she must already be servicing men on a regular basis. "Well it was a good job you told me you prostituted for him, and not some guy you'd picked up, Chuks would have used the cat on you, if he found out. He doesn't like people knowing he uses unregistered girls."

Karen had come to a halt. "You won't tell him, will you?"

"I'm still thinking about that. So how long have you been with him?" Shaun asked.

Karen had no idea. "I don't know. It must be a long time. I can't seem to remember doing anything else."

"So has Chuks got you working tonight, or is it your night off?"

She thought for a moment. "I don't have this night off you talk about."

"Then you're available?"

Karen didn't hesitate in answering. "I'm not really sure; you see, Chuks said he'd bring men, but he hadn't come, so I thought I'd got it wrong, and I was supposed to find men myself."

Turning to face Karen, he looked her up and down, before grasping her shoulders and pulling her closer. Then running his hands down her back, he pulled away after gripping the cheeks of her bottom with both hands. Karen didn't object, standing still allowing him to do that. "If Chuks has left you alone, rather than bring men to you, then he'd expect you to find them. You're a bit old for me, but I'm after a shag, and you've a tight bottom so you'll have to do. Your payment will be for me keeping my mouth shut."

Karen was put out; she didn't think she looked that old, not that she could actually remember how old she was. "I'm okay with you shagging me. Thank you for not telling Chuks. Shall we go to your room?"

He gave a forced laugh. "I want to fuck you, not fucking live with you. We'll go to the beach; there's a few small tourist boats piled up for the night; we can go behind them?"

Karen was taken aback by his suggestion. "I'm not going to get undressed on the beach, with people walking past all the time."

Shaun grinned. "Are you for real? You're a fucking prostitute, already being shagged by anything with a dick. Then with what little you have on, getting undressed quickly is not exactly difficult."

"I know that, but where Chuks keeps me, at least I have a room to undress in; I don't do it in public."

"I see, so you have this belief; I'd want to treat you in a way I would a real girlfriend?"

Karen wasn't sure what a girlfriend was, but a girlfriend must be special, by the way he was talking. "Why not, I'm not only letting you shag me, but will also show how affectionate and submissive I can be, like a girlfriend."

Suddenly he moved forward, gripping her shoulders with his hands. "What's all this fucking affectionate shit? I wouldn't want a prostitute for a girlfriend. I wouldn't even want to kiss you, after the amount of dicks you've probably sucked off. I only want a quick shag, so you get your fucking knickers off and bend over," he demanded aggressively, then shrugged indifferently. "But it's up to you, I'm not that desperate, forget I asked. I'll give Chuks a call, and keep hold of you till he comes. When I tell him what you've been up to, then how you refused to shag, expect the cat, or he may use the rod on you."

She looked alarmed, the memory of the punishment room, in particular the electric rod, was still very real in her mind. "Please don't tell Chuks, he punishes me for simply saying the wrong word. If I'm just lifting my dress out of sight of the road, I'll do as you ask."

"In that case, let's go," he demanded, grasping her hand, virtually dragging her onto the beach towards the few tourist rowboats tied up. Soon they were on the dark side, out of sight of people walking along the seafront.

"Right, get yourself ready, I may decide to finish up your arse, so make sure you lubricate yourself well."

Karen stood there, not moving. "I don't have anything like that with me," she said softly.

Slipping his hand into his pocket, he drew out a tube, as well as a condom. "Then it's a good job I do, so while I get this condom on, stuff some jelly up your arse."

Karen removed her knickers, putting them inside her handbag, then rubbed a little of the jelly around her entrance and up her back passage, the way Chuks had done to her each day.

Even before Karen had screwed the cap back on the tube, Shaun had turned her round to face the boats, pushing her dress up, exposing her bottom. Moments later he had her bent down, gripping her hips firmly, pushing up inside her. Karen was holding onto the top edge of a boat, stopping him pushing her forward and smashing her head on the side, as he took her aggressively from behind. Within minutes, he pulled out. She thought it was over; it wasn't, he was already trying to force himself up her backside. He was hurting her, so she began struggling, pulling away from him.

He abruptly stopped, grabbed a lump of her dress with one hand, preventing her from moving away any further. "Playing hard to get are we? Let's see if a little house punishment will bring you into line," he said aggressively, at the same time reaching down with his other hand, pulling one of his trainers off, then immediately laying into her bottom and top of her legs with the trainer. His punishment was hard, painful and relentless.

Karen never expected this, it took her back to the punishment room. Shaun could be Chuks, knowing the only way he'd stop was if she succumbed to his demands. "Please, you're hurting me that's all, I'm not trying to prevent your going up my backside, you can, just stop hitting me," she implored.

He didn't give up at once, requiring her to experience punishment, so next time she would do anything he wanted of her without question. Then he broke off, pushing her away. "Looks like you've been having it easy, working the hotels. From now on, if a man wants you up the arse, you let him. If I, the same as Chuks, tell you to do anything, you do it. Understand?" he said aggressively.

"Yes, it won't happen again," she answered meekly, tears trickling down her cheek.

"Then let's get rid of the fucking dress, it's in the way," he retorted, at the same time moving closer, grasping her dress, pulling it up over her head and off her arms, throwing it to the ground, leaving her naked. Karen never objected; the punishment and fear in her mind were overwhelming any objection, or retaliation she could muster. She was really scared of this man, the same as with Chuks. "What are you waiting for? Fucking turn around and hold onto the boat, struggle again, I'll really lay into you," he shouted at her.

She gripped the edge of the boat. Shaun moved behind, kicked her legs further apart as he started pushing himself up. Once inside he reached round her body, holding her breast, preventing her from pulling away again. Karen just held on, her eyes closed, clenching her buttocks, trying to make him come quickly, so he'd pull out of her. This was as bad as Chuks in the basement.

Finally, he finished, allowing her to collect the dress, pulling it on quickly, leaving her knickers off until she could clean herself later.

"I now know why Chuks keeps you, you're not a bad shag, nice and tight both ways; I've loved the experience. If you're still around the hotel for the next few days and see me at the bar, don't come near me. I'll come to you if I want a repeat. Do you understand?"

"I understand if you'd rather us not be seen together. Not that I can see what's wrong with me."

He shrugged with indifference. "Whatever. Anyway, Chuks will expect you to be working. The nightclub will be packed by now, so you'll get plenty of takers. They've a disabled toilet behind the stage no one uses. Take your clients in there, it's large enough. Most are drunk, so you make all the noises, urge them on, they'll come quicker. He'll be expecting you to service at least ten, even fifteen, before the club closes, charging ten dollars a blow, fifty a shag, with an extra twenty-five if they want to go up your arse to finish off."

Karen remembered that Chuks had mentioned ten men, except she knew she couldn't cope with that many if they were like Shaun. But she didn't tell him; he might call Chuks, or may even go with her, to make sure she did as he said. So she decided to play along. "Thank you for telling me about the toilet. Can I keep the tube and have you any more of those things you put on?"

He frowned. "You mean a condom?" he asked.

"Yes, if that's what they are called."

"You can have the tube, I've got one more, but condoms, you get your own, most don't want to use them. I always do when I'm

341

shagging a pro; you don't know if they have lice, or even the pox."

Karen looked at him with indignation. "I don't think I have this pox, or lice thank you."

He laughed. "Maybe not yet, but you will. You'd better get Chuks to shave your fanny, unless you want lice crawling around in it. Anyway clear off, I'll look in on you later, to make sure you're working hard."

Karen walked away, except rather than head towards the nightclub Shaun had told her about, she decided to return to the room and talk to the other girl. After all, she'd been with one client tonight, in her mind that was enough, outside a bedroom that is. At least she could tell Chuks she'd tried, but needed him to look after her.

***

Back inside the hotel, she walked through the reception area into a lift. A couple followed her in.

"What floor?" the man asked, his fingers hovering over the buttons.

She stood there unable to remember, quickly pulling the key card from her bag. Looking at the card, for security reasons it had no indication of the room number, just the name of the hotel and she'd forgotten which floor she was on, or even the number of the room.

"I'm not sure. I'll have to go and ask," she replied,

He pushed the door open button, and she went back into the reception area.

There she hesitated, who should she say she was? Rummaging through her bag, she pulled out a passport. It stated she was someone called Karen Marshall, even the photo looked like her, and she seemed to recognise the name, but it wasn't her name. Then if she went to reception, who should she say she was, Amber, which was her real name, then Amber who, or was she this Karen Marshall as the passport said? Either way, she couldn't understand how she could go to the reception asking what room the key fitted. The room may even be in the other girl's name and not in hers at all.

Karen didn't know what she should do. She needed help, the only person she could think of, who would help her, was Chuks; even then she'd no idea how to find him. All she could hope was that he'd find her, then take her back to her room.

With not being able to go to the room, Karen instead went to the ladies, cleaning herself as best she could, before replacing her knickers. Leaving the hotel, she crossed the road to the seafront, wandering aimlessly, before giving up and sitting down on a bench, looking out to sea. How long she sat there, she had no idea. A few lads and older men had made comments as they walked past her towards the nightclub, but Karen had not answered back, or even tried to get them to shag her in exchange for money. Although Shaun had specifically told her to do that, she had no intention of going out on the beach with different men, for her it had to be a hotel room or nothing. Walking slowly back to the hotel and sitting at the bar, she ordered a drink, paying with what little cash was left in her purse, she had nowhere else to go.

"We're closing up love, the nightclub's open till three, if you want to drink," the bartender told her, as he took her empty glass.

"Thank you, which way is it?"

"Down that way," he replied, pointing in the direction she had come.

Karen didn't really want to go to the club, but with nowhere else to go, then needing Shaun to call Chuks to collect her, she couldn't see an option. For him to do that, she had to show Shaun she'd been selling herself, as was expected, otherwise if he told Chuks she'd done nothing, he'd take her to the punishment room. That was something she didn't want to happen.

Walking along the seafront, she could already hear the music, with lots of people milling around outside the club, as she got closer. Trying to avoid them, she joined the queue, waiting to get inside; soon she was at the entrance.

"Ten dollars, love," the man said at the door.

Opening her purse, she found it was almost empty, with only a few low-value coins left. Her stopping off for a drink at the hotel bar had taken all the money. "I've not got enough, I've run out of cash," she told him.

"Without money, you don't go in, so get lost," he retorted.

Karen didn't know what to say, she could hardly tell him she'd pay later, with what she'd try to earn inside the club, with everyone listening. Karen walked quickly away, aware of other people waiting to get in. She considered approaching the men hanging around outside, but most were not even in their twenties; more interested in the younger girls, who were laughing and shouting; most completely off their heads with drugs and drink.

Deciding she could get herself in deep trouble, maybe even gang-raped, by saying what she was, Karen left the area, walking aimlessly along the seafront. She'd been expecting Chuks to be waiting to take her back. Even her room and mattress were better than this, but he wasn't, she was alone. She down onto the beach, hoping to find a sun lounger to sleep on, but the only ones she could find were all chained up securely, so she ended up back at the boats where Shaun had taken her. She pulled out an old newspaper, stuffed between the boats, laying it down before sitting on it, leaning against a wooden marker jutting out of the sand.

Whether it was instinct, or self-preservation from past experience, Karen had no idea, except she pushed her hands into the soft sand, making a hole. Removing her ring and bracelet, she slipped them inside her handbag and dropped the bag in the hole, covering it with sand. Karen lay back, gazing up at the stars, but not really seeing them, before closing her eyes. The depression caused by the hopelessness of her situation, her lack of identity, not knowing who she was, or where she came from, was weighing heavily on her mind. The only future she could see was to be treated in the way Shaun had done. If this was prostitution, it was something she was prepared to do, for self-preservation, but never as a way of life, she'd rather be dead than do that all the time. Karen was listening to the waves crashing onto the beach, considering how far she could swim out away from the shore, before she could swim no further. She was now very close to taking that final swim, never to return.

***

How long she lay there, Karen had no idea, but she was brought out of her thoughts by someone yelling at her.

"I said wake-up, we want money," a man was shouting, at the same time kicking her in the side, until she responded, then he stood back.

Karen sat up, there were two Turkish men of around twenty standing there, looking down at her. "Don't we all, I'm broke," she retorted

He laughed harshly. "If that's the case, we'll have that watch you're wearing, then as a bonus, we'll both give you a good shagging."

Karen just stood there. "I don't shag for free; it'll cost you fifty dollars each. Cash in advance," she replied, remembering what Shaun had told her she should charge.

The lad looked at his partner. "It's a fucking prostitute, asking fifty dollars a pop," he said to his friend, then began to laugh, before looking back at Karen. "I'm not putting my dick up a pox ridden fanny, besides, you're old enough to be my mother. But I still want the watch. Refuse and expect a few slashes across the face," he demanded.

He took out a flick knife from his pocket, snapping it open; its four-inch blade glittered in the light from the seafront illuminations. As Karen stood watching him, the fear and hopelessness of her situation that had been engulfing her before they came, were gone. This lad was threatening her life; that was something no one did. How she knew that, besides having no idea why she'd no fear of the lad holding the knife. "So the only item of value I've got, and which I may need to feed myself, you intend to take off me? Get lost, I'm giving you nothing."

The lad with the knife didn't hesitate, he lunged forward. Within moments of his coming at her, she'd side-stepped, at the same time wrenching his arm up and snapping it like a twig, the knife dropping harmlessly to the ground. As he screamed in pain, she followed the knife down, snatching it up. However, the other lad had also brought out a knife and was about to help his partner. Karen saw this; her reaction was fast and deadly, throwing the knife she'd picked up at the other lad. The knife embedded itself in his chest. He dropped his own knife, already he was feeling faint, as he stumbled away with his injured mate following. Both were shouting obscenities back at her, but weren't prepared to take her on again.

Karen walked over, picked the discarded knife up, snapping it shut. Then pulling her bag from in the sand, she droped it in, before burying the bag once more. At least now she had a weapon, if any other muggers decided to rob her. However, the shock of the lads threatening her, the adrenaline rush, was also all she needed to snap her out of her despair; it had become the catalyst for breaking down the barriers inside her mind, beginning to bring her thoughts together once more. This was a very small step, but at least she was thinking beyond Chuks.

Chapter Sixty-Five

Igbo went through to the specials lounge to see Iroatu, who was sorting clients for the girls. He took him to one side.

"With Chuks not coming back to take Charlene to the hotel, I sent the lads to see if he'd problems at the farm. They've just returned. Chuks is dead and Amber's missing. They've got him out, burying him at the back of the farm. We don't want the police sniffing around."

Iroatu looked scared. "I bloody knew this would happen. So what do we do now, she'll hit us hard, that's for certain, after what Chuks has been doing with her."

"We bail, go back to Nigeria and live like kings. We've got close to five million stashed, to split only two ways now. Pula won't be here for a few days to collect his payment. So it's all ours."

"What about the three illegals?"

"Take them to the farm and cut their throats. There's no link to us there. It's rented by Pula, as his stop-off for girls coming in from Asia. Let him sort out the bodies."

"So when do we go?"

"Tonight. While you close up, I'll pack my car. You take the van with the girls to the farm; I'll follow. Then leaving the van at the farm, we'll drive overnight to Syria. We'll easily get over the border and pick up a plane direct to Nigeria. I've family in customs at the airport. They'll get us into the country without any bag searches."

Iroatu looked at his watch. "There's only two left, most of the girls have gone home. Give it an hour, and I'll be ready. To tell you the truth, I'm glad to be getting out. Chuks was getting paranoid about Amber, already he had earmarked her for some of the more expensive clients. Believed she would be earning six hundred a pop. He was in cuckoo-land, that girl would always be very dangerous."

"I agree with you. We should never have used chewy; it's too slow to build up before you can overdose. If we'd used cocaine like I wanted to blow her mind out, cut and dyed her hair, then put her on the floor, she'd be earning now. Anyway I'll go and pack."

At that moment, Igbo's mobile began to ring. He looked at the caller and pressed the answer button. "What do you want, Shaun, isn't this your night off?"

"Yes, but I'm looking for Chuks. He's not answering his phone, is he with you?"

"No, why do you want him?"

"I was at the Clarian Hotel sussing a girl out for taking to the nightclub. She turned out to be one of his girls, Amber, even told me she worked for him. I've never seen her before; does she work the hotels? because if she does, Chuks should be telling her not to go blabbing that she works for him, and besides, keep her away from the Clarian; they'll not put up with it and call the police. Anyway, I've sent her to work the nightclub. Can you let Chuks know?"

"Hold on," Igbo told him, then muted the call. "Shaun's found Karen. Says she's trying to pickup around the Clarian Hotel, calling herself Amber; so maybe the chewy did work and her mind's blown, or she needs money to get out of the country. How she's ended up there is anyone's guess."

Iroatu shook his head; he was confused. "We should get rid of that girl once and for all. Tell Shaun to take her on the beach, then slit her throat. Offer him twenty-five grand, after all, we won't be here to pay it."

Igbo nodded and took the mobile off mute. "Shaun, the girl's fucked. Chuks is pissed off with her, besides her being too old for what we want. How would you like to earn twenty-five grand in cash?"

"What do you want me to do?"

"Take Amber out on the beach; make it look like a robbery, maybe even rape, then knife her. We can't have her blabbing around, like she's doing."

"I agree; it was lucky I picked her up. I'll see to it. When do I get paid?"

"Come in tomorrow sometime and see Iroatu."

Chapter Sixty-Six

Shaun had been sitting in his car when he'd called the brothel and spoken to Igbo. He reached into the glove-box and took out a flick-knife, hesitated for a second before also taking hold of a pair of handcuffs that he'd taken from the brothel, to use with girls he picked up, for a bit of fun. He decided if she was being difficult and wouldn't go back down along the beach, they may be useful. He flicked the knife a few times; it had a good feel and reminded him of being part of a street gang in West London. The job at the brothel had come about with the Nigerians getting to know him, after he'd moved from gang member to doorman, in the late- night drinking bars around the West End of London. He'd no qualms about killing Amber, although he might give her a final shag before cutting her throat.

Locking the car door, Shaun hurried down the seafront towards the club. Mat, the doorman and his mates were on the door.

"Here he comes, to pick up a girl for his usual nightly shag. I don't know how you do it, Shaun," Mat mocked.

Shaun just grinned. "Not tonight. I'm looking for a girl who came here earlier. She'd be alone, around thirty, five ten, slim, her hair tied back, with blue eyes, wearing a short flared blue dress."

He thought about it for a moment. "There was a girl in a blue dress. She'd no money, so we told her to clear off, we get loads like that."

"Which way did she go?"

"Towards the beach, I think."

"Thanks, Mat, I'll be around tomorrow and buy you a drink."

"Any time, Shaun. After you finish with her, send her my way, she looked my type."

"Will do," he called back.

Shaun walked along the front slowly, looking around, trying to find her, certain that if she was not hanging around the club entrance, she could easily be further along the beach. Then he had an idea, she could have returned to the boats and be working the punters coming back from the club. At least she had somewhere to take them. He began to run in that direction. Already, as he drew near, he could see the shadow of a single figure sitting on the sand. Once closer, he was certain it was Amber, she was sitting on a newspaper, gazing out to sea.

"What the fuck are you doing here, I told you to go to the club and service the drunks?" Shaun demanded, looking down at her.

Karen shrugged. "They wouldn't let me in, I'm broke and can't even remember the number of the room I was supposed to be sleeping in. Chuks hasn't turned up, so I'm on the beach for the night."

"Are you fucking stupid, as well as thick? If you'd explained to the doorman that you were with me, and I was coming later, he'd have let you in for free."

"Then you should have told me I could do that. If I'd mentioned Chuks to other men, you said I'd have been punished, how did I know you wouldn't have done the same, if I'd mentioned you?"

"So why aren't you working outside the club, if you couldn't get in?" he demanded, ignoring her logic.

Karen glared at him for a moment. "If you hadn't noticed, there were loads of girls, as young as sixteen, most out of their heads on drugs, many so drunk; the men standing around could have taken them for free. I'm nearly twice their age, so why would they go with someone they had to pay for?"

"I don't believe you; in fact you could have worked from here, picking up clients on the road. So did you have any real intention of working the fucking club, or is all this excuses coming out of your mouth?"

"Yes, I'd an intention; it's what Chuks expects in exchange for food and somewhere to live," she hesitated. "But I can't do it on my own; will you call Chuks for me? I'll even take the punishment I deserve, for not doing what you told me to do."

Shaun was annoyed. He'd the intention of robbing her of anything she'd made, before he slit her throat, except she'd earned nothing. Pushing aside his original intention of shagging her once more, he knew at this time of night there would be no problem in obtaining clients, with opportunities to make even more money, before killing her. Except to do this he had to leave her alone to fetch them. If she were lying, she'd more than likely wander off.

350

"You don't get it, do you?"

"Get what?"

"I work for the Nigerians, the same as you. It's my job, not only to look after the safety of the girls, but make sure they stay in line. You've already had a slapping for not performing, even with me; do you want a fucking repeat?"

Already scared of Shaun, the last thing she wanted was him laying into her with the trainer again. "I don't need to be threatened all the time. Just give me ten dollars to get in, and I'll work," she replied, with a resigned expression.

"No, you're not to be trusted; I find the fucking clients; you service them."

Although inwardly relieved that he intended to go with her, his reply placed Karen in a dilemma. With no real intention of picking up a client once inside the club, but now with him there, she couldn't see a way to avoid it. "If you want," she answered softly.

He laughed harshly. "I do want. So expect to work your fucking fanny off. Stand up."

She stood and was just about to collect her bag, still hidden under the sand a short distance away, when Shaun grabbed her hand. He pulled the handcuffs from his pocket, quickly snapping one handcuff on the wrist of the hand he held. The other handcuff he attached to a rope tied around the boats. He slipped the handcuff up and down the rope, to make sure it gave her enough movement, besides being secure.

"What are you doing, I thought we were going to the club?" Karen asked, alarmed at being handcuffed.

"When did I say that? I said I'd find you the clients; you work from here. The handcuffs are to make sure you don't wander away; now face the boats, hold onto them and bend down."

Karen gave him a weak smile. "I see, you want to take me again, there's no clients, just you?"

"I said hold the fucking boat and bend over," he demanded, ignoring her comment.

Karen did as she was told; she could cope with one man.

Lifting the dress, he pushed her knickers clear of her bottom, then unseen by Karen, he promptly got hold of his trainer, grabbed a chunk of her dress as he'd done earlier, so she couldn't move, then laid into her. The punishment was severe and unforgiving. Karen, taken by surprise fell to the ground, trying her best to escape, but restrained by the handcuffs. Shaun followed her down, now with her flat on her face, he continued hitting her across her legs and bottom. He wanted her submissive, scared of him and ready to service a constant stream of customers. On Karen's part, she could only grip her buttocks tightly together, trying to reduce the stinging pain from the hits, begging him to stop.

Suddenly he did. "That's for pissing about and not doing as you were told. Think yourself lucky I wasn't Chuks, he'd have had you strung up at the house and had you gang-raped. Where's the fucking tube of jelly I gave you?"

Karen's distress was very obvious, tears running down her face as she pulled her knickers back up, the constant punishments wearing her down. Even so, she didn't want Shaun to go into her bag for the tube. Inside was the flick-knife. If Shaun found it, she'd be defenceless. She already had a feeling that he'd just leave her on the beach handcuffed, after he'd run out of clients. She may need that knife to release herself, if that was his plan. "I don't know, I've left it somewhere, but I can't remember where," she lied, her voice breaking.

He laughed harshly. "Another fucking excuse then, it's a fucking good job I've more," he said, pulling out a tube from his pocket, handing it to her. "Put plenty on, unless you want a fanny and arse so sore by the end of the night, you'll barely be able to walk tomorrow."

He watched for a moment as she opened the tube, before pulling her dress up and slipping her knickers off.

"While you do that, I'll go and find your first shag. When I bring him, take the fucking dress off so he can see what he's getting. Then make sure you give him a good time."

"I do know what to do, but I'm not standing around naked all night," she answered, with a resigned expression on her face. How she wished she'd never gone out tonight, it was turning into a nightmare.

He simply shrugged. "Please yourself, put it back on between clients if you want, not that you'll have much time. So have we any more fucking excuses?"

"No."

"That's good. Try to be difficult with the client, you'll find my trainer across your backside." Then he walked away.

Once out of sight, Karen tried to get her bag, still hidden under the sand. If she could get it, she could cut the rope and escape, before he came back. Unable to reach it, even with stretching her arm, because of the constraint of the handcuffs, she kicked her shoes off and began to dig the sand around the bag with her toes. It was slow going and difficult. Then she heard voices; Shaun was on his way back with a man of about forty. Quickly she covered the hole with her foot and stood.

"Get your fucking dress off when I bring a client; don't let me tell you again," Shaun demanded as he walked towards her.

Karen unfastened the straps and stepped out of the dress, pushing it to one side. She felt acutely embarrassed with Shaun at her side, as he turned her round to face the man, then slapped her bottom once. "Like I promised you, nice long legs leading up to her tight fanny. If you want to finish off up her backside, she'll struggle, even try to stop you, but give her a few slaps, it'll make her submissive, and so she'll really grip you with the buttocks," he told him, before turning to Karen, his voice low. "Get in position. Remember, he's paid for ten minutes, so you let him do whatever he wants to you. Make it difficult, don't give him a good time... you know what to expect when I come back."

Karen said nothing; she just stood there not moving, waiting to be told how he wanted her.

The man didn't delay, turning her to face the boats, telling her to bend down, with her legs well apart. Soon he was gripping her hips as he worked her hard.

Even before he'd finished, Shaun was back with another man. They both watched as the first man finally pulled out from her. He had a big grin on his face. "You're right, Shaun, she's a tight shag. If she's here tomorrow night, I'll have her again." Then he walked away back up the beach.

Karen hadn't even time to tidy herself, before the man who'd

353

been waiting his turn, turned her around to face him, pushing his jeans down, demanding she start with a blowjob before he'd take her from the front.

Shaun was again back with yet another man, except this man was obviously drunk. Karen was still servicing the previous one.

"Come on, Amber, don't keep your client waiting," he mocked. "You're not getting through them fast enough; that's twice I've come back and you're still shagging. At this rate, you'll have yourself a queue. The club's closed, and they're piling out." Then he walked away again.

As soon as the man finished with Karen, the drunk took his place. This time, the man was drooling all over her, his breath knocking her sick, trying to kiss her, holding her breasts, hurting her. His pants were already at his feet, his penis not even hard. She'd had enough, bringing her knee up into his crotch; he pulled away gasping, then threw up. "Fuck off, sober yourself up, then come back if you still want your shag," she yelled at him, afraid if she didn't at least offer, he'd tell Shaun.

"I'll be back; you'll see," he slurred, pointing his finger at her after pulling his pants up, before staggering away towards the water.

Shaun still wasn't back after the man left. Karen didn't dwell on her discomfort and disgust at what was happening to her, but quickly put her dress back on, then tried again for the bag. She was determined to get it; there was no way she could cope with what Shaun was having her do. This time she succeeded in working her foot between the bag and the strap, pulling it towards her, until she was able to grab it. Karen was just about to open the bag and cut the rope, when she saw Shaun coming back down the beach, with another man in his forties. It gave her only enough time to make a hole in the soft sand and hide the bag, before standing and removing her dress. She grabbed the tube and rubbed more jelly between her legs and up her bottom.

This man was rough, pushing her hard against the side of the boat, gripping and squeezing her breasts until she was gasping in pain, before he began forcing himself inside her. After he'd finished, he stood back, then began to urinate over her, laughing at her verbal objections.

Shaun was standing a short distance away watching, but did nothing to stop the man doing this. Once he'd gone, Shaun came closer. He picked the newspaper up, stuffing it into her hand. "Wipe the piss off your legs; then tidy yourself up, you look a mess. When I come back, you'd better be greased up well. You've got yourself a two-up, wanting to go up your fanny and arse at the same time; I've agreed, and they've gone for money from the machine."

Karen wiped herself, pulling the dress back on as he spoke. She wanted to object, tell him she wouldn't do it. Somehow she had to get herself free before they came. She was appalled at the prospect of what they intended to do with her.

"How many more are going to shag me tonight?" she asked, trying to make it seem as if she was prepared to go on.

"Not many, maybe five or six, after the lads. That's if you move your arse faster and get them to come quicker." He glanced at his watch. "They should be back now, I'll get them."

With him walking away and no longer watching, Karen dropped to the ground, digging in the sand with her hands for the bag. She had no intention of taking that level of abuse, whatever he thought. Once she had the bag, Karen pulled the knife out and cut the rope, releasing the handcuffs. At once, she stood up.

"I've had it for tonight; the last one was tough enough, urinating over me, and you can forget this perverted idea of two taking me at the same time, or even the six following, it's not going to happen," she yelled after him.

He stopped and turned, before beginning to walk back slowly towards her. "You're a fucking prostitute, it's what you do," he shouted.

"I know what I am, but that doesn't mean I should accept perversion, or abuse," she retorted.

"We own you, you have no say in what you do or do not do. As it is, all that's left tonight are the drunks, who can't get anything else. As for being pissed on, most can't hold it in, with a belly full of beer in their gut after shagging; so don't give me shit, that it's never happened to you before? But I warned you earlier, refuse to service a client and expect punishment. But not a trainer, I'll cut you up, giving you a permanent reminder. After all, they won't be looking at your face while they're shagging you."

Karen never replied, just began backing away. He couldn't understand how she'd released herself, but he'd come to a halt, standing there watching her pathetic attempt to put distance between them. In all likelihood, he decided, she was intending to make a run for it. He was savouring the moment when he'd catch her up and pull the blade across her throat.

"I see you've got yourself free, it'll do you no good, Amber. You won't get far, before I catch you."

Karen was now away from the boats. She smiled. "I'm not running. We both now have knives. Perhaps, if I'm lucky, I get to kill you, rather than you kill me."

Shaun couldn't believe what he was hearing; Amber was actually threatening him. "One last chance, Amber, shag, or you die? I wasn't in a street gang for years, to turn away from a fight; if it wasn't so one-sided, I'd feel sorry for you, but I don't."

She shrugged indifferently. "In that case, I die, anything's better than this life."

He didn't delay but came for her. Already she had seen the way he stood with the knife in his right hand. It was too far in front of him; the thrust distance would be short; his wrist exposed. The way he'd positioned himself was as if he saw her as no threat. Karen dropped the arm of her hand holding the knife.

Shaun saw her arm drop. He smiled inwardly; this girl knew nothing about fighting with knives, it was far too low, she wouldn't be able to raise it quickly enough, with any strength, to penetrate his skin.

As for Karen, she knew exactly what she was doing, as he lunged forward. Her sidestep was slow, allowing him to follow, believing he had her.

Shaun's arm, by this time, was virtually outstretched, intending not to thrust with the knife, but use the forward inertia of his body, to crash into her, pushing the knife straight into her heart. She had no way to protect herself with her weapon down.

Karen's side-step was just the beginning, she also, with surprising speed, turned at the very last moment, sideways; with the outstretched knife of Shaun's passing harmlessly inches past her. Shaun tried to correct, but he was too late. Karen had brought her own knife up very fast, not to penetrate his skin as he'd believed, but to slice deep into Shaun's wrist, severing arteries. Blood poured out; he felt momentarily faint, as she avoided his stumble, sinking her blade into his liver and twisting it, to increase the severity of the injury, as he passed her. Then Karen stepped back, ready to defend herself, if she'd not disabled him sufficiently. But she had; Shaun collapsed onto the ground. Already blood was beginning to pool around him.

"You're dead, Shaun, or soon will be. I've burst your liver; the blood will already be pumping into your guts, as well as out of the wound. Now throw me the key for the handcuffs, or expect me to slit your throat."

He pulled the key from his pocket and threw it over to her; very nervous of this girl, stunned at how fast she'd been with the knife. But the loss of blood was making him feel decidedly dizzy, knowing that she was right, he was dying, unless he could find help. Except, while she stood around, he couldn't do that.

Karen picked the key up and released the handcuffs. Then retrieving her bag, she began to walk away.

"Who the hell are you, I've never seen a girl able to wield a knife like you?" he called after her.

Karen stopped, turning round to watch him trying to stem the blood oozing from his wound. "I wish I knew. You've taken not only every bit of dignity I had left, but also my pride, besides treating me like trash. If this is what you put specials that work in the house through, then I relish that fact you will die; people such as you deserve nothing less. As for Chuks, the drug he kept giving me has destroyed my memories. I'm not even sure if I've family, where I live, or what I did for a living. You can't even begin to imagine how that feels, to know nothing about yourself, or your past." She sighed. "Now I have to find out how to live again, how to survive and it won't include drunks fucking me on the beach, or anywhere else for that matter. You've certainly opened my eyes. So I intend to wait for Chuks, then kill him, the same as you. You see, when threatened, I will retaliate. As for the skills you seem to believe I have, I've no idea how I have them; except, I will use whatever I have at my disposal to protect me."

Chapter Sixty-Seven

Sherry's approach to the brothel was from the back, at just after one in the morning. With her previous drive around the area, she knew the house was set in such a way, that the one behind shared the same yard area. A heavy single wooden door was the only external entrance to the shared yard, and it was securely fastened from the inside. Sherry suspected earlier the house sharing the yard was part of the brothel, maybe the residence of the Nigerians. Either way she needed to get in the yard. Scaling the six foot wall with little effort would be easy, if it hadn't been for the rows of upturned broken bottles with jagged edges along the top. She returned to the hire car bringing back the car mats. Throwing them over the wall on top of each other, in order to afford protection from the glass, she was soon inside. Sherry stood there confused. The door to the brothel was wide open, so too was the door to the other house. She switched the safety off her gun, moving silently into the brothel. It was strangely quiet, but she'd not gone many feet before the telltale red laser lights of assault weapons were resting on her chest.

"Make your weapon safe Corporal Malloy, then lower your gun," a male voice came from in front of her.

Sherry couldn't believe she could have walked into such a simple trap. But she had no option but to do as he said, so she clicked the safety on, before pointing her gun to the floor.

"That's a sensible girl; now for the record, state your full name and unit."

"Corporal Sherry Malloy, a soldier from Unit T's Dark Angel."

Suddenly the lights were switched on, and Sherry was facing two soldiers in all black, both wore helmets with visors and radios fitted.

One took his helmet off and offered his hand to her. "Lieutenant Garcia, commander of a GIGN unit."

Sherry knew all about GIGN units. An elite parachute squadron of the French Gendarmerie Nationale. "I may seem a little stupid by my question, but why are you here?"

"Why are you?" he asked, turning the question around for her to answer.

"I'm on a search and rescue operation."

"So Unit T is now sending Dark Angel soldiers out on rescue missions alone are they? Trying to save a few euros?"

She shook her head slightly. "No. My colonel was captured; I had an idea where she could be, so I came to get her out."

He sighed. "You already have her out, which begs the question as to why you're back. Come with me to the lounge, corporal, we need to talk. The brothel is empty; the birds have flown the nest."

They went through and sat down.

"May I call you Sherry?"

She shrugged. "You may as well; you seem to know all about me."

"Let me explain, Sherry. Following Lieutenant Clavier's murder, our intelligence unit looked into it. This was one of our men; we wanted to know the real reason why he died. They weren't convinced he was robbed, as the local police were claiming. Then after the hotel manager claimed he'd checked in and stayed at the hotel alone, we found he'd actually entered the country with your colonel, Karen Harris, except she'd used her other name, Marshall. First checking if she was back in France and finding she wasn't, we suspected he'd been killed to get to her. Whoever had her, was not putting her up for ransom, but keeping her capture very quiet. We were sent in to find her and the killer of Lieutenant Clavier. We arrived yesterday, spoke to the hotel manager at length and with a little persuasion, found that the Nigerians who killed so many innocent children in London, were running this brothel. Then it all added up as to why your colonel was here, and that Lieutenant Clavier was helping her. Am I correct so far?"

"Yes, but the unit didn't know about this operation, she only confided in me, in case something went wrong."

"Something went seriously wrong, Sherry. So Lieutenant Clavier's murder was the catalyst for you coming?"

Sherry shook her head sadly. "No, the lack of a text from Karen was the reason I am here. But I had to get into their bedroom to confirm she was in trouble and hadn't remained covert, even with Lieutenant Clavier dead."

"So early yesterday, you were weighing up just how to get into this brothel?"

"I was, but Chuks, one of the Nigerians on my list, came out, so I followed him. I figured I could take him out and leave just two inside."

"We know, we followed you."

Her eyes went big and round. "You did? I never saw anyone."

"Sherry, with the best will in the world you were trained for Afghanistan as a combat incursion soldier. You would never have seen us."

"So did you know Karen was in the farmhouse?" Sherry asked.

"Yes, we'd followed Chuks the night before and like you checked the skip. We then knew someone was inside and suspected it to be Karen. We were planning to bring her out later today, besides take down the Nigerians. It was then you appeared; you did a bloody good job in releasing Karen, but a bloody lousy job in alerting the other two of a possible Unit T presence."

"Why didn't you do something?"

"We had no idea who you were until we sent a photo of you back to our intelligence unit. They told us your name, but more importantly that you were a Dark Angel soldier. At first we thought there were more of you here, but could find no trace of anyone else. By then it was too late to intervene, you'd already bedded down in the farmhouse waiting, I presume, to ambush Chuks. We wouldn't have been able to get near you, without a possible shoot-out. But why didn't you bring Karen out earlier?"

She looked slightly embarrassed. "I couldn't, she had ankle irons on, and there were no keys, so I just set up an ambush and waited. But by doing that, it seems they've escaped. Karen's in no fit state at the moment to tell me what happened with Lieutenant Clavier. She was heavily sedated." Sherry had no intention of telling them how serious a condition Karen was really in.

He shrugged. "It's academic as to who killed him. They took the underage girls from here to the farm earlier. We suspected they were bailing and covering their tracks; probably going to kill the girls as they'd done in London. Either way, it didn't really matter. We had our orders; both were taken out when they arrived. The girls were from

Africa; we will be taking them to France with us to start a new life, they deserve that opportunity, rather than to be returned to Africa and probably more abuse."

Sherry sighed. "Thank you, for sorting out my mess. I did my best, but like you say I'm just a foot soldier and not a very good one at that."

He grasped her hand and squeezed. "No, Sherry, you are. Single-handedly, you rescued your commander, with just a handgun, from a very brutal and dangerous trafficker. Then, not content with that, you came in here intent on completing your assignment, again risking your life. We'd be proud to have a soldier in our unit like you. In normal operations, you'd have been in line for military recognition and would have deserved it. As it is, this operation never happened. You never met us; even Karen must never know we were here. Karen was also never here and never abducted, she has to be told that. Lieutenant Clavier was subject to a brutal attack by a robber as the police said. You've just had a couple of days' holiday in Istanbul. Get Karen home, insist she has a doctor check her out and keep a close eye on her. If they have tried to manipulate her with drugs, she will be exhibiting irrational thoughts and actions for a while. Get her to call the unit, tell them you and her are on extended leave for a month. After all, you're both very wealthy, so you can afford a decent break."

Sherry nodded. "You're right, she is irrational in her thinking, so I'll stick to her like glue till she comes out of it. But how do you know so much about us?"

"You both live in our country. Karen is not only your commander; she is also a professional killer, extremely dangerous, and as you've probably found in this operation, a little unstable. With millions of pounds in a Swiss bank unaccounted for, the decision was made to keep a very close eye on the girl. You, as her friend, have also been investigated. There again, we find a girl with over a million pounds in her bank. Both of you come from a home environment that could not explain such sums."

"We can both explain it, and the British government knows where it came from."

"Perhaps, Sherry, but they don't tell us, anyway, you need to know one more thing, the bag at the side of the door contains a very large sum of money, I estimate getting on for four to five million dollars. Every penny of it will be placed in Karen's charity, apart from a little to assist the three girls we're taking to France with us. There are so many victims that rely on her charity, to help them get back on their feet."

Sherry stood, looking down at him. "You can be sure Karen will put the money to good use. Her charity helped me, when I was at rock bottom. Goodbye, Lieutenant, it's been nice meeting you and thank you for completing my task. Those men were worse than beasts; they didn't deserve to live."

"Look after yourself, Sherry; we will meet again one day. A word of advice: don't go down the same route as Karen; she's a loner, a cold-blooded killer and a very stupid one at that. You're a good incursion soldier, not a covert operator, stay that way. Karen's world is not yours; you're out of your depth. Such operations will get you killed, the same, unfortunately as Lieutenant Clavier, when he tried to follow her."

Chapter Sixty-Eight

Sherry returned to the hotel, going directly to the bedroom. Leaving the lights off, so as not to wake Karen, she went through to the bathroom. After cleaning her teeth and a quick wash, she did her usual thing of jamming the door with a chair, before going to the bed. She stared at the bed for a moment, then turned the light on, Karen wasn't there.

"Bloody hell, where's she gone now?" she said aloud, at the same time grabbing her jeans and pulling them back on, before donning her tee-shirt and leaving the bedroom, determined to go and find her.

She went down to reception; only the night porter was on, he was talking to another man.

"Can I help you, miss?" he asked.

"I'm looking for my friend. She is my height and build, brown hair, and very attractive."

He shook his head. "There are lots of nice-looking girls in the hotel." Then he turned to the other man, talking in their own language. The man came forward and began to speak. "This girl, would she be alone, with really stunning blue eyes?" he asked.

"Yes, have you seen her?"

"She was at the bar; we were closing, so I suggested she went to the nightclub for a drink."

Sherry thanked him and ran off. Soon she was at the club entrance.

"We're closing in half an hour, love. You can go in if you want," the doorman said.

Sherry thanked him and went inside. She checked the fast-emptying club, even the toilets, but Karen was not there. She was becoming very worried. She shouldn't have left her, but there had been no option. Although if she'd known then what she knew now, she hadn't really needed to leave Karen anyway.

Spending time walking along the seafront, Sherry even went down to the beach, but Karen was nowhere to be found. By three, she'd given up and returned to the hotel. As she walked through the hotel lobby, the night porter called her over.

"Have you found your friend?"

"No, I'm not sure what to do now."

"I'll call the police a little later for you and see if she's been picked up. They often pick up girls sleeping it off on the beach after coming out of the clubs. It's for their own safety, but they are kept overnight in a cell and are fined the following morning."

"Thank you, I'll be in my room if you find out anything."

Chapter Sixty-Nine

Sherry didn't sleep very well; she was really concerned, but wasn't sure how to approach anyone about Karen. She was aware that if Karen was still confused, she'd not answer, or admit her real name, and neither would she be able to prove that she was Amber. By the morning, there had still been no call from the desk, so Sherry showered and dressed. At half-past eight, she was making her way down to reception, asking if the night porter had left a message. He hadn't, so she went outside, found a seat, then joined a small queue at the breakfast buffet.

Carrying fruit juice and cereal back to the table, Sherry had only just begun eating when she froze. Karen had come into the breakfast area, looked around, then walked deliberately over to her.

"It's about time you emerged, I'm bloody starving," Karen said, as she sat down.

"Where the hell did you get to last night?" she demanded, "I've been out my mind with worry."

Karen looked at Sherry for a moment. "Sleeping rough, why?"

"Because we had a room in the hotel, that's why."

Karen took the hotel room card out of her bag, showing it Sherry. "I know that, but I'd forgotten the room number and this card didn't help, with only the hotel name printed on it. How could I go to the reception and ask what room I was in, when I didn't even know who'd booked the bloody room. Besides that, I've no money, I'm completely broke."

The waiter came over and filled both their cups with coffee and left. Karen got up and collected cereals and orange juice before returning.

"So what name are you calling yourself today?" Sherry asked, with a trace of annoyance in her voice.

Karen looked confused. "Amber, why should I change it to something else? I like my name."

"Amber who; you do have a surname don't you?" Sherry wanted to know, while she carried on with her cereal.

Karen sighed. "Why shouldn't I? It's just that I've had a little confusion with my name, well a lot really. I know my name's Amber, but a bloody passport in my bag has my picture on it, with the name Karen Marshall. Anyway my name is the least of my problems. I don't think I should be here and last night I would have got in touch with Chuks, so he could come and get me, but I didn't know how to contact him. Now you're here, and you work for him as well, you can call him for me?"

Karen was annoyed that Chuks hadn't turned up to collect her last night. Already stressed over what Shaun had made her do, she inteded to kill Chuks. She decided on this, because she couldn't believe she'd been servicing clients, similar to what Shaun had brought, in the past. She was sure she'd have remembered the constant abuse of her body, when in just over half an hour four men had already taken her. At that rate, she'd have been servicing close on twenty or thirty men a night, something she'd never have forgotten. It was with these thoughts, Karen now suspected, but wasn't certain, that Chuks' punishments, the drug chewy, followed by constant demands on her body, had been in preparation for this life. So with Chuks not coming, she'd been unable to confront him, leaving her confused and in a position where she'd had to move around the beach, avoiding the local police vehicles that went up and down for most of the night. She'd also watched Shaun crawl to the road, trying to find somebody to help him. One man had, with an ambulance eventually turning up. But she knew it was too late; already he'd slipped into unconsciousness, before he was taken away. It was obvious with what little they did for him; they didn't consider it worthwhile. Before daylight, she'd made her way to the water's edge, cleaned herself up and put her knickers back on. As people began to move around the hotel and breakfast area, she'd made her way back into the hotel complex, hanging about, waiting for this girl sitting with her now, to come down for breakfast. Karen was brought out of her thoughts when Sherry spoke.

"That would be a little difficult. Unless you're considering ending this mortal life and are on your way to hell, rather than heaven. I put two bullets in him. I also don't work for him."

Karen still had the feeling that the girl sitting here worked at the brothel, even if she didn't directly work for Chuks. Because of that, she had no intention of admitting her decision to no longer live the life of a prostitute. With that doubt in her mind, she decided to play along. "Thanks very much for that, now what do I do; I tried last night to get clients like he said I should. All I got was one of the house minders who had me for free." Karen didn't intend to tell her of the other men Shaun had forced on her, or even the punishments. Acutely embarrassed at the way she'd allowed herself to be taken in by him, she just wanted to forget it. "I couldn't get into the nightclub to find ones who'd actually pay me. I don't suppose you'll be staying around here, which means I'll not even have a room to come back to, so I'll end up on the beach again."

Sherry had finished her cereal and was sipping her coffee. "So with your being dressed with very little on and not the usual jeans, besides make-up that makes you look like a clown, you're telling me you went out last night with the intention of selling yourself?"

Karen looked around nervously. "Listen, can't you keep your voice down, Shaun told me this hotel would have us removed if they knew we were prostitutes. But yes, I went out, the same as you, it's what we do."

Sherry was silent for a time; eventually she finished off her coffee and stood up, pulling a pen from her bag. She took a paper napkin and wrote a floor and room number on it, handing it to her. "We need to talk, Amber. Finish your breakfast and come to our room."

"I'll do that, but before you go, could you lend me a few dollars? I'll pay you back later when the bars open and I can begin to earn some money. I want to call at the chemist and get a morning-after pill?" The admission of the intention to earn money, when the bars opened, was a lie, but she needed to make sure she wasn't pregnant after last night.

Sherry moved closer and grasped her hand. "Forget pills, Amber, you can't get pregnant. Drugs in the past have destroyed that chance; I'll see you in the room."

Karen watched her go, there were tears trickling down her face. She'd not even realised she was infertile. Her world was falling apart, and she could do nothing to stop it. Even this girl didn't tell her what she was called; she now doubted she'd actually go back to the room, probably just leave her like she had last night.

Ten minutes later, Karen, after finishing her breakfast, returned to the room. She was surprised to find Sherry there. "I didn't think you'd be here, thought you would bail on me. Anyway, I'm having a shower. If you're still around when I've finished, we'll talk."

Sherry frowned. "What's this, you didn't think I'd be here, or wonder if I'm still around? It's my bloody room; I paid for it."

Karen didn't comment, just rummaged through her suitcase, selecting something to wear, then went through to the bathroom.

**

"Right, what do you want?" Karen asked, coming out of the bathroom, dressed in jeans and tee-shirt, still rubbing her hair with a towel.

"I think, Amber, you'd better sit down and listen," Sherry told her.

Karen shrugged. "If you want, but whatever you say, I've made my mind up, I've no intention of working as a prostitute like you again."

Sherry rolled her eyes back in despair; this was going to be difficult. They both walked through to the balcony, sitting down on loungers.

"Okay, tell me what you want to talk about?" Karen asked.

"For a start, get it out of your thick head, once and for all, I'm not a prostitute and never have been. I'm a soldier, attached to a European special services unit."

"That's a bit far-fetched. You don't look like a soldier, not that I really know what a soldier is, or would look like."

Sherry ignored the comment about her not knowing what a soldier was. "You mean I don't look like a 'Rambo', not many of us do. But I'll prove it to you," she said, leaving the balcony to fetch her bag. Bringing it through, she pulled out her purse, removed her ID then handed it to Karen. "I assume you can still read?" she demanded, with a tinge of sarcasm in her voice.

Karen said nothing, just gave her a withering look, before handing back the ID.

"I suppose, with you saying downstairs that you killed Chuks, it must be true, the ID does say you're a Unit T soldier? I'm also sorry

368

for thinking you were a prostitute, I just assumed you were the same as me."

"It's forgotten. But I killed Chuks to help you get out. You're also not a prostitute and never have been; you're a soldier, the same as me, and came here to take out the Nigerians, including Chuks. You failed, and they captured you. Another soldier with you, called Hamon, was killed. Once they had you, I think Chuks must have put you on some kind of drug, that's seriously affected your memory. I suspect he wanted you to believe you prostituted for a living, so later he could put you to work. By what you said at breakfast, he did quite a good job, if you went out last night believing that's what you do."

Karen was looking down, playing with her fingers. "You're telling me that bloody drugs were able to have Chuks make me believe I was a prostitute?" she whispered.

"In a nutshell, yes; you should have stayed in here and never gone out. You didn't, paying for it, pretty harshly by the sound of it."

Karen sighed. "I began to realise that, once I was out. It all seemed so strange, as if I didn't really know what I was doing, or how to stop it. Except, my fear of Chuks pushed me on. Now, what you're saying sounds so bizarre as to be a complete fabrication; except, I can see some truth in it. As for my past, I'm struggling to recall if I've ever had one. It's like waking up, believing that this day is the start of your life." She paused, looking up at Sherry. "So what happens now?"

"It's time to come back to reality, by trusting me and accepting what I'm going to say to you. You're not short of money; in fact you have more than enough never to work again, besides a nice home and family. I reckon we should try and get you your old life back? I've got some leave due, the same as you. We could go away; spend time together talking through your past, then you may begin to remember again. If you can't, you'll have to admit to the unit's doctor what happened. He's bound to have you assessed, in order to make sure you're actually capable of staying in the army; maybe he'll recommend that you resign. We will only consider that route as a last resort."

Karen sat for a short time, thinking about what Sherry had said. Then she looked at her. "Why are you doing this for me? You've done your job, killed this man, why don't you just go away and let me sort my own life out?"

Sherry looked a little put out. "I will if you want, that's your decision, my military work is done here. The truth is you've helped me in the past; when I was at rock bottom. My mum was on the game and a drunk. At sixteen, I'd already been taken by people similar to Chuks, and forced into prostitution, the same as they tried to do with you. You came for me, now I've done the same for you. You also gave me my self-respect back, my dignity, always treating me as an equal and not shit. You're my best friend; I've no one else. I just want to try to get the Karen back I love so much."

Karen was still looking at Sherry. "I'd like to try to get my memory back. What are a few weeks? If it doesn't work, I can always go home to begin a new life?"

Sherry was relieved; the last thing she wanted was to admit to the unit, any connection with the brothel or the Nigerians. This was an unauthorised operation. She had killed as a civilian, not in self-defence. Her army status wouldn't protect her from prosecution, if they found out. "Great, I'll arrange it, but from now on you use your real name, Karen, the same as on the passport. Amber was a prostitute, she dies before we leave this room, agreed?"

"She died last night, Sherry; she won't be coming back in my life, believe me."

"Yes well, it goes further. You were never taken, and I never came for you."

Karen almost laughed. "That's easy; I can't even remember being taken. I'd even struggle to remember this room number, without carrying around the paper you wrote it on."

Chapter Seventy - Four Weeks Later

"Mum, dad, are you ready yet, the taxi's here?" Sophie shouted up the stairs.

"Just coming," her mother replied.

Five minutes later they were sitting in a taxi.

"I'm really looking forward to this show; it was good of Karen to send the tickets," Kevin, Karen's father said, sitting in the seat alongside the driver, looking back at his wife and Sophie.

"You're right; it's a shame she couldn't be with us. Did you finally get to speak to her, dad?" Sophie asked.

He shook his head. "No, I didn't manage to. Stanley told me she wasn't available. I even asked him about the tickets that had come in the post, also the dinner booked afterwards, wondering if he'd sent them on her behalf. But he told me he hadn't, they must have come directly from Karen. I had the impression he'd no real idea where she was, but didn't like to say."

"What do you think, mum, do you think tonight's a way to try to placate us, because she's not been in touch over the last couple of months?"

"You know Karen, love. She's often very busy and can lose all track of time. Except I do worry when she's quiet for so long."

"I suppose, but it would be nice if she came home for Christmas. We've not had a family gathering for a couple of years now."

At that moment they arrived outside the theatre, more comments about Karen were put to one side.

***

Later in the restaurant, the talk came back to Karen.

"Well I'll give Karen her due, she really knows how to turn a dull Friday night into a brilliant one," Sophie said, finishing off her coffee.

Kevin just laughed. "I've got to agree there. The best seats in the house, followed by a really good dinner. She must have good contacts to do that." Then he looked at his watch. "The taxi home is booked for eleven-thirty; does anyone want a brandy to complete the night then?"

Leaving a little later, the taxi waiting for them was a standard black cab. It didn't wait around, so as soon as they climbed inside, it was off.

They had been travelling for ten minutes when Kevin frowned. "Do you suppose he knows where he's going? We should have turned three roads back."

Karen's mother also frowned. "I hope it's not another of Karen's surprises and we're on our way to a nightclub?"

Kevin leaned forward and tapped the glass. "Driver, you missed the turning," he shouted.

However, the driver never commented but carried on.

Kevin attempted to open the dividing window, but it was firmly locked. Then he tried to pull down the windows, again they were locked, even the doors wouldn't open. Panic was setting in, when suddenly the cab turned off the road, going down a narrow lane, coming to a halt in a picnic area. A large black car was already parked there. Two men were standing smoking at its side.

One walked over and pulled the cab door open. "All of you out," he demanded.

They climbed out, and the cab drove away.

"What do you want, where are we?" Kevin asked, now obviously concerned and very confused.

However, the man pulled a gun. "On your knees, hands behind your head, or I'll put a bullet in your daughter."

They were terrified, but all did as he demanded.

The other man approached. He stood looking coolly down at them. "The name's Maksim. You won't know me, but I can assure you, your daughter Karen knows me."

"If it's Karen you're looking for, you can see she's not with us, so what do you want?" Kevin asked.

"All in good time. Karen's been a very stupid girl, thought she could renege on a deal she'd made with the Russian mafia. In fact, she's walked away with five million of our money, besides destroying a shipment of cocaine worth upwards of a billion to us."

"What's Karen's professional life got to do with us, she never tells us anything?" Kevin wanted to know.

He shrugged indifferently. "Nothing, nothing at all; but first I want to know where she is?"

"We were asking each other the same on the way to the theatre; Karen hasn't spoken to us for nearly two months," Kevin replied.

"I can't believe a daughter would leave it two months and not call home. So let's jog your memory, with not just a threat, but a promise to put a bullet in your daughter's head. When has she last talked to any of you?"

Kevin, knowing Karen would not expect them to try to hide anything to protect her, as she was well able to protect herself, answered in desperation."I'm not prepared to risk Sophie's life, by telling you lies. This is typical of Karen; often she can't call when she's on an operation. We're just a normal family, if you have problems with Karen, then sort them out with her, we can't help. We're not party to anything that goes on outside her military life."

Maksim sighed deeply. "Then we have a dilemma. You see; we cannot let someone make us look like fools. To control requires being firm, decisive, having people in fear of us; otherwise more of our associates would believe they too could take from us."

"I can understand you need to keep a firm hand, in any business. But why take it out on us, because your dealings with Unit T and Karen haven't gone to plan? We cannot do anything for you, even she wouldn't listen to us as far as her military life goes," Kevin answered.

"That is right of course, but it isn't Unit T hanging on to our money, it's your daughter Karen. So as her family, you will pay the price of her stupidity. She will have to live with the consequences of that for the rest of her life. I hope she thinks five million was worth taking from us?"

"Why would she want your money, Karen's already got millions of her own?" Sophie cut in, hoping Maksim didn't know this.

"We're aware Karen's wealthy, but that seems not to have prevented her wanting to add to her wealth, at our expense. So like I said, you will all pay for her greed."

"When you keep saying pay, we don't have that sort of money. But if it's Sophie you're considering using as a hostage, please take me instead, Karen will still deal with you," Kevin begged.

He sniggered. "We don't want the money; it is of no importance;

her word, her agreement with us is more important. She has broken her word, believes she can treat us like fools, and is to be punished for such arrogance. We have decided this payment is to be made by her loved ones, as a stark reminder to her, for the rest of her life, that it was her who signed your death warrants."

Before any of them realised the significance of what Maksim was saying, he pulled a gun from his pocket, shooting both Kevin and his wife through the head. Sophie, at first, stared in absolute horror, seeing her parents shot, before going into hysterics. They expected this; she was quickly overcome by Maksim and the other man. They held her down firmly, her face was slapped hard a number of times, quietening her, tears streaming down her cheeks.

"As for you, Sophie, you are not quite due to leave this mortal earth, you're coming with us, to be put to work in one of our brothels. Expect to be servicing upwards of ten men a day, until no man is prepared to take you, then you will follow your parents' fate. Plenty of time, I expect, for you to build up hatred for your sister, as to what she has brought on the family, because of her greed."

While Maksim talked, the other man pulled a case from his pocket and drew out a syringe, already pre-filled. Pulling her dress up, he pushed the needle of the syringe into the upper side of Sophie's leg. Moments later, her head began to spin, before her eyes closed. Sophie was carried to the car.

Maksim threw his cigarette to the ground, looking at the other man with him. "Well at least they had a good night, courtesy of us. I hope Karen appreciates our calling card?"

He looked back at Maksim. "I suppose you realise when she finds it was us who killed her parents, she will attempt to take out the cartel, or even if she can't, she'll make it impossible for us to operate in Europe?"

"Yes, Ignatius did warn the leaders, but his advice was ignored. Ignatius is only just hanging on to his own life, because he told them the money would be returned. We found out from Pular that it was unlikely, after one of the men Ignatius sent sold Karen down the river, with the Nigerians taking her. How she escaped and killed the Nigerians, we don't know, but she did. Since then, she's disappeared, along with our money. Maybe she believes that's the cost to us, for telling the Nigerians she was there, I don't know. Even so, she should have contacted Ignatius, laid down the facts and made a different arrangement. She could have even insisted the man who turned her over to the Nigerians, must pay, before she returned the money. But she did none of those things, preferring to ignore us. It was decided Karen must be taught a lesson she will never forget. Then the next time she tries to make a deal with us, she will keep to it no matter what."

Chapter Seventy-One

Sherry and Karen had taken a scheduled flight from Istanbul to London, except they didn't stay there, booking an internal flight to Glasgow, hiring a car at the airport. Karen had credit cards, but couldn't remember what her pin numbers were, so all the costs went on Sherry's account. They left Glasgow after staying one night and hitting the shops for warmer and more practical clothes; both girls only had clothes with them for a far warmer climate. Planning a route to take them further north, through the Scottish Highlands, Sherry booked accommodation at tourist information centres, so they never had to look around for a place to stay. With arranged leave, by text from Karen to Stanley, put together by Sherry, of six weeks, they intended to stay in Scotland for at least four of these weeks, then decide where to go from there. Sherry had deliberately chosen a route away from large towns with their usual distractions.

Their stay in any area was short, before moving on. The accommodation was bed and breakfast, mostly in private houses, with any hotels they stayed in small, and out of the towns. It was inevitable that people would recognise Karen, most wanting autographs, others would offer her a drink at the bar, tell her how good a job she was doing. However, it wasn't everywhere, just the odd time when they were in a shop, or sitting in a hotel bar at night.

Karen seemed to take it all in her stride, at times Sherry even believed that Karen was fully recovered, from the way she'd speak to people, then an odd word would tell her that she was not right, as if she was just agreeing with what people said to her.

The fourth week they had taken a car ferry to the Outer Hebrides, with the intention of island hopping. Sherry knew a great deal about the area. When she was a child she never had holidays, so she'd sit in her room reading about different parts of the world and dream she was there. Now with money, she wanted to visit the places she'd dreamed about for herself.

The weeks before, while they explored the mainland, she told Karen all about what she knew of her life. Karen would listen quietly, saying very little. Now on the island of Barra, they were in the lounge of a small hotel. It was raining outside and very cold, so they were happy just sitting in front of the open fire, in the hotel lounge.

Both girls were far more relaxed; Karen had become more talkative, close, in lots of ways, to what she used to be like.

"So now we're four weeks into our leave, how do you think you're doing?" Sherry asked. She had deliberately not broached this question sooner, not wanting to push Karen, just allowing her to come around in her own time. Hoping by now, she'd have been telling her how she felt, but she hadn't.

"I'm okay in myself, and really enjoying the holiday, besides managing to put back together a great deal of my life. I think knowing Chuks is dead, his hold over me has just evaporated, allowing me to think beyond the box once again. Even without you telling me I had family, I knew I had. The problem I've still got, is most of my thoughts seem to be like immediate happenings, if I try to think back to when I was maybe sixteen or even eighteen, that's where it gets confusing."

"In what way?"

"I don't know really how to explain it. I think it must have been a very traumatic time in my life, a time I suspect I prefer to forget. The drug must have contributed to helping me to forget what I wanted to, now I'm unable to bring anything together."

"That's got to be good in one way. You've had a tough time in the past, Karen; I understand the worst part of your life was when you were just eighteen. But more importantly, do you now accept you're an officer in Unit T?"

"Yes I do. I also feel confident in having to lead an operation, as any officer would be expected to do. Except names go out of my head very fast, and I struggle to remember them again. I'd have to be very careful, maybe even make notes. I'd look silly giving an order, then forgetting what I'd ordered."

Sherry smiled. "I'm always doing that. Some of the exams I had in the army I really struggled with. So I did one of those memory courses you see on the net, to try to get my memory better."

"Did it work?"

"Sort of, you have to associate words with pictures, apparently the brain handles pictures better than words, so it doesn't matter how stupid the picture you imagine, in fact it's better that way. Like with my sergeant called Freeman, I was always forgetting his name, when I was filling in forms. I made up a picture in my mind, of a man bursting out of a box upside down naked, with only an army hat on. Looking at it as the man's freedom from the box, so it was freeman. The problem was, I'd often giggle when I looked at him, with the silly picture in my mind, people would look at me as if I was stupid, but I never forgot his name again."

Karen frowned thoughtfully. "I think I'll try that. Anyway are we going to the local Saturday dance tonight? Annis, when she was serving breakfast this morning, was insistent we experienced céilidh music while we're here."

"It's up to you, Karen. This is your call; you know how you feel. Although, Annis did say she'd teach us the basic steps this afternoon, so we could get into the dancing quicker. I'd like to do that at least."

"Then we'll go, it could be fun."

***

The small hall was packed. To Karen, it seemed like everyone on the island had turned up. Both she and Sherry were wearing dresses that were tight round the body, flared slightly in the skirt and quite short. Taller than the average girl, even without the high heels they were wearing, they both looked and felt good. Sherry had held back a little as they entered the hall, letting Karen go ahead. She was impressed, with what she'd been through, Karen still looked stunningly attractive, portraying a manner as if she'd not a care in the world. Now in the hall, everyone was turning to look at her, when she walked in. Sherry was proud of being her friend, a girl who had never looked down on her. She was also a girl who had everything to live for, who was not only titled, but probably the most famous soldier in the world; and yet, this was also a girl who would turn her back on it all, to rescue one child. She was glad she had been able to rescue Karen, before the Nigerians had destroyed her.

Given a drink from a large glass bowl set in the centre of the drinks table, they also received a word of warning, not to keep coming back too often, if they wanted to stand by the end of the night. Soon they were on the dance floor; accompanied by a seemingly unending supply of men wanting to dance with them.

Sherry was really struck with a local lad called Alasteir, spending longer with him than others who'd asked her to dance. She came up to Karen, who was collecting yet another refill from the glass bowl.

"Alasteir has asked me to see his dad's farm tomorrow. Would you mind if I went?"

"Why should I, it's your leave as well, and he does look a hunk."

"You're sure you'll be okay on your own?"

"Sherry, I need to get back into living my life, you know? I'll just take a walk along the beach. Give me time to think and put my life into perspective. I'm seriously considering resigning, calling it a day and trying to live a normal life from now on. Like you say, I've money, so I don't really need to work."

Sherry grinned. "If you do, can I come with you? We could go backpacking, see loads of countries, it'd be really good fun," she said, her eyes sparkling with excitement.

"I wasn't thinking of the backpacking type of living, but you're right, it could be good fun, I may just take you up on that. Now go and find Alasteir, before another girl takes him."

***

The following morning, after what proved to be a fantastic night, both girls went down to breakfast decidedly fragile. Annis, who usually served them, wasn't there, her husband was serving that morning.

After breakfast, Karen had wrapped herself up in warm clothes, collected a lunch pack and left the hotel alone, in their hire car. Sherry was mooching around in the hall, looking at the leaflets, waiting for Alasteir to collect her.

Annis's car drew up outside the hotel; she climbed out quickly, carrying a newspaper and shopping bags, hurrying inside.

"Good morning, Sherry, is Karen around?" she asked, looking flustered and concerned.

Sherry shook her head. "You've barely missed her, she's out for the day. Told me she was going walking, to take a few pictures of the wildlife. Can I help?"

Annis handed her the morning paper, flown in from the mainland earlier on. "You need to read this. I understand the ferry, due in at ten,

379

is packed with reporters. How they found out Karen was here, I've no idea, but they have."

Sherry opened the folded paper, staring at the headlines. A cold shiver ran up inside her, her body actually shaking. "Oh my god, this can't be happening," she stuttered.

'Karen Harris's parents found dead' was the headline. 'Police, last night, confirmed that the middle-aged couple, found dead in a local beauty spot yesterday, by a woman walking her dog, were indeed Mr and Mrs Marshall, the parents of Lieutenant Colonel Karen Harris, commander of Unit T. According to local sources, police are treating this as a possible reprisal killing; both had been shot in the head, with none of their valuables taken. Karen's older sister Sophie, believed to have been with them, is missing; raising the possibility that whoever has done this, may have taken her. Police, as well as Unit T, are desperately trying to contact Karen, both very worried about her safety. We understand she is on extended leave, touring with another girl from the same unit, possibly in the UK…'

"Oh, my god, this can't be happening, I need to find her before the reporters," she stammered, tears already forming in her eyes. She looked at Annis. "May I use your telephone, to call our unit, ours are upstairs on charge, both batteries were flat?"

"Of course. You can use the one in my office."

Left alone in the tiny room, Annis called her office; Sherry began to dial the unit's number. When the switchboard answered, Sherry gave her the name and code number. Immediately she was connected to Stanley.

"Sherry, is Karen with you?" Stanley asked.

"Yes, but she's gone out, she's also not got her phone with her. I don't know what to do, Stanley, how do you tell someone their mum and dad is dead, besides her sister missing?" she said, her voice breaking.

"Pull yourself together, Sherry. We don't know what happened, or if they were looking for Karen. She could be in great danger, are both of you armed?"

"No Stanley, this is our holiday, not work or an operation."

"I realise that, but this is very unusual for Karen, in fact, unheard of, not to be armed. She is all right isn't she? I haven't spoken to her for some time now, which is unusual in itself. There's nothing you're not telling me is there, Sherry?"

"Like what?" she asked, tongue in cheek, but the tone of her voice gave her away.

"Then there is. I want the truth. What has been going on, why did you both suddenly request long leave?" he demanded.

"Karen hasn't been very well. I think she was depressed, needed a holiday away from it all. But she's okay now."

"You should have told me this, Sherry. Karen's a commander of a strike force, we can't have her in control, if she is not up to it. If you believe she will have even an inkling of who has done this, I want to know. You of all people should understand how unpredictable and dangerous she can be, so I need as much information in advance as possible, to have it followed up."

Sherry hesitated then decided to tell him. "I do understand. All I know was she had dealings with the Russian Mafia. Some sort of exchange deal I think. I don't know if this was sorted out, but I know of nothing else that might have a bearing."

"What kind of deal?"

"She never told me, even though I'm her friend. When it comes to work, she's more likely to tell you, rather than me."

"Possibly, except in this case she hasn't. Anyway, according to the number you're calling from, it seems you're on the island of Barra. We can't land any of our aircraft there, so I'll charter a helicopter from Glasgow and send two armed soldiers for your protection. I want you both back at the unit, I need to understand the possible background to these murders and abduction, to move on and perhaps find Sophie. So get the mobiles charged up, I'll be in touch."

"Thank you, Stanley, I'll go and find her, before the reporters do."

When she came out the office, Alastair was stood there waiting. He put his arms around her, pulling her close. "Annis has just told me, Sherry. The entire island will be devastated by the news; Karen had endeared herself to everyone on the island last night. Is there anything I can do, or would you rather I left?"

Tears were running down her face, as she drew back. "I need you to help me find her, Alastair, if you would? I couldn't bear it for her to find out from the reporters."

"That goes without saying, Sherry, have you any idea where she intended to go?"

She shook her head.

He smiled, taking her hand. "Come on, I'll make a few calls. There's one thing about this island; she'll not get far without an islander seeing her."

Chapter Seventy-Two

When Karen left the hotel, she travelled along the coast, turning off down a track and parking up in a small clearing by the side of the road. There, with her lunch pack and camera, she set off down to the beach below, intent on watching the seals.

Karen had been sitting on the beach for over an hour, watching the seals bobbing about in the water, some even coming ashore and looking at her. At that moment, she could have been the only person in the world. In the last weeks she'd not had any real time alone, now she had, already she was considering just where to go from here. Foremost in her mind was whether she'd the drive, the passion, to remain in Unit T. Then, while she had difficulty in associating names to faces, unless confronted with that person, there was no such loss of memory as to what she did at Unit T. In fact, she could remember in detail many operations she'd taken part in, or even commanded. Except, if she could remember those so vividly, why not her home, her private life? There, she could remember nothing about the house, the location. It also sounded very large and already she felt frightened of walking inside, not even knowing where to find the lounge, or the bedroom where she slept. This was the same when it came to her family. Although Sherry had told her their names, and where they lived, Sherry had no photographs to show her, leaving Karen with no pictures in her mind as to what they looked like, or even when she last saw them. Because of this, she held no affinity to them, as a daughter should for their parents. As far as she was concerned, they could have been anyone off the street, who told her they were her mum and dad; that was how little she remembered about them. Even her sister Sophie, who according to Sherry, spent a great deal of time at her home, meant nothing, apart from her being single, the same as her, and older. Karen knew, deep inside, Chuks had partially succeeded in his attempt to change her forever. Her statement last night about resigning had been no whim. As she sat there, Karen was already looking forward to a future where she could live again; maybe go back to her parents, try to build a relationship once more with her family. Then away from the pressures of being a commander, she may even meet someone who wanted to be with her. Karen hoped so; she didn't want to be alone for the remainder of her life.

***

Sherry, with Alasteir's help, found Karen still sitting on the beach watching the seals. He waited at the top of the ridge while Sherry made her way down to Karen, with the paper in her hand.

"Hi, have you bailed from Alastair, and come to join me? The seals are really funny; one's even pinched a piece of my sandwich," Karen asked, as Sherry sat down at her side.

"We need to return to Unit T, Karen. Stanley's sending a helicopter to pick us up," she said soberly.

"But we've got another two weeks, besides, I don't think I'm going back. Like I said last night, I'm going to resign."

Sherry pushed the paper into her hands. "We really do have to go back, please read the headlines."

Karen looked at the paper for some time. Each word she read, didn't build up anger, or stir emotional feelings which would normally lead to someone breaking down, the words had the opposite effect. More and more memories of her past were flowing back, from happier times when she was a child, to the times of stress, with her parents always getting at her, because of what she'd decided to do with her life. Finally Karen shrugged with obvious indifference. "So who told you I needed to go back to unit?"

"Stanley, I called him because they were searching for you and I wanted to tell them you were safe. He wanted you back, to discuss what's been going on and look into Sophie's possible abduction."

Karen just looked at her. "Who the hell do you think you are? I'm the commanding officer here, not you. Until you'd talked to me, you should have called no one. Then Stanley's a civilian, he works for me; he does not tell me what I should, or shouldn't do."

Sherry was close to tears at the way Karen was talking. "I'm sorry, I just panicked, this is your family we're talking about, so whoever did it could be looking for you. Already reporters are coming, one may not even be a reporter but an assassin."

Karen simply shrugged. "Then let him come. Besides, my family's already dead so running around like a headless chicken won't

384

bring them back. Anyway, what were you expecting, I'd break down and cry?"

"If you want the truth, then yes, it's not normal if you don't, I cried for my mum."

"Well that's you and not me. So you believe I'm not normal. Do you think that it might just be because I live in a world where death is so much a part, what emotions it generates, rolls off you?"

"Then if you think so little of losing your parents, what about Sophie, she needs your help."

Karen nodded her head up and down slowly. "Sophie will need help; the same as hundreds of others taken by traffickers. She, like them, will have to wait, our priority is to take down the trafficking cartel that has taken her; even you know that victims are incidental."

Sherry put her hands to her head. "I can't believe I'm hearing this. I came for you; the same as you did for me. You can't be considering wanting to finish your leave, before even starting to look for Sophie, can you?"

"I am actually. Sophie has been warned many times of the very high risk to her, because of my position. She was offered a new name, a new life; I even offered her a home where she'd be safe. The same went for mum and dad. They all chose to ignore the risks, turning me down, in fact, laughing at my concerns; virtually accusing me of being paranoid. Now they, like Sophie, have paid the price. Will I look for her? Of course I will, but it may take time and until then she'll be abused, raped and put to work, not killed. If they wanted to do that, she'd be dead already."

"So what do we do?"

"You call Stanley and cancel any rescue plan for me. Then you finish your day with Alastair, the same as I'll finish my day here, enjoying the seals."

"You can't be serious? I'm not prepared to do that."

"Then you meet the bloody helicopter he's sending; I'll not be on it, and I will return only after my leave is finished."

"If I do, then I'll tell them everything. You're not right in the head. They'll lock you up."

"They won't, trust me. You see; I'll pass any test they throw at me; that's if anyone actually has the nerve to attempt to suspend a senior officer on your say-so. I was on holiday with my boyfriend; I was snatched, he was killed and you found me. You didn't inform the local police and have me rescued; you shot a man. Except, it wasn't as a Unit T soldier, acting under orders, even from me, but as a civilian. You're already close to facing court-martial, for disobeying an order from your commander. Think about that, Sherry, because take the route you're threatening, you may also run the risk of being sent back to Turkey to face a murder charge."

Sherry was scared. With her working-class background and limited education, she had no idea if what Karen was telling her was correct. Karen was far more cunning than she'd ever be; because of this Sherry had no choice but to believe what she was saying. "Why are you talking to me this way? I thought we were friends; I'd do anything for you, you know that?"

"We are still friends. I'd also do anything for you, never forget that. But work-wise, I'm still your commanding officer. Anything military, as you know, should have been passed by me. Neither you, nor Stanley, can authorise military operations without at the very least the lieutenant standing in for me agreeing. Then if he's aware I'm available for consulting, particularly if the operation's directed towards me, he'd be a very foolish man to order it without my agreement. Now call Stanley and cancel everything. He waits, like everyone else, until I make a decision as to where to go from here."

"I'll do that, Karen, and I'm sorry that I overstepped my authority, it won't happen again, but is this decision of yours in leaving the unit still going to happen?"

Karen remained silent for a moment, then sighed. "It's forgotten, Sherry. As for my future, I've been sitting here seriously considering resigning, to be with my family, try to get my life back. Once more, God has decided he's not finished with me, again seeing fit to have people I love, as in the past, taken away from me. Will I resign?" she hesitated. "I can't. I've nowhere to go. As for the future, I'll continue moving from crisis to crisis. But believe this, whatever I do won't be clouded with emotion, desperation, it will be driven by decisions that will lead me to the killer and the people who gave the order."

Again she paused, looking out across the water, her voice a voice of determination. "They may have thought they could break me, destroy my resolve by murdering my family. It won't; they have failed, now they will pay for that failure with their own lives."

Books by the Same Author

For full up to date information:
http://www.keithhoare.com

Lightning Source UK Ltd.
Milton Keynes UK
UKOW04f2331110714

234974UK00001B/1/P